the Sleeping Serpent

LUNA SAINT CLAIRE & VIRGINIA BOWEN

A COMPELLED NOVEL

WWW.COMPELLEDBOOKS.COM

Published by Compelled Books
www.compelledbooks.com

The Sleeping Serpent is a work of fiction. All characters appearing in this work are fictitious. Any resemblance to actual persons, living or dead, or events that took place, is entirely coincidental. Any names, characters, places, events and incidents are either the products of the author's imagination, or used in a fictitious manner.

Cover photograph © Arman Zhenikeyev/Corbis
Cover Design by Ilene Segal

Library of Congress Control Number: 2015935572

ISBN 978-1-928816-76-8
ISBN 978-1-928816-77-5 (ebook)

Please follow #TheSleepingSerpent
Facebook, Instagram, Pinterest, Twitter & Tumblr

FOREWORD

Vampires are real. I'm not referring to the kind with blood and fangs, but rather emotional vampires—narcissists—the ones who use manipulation and compulsion to seduce. Charismatic and magnetic, they appear innocent in their motives, gaining your trust with affection and compliments. Truth is, they have targeted you. Within five minutes of meeting his prey, a narcissist has identified your vulnerabilities. It can be as simple as telling you how beautiful you are.

If I ask you, "Could you succumb to the seduction of a sociopath? Would you allow a man to verbally or even physically abuse you? Would you risk your job, and permit him to reduce your self-esteem to nothing?" I'm certain you would say no. But the process is slow—almost imperceptible. Before you know it, you're hooked.

Initially, a narcissist is infatuated and idolizes his target, mirroring what he knows you want him to be. Captivated by what you perceive to be the perfect mate, you quickly fall under his spell. Most people get into relationships for love, but narcissists lack empathy and do not have the ability to feel love. Their self-worth is dependent on the admiration of others. Their targets must be attractive, intelligent, and accomplished. The greater the status, the better to provide what's called narcissistic supply, be it money, tangible goods, services, or status.

Once a narcissist has you entangled in their web, the bond is difficult to break. Just like in a vampire story, you are inexorably bound. Bewitched. Compelled. Because they are emotionally unstable, being in a relationship with a narcissist is like a roller coaster ride. He is charming and passionate, yet nothing satisfies him. He is needy and controlling, making you feel desired and important to him. Once assured of your devotion he becomes verbally abusive, berating, finding fault and punishing you—imposing unreasonable demands to prove your love. Not wanting to lose a source of valuable supply, the narcissist skillfully pours on the charm and romance in doses just large enough to keep you on the hook.

Emotionally devastated and conditioned to think less of yourself, you hold fast to the fantasy, unaware that it is all smoke and mirrors, and work to restore the initial ecstasy you once felt. There was excitement. Elation. Gratification. Passion. A flood of feelings that were thrilling. But in a relationship with a narcissist, there will never be love.

All is clouded by desire: as fire by smoke, as a mirror by dust...
Through these it blinds the soul.

The Bhagavad Gita

1

The breath of the passengers created a layer of condensation on the windows of the plane obscuring his view of the city. Nicolás wiped the window with the sleeve of his jacket to get a clear view. Looking out, he surveyed the landscape with a shiver of delight. The vast expanse of Southern California…mountains, deserts, canyons, and plateaus appeared rugged and unwelcoming, yet magnetic to all seeking wealth and celebrity. Los Angeles, and the promise of a fresh life, stretched deliciously below him.

He hadn't actually wanted to leave New York, but circumstances had forced him to seek a new home. As an intuitive man, Nicolás had an innate sense of when it was time to move on, and that time had come for him in more places than he cared to remember. Still, each move brought a certain tingle of anticipation. He craved novelty… new life…new energy. Most of all, he craved new women.

o   o   o

Walking into the dimly lit restaurant, Luna took a moment for her eyes to adjust. The elderly pianist was warming up with the Liszt paraphrase from Verdi's *Rigoletto*, and though she wasn't as brilliant as Cziffra, the runs were bright and agile. Luna had been coming to this Hollywood haunt for decades, ever since moving to Los Angeles when she was in her twenties and working as assistant to an Academy Award-winning costume designer. The front room of La Forza was packed with regulars eating at the bar, and Luna wove her way toward the reservation desk, past a long farmhouse table filled with noisy locals. A large wooden hutch behind them displayed the restaurant's renowned cookbooks, exclusive bottles of olive oil, and Sicilian sea salt. Shelves mounted on ochre-colored plaster walls held antique crockery and colorful majolica plates, warmly illuminated by candlelight and copper chandeliers. The charming ambiance, reminiscent of a general store tucked into the hills of Tuscany, always comforted her.

Seeing Luna and her husband, Tyler, enter the restaurant along with four friends, the owner, Mario, rushed over to greet them. "Luna! Bella, where have you been? I'm so glad you came!" Mario exuberantly gave double-cheek kisses to all the women, embraced Tyler, and vigorously shook the other men's hands. "We have a wonderful mezzo visiting us from Paris Opera. She'll be singing the aria from *Carmen* tonight!" Such animated enthusiasm had helped make La Forza the enduring institution it now was.

Luna thought he looked better than when she last saw him. His middle-aged pasty and portly look had been replaced with a shaved head and a leaner, more muscular body. Chatting nonstop, he led them to a rustic wood table with mismatched primitive spindle-back chairs. An earthenware milk pitcher filled with thistles and wildflowers provided privacy from a nearby table. The piano area, where the guest singers would perform, was just far enough away to not inhibit conversation. Once everyone was comfortably seated, Mario drew up an extra chair near Luna to catch up on industry gossip.

Luna's latest job was the new hit series *Going My Way*, about four young, artistic women living in L.A., trying to navigate their careers and love lives. Luna described it as *Sex and the City* meets *Entourage*. As head costume designer, she applied her eclectic style, using trendy designers and vintage clothing to create cool looks. Having received critical acclaim for the first season, Luna was counting on this series to be the defining project of her career, earning her the Emmy she had long coveted but had so far eluded her.

Feeling a bit guilty, she lamented, "I'm sorry I haven't been here in a while, but I've just been so busy on the show."

Always charming, Mario teased flirtatiously, "Ah…where does the time go, bella? I remember you waltzing in like an exquisite butterfly, and all the heads would turn to stare. So pretty—and sexy!"

Luna laughed and tossed her long, chestnut-brown hair off her shoulders, shaking her head as if considering whether his recollection was correct. Tonight she wore L.A.-based designer Paige black skinny jeans with a Roberto Cavalli embellished silk tank and her signature turquoise and sterling silver Native American jewelry.

"Now look at you—a big time costume designer!" he voiced robustly, then asked, "How are things going?"

"They're great! The show got good reviews."

Switching the focus to Mario, she smiled, "It's good to see you looking so well."

"I wasn't doing so well last year. You remember." A twinge of sadness passed over his face, and it struck Luna that it had been nearly a year since the passing of his longtime friend and partner. "Time just seems to take a lot away from us, eh, bella?" he added quietly.

Luna nodded. He'd hit a nerve, but she concealed her chagrin. His voice receded into the background as she remembered herself in the past, catching the admiring glances of men. She tried to reconcile that Luna with the present day, telling herself she was a successful, happily married woman—and still attractive.

Mario piped up enthusiastically, "Do you remember my friend, Roberto, the wine distributor?"

Luna wasn't sure, but nodded anyway.

"His son, Nicolás, is coming tonight. He opened a yoga studio here in L.A. You should go. You'll feel younger…trust me!"

Startled that it seemed Mario had read her thoughts, she responded defensively, "I'm so busy, Mario. There isn't much time left in the day for myself." But then she sighed and conceded, "I do need to sleep more, though, and take a vacation!"

Mario leaned in to whisper, "You know, when I started doing yoga, my sex life improved. I have a young lady—and I keep her *very* happy." He grinned and winked.

Luna blushed a little and looked over at Tyler, hoping he would rescue her. Seeing her searching for an escape, Mario finished, "I'll bring him over to your table. He should be here soon."

Picking up the familiar menu, Luna debated what to order. She wanted the seafood lasagna, but thought about the thick layers of cheese and briefly considered a salad. Sadly, she reflected on Mario's words. *What did he mean I **used to be** pretty and sexy? I'm wearing skinny jeans and a tank top, how is that not sexy? Granted, the top is long and loose-fitting…camouflaging,* she ruminated. But when the waiter refilled her wine glass and asked for her order, she pointed to the lasagna. Moments later, the singers assembled around the piano to begin a lively, popular aria from *Rigoletto*, and some tables sang along.

She allowed the wine and music to transport her, until something in the corner of her eye caught her attention. An attractive man stood next to the reservation desk texting on his cell phone. The greeter, a pretty young woman, apparently knew him, since she kept leaning in closely and touching his arm. But intent on his phone, he kept his head down, ignoring a thick forelock of long, layered hair curtaining his eyes. Perfectly ripped jeans revealed the tanned olive skin of his muscular thighs, while a half tucked in, tight-fitting, black T-shirt displayed a large, silver dragon's head belt buckle, accentuating his nice package below. A well-worn, vintage black leather motorcycle jacket slung over his shoulder with one hand completed the captivating, sexy image. Always the costume designer, Luna made a mental note to distress the jeans of one of the male characters on the show in exactly the same way. She found herself staring too long at the exotic man, and his eyes raised to meet hers. Instead of looking back down, he kept them firmly locked with hers, until he shoved his phone into the jacket pocket and walked in to warmly greet Mario with a big bear hug.

After escorting the stranger to the table, Mario dragged up another chair from nearby so they could join Luna's party. When Mario introduced him as Nicolás, Luna shifted in her chair uncomfortably, pushing her hair back. *He must be used to women gawking at him,* she rationalized. He hung his jacket on the back of the chair, then took Luna's hand and his eyes danced as he said, "Nice to meet you. Call me Nico." He sat down assuredly. At that moment, the server arrived with their entrées and placed the large plate of seafood lasagna in front of Luna. Feeling her face get hot, she tried to sound casual when she asked Nico, "Would you like to share this with me? It's far too much for me to eat!"

Aware of her ruse, Nico winked, "Sure, I'd love to share with you."

The words flowed mellifluously off his tongue.

His voice was soft, with a musical quality, and Luna puzzled over his accent. Unlike the Spanish she was accustomed to hearing in L.A., there was no roll to his Rs and no lisp on Cs. Most strikingly, when he spoke of something exciting to him, she detected a hint of an Italian accent. After telling her about the new studio, he began gently pressing her with questions about her job and inquiring where she lived and worked and whether she was married.

Luna pointedly introduced Tyler, who was splitting his attention between the singers and their dinner guests and reported that Nico taught yoga and was explaining the benefits. However, Nico's gaze remained focused on her. Soon, the rest of the table fell into a haze in the background, leaving the two of them in a cozy cocoon. Locking eyes with her, Nico asked if she practiced yoga. She replied, "I was a ballet dancer when I was young." Pausing to wonder at the magnetism of his unwavering gaze, she nearly forgot to answer his question. "But I have taken yoga classes on and off."

Nico murmured a low "Uh-hmm," then cleared his throat. "Well, Luna, the purpose of yoga is not just physical discipline. Yoga is also a meditation, meant to help us reach a higher consciousness. Did you know yoga is integral to Hindu philosophy?"

The chairs were packed tightly at the table, and Nico's arm occasionally brushed Luna's as they picked up their glasses to drink. She felt a strange electricity sparking off his warm, olive skin. His hair covered his neck, just touching the collar of his T-shirt in soft waves. When he angled his body to address her directly, she noticed his eyes, dark green with flecks of yellow in the iris; they didn't so much sparkle as glow, teasing her with some closely held secret.

Being married to Tyler, a philosophy professor, she was careful not to come across as a know-it-all. So, smiling, she deftly applied her talent for disarming self-important movie stars. "Well, yes, I know yoga is more than physical postures. I believe its fundamental underlying principle is mastering the mind." She glanced over at Tyler attempting to engage him in their conversation, but he was engrossed in soccer talk with the other men.

Nico gazed at her as if she were an exotic bird he'd never seen before and was trying to fix in his memory.

Feeling put off by his intense scrutiny, yet curious to know why Mario felt so strongly that she should hire him, Luna gently asked, "What do you do, exactly?"

Nico leaned in closely, almost too close. His tone and cadence were hypnotic, "I'd already been practicing yoga for many years when I made a trip to study with the paqos—the mystics of the Q'ero tribe—in the Andes. As with yoga, these mystics also practice meditation and controlling the body's energy, or *kawsay*. I felt a strong connection with the paqos and stayed to study their ways, and what I learned from them is why I opened a studio combining yoga and energy healing. My methods help people alleviate stress, which in turn puts the body's systems, like hormones and metabolism, back into alignment. Plus, my program makes you look and feel younger."

Luna was skeptical, but not because he studied energy healing with native tribes; after all, Luna herself had Mohawk blood in her veins. She knew quite a lot about the healing properties of herbs, as well as sacred ceremonies. Something else about Nico made her a little uneasy. Maybe it was his Latin machismo vibe, or his body language. But Tyler had been saying she needed to take better care of herself, warning she was wearing herself down. And those comments from Mario had hurt her feelings; how he'd described her as "pretty" and "sexy" in the past tense. Although Nico wasn't being overtly pushy, there was a part of her that couldn't say no. *Besides, there's no harm in trying something new*, she decided.

o   o   o

Nico had wanted a tony Beverly Hills address somewhere within the triangle of Wilshire, Santa Monica, and Canon, but was forced to settle in Studio City for now. With the help of his longtime childhood friend, who happened to be one of the top restaurant and club developers in L.A., he'd found this space nearly ready for him to move in. The studio had formerly been a martial arts school, so mirrored walls were already installed. Before his arrival, he'd had the hardwood floors refinished and the locker room spiffed up to almost elegant status—essential to the type of women he wanted as clients.

He creatively designed a warm and mysterious space, using dark ox-blood-red paint, dramatic lighting, and liquid music.

Nico hung his collection of photos from the time he lived in the Andes with the Q'ero and the spa where he'd worked in Kerala, India. Stepping back, he admired a photograph showing his ripped and bronzed body taken back when he surfed and took daily runs on the beach. *Well, sunny California will be a nice change from New York City,* he thought to himself. He had a good feeling about moving here, especially the opportunities he would welcome.

Word spread quickly, and classes at Amaru Yoga instantly filled with actors and studio personnel. Calling on his friend, Paolo, for yet another favor and promising to pay him in a month, Nico persuaded him to send someone over to install his sound system. He went to his laptop and turned up the volume on Spotify in expectation of the class soon arriving. Nico prided himself on his playlists of unusual music, and his mixes were already getting positive comments from discerning clients. "Kafez (Dusk Mix)," by Nuria Lita from the *Destination Marrakesh* album, played while his evening session filed in. Nico did a quick head count as the last person squeezed her mat between two other students in the back. His studio had been open for business only a short while, and already forty people were in this class. He realized he would have to set up his online registration to limit attendance to that number. Pleased with the progress he was making, he confidently sauntered the room in bare feet, his black yoga pants hugging his taut butt and thighs and accentuating his lean, muscular build as he approvingly admired the clientele of mostly attractive young women.

"Namaste," he called out powerfully in a low, musical incantation. All eyes rested on him reverently; the sides of his mouth turned up slightly as he bathed in their admiration, soaking up the positive energy they emitted. He checked himself to ensure he gave each student a soft, gentle, and reassuring smile.

"Namaste," they chanted back to him. The ethereal voice of Deva Premal filled the room while Nico led the session. Working in Kerala, where yoga was as normal as breathing, he had taught international master classes. He thought California had too many hippie dippy wannabe yoga instructors, and with his knowledge, experience, and power, he'd have no problem capturing the cream of L.A.

When he called out "Namaste" again to close the class, "Magnetic" by Tabla Beat Science, from the *Tala Matrix* album, was playing. As he'd come to expect, students asked about the music, and he made a mental note to provide his playlists as handouts.

"Cherie," Nico called out to a strikingly beautiful young woman of mysterious heritage. He'd paused to think about how to pronounce her name before saying it aloud. It wasn't Sherry, like the beverage, and it wasn't cherry, like the fruit. It was sort of French sounding and a bit annoying, he thought. But she had an excellent eye for design and was hot as hell in bed. That perfect ass and those full lips got him hard at just the thought. Her bronze skin tone hinted at African American descent, with definitely some Asian blood giving her the most exotic, delicate features. She nonchalantly approached Nico, coming to stand too close in front of him. Feeling her heat penetrate the air between them, he took one step back, silently rebuking her. Careful of his image and reputation, he didn't want the other students to see him being too friendly with anyone. Then, to soften the sting of his nonverbal admonishment, he smiled charmingly. "Can you help me in the back for a little bit? I need your trained eye to hang some artwork."

"Sure. You want me to go shower first?" Trying not to seem too eager, she phrased it with a combination of discretion and apathy.

"That would be a good idea. Come find me when you're done." He turned on his heels, heading for the apartment, where he set the tea kettle on the stove to heat up water. He'd met Cherie at one of the clubs. Paolo had introduced them, saying she was an event planner for his company. The music was pounding loudly, and Nico took her hand, kissing the back of her knuckles and letting his lips linger for a moment before looking into her eyes. Women loved that chivalrous mannerism. Her golden eyes sparkled like imperial topaz, and Nico leaned in to capture her attention, asking her to explain what, exactly, an event planner does. Cherie explained how she tailors the look and feel of an event to the hosting company's brand identity. Nico nodded, considering she must have a flair for design, and that her clients had to have big bucks to afford private parties at these clubs. He would invite her to a session at Amaru, and she could refer her clients to him. They hit it off, dancing and getting a bit too high, ending up partying in the executive bathroom. Having the pass code for the private bathroom was useful; there was never a line, and it was much cleaner. Also, following a girl in was naughty and titillating, like that Usher song, "Love in This Club." He could tell it wasn't her first time; she was totally into it. After a few lines of coke, he leaned her over the sink and fucked her from behind, holding onto that sweet ass.

Nico was in the kitchen brewing his special tea when Cherie came into the apartment. This time when she stepped into his personal space, he placed his hands on her perfect ass and pulled her tight against his groin, his cock twitching at her proximity.

"Nico, do you really want me to hang artwork?" she cooed, fixing her golden eyes on his.

He'd never seen eyes that color on a human, only on cats—and owls. Handing her a mug of tea, he answered, "Yeah, I really do need your help hanging this oil painting. My uncle painted it. It's my grandmother. Do you like it?"

She took a big sip of the tea, inhaling the aroma deeply, and taking a step back, tipped her head to one side and then the other before answering him. "I do like it, very much. I like that it's impressionistic, not a rendered portrait. It has a lot of character. Where do you want to hang it?"

"Where do you think I should hang it? You're the expert, right?"

Scoping out the room, she headed to the counter where Nico was standing. "You're always at this counter either cooking or eating. So I would hang it over there." She walked about eight paces to an empty wall visible from the kitchen. "You can see your grandmother all the time. It's a large enough painting to stand alone there."

"Hold it up for me, can you?" he asked, considering her idea thoughtfully.

She grasped the painting in both hands and placed it against the wall so her eyes fell about dead center.

"I can't see through you!" he complained.

"Nico, it's big and heavy! Just pretend I'm transparent!"

"Ha!" he laughed. "It's good there. I trust you. Let me get a nail and hammer."

Without any deliberation, Cherie hung the painting. Back in the kitchen, she eyed it approvingly while finishing her mug of tea.

"I like it. It looks good there." Nico paused, thinking. "I have this tapestry. Where would you hang *it*?" He showed her a finely woven scene of mountains she assumed were the Andes.

"Wow, Nico—this is beautiful. How about on the wall behind your bed?"

Cherie took off her shoes and stood on the bed, holding it over her head, "What do you think?"

He chuckled, "I think your ass is divine, and I can't wait to fuck it."

Turning to look over her shoulder, she almost fell down with the tapestry in her arms. "Go get me three long nails," she playfully ordered.

As she gingerly rested the tapestry now attached to a dowel on top of the nails, she used her best authoritative tone, "Just be careful you don't knock it off the wall. Come, look at it from here."

Still barefoot from class, Nico climbed onto the bed and tugged her down. "You are so bossy!" he teased. Straddling her playfully, he pinned her arms over her head and kissed her forcefully, pushing his tongue into her mouth and swirling it around hers. Then, tearing his mouth away, he chided breathlessly, "Now it's my turn to teach *you* something."

Sliding his hand up her thigh and under the short, flirty floral dress, he could feel the heat of her pussy under the boy shorts she was wearing. She was a tantalizing blend of exotic beauty and androgynous child. "Mmm…how sexy. You're wearing boy underpants."

"They aren't boys'!" She squirmed at his touch, then whispered provocatively, "If you don't like them, I'll take them off now."

"Allow me," he purred. As he pulled them down, a soft cry escaped her lips. The chiffon minidress was now bunched around her waist, her bottom bare. Nico admired her long, lean body and perfect skin the color of toasted caramel, "I like this little flower girl dress," he said, his voice low and gravelly. "You're like a child."

Pushing the dress up higher, he cupped her small but perfectly round breasts, still confined underneath a white cotton eyelet bra. She moaned when he squeezed hard, his thumb pressing her erect nipples now straining at the fabric. Lifting the bra up, he bent his head down and licked them, savoring the sweet taste of her freshly washed skin. Trailing his tongue over her breasts, he tentatively flicked the dark stems, coaxing them to further rigidity. Taking a nipple into his mouth, he sucked hard until she cried out.

"Mmmm…you have the longest nipples in the world," he sighed. Rolling the hard bud between his lips, he asked earnestly, as if needing her approval, "You like when I play with your tits?"

She groaned, her nipples on fire. "Yes! Very much." Her back arched up to him, begging for more.

He wanted to slam his hard cock into her. But it was even better having her captive and vulnerable, pleading for him.

"I want you to fuck me—now," she begged, squirming under him. His hands clasped her wrists tightly, pressing them into the mattress, while her hips bucked as if she were trying to free herself.

But he wanted her frantic.

"Where do you think you're going?" he asked menacingly.

She tugged at his hands, and after a moment's consideration, he freed her. Staring at the enormous bulge beneath the thin fabric of his yoga pants and licking her lips, she looked up innocently into his lust-filled eyes, where the yellow flecks threw lightning bolts of anticipation. "You want my cock?" he asked huskily.

She nodded. Her almond-shaped eyes, spaced perfectly on her angelic face, pleaded with him. He couldn't contain himself much longer. Yanking his pants down, he kicked them off.

She'd already guessed he wasn't wearing underwear, knowing that was why no one took their eyes off him in class. He stroked his cock firmly, with slow, strong pulls. "Open that luscious mouth for me, baby."

Positioning her at the edge of the bed, he held her head and pushed eagerly into her mouth. "God, baby. Those lips are exquisite around me," he growled, sliding over her velvet tongue.

Locking her eyes onto his, she wrapped her fingers around the width of his manhood and began pleasuring him. Pulling firmly toward his root, she slowly drew her hand back, sliding her wet palm over the head of his cock. Rubbing the tip over her lips, she smiled innocently up at him, her eyes burning into his, before placing him back into her mouth and sucking until her cheeks hollowed. Her tongue twirled deftly around his mushroomed head as she licked precum from the slit before guiding him deep into the back of her throat—her humming, low and sexy, sent vibrations around him. Gripping the backs of his thighs, she took him deeper, contracting her throat to gently squeeze the thick shaft. He groaned, his hips rocketing as he gathered fists full of her hair, and his head lolled back in ecstasy.

Releasing her, he pulled out so she could catch her breath, running his finger along her jawline and over her lips. "Open," his voice was strangled, but commanding. He pushed back into her mouth and fucked it slowly, sliding deep into the back of her throat before pulling out—until just the tip stayed between her full lips.

Lavishly, as if it was her last meal, she licked and sucked him hungrily, feeling his climax building to a crescendo. The veins on his forehead bulged, and his breathing became ragged as her hands trailed down from his clenched buttocks to fondle his balls, then moved to the rim of his anus. She looked up. His eyes were closed, and she could hear him purring loudly from deep inside his chest, like a mountain lion she had tamed.

Suddenly, he pulled out of her mouth. "Turn over, give me your ass," he growled, his voice raspy and anguished. Cherie turned and positioned herself on her knees at the end of the bed, her wet, glistening pink pussy bared to him. "So beautiful…like a pink flower." His hypnotic voice washed over her.

With urgent desperation, he hoisted her ass into the air, his fingers digging into her hips to hold her steady. She gasped sharply as he penetrated her and was enveloped by the slick, wet walls of her pussy.

"Oh God, baby…you're so tight! Like a virgin," he gasped. Her pussy quivered as she grew wetter around him, and a whimper escaped her lips.

At first he fucked her gently, luxuriating in the blissful sensation of her tight muscles around his cock and watching his dick disappear from sight, then reappear, covered in her juices. He loved fucking her from behind. Her ass was perfect—high, round, dark-skinned, without a single blemish. She had gone to one of the expensive Asian salons for a full Brazilian and was as bare as a newborn baby. He rocked into her, plunging deep inside and repeatedly rolling over her hot spot, massaging it into submission, before pulling out until only the tip remained inside her.

Crying out in a frenzy, she lifted her ass and wiggled it, pleading with him, "God, Nico. You're such a tease—fuck me!" she begged.

His touch was electrifying—each stroke measured and strategically placed to send her to the edge and bring her back again. She wanted—needed—him inside her, filling her over and over. His rough, selfish urgency made her feel supremely desirable. Yet he was attentive, knowing exactly what she needed—what she wanted—so that when she came, it would be an orgasm that was nonpareil.

Her begging, pleading, and whining fueled his lust. Thrusting back into her, he pumped hard and fast. She panted, her legs stiffening, and then he felt her go liquid around him. He reached around to finger her pussy, collecting her wetness on his hands and fondling her swollen clit, sending shock waves ricocheting through her body. Bringing his fingers up to his nose, he inhaled her scent deeply. It was both musky and sweet, a mix of wild animal and fragrant herbs. Losing control, he gripped her ass, his thumbs leaving an impression in her flesh as he powered into her. The sound of his thighs slapping her ass over and over while he fucked her long and hard filled the room. Feeling her pulsing, the waves of another orgasm surging over his cock, his eyes glazed over and the room dissolved around him. He couldn't hold on and spent hot jets of cum over the walls of her pussy.

Lying on his bed recovering, Cherie rested her head on his chest, listening to his racing heart. Then, as his breathing became normal, she shifted her body to get up.

"Where are you going?" Nico asked.

"Home. I have things to do and an early day tomorrow."

"Oh, I thought you would stay for dinner."

"Next time. Invite me. You know—in advance."

"I never know what I'm doing. You know that."

She got up, tugging her bra back down over her breasts. She found her boy shorts on the floor and pulled them on. After slipping on her shoes, she walked over and kissed the top of his head. Still lying on the bed, he watched her preparing to leave. As she headed for the door, she turned and looked above the bed. Smiling, she said, "The tapestry is beautiful, Nico."

He grinned wickedly. "Thanks for helping me."

∘ ∘ ∘

Sitting on one of the black barstools at a large wraparound counter in front of the open kitchen, Olivia busily inserted the evening's specials into the dinner menu. Plato Picante, a trendy restaurant in Studio City was an open and airy restaurant known for authentic Mexican cuisine. Olivia knew she was lucky to have found a job where she met interesting people in the entertainment industry who occasionally left big tips after ordering the best margaritas in town. Being midafternoon, the restaurant was almost empty. Sunlight poured through large glass windows onto the dozens of potted palms and ficus trees dotting the dining room. She was softly rehearsing her part in the "Sull'aria" duet from *Le nozze di Figaro* when the lunch chef interrupted to say a customer had seated himself at one of the outdoor tables, under a red umbrella. Clutching her pencil and notepad, she quickly darted past a lingering group of girls she recognized from school and headed toward the waiting man with a sigh—a sigh of quiet desperation. Her thoughts wandered, *was it Thoreau who wrote that? That quote about most people leading lives of quiet desperation...*

Olivia hadn't tried to be different, but as the only child of a Mexican housekeeper, she had struggled to fit in with L.A.'s nobility at Harvard-Westlake School. Instead of dreaming about society parties and shopping at Fred Segal, she fantasized herself an opera diva, bouquets being tossed to her onstage as the audience yelled "brava"— quite unusual given her age and upbringing in urban Los Angeles, where kids mostly dreamed about becoming the next Rihanna.

Olivia's long, curly, brown hair was loosely tied back in a low ponytail, and several wayward strands had escaped to frame her oval face. Her full lips were too pale, and her translucent, violet-colored eyes looked tired. She didn't know it, but the customer's keen talent for reading people combined with her appearance told him much more about her than she would have liked.

"May I take your order?" she asked mechanically. When the customer said nothing, she looked at him.

He stared into her eyes, and she faltered. *He's not so much handsome as…*her thoughts paused while she searched for the right description…*magnetic. That's the word,* she decided.

As if meaning to purposely break her trance, he spoke up, "What do you recommend?" The prosaic tone and topic seemed out of place and made her feel a bit disoriented.

She finally found her voice, "Well, I really love the mole poblano con pollo tacos."

"I'll trust your taste, then." He smiled enigmatically, closing the menu decisively and handing it to her.

"What would you like to drink? Maybe iced tea?"

"Yes, please. That would be very nice."

She rushed away, uncertain why she felt so flustered. After giving the order to the chef, she delivered his iced tea. He looked up, and their eyes locked for just a moment before she turned away and hurried back to the counter. She continued her task of placing specials into menus, angling her seat sideways so she could see if he signaled for her. When the order was ready, she walked it over to him and casually said, "Enjoy." Again, his eyes penetrated hers, and she tried to hold his gaze, but nervously looked to the floor before returning to her post at the counter.

Watching him from under her eyelashes, she noticed he ate a bit too quickly and was simultaneously texting on his phone. His dark hair fell over his face, and he swiped it back with his hand absentmindedly, like a preening bird. He was wearing slim, black yoga pants and vintage-inspired black plimsolls stamped with a red laurel wreath. The words Amaru Yoga were printed in red letters on his black T-shirt, and she thought the name seemed familiar, yet she had never noticed him before. Certainly she would have remembered someone this dreamy. Thoroughly immersed in his iPhone, he ate inattentively, his feet supinated—shuffling as if keeping time to a song with a good beat though he wasn't wearing earbuds. To Olivia, he seemed like an adorable little boy, somewhat unsure of himself. Admonishing herself for staring, she finished placing the last insert into the menu.

Leaning over the counter, the chef teased, "What's with you and Romeo over there?"

Embarrassed, she shrugged and feigned nonchalance. "I dunno, he's kind of weird. I think he's one of those 'I'm so cool because I'm foreign' types."

When she noticed the handsome stranger had finished eating, she returned to drop off the check. Her shyness overtook her, and she automatically mumbled, "Thanks. Come again." After placing the bill on the table she attempted to scurry away. But he caught her gently by the elbow to stop her leaving, and his touch felt hot and prickly, like a shock from a doorknob in winter.

"Sorry, I didn't mean to startle you. I just wanted to invite you to visit my new yoga studio, Amaru. Across the street." He pointed to the other side of Ventura Blvd.

Only then did Olivia remember where she had seen the name, noticing the For Lease sign had been replaced by one reading Amaru Yoga. "I thought I recalled the name on your T-shirt. I must've seen the new sign when I was coming to work."

Pleased she had noticed the studio name, he continued, "This is only a temporary location. I'll be moving to Beverly Hills soon. I'm a yoga master, but Amaru's not an ordinary yoga studio. I cater to celebrities and perform healing ceremonies." He paused to ensure Olivia met his gaze. "There are many people in need of my help here in L.A., don't you think?" He flashed a captivating grin at her.

Olivia couldn't help chuckling. "Definitely true!"

His eyes twinkled with sly flirtatiousness. "Then you'll come?" he asked.

She returned his smile and nodded. The stranger's gaze was making her pulse race and her hands sweat. Seeking an escape, she uttered, "I'm sorry. The restaurant's getting busy."

He interrupted her, "By the way, I'm Nico Romero." Tilting his head, he smiled wryly. "And you are?"

She looked up and immediately wished she hadn't. Staring into those unnaturally deep green eyes, she had the sensation of a drifting descent into…something.

"Olivia," she answered. Her voice sounded to her like someone else's, submerged in water.

An awkwardly long pause followed before she dimly heard him ask, "Olivia, what gives you joy in life? What's your passion?"

Rolling her eyes, she blurted, "I want to be an opera singer."

"No, no, Olivia," Nico replied with sincere interest. "You *are* an opera singer. Say it that way. It's very important." He searched for something in her face, but she wasn't sure what.

Self-consciously, she shrugged her shoulders and replied in a small voice, "I am an opera singer," adding an uptick at the end that made it sound more like a question.

Nico's lips twitched into a hint of a smile. "Better, but not with belief—yet. I'll help you with that."

His confidence and certainty kind of irritated her, yet she also inexplicably felt drawn to him. An insecure, little girl part of her wanted so badly to believe he could keep that promise.

Returning later to collect the check where he had been sitting, Olivia found he had left just enough to cover the bill and a pass to Amaru Yoga Studio. "Cheapskate!" she mumbled to herself. Picking up the pass, she saw he'd written something on the back, "You *are* an opera singer, princesita. I will help you claim your dream." Tucking the pass into her pocket, she mused. She hadn't gotten a tip, but at least she'd gotten a free yoga session.

2

On her way to Nico's studio, Luna wondered why her mouth was dry and her jaw tensed. In her career, she had become a trusted confidante to Hollywood's elite; even the most self-obsessed movie stars entrusted her with their image. Certainly, meeting with a hot Latin man should not make her nervous. Plus, she was curious to see if yoga could be the magic bullet that would turn back her clock.

Driving to Amaru brought to mind the first time she had taken a ballet lesson. She must have been around four years old—hiding behind her mother, peering out at the older girls. Standing in front of the mirror, Luna's eyes remained fixed on the ballet mistress, who moved like a magical bird and had arms like the wings of an angel. Luna wanted to be just like her, so she memorized every tilt of the head and placement of fingers. Listening to the piano player, Luna mirrored the steps of the girl in front of her, embarrassed when the teacher stopped to adjust her placement. Soon she learned corrections were given only to girls the teacher believed had promise, and Luna still vividly remembered the day when a new girl was placed behind *her*. She cherished those moments, working diligently to be recognized. Not until she became a relatively successful costume designer did she realize ballet had given her the focus and perseverance to listen, learn, observe, and work hard to get noticed.

Pulling into a parking space at Amaru Yoga, she felt a small flutter in her belly. She'd had that same feeling when the piano began and she attempted her first plie. Inside, Nico greeted her warmly with a kiss on each cheek. Luna found that custom charming, if slightly awkward because she never knew which cheek came first.

Nico's loose, black yoga pants hung just right on his slim hips.

A white T-shirt with graphic tribal snake design revealed his broad shoulders and chest and provided contrast to the warm skin tone of his strong arms. Nico moved gracefully, like a dancer, showing her around the studio space with pride, telling her how the floors had been rescued from an old church in his hometown in Argentina. Luna found herself taking him in, then looked away, red-faced, when she realized that although his sweats were loose, the fabric clung to the perfect form of his manhood. Laughing at herself, she wondered if her scrutiny came from being a woman or a costume designer.

Pushing those thoughts aside, she focused on the music playing in the background—light, breathy tones of flutes combined with gentle and soft drumming immediately soothed her. "What is that you're playing?" she asked. Nico replied that he'd created a station on Spotify he called "Healing Flutes of the Andes," because it rooted him in the mountains where he felt physically and spiritually connected.

He escorted Luna into a little chamber painted a dark oxblood red surprisingly similar to the color of her den at home, with oversized woven tapestry pillows surrounding a low slate table. A shelf on one wall held stone artifacts and primitively carved bowls. Gesturing for her to sit down, he poured them each a mug of tea from a black iron teapot. Still a bit nervous, Luna got up and walked to a gallery of framed photos on the wall facing her. They depicted Nico with local Indians in brightly colored costumes; the majestic Andes Mountains provided a backdrop.

Luna inquired about a picture of him sitting in a circle, a drummer in the center. He replied, "I asked permission for that photo to be taken before we started the ceremony. That's where I learned everything about healing and how to find the cause of illness, not to just treat symptoms." Then getting down to the business at hand, he prompted, "What is your life like? What brings you joy?"

Luna spoke rapidly, almost too quickly, describing a typically stressful day of eating quickly while working, getting home late, and drinking wine to unwind before the next day's repeat performance.

When she finally slowed down, Nico handed her another mug of tea—a fragrant concoction of herbs and lemon. The aroma and warmth comforted and relaxed her. Settling down, she looked up and saw his eyes—they glowed. "Luna, you are like the mouse running in the wheel—and missing everything around you. There is more to life."

Luna inhaled deeply, then sighed.

Nico continued, "Yoga's only one part of my program. Most important is energy healing, which is curing disease by dealing with the root of the problem. Then yoga gets you in harmony with the universe and you can channel the energy." He took a sip of his tea before continuing, "First, we must clean the mind, body, and spirit. I'll completely undo all the damage, imbalances, and illnesses that have controlled your body for decades. You'll be completely cured for life, and look as young and beautiful as I know you were in your twenties. All this—literally saving your life—for only $10,000."

Luna balked, incredulous. She replied bluntly, "Wow—that's some pricey plan. How exactly does it work?"

Unfazed, Nico answered evenly and warmly, without any sleazy, assertive sales pitch, "My program is for energy work. This includes a diagnosis, cleanse, private healing, and yoga sessions. After three or four weeks, you'll be healed, looking and feeling young and full of vitality. When your initial program is complete, you continue maintenance sessions with me."

Logically, Luna was aware the cost was extravagant, even for her. How could she justify so much money to Tyler? Why was she even considering it? Just then, Nico's iPhone vibrated, and he excused himself to take the call.

Feeling a warm spot in her stomach and an unusual flutter sensation, she wondered, was it the tea? The mystical sound of flutes filled her head. Looking up at the wall of photos, her eye stopped on one of Nico with his arm draped around a smiling Indian man in native costume who stood only as high as Nico's shoulder. Nico's mesmerizing eyes shone out at her from the photo. Maybe this program would work. She had tried to commit to the gym and too many diets to count. Maybe *this* would be the change she needed. When Nico returned to the chamber, she already had her checkbook out.

o   o   o

Preparing for her first session with Nico, Luna changed into yoga pants and a loose-fitting T-shirt, emulating what he had worn when she met with him. Nico had said he would know exactly what she needed after the ceremony, and though she hadn't said anything, the word ceremony was flipping her out. When she arrived and he again greeted her with the double-cheek kiss, she made a mental note that it was right cheek first. Then she thought, *With a ceremony looming, why am I focusing on cheek order?*

They moved into the room Nico called the chamber, which that evening was lit only by candlelight. Nico explained, "I see better in the dark during a ceremony."

She looked around. A black metal teapot sat on the slate table alongside two mugs, just as before. The sound of a solitary flute accompanied by flowing water, though slightly mournful, immediately calmed her senses. Nico sat on one of the large pillows and gestured for her to do the same, handing her a mug of tea. Taking it, she asked, "What kind of tea is this anyway?"

He replied, "It's to relax you and awaken your spirit body. Now close your eyes, drink the tea, and focus on the music. I'm going to prepare a smoke cleanse."

Closing her eyes as instructed, she caught the aroma of a fragrant herb she recognized as sage, used by many native tribes to remove bad energy.

Nico softly sang along with the music—more of a low chant than singing, but not in Spanish. Having done a bit of Googling, she assumed it to be Quechua, the language of the Q'ero. Her eyes were closed, but she felt a light breeze and heard a soft rattle as he guided the smoke up the front of her body and over her head with a feather wand. She knew about smudging, so didn't find it strange or uncomfortable and made a mental note to tell him about her Mohawk ancestry.

When he said she could open her eyes, she saw Nico had spread a sheet of white paper on the table and placed one red and one white carnation face up on it. A large oyster shell lay in the middle. She watched as he took three small, oval leaves in his fingers and pressed them to his lips as if kissing them, at the same time whispering something softly in Quechua.

Placing them around the shell, he addressed her, "This ceremony is called a despacho, an offering to Mother Earth, Pachamama. We're requesting her guidance and asking her to remove negative spirits. It's an exchange, so we make her a beautiful and powerful offering."

Moving to a shelf laden with uncommon artifacts, Nico retrieved several jars and boxes, returning and placing them on the table. When he sprinkled cornmeal over the flowers, Luna almost said aloud she knew it was the accepted gift to Mother Earth. One by one, Nico placed items on the paper in a decorative fashion. She recognized pale green sage for purification and golden brown tobacco, the favored gift to the Great Spirit. Opening a box containing many compartments holding bits of gemstones, he removed three pieces she recognized as turquoise, agate, and amethyst. Analyzing each step and every element, she reprimanded herself for not being in the moment.

From an artifact depicting the head of a strange man/god, Nico removed what Luna was certain was bone. After pouring oil from a glass jar, he produced a pair of scissors and asked if he could cut a few strands of her hair. Feeling that warm flutter in a place deep in her stomach, she could only nod. He gently lifted a few strands and snipped once, placing the cuttings ceremoniously on the seashell. Then, choosing a feather from a bouquet-like display on the table, he placed it across the top of the shell.

From Ziploc bags, so different from the ceremonial objects before, Nico added alphabet noodles and brightly colored candy she recognized as Mentos and Skittles. She admired how pretty it was with the candy, but then he did something that caused her to gasp. Taking a small pocketknife, he pricked his finger and sprinkled droplets of blood on the four corners of the arrangement. She looked inquiringly at him, but he was again softly chanting, lost in trance as he folded the paper, encapsulating the gift to Pachamama. Tying the bundle with string to secure it tightly, he then added a red ribbon for decoration.

Helping her to her feet, he murmured, "Stand up." Chanting softly, he placed the despacho over her solar plexus, tapping there several times before sweeping it over her body, as if painting her from head to toe. After each pass, he brought the bundle to his lips and whistled, shaking the bundle vigorously. Though aware she was in Nico's chamber, she felt her spirit body had been transported to a time and place long ago when she was more alive and free.

Taking her hands in his, Nico gently brought her back to the present saying, "We're not quite finished. The gift has to be delivered." He moved toward a corner of the chamber where a fireplace with a copper flue sat. Luna hadn't noticed it on her last visit because it had been concealed by a painted screen depicting the Andes and apparently had been uncovered for this occasion. Striking a long match on the slate table, Nico lit a fire and placed the offering on it. Turning their backs to it, he explained, "We can't watch Pachamama consume her gift." With the ceremony now over, he embraced her, whispering something in Quechua that she did not understand. After she got her bearings, all she could say was, "Wow! That was incredible."

The authenticity of the ceremony reminded her of the visit she had made to the Kahnawake reserve in hopes of getting closer to her origins. Adopted as a baby, she always had a burning curiosity about her Native American heritage. Her parents had only told her she'd come from an Indian reservation where she couldn't be cared for and that she was special. Not wanting them to think her ungrateful, she never pressed for details, and it was long after her mother had passed away before she delved into records and discovered her great-great grandfather, a French fur trapper, had married a native woman.

Feeling restored, she asked, "What did the gemstones represent?"

"Various minerals resonate with different energy. Come with me, and I'll explain while I check my messages." He took her hand to lead her into his office, causing that fiery flutter in her belly again—like a thousand butterflies beating their wings. At his desk, he talked while busily clicking back and forth between e-mail and the text messages on his phone. "Turquoise is for protection, good fortune, and a fresh start. Amethyst is a request for higher knowledge, courage, and self-esteem." He paused, looking her in the eye, "You have all this within yourself already, Luna, but we ask Pachamama to give you access to it by offering her amethyst."

Luna was ambivalent about the crystal energy thing; she remembered when it had been a popular fad in the '90s and everyone had purchased crystal pendants. But now, listening to Nico speak with conviction about each stone's significance and energy, she felt more inclined to embrace the concept. Besides, she liked the stones he'd chosen, especially because most of her everyday jewelry was silver and turquoise, so it seemed totally appropriate to her. Come to think of it, she also had a pair of amethyst earrings she rarely wore. Learning the power of their energy, she decided to make a point of wearing them more often.

After being distracted by an e-mail, Nico continued, "And the agate was a request to raise your consciousness and give you emotional and physical balance."

Luna stood up straight, arching her eyebrows. "Tyler gave me a bronze seahorse necklace with agate beads for my birthday. No wonder I always feel better when I wear it," she exclaimed.

Nico grinned as he began scrolling through his Facebook photos. "I love seahorses! They're a symbol of delicacy and balance. The sea itself is very special to me. Last year, when I went home, I found a live seahorse on the beach." Then suddenly landing on a photo, he chimed enthusiastically, "Look, here it is! See, I took a picture."

Luna leaned over his shoulder to see, then realizing how close their faces were, felt uncomfortable and changed the subject. "So, what's the deal with the Mentos and Skittles?" she giggled nervously, stepping a little bit away from him.

He threw his head back, laughing, "Why, Luna, spirits like sugar! Didn't you know?"

His playful innocence erased any apprehension she still felt. Sneaking a peek at the screen, she saw photos of Nico on the beach, bronzed and revealing ripped abs in each one. She'd had no idea you could get such a well-built body from yoga. But before she had a chance to comment, Nico grabbed his phone, noticing a text. Turning, he casually dismissed her, "Come again on Monday—at noon." He acted like there was no reason she might be unable to show up any time he commanded.

Luna hesitated. She usually got to work early in the morning, and rarely left before 7:00 p.m. But she found herself acquiescing, reasoning that she'd tell Sam, her assistant, she had a doctor's appointment. After noting the appointment in her calendar, she was surprised when Nico followed her out the door and walked her to her car. This time, when he gave her the double-cheek kiss, the simple ritual felt like a blessing.

In her dark green Land Rover, she turned the ignition without closing the door, then powered down her window. Shutting the door for her, Nico leaned in, his thick black hair falling onto her shoulder as he scrutinized the contents of her car. Bags of clothes sat on her backseat, items she'd picked up for the cast at a vintage store. "Where'd you get those clothes?" he asked. "Do they have any cool leather jackets there, you think?" Luna told him about her favorite shop, which was right there on Ventura. He nodded thoughtfully, then brightened. Taking her hand and kissing it, he said, "Drive carefully, Luna bella. You need to go that way," he pointed, "to get to Laurel Canyon." She internally rolled her eyes; did he forget she had lived here her entire adult life and he'd just moved here? *He's so controlling,* she thought, but then decided he probably was just being caring, which was kind of sweet.

o   o   o

Luna quickly ran through the talent's wardrobe, feeling especially good about the selections she'd put together. Engrossed with show preparations, she was perplexed when Sam said she'd be late for her doctor's appointment. *What doctor's appointment?* she thought, then remembered she was due at Nico's studio. Hoping her momentary pause of confusion wasn't apparent, she gave Sam a list of tasks to be handled while she was gone, and hurried out of the office.

Nico greeted Luna with sexy, sleepy-looking eyes and bed head hair. Having finally remembered the order, she welcomed the cheek kisses without hesitation and deeply inhaled his lovely, warm, citrus and wood scent, wondering how someone could always look so hot and seductive.

"Come, bella," he said, leading her into the yoga studio.

He got right down to business, explaining, "Kundalini Yoga raises the vibration of your body's energy to a higher frequency, awakening your inner power and raising your awareness. You become one with the universal force." He was so close, she could feel the heat emanating from his body. "The chakras are your energy centers. They control different parts of your life experience, so a smooth connection throughout your body is vital. To open the pathways between them, we do the energy work of Kundalini." Placing one palm firmly on the small of her back and one finger from the other hand very low on her abdomen, he went on, "There are seven chakras."

The sudden contact startled her. Either Nico didn't notice, or he pretended not to. "Kundalini is the untapped energy, called prana, coiled like a snake at the bottom of the spine in the root chakra." He slowly dragged his finger up the front of her body and continued, "The kriyas—exercises—performed during sessions will move the prana into your heart chakra." He stopped between her breasts just long enough for her skin to grow hot. Then, placing his finger gently on her forehead, he said, "Finally, the prana is moved into your third eye." He paused, gazing deeply into her eyes and added, "Any blockage in your chakras will distort the flow of energy and limit the possibilities in your life."

Luna was mesmerized by his soothing, hypnotic voice. "Let's begin with the Sat Nam kriya, a very potent seed mantra. In the Sat Nam kriya, the force of your breath moves the mantra—the chant— and that creates waves of the mind. They're how you move energy through your body. By using your breath to open and balance each chakra, eventually they all open."

He paused to confirm she was still following him. When she nodded her understanding, he went on, "The mantra for this kriya is Sat Nam, which means 'my true identity; my true divine nature.'"

Lilting flutes and soft drums flowed pleasantly through the room in surround sound. Nico watched her carefully as they performed the Sat Nam kriya together, and seeing she was struggling to keep her arms in the upright position, knelt in front of her. Holding her arms over her head, he placed his hands on her shoulders to move them slightly until they were just across her ears. Finally, he slid his hand under her buttocks, ensuring her heels were in just the right spot to activate the pressure point. His familiarity both unnerved and electrified Luna, but she tried to stay focused on his instruction. He told her to start the Sat Nam kriya again, and as she said Sat, he placed his hand over her navel.

Again, she felt the electricity of his touch, and finding his tone seductive, she was eager to please him. When she said Nam and he released the pressure of his hand, she felt a little pang of disappointment. "Don't be shy, Luna. Repeat and use more force. Your breath is sweet." She wondered what he meant by that, but didn't ask. "I'm here to teach you. Breathing is essential to Kundalini, and this is a very fundamental kriya. We'll master it together."

He took her arm, "Now let's go into the chamber and get some tea."

Within a few minutes of sipping the warm concoction, she realized she felt more energized and surprisingly happy. She looked at him inquiringly. "What's in this wonderful tea you make me?"

He smiled cryptically. "It's special. I get it from home."

His phone was vibrating constantly now, and she wondered what was going on, realizing he must not have had it with him during their session. Now he was distracted, and she needed to get back to the studio, so she said a quick good-bye. Without looking up from the phone, he called over his shoulder, "Be here again tomorrow at 11:00 a.m."

"Sorry, Nico. Tomorrow is a very busy day. The actors are coming in for wardrobe fittings. Could I come in the evening instead?"

Baffled, he paused before replying, "Sure, that would be fine. Come at seven. You can watch me teach a class."

Olivia's dream intensified. Her Great Dane, Brontë, shifted her position away from her human's twitching legs. The man in Olivia's dream approached to take her into his arms in the kind of sweeping embrace novelists never accurately describe. Her breath paused. His touch had an electrical intensity, making her entire body tingle with desire, and fulfilling her in indescribable ways. Suddenly, she jerked into wakefulness. *What was that noise?* The thought bubbled into the part of her brain that was not home to her sense of self, as though her mind had a separate life apart from her consciousness. She listened intently to the blackness outside. There it was—a low nicker from Casper. Trying not to disturb Brontë, who was now snoring softly on top of the covers next to her, she crept out of the bed and padded carefully to the window, then pressed her ear against the glass.

Casper, her Arab/Quarter Horse, had been a gift from Kathy, who employed Olivia's mother, Emma, as manager of the estate, overseeing staff and discretely handling family affairs. Olivia and Emma lived in a guest house on the estate, just outside of L.A., where the wealthy and famous chose to live for more open space and privacy. Kathy was descended from one of California's old money families, and with no children of her own, she had become a benefactor to Olivia.

Casper nickered again—a very low, cautious call to Olivia. She grabbed her jeans and sweatshirt off the chair, and tugged them on. Outside, the moonlight cast a bluish glow almost more visible than the lights from the city. She loved this kind of night, when it was blissfully quiet. Nearing Casper's paddock, she paused and listened again.

Silence. In fact, it was *too* silent.

Something caught her attention at the very edge of her peripheral vision. Instinctively holding her breath, she turned her head slowly, suppressing the urge to blink until the image came into focus.

Underneath the eaves of the barn, a coyote eyed her from his position next to the bales of hay. Blinking a few times to clear her vision, she saw the coyote remained impossibly still; flecks of gold in his eyes glittered in the reflected light. They just watched each other for what seemed to be hours.

When Casper nickered softly again, Olivia jumped, nearly toppling over. She'd almost forgotten why she'd come outside, as if the only reason for her presence there now was to commune with the coyote—one of the few species of wildlife in this Valley-adjacent area. She realized the coyote must be why Casper had called for reinforcements. Reaching her hand out to give the horse a scratch under his chin, she cooed, "It's OK sweetie." Casper inhaled with a little whuff, then let out a very long sigh. Glancing back toward the barn, she noticed the coyote had grown bored with her and was now watching something—probably a mouse—among the hay bales.

o   o   o

Olivia stood in the shower, hot water cascading down her back. Lathering her hair with a mango scented shampoo, she belted out "Angel of Music" from *Phantom of the Opera*, while deliberately shaving her legs, and wondered why she was focusing on this ritual.

A small voice in her head offered up thoughts about Nico's impressively masculine body and dark, sultry looks, but she quickly pushed them aside. Returning to her bedroom, she wondered what she should wear to a yoga studio. Rifling through her dresser drawers, she finally settled on a pair of old leggings.

Nico's studio was in a prime area on Ventura, so Olivia anticipated trouble finding a parking spot. Checking the clock on her dashboard, she worried about the time, but when she turned the corner, she saw the parking lot right behind Amaru Yoga.

Stepping into Amaru, she saw a class was just ending, and students were still seated cross-legged in what she guessed was the lotus position. The room was eerily quiet, and looking to the front of the class she saw Nico's eyes fixed on her. Feeling her face heat up, she turned away and tiptoed over to a table of literature about the studio. She picked up a brochure and pretended to read, but her mind wasn't absorbing the words on the page. She was thinking about Nico's penetrating stare and his beautiful hands with their long, elegant fingers. Thankfully, it wasn't long before she heard Nico say "Namaste," and the class replied. She turned and watched the students gather their bags and mats and head out the door.

Looking where Nico had been standing, she saw he was no longer at the front of the room, but she hadn't seen him move. When someone brushed the small of her back, she flinched. Nico had managed to sneak up behind her. Alarmed, she turned to face him, and saw he was staring at her warmly, his eyes dancing with a hint of amusement. "I'm sorry, *princesa*, I didn't mean to startle you. Did you not hear me?"

She replied quickly, "Do you always sneak up on people? I think maybe you do."

He laughed, a rich, deep, and surprisingly sexy laugh. "Oh, Olivia, you'll be a wonderful student," he replied, without answering her question. "Come, let's begin your training with learning to breathe."

Trailing him to the mats, where they sat cross-legged facing each other, she was exasperated. "Nico, I'm an opera singer! I *know* how to breathe already!"

A Cheshire-cat grin crossed his face, "Excellent, Olivia! You said you *are* an opera singer. See, I've already helped you."

She realized she had, indeed, made a positive statement of her talent. Gratified, she returned his grin, and her resistance to his charm melted away.

He began, "I know you've been trained how to breathe for singing, of course, *querida*. But I will teach you how to harness the fire of your sexual energy to give great power to your voice."

Sexual energy? she thought, shocked. "What do you mean…exactly…I mean, by harnessing sexual energy?" She felt herself beginning to blush.

"Your sexual energy is held here, in your sacral chakra." His fingers pressed firmly into her flesh at the very top of her buttocks. "Certainly you must know that sexual energy is creative energy too, no?"

He paused, and she realized he actually expected an answer. She nodded her head. "I'd never really thought about it, but I guess that makes sense."

Nico eyed her closely, his face giving no hint of what he was thinking, though it was clear he was pondering something about her. The corners of his mouth twitched up as if he knew some secret thing about her that he wasn't going to share. Instead, he continued, "Well, yes, Olivia, sex itself is creative energy. Some artists abstain from sex in order to create." As he was speaking, a lock of hair had fallen over one eye. Now he peered at Olivia from underneath the errant curl, the golden sparks in his eyes shimmered. "For me, sex stimulates creativity."

Her heart quivered wildly, and she was certain he knew secrets about her she didn't even dare to consider. Intensely drawn to him, she remained silent as he continued the lesson.

"Through our kriyas, we harness the powers of the chakras to direct our energy. Because you're an opera singer, we'll focus on harnessing your sexual energy to bring forth your most powerful creative voice. Now let's chant the Sat Nam mantra while breathing deeply, from your solar plexus. I'm sure you know how to do that, right?"

She nodded.

Closing her eyes, she matched her breathing to his and chanted along with him. The sound of their voices commingling—soothing and hypnotic—induced a transcendental state that permeated her spirit, connecting her to him.

When Nico spoke, Olivia's eyes fluttered open.

Her breathing had become shallow and rapid, and he listened, cocking his head alluringly. Without comment, he went on, "Let me teach you the Breath of Fire—*Kapala Bati.*" The exotic words tripped off his tongue like the primal beat of a timba drum. "This kriya for powerful breath pulls the energy from your sacral chakra, here," he placed one hand low on her belly as he spoke.

His touch was a sudden fire burning through her clothes, causing an intense heat to spark between her legs and deep within her belly, as if her womb had been placed under a heat lamp. While erotic, there was also something more potent about it, but she couldn't quite grasp what that something was. Nico ran his hand slowly up her body until he reached the spot between her breasts, where he paused. As his hand moved, so did the burning she felt inside. She would have gasped were it not for the tightness within her that had begun when he touched her.

"Here," he purred, "is the heart chakra. We want to draw your sexual energy through the heart to add emotional power and love to your voice."

Olivia wondered if Nico let his hand linger between the breasts of every woman he worked with, or if he was seducing her. As if she'd spoken the thought out loud, he seemed to reply, "Querida, you are a very beautiful woman. Do not think I'm unaware of the nearness of your perfect, round breasts."

She felt a hot, deep, redness rush up her neck and face. His Cheshire-cat grin returned. "I'll never be inappropriate with you, however. That is, unless you want it."

Olivia felt an urge to throw herself on him, and the idea frightened her. She suspected he might be toying with her. His eyes mocked playfully, and his provocative words goaded her. Thoughts raced wildly through her head. *Could he really be seducing me?* Unsure of herself, she panicked and froze—discovering she could not move, nor utter a sound. Her desire was pent up in a tight knot inside her stomach. Unable to contain herself, she lifted her gaze and fell into the dark, green pools of his eyes.

"Very good. That will be all for today."

She tried not to look too disappointed their session was over.

Taking her by the hand, he helped her stand, asking if she would like to have some tea and keep him company before his next session. She eagerly accepted the invitation, and they moved to a door leading into his apartment.

Putting the kettle on his little stove, he asked, "How do you feel?"

Reticently, she put her head down and shyly uttered a simple, "OK."

"Just OK?" he purred, reaching out and placing one finger under her chin to tilt her face up.

Olivia swallowed, adding in a tiny voice, "Well, yes, I feel great, actually. I liked it…" Then, feeling awkward, she added, "Is the tea ready?"

The corners of his mouth turned up enigmatically. After placing a cup of tea in front of her, he took his cup over to the sofa and picked up his guitar. He fingered the strings quickly, the rhythm of the introductory refrain playful and contagious. Olivia immediately swayed with the melody. His eyes twinkled as he launched into the song, dramatically chanting the opening words "Hable me" to her.

The music was a welcomed diversion, and she brightened at hearing the familiar song. "I love the Gipsy Kings!" she said, moving over to the sofa to sit next to him.

Their eyes remained locked as he serenaded her expressively in Spanish, and his shoulders danced to the tempo.

Her heart melted at the thought he had chosen this song deliberately, and that the words were meant for her, "Love me, like I flirt with you. Love me, like I love you." His voice trembled in a heart-rending way, giving her goose bumps. When the chorus came around again, she joined in, her wistful and slightly melancholic voice ringing out an octave higher, perfectly accompanying his anguished and pleading tone. Their voices blending in song was the closest she could think of to what it would be like making love with him. The lyrics, "It's like a dream, and it will return," seemed poignant.

When they had finished the song, Nico's eyes lingered on hers before moving to her lips, then resting on her breasts. Lavishly admiring her, his lips curled in a surreptitious smile. "I'll get you a job singing at La Forza, my uncle's restaurant."

Olivia had hoped for something more romantic, but his approval was ample reward.

o   o   o

Luna and Sam hadn't stopped all day. Racks of clothes stood all around them, with tickets bearing scene numbers and actors' names attached to each outfit. Now it was 6:00 p.m. and they were almost done. Luna hadn't had time to think about Nico, but now she was getting antsy to leave. Picturing his smoky green eyes, she decided to head over to his studio, and asked Sam to wrap up for the day.

At a red light, she turned up the volume of Van Morrison's "Moondance," and reached into her handbag on the seat next to her, fingering the little pouch she had quickly placed inside. While putting together looks for the show, she had come across a silver Om pendant on a black leather cord. The accessory closet in the wardrobe room overflowed with jewelry and trinkets—none of it particularly valuable. Knowing Om represents all that is sacred, the talisman seemed appropriate to the work she was doing with Nico. *It will look very sexy on his warm olive skin,* she thought, remembering the feel of his hard chest and strong arms when he had embraced her after the despacho ceremony. She hoped he would like the pendant, and accept it as a token of her friendship and gratitude. She hesitated slightly. After all, she was paying a lot of money for his services. Why was she giving him a gift after knowing him so short a time? But she liked him and enjoyed being in his company.

The traffic was lighter than she expected, and arriving at the studio early, she followed the sound of meditative music. A class of about ten people stood in a lunge, arms above their heads and hands in prayer position. Feeling a little voyeuristic just watching, she went into the chamber to wait. Looking at the wall of artifacts where Nico had retrieved all the items for the despacho, she noticed they were lovely pieces, just like ones in a museum. Hearing Nico's phone vibrating, Luna thought how glad she was he didn't bring it into their sessions. She was dependent on her smartphone, and accustomed to urgent phone calls and text messages from the studio and actors' agents with demands and schedule changes, but she wondered what could be so urgent about Nico's business. His studio was always peaceful and mystical, yet he often seemed anxious.

Walking into the chamber, Nico greeted her with the now familiar double-cheek kiss, and she hugged him, startling herself with the unexpected display of intimacy. He took a quick look at his phone to check missed calls and text messages, then put it down looking mildly annoyed and said, "Come, bella, let's begin your session."

Taking her hand, he escorted her into the studio, where his Spotify channel was still playing. Luna tried to concentrate, but he seemed distracted, and his eyes lacked their usual intensity. She could hear his breathing, tense and shallow.

During the Sat Nam kriya, he placed his firm hand on her belly, coaching her to be more emphatic on Sat and relax on Nam. "Good, Luna," he said. "You're not as shy about having a forceful expression in your breathing. I'm pleased." She brightened at his praise.

When her session had ended, and she was gathering her belongings, Nico said, "I haven't eaten anything all day. Would you like to come with me to my friend's restaurant?"

Remembering the Om necklace, she thought it would be a good opportunity to give it to him. "Sure, I'm hungry, too," she called out happily.

Nico held the door open for her. "It's just a mile down the road. Let's take your car."

The restaurant was a cute little café with salads, pizza, and pasta, which all sounded like good comfort food to her. When the waiter approached, Nico waved off the menus, ordering a big arugula salad with cucumbers, vinegar, and olive oil, and one large pizza. Luna watched how he relished his food, eating with passion. Sipping her water with lemon, she thought a glass of wine would be good, but almost immediately focused back on Nico, intoxicated by him instead. He was a great storyteller, entertaining her with tales about a job he had in Argentina selling copies of fine art door to door.

"I wasn't allowed to leave without selling something. So, because I *had* to, I surveyed their house to get a feel for what they would like, then persuaded them to buy whatever I presented." He sounded so confident. "Because *I* was convinced they needed the artwork, they were too. I won the top sales award for the company!" he added triumphantly.

She laughed. "I can easily see how you can command a room, convincing anyone of anything you like," she said sincerely. Hearing Nico's story, it dawned on her that she shared this talent. Her job required a delicate balance of pleasing the actors and the director, while coming up with the right look for the characters.

As though he'd read her mind, he gazed deeply into her eyes. "Bella Luna, I think we have a lot in common. You're a very beautiful woman. I'll help you awaken inside, and be younger and more beautiful than you've ever been," he cooed.

Unable to hold his gaze, she looked down, a bit self-conscious. Then, calling on her professional self, she looked up right into his eyes and declared, "You know, let's cut the crap. I'll help you, and you'll help me."

Nico chuckled, then nodded, his hair falling over his mesmerizing eyes.

Those eyes know many things, Luna thought, *and have seen many things*. She wondered about his past and all the places he had been. Reaching into her handbag, she took out the little mesh pouch with the Om necklace and handed it to him unceremoniously. "This is a little something I thought you may like."

With ritualistic attention, he removed the necklace from the pouch. Contemplating, his head bowed, he studied the silver pendant while slowly rubbing his thumb over the raised Om symbol as though trying to release the genie within. Looking up, he fixed a penetrating gaze on her as he carefully placed the leather cord around his neck and grinned. "I love it—this means a lot to me. I'll wear it always."

o   o   o

Olivia rummaged in her closet for what to wear to La Forza. She was nervous, though she wasn't certain whether it was because she'd be singing, or because she'd see Nico. There was now a pile of clothes on the bed, and nothing seemed right. The girls she had gone to school with wore all the newest styles, but Olivia didn't try to compete with them. She didn't have the money, and the frivolity of shopping as entertainment didn't appeal to her.

Deciding between a floral dress from H&M and the J.Crew lace miniskirt she'd gotten for graduation, she chose the latter so she could pair it with a new periwinkle peasant-style blouse that complemented the color of her eyes. The tiny mother-of-pearl buttons were meant to be left undone, revealing the curves of her breasts, which

Nico had admired so overtly.

"Love you, sweetie," she cooed, giving Brontë a kiss on the head. Plucking the car keys off a hook by the door, she headed out, thankful she had cleaned her blue Mini Cooper earlier that day since La Forza had only valet parking.

She entered the dark restaurant and paused to let her eyes adjust in the dim light. Spotting Nico chatting intimately with an exotic looking dark-haired woman, she felt a sharp pang and tightening in her belly until she realized the woman was much older. Nico quickly made an introduction. "Olivia, this is Luna," he gestured to the woman, "and her husband, Tyler."

Olivia was greatly relieved to hear "her husband," and shook their hands.

While sharing eggplant parmigiana and a bottle of wine before her performance, she told Nico how Kathy had become like a fairy godmother, financing Olivia's privileged schooling, and giving her entrée to opportunities she would not otherwise have had. Regardless, she still worked to help pay her way, not wanting to take advantage of Kathy's generosity.

Hearing her name announced, Olivia's stomach leaped, but Nico encouraged, "Princesita, remember your breathing. And remember you *are* an opera singer." He held her eyes. "And you look incredibly beautiful tonight." His eyes fell to her cleavage.

Delighted by his admiration, she coquettishly twirled one of the long errant tendrils that had escaped her loose side braid around her finger. Feeling confident, she looked around the restaurant and caught Nico's eye as she began Violetta's aria "Sempre Libera" from *La Traviata*. She sang softly, allowing the tempo of the aria to take shape. Her coloratura voice lilted perfectly as she sang "dee volare," and soon the diners were singing along.

After perfectly hitting the final high E flat, many people stood to applaud and shout "Bravo." She couldn't hold back a huge smile as she curtsied, certain this was her best performance of the famous aria. She noticed Luna nodding her approval as she passed their table. Hugging her, Nico purred into her ear, "You see, you *are* an opera singer."

Olivia's head swam with his compliment.

Mario, delighted at having found a new star to sing at his restaurant, brought over a bottle of champagne to celebrate, and after
drinking several glasses, Nico shared some solemn news. "I'm sorry
to say this now, but my mother is very ill, and I have to go to Argentina as soon as I can."

Mario shook his head. He'd known of her illness for years, but
hoped this day would not come soon. Olivia's face fell. Reaching for
Nico's hand, she consoled, "I'm so sorry. What can I do to help?"

Nico's brow furrowed, then he looked up, his eyes piercing hers
with longing. "I don't want to lose you. Wait for me."

Later, they stood in silence while the valet collected Olivia's Mini
Cooper. After handing over the tip, she got in and was buckling her
seatbelt when Nico suddenly swooped into the passenger seat, directing her to pull the car to an unlit corner of the parking lot.

He reached over to turn off the headlights and leaned into her.
Nuzzling his face in her hair, he murmured wistfully, "I'll miss your
sweet smell, princesita." The whispering sensation of his breath on
her neck and in her ear made her swoon. Nudging her face gently
with his nose, he sighed her name as his mouth found hers. Her
breath grew desperate when his hot lips explored the outlines of her
mouth, and she felt a warm wetness forming between her legs. Until
that moment, Olivia had no idea a simple kiss, without tongues,
could have so much effect. Tentatively, she threaded her fingers into
his hair, giving herself over to the passion consuming her. Letting out
a pleading groan, Nico pushed his tongue into her mouth, deliciously dancing it around hers. She shuddered, the unfamiliar sensation
making her pussy quiver and her clit throb.

Nico's fingers drifted into her blouse and she whimpered softly,
lifting her body to him welcomingly. Her nipples instantly hardened
as he fondled her breasts through her bra. Then deftly reaching into
the lace cup, he lifted one breast to his mouth and softly flicked
his tongue across the nipple. Moaning, she held his head with both
hands, arching into him as he licked and teased. "You taste so sweet,"
he purred, his lips tugging on the puckered stem. "I've been dreaming of your perfect tits."

Pulling his head up, she hungrily pressed her lips to his, encouraging his ardor. Probing his mouth with her tongue, she imagined it was his cock inside her pussy. Gingerly, he placed his hand on her knee, then slowly slid his palm up the inside of her thigh and underneath her skirt, stopping as he neared her panties. She inhaled sharply in ecstasy, the fires of her lust burning. Crying out, she opened her thighs wider, giving him a hot, wet invitation.

Emitting a strangled groan, he abruptly withdrew his hand.

Olivia squirmed in frustration. Her entire body ached with desire.

Lost in thought, he mused, "Look, we've fogged up the windows." Turning back to her, he ceremoniously placed her breast back into her bra as if it were a valuable artifact he was careful not to break. Gazing intently into her eyes, he tucked a ringlet behind her ear and murmured huskily, "Olivia, you are hard to resist. I want so badly to fuck you now. You'll wait for me, won't you?"

She nodded, then self-consciously lowered her gaze. "Will you write to me?"

"Every day."

He got out of the car and strode away without looking back, while hot tears fell from her eyes.

4

Tyler's class schedule had been heavier than normal, and lately, weekends were dedicated to writing his blog and working on the book. He was at his desk when Luna interrupted, "Do you want to go to the farmer's market later, then we can stop by The Parlor for guacamole and a beer and watch soccer?"

Looking up, Tyler was at first annoyed she'd broken his train of thought. "I have to finish this today. I'm jammed. Text me later and I'll let you know."

Luna was about to turn and go when he commented, "I see you're going to yoga." He'd stated the obvious, seeing she wore black practice pants and a tank top depicting Ganesh, the elephant-headed Hindu god of protection. "What time will you be home?"

She sighed, "If you would make plans to do something with me, I'd come straight home."

He struggled with that idea for a second before waving her away. "Call me later. I'll try to finish and get this posted." Then he turned his attention back to the computer screen.

Even in his late forties, Tyler had a youthful appearance. At six feet two, he was lean and well-built, with a Ralph Lauren model appearance and dazzling smile that drew admiring looks from women, including his students. When they had first started dating, Luna couldn't help feeling threatened. The men she had previously been involved with had been players, and she'd been burned too many times. When Tyler confessed after only a few weeks that he was dating her exclusively, she surprised herself by jumping in with both feet and never looking back.

She would have liked for him to commit to her plan, or even

come up with one of his own. Instead, she murmured, "OK, I'll call you," and left. She'd packed well-worn boyfriend jeans and a black crocheted Free People top into a Ralph Lauren kilim tote bag, glad it was a weekend so she didn't have to skip out on work with more vague excuses.

Sensing her disappointment, Tyler called out, "Luna?" When she came back, he apologized. "I'm sorry I've been so busy. Let's do something tomorrow. We can go for a run and have an early dinner. How about sushi?"

She leaned over, putting her head between him and the screen, and gave him a kiss. "I love you, honey. Of course, that would be great. I'll call you later." At the door, she added as an afterthought, "So today I might hang with Nico if he's not doing anything."

Tyler smiled, but she wasn't sure how genuinely. As she turned to leave, he said, without sounding judgmental, "I guess you have yourself a new project, huh?"

She chuckled and shrugged. "I suppose maybe I do." Having found it all very exciting, she'd told him every detail she could recall about the despacho ceremony, Nico's life, and Kundalini Yoga, adding that Nico seemed lonely and needed a good friend.

Not sure if she might get cold, she put on her favorite Nigel Preston & Knight stone suede fringed jacket and left.

o   o   o

Following Nico's voice, Luna found him in the office, yelling in Spanish at someone on the phone. Looking up, he gestured for her to come in and sit down. He had on a simple black T-shirt, and she was happy to see he wore the Om necklace. After a few more minutes, he said "Besos," and hung up.

Running his fingers through his hair and gently tugging at the roots, he gazed up at her. She saw his eyes were moist. "I don't know what to do, bella. That was my sister. She said my mother is getting worse." He walked over to a hot kettle and poured her a mug of tea, then refilled his own. "I'm going to have to go home and nurse her back to health again. She won't take her medication and wants to give up; she's tired."

In a flash, she was back in sixth grade, overhearing those words, "She's tired," spoken between her father and relatives. Luna didn't know what to say. Nico spoke as though she knew what he was talking about, but she didn't. After a moment's thought, she replied, "If your mother needs you, Nico, you should go to her right away."

He nodded thoughtfully.

Then she asked, "Is it just you and your sister? Does your sister live with your mother?"

He gazed down pensively at his hands and answered quietly, "Yes, she lives with my mother and Ita, my grandmother, in San Telmo. The house has been in the family for generations. There's also our beach house in Pinamar from my mother's family. That's where I found the seahorse." His eyes grew distant. "I loved being there when I was a boy."

"How did you end up here, Nico?"

His face darkened. "When I was four, my parents split up, and my dad moved to New York City. He visited us in the summer, then I was sent to live with him when I was around ten. My mom wasn't around much, and I started getting into trouble." He snuffed, "My dad had a restaurant and worked all the time. And his girlfriend didn't want me around."

Though encouraging him to continue, she winced at the thought of little Nico being sent away to a foreign country. It stirred up memories of the copious neighbors who took her in after school, waiting for her father to get home from work and collect her.

Nico's voice curtailed her reflection. "When I finished high school, I went back and taught yoga in Buenos Aires and then at my friend's resort in Kerala, India. But I felt there was something more I needed to do with my life, so I went to live with the Q'ero. I took tourists up for healing ceremonies with the paqos and learned all I could from them before moving back to New York."

Worriedly, he questioned, "How can I go to Argentina now? I have a following, and I need to save money for the studio in Beverly Hills."

Not wanting to pry, Luna didn't ask what illness his mother had. Instead, she simply reiterated, "You really should go be with your mom, Nico. We never know the time that is given to us. I lost my mom when I was eleven…"

Taking her hand, he kissed the back of it softly. "Bella—I did not know this…you're such a good person. I feel lucky I met you and that we're friends."

The touch of his lips on her skin sent a jolt of electricity through her, awakening a swarm of fire butterflies in her belly. She hadn't thought about whether they were friends, but had sensed there was some kind of powerful connection between them. She was accustomed to people bonding with her quickly because her work required it, but this was different. Maybe she was meant to be here for him at this difficult time. She thought Nico was sweet, but he seemed lonely despite being surrounded by people, almost all of whom were women.

He didn't seem in a hurry to do her session, and she dutifully listened to him as they drank tea.

"Ita's getting old now. Who's going to take care of her if my mom's no longer…" he paused, taking another sip of tea. "No, I have to get a plane ticket today. On such short notice, I'm sure it'll be very expensive."

Before Luna could reply or reassure Nico his decision to go home was the right one, he leaped up, saying, "Let's do the session now." Taking her hand, he led her into the studio, where he set the lights on low, then went over to the sound system to select a playlist.

Feeling less inhibited, Luna thought she was already seeing benefits from this work with him.

Nico sat down next to her. "Let's begin with a small meditation to focus and call on your higher self to do your best. The mantra is Ong Namo Guru Dev Namo. OK?"

She nodded, and they began the meditation together.

His lulling voice guided her through the kriyas. "The *Muladhara*, the root chakra, is our standing in the world—it's our security and survival chakra. But the shadow side of this chakra is our fear, resentment, and insecurity. Let's move the prana up and out of the root chakra." He paused, carefully watching her as she did the kriya, then continued, "The spinal flex is like the cat/cow kriya, except seated in

Easy Pose." His cadence made the words sound like poetry, yet Luna was sure he wasn't aware of doing so. "Place your hands on your ankles. Now roll your pelvis forward as you inhale and roll back on the exhale. Then do the Breath of Fire, but not too fast. Keep your breathing even. That's right," he encouraged her.

Doing the Breath of Fire while swiveling her pelvis upward and back fired up Luna's sex organs, and she found herself uncomfortably aroused. Suddenly, the sensation was so intense and unexpected, she felt a wetness between her legs, and her face flushed. She hoped Nico hadn't noticed what had just happened, and was relieved when he announced they would finish with a brief meditation.

After the session, he enjoined, "Come Luna, I'm going to make my special empanadas." It appeared she had no choice but to join him. Discovering the door off his office led to Nico's private residence, Luna thought, *This will be interesting.* The small kitchen had a counter that opened onto the living room, and she could see his bedroom through another doorway. The walls were painted a deep red, like the chamber, and an assortment of tribal rugs covered the dark wood floors. Kilim pillows and a colorful horse blanket decorated the sofa. The iron and glass coffee table was stacked with large format photography books on the Q'ero and shamanism, and an illustrated book of Kundalini Yoga; a large reference book titled *Native Ethnobotany* lay nearby. Luna believed people's books give silent insight into their soul, and Nico's were no surprise. Also on the table sat an oversized, primitively carved wooden bowl containing beautiful feathers, a bundle of sage, and a few conch and nautilus shells. She was delighted at how similar his sensibility was to hers.

As she meandered around the room taking it all in, Nico pulled out a large cast iron skillet and took some chopped meat from the fridge. Soon, the smell of onions cooking wafted through the room. While he was busy, she used the time to continue absorbing clues into Nico's true self. Just as in his chamber, the shelves in his apartment held photos, artifacts, pottery, and wood carvings from his travels. Every table had at least one candle. Through the doorway into the bedroom, she could see a large tapestry hanging over the bed. One of several oil paintings Luna found compelling depicted a cobblestone street she assumed was in old Buenos Aires. Another was a portrait of a smiling elderly woman with dark hair and penetrating eyes. Nico walked over as she stared at the woman in the painting. "That's my Ita," he said. "My uncle, her oldest son, did that recently. He's a well-known painter throughout South America and Europe. When I decided to come back to the States, he gave it to me, saying I needed to have Ita with me."

He reached out to take her hand. "Come, I'll teach you to make traditional Argentine empanadas."

She watched as he gently kneaded the dough. His hands were firm, but gentle, his long fingers moving gracefully until the consistency was perfect. On the counter, he unfurled some parchment paper, reminding her briefly of the despacho ceremony. After rolling out the dough, he cut out circles with a round metal cookie cutter.

Looking at the bowl of ground beef he had seasoned with paprika, cumin, salt, and pepper, she asked, "Do you eat a lot of red meat?"

He laughed out loud, his hair flopping in his face. "Of course, bella. I'm from Argentina! I grew up with the finest steaks in the world. Look, I'll put these roasted peppers and cooked onions in with the meat, then fold it all up in the dough, pinching them closed, like this," he demonstrated. "But you can put all kinds of fillings in them. Ita used a different pattern—*repulgue*—when she pinched the edges so she'd know what was inside. Otherwise, we kids would break all of them open till we found what we wanted." He heated some oil in the skillet and gently placed the empanadas in the oil, then instructed her, "Watch that they don't burn while I make more."

They sat at the counter, feasting on the empanadas, which were so delicious Luna wasn't shy about eating several. Nico watched her eat while he regaled her with stories of fishing in the sea with just a snorkel and a spear, later roasting octopus on an open fire. "You have to know where the octopus hide, then hold your breath for a really long time as you scare them out of their hiding places and catch them with your spear," he described for her, standing and moving about with an imaginary spear in hand.

He was so animated when he spoke, Luna took pleasure in watching him talk and eat, the large veins of his forearms and biceps growing as he moved to bring a golden empanada to his lips. When they were finished, Luna took their plates to the sink and began cleaning up. As she worked, her back was to the living room, and soon she heard a lovely guitar melody. Turning to look, she saw it was Nico and not a recording. As she listened to him singing in Spanish, she felt as if she were in a dream. Who was she? Here she was in the home of an alluring, younger man she barely knew, eating a lunch he'd cooked, washing his dishes, and now he was playing guitar and singing to her in Spanish. She chuckled to herself. If she told this story to any one of her friends they wouldn't even believe her.

Content listening to him play and sing, she took an extra-long time putting everything away. With his neck and strong shoulders bent over the guitar, she watched his graceful hands finger the strings. She recognized the song as the traditional folk story "La Llorona." Seemingly lost in memories, his performance wasn't for her so much as a form of meditation for himself. Emphasizing the words with passion, his voice was deep and gravely, while at the same time the sound of the double "L" in "Llorona" had a slurry softness. When he tried hitting the high notes on "Picante pero sabroso," his voice cracked slightly, just enough to sound sexy in a pleading sort of way. He didn't seem aware she was even in the room, so she sat on one of the stools at the kitchen bar, just far enough away to not penetrate his space.

When he finished the song, he put the guitar down across his lap and looked up at her from beneath the thick, dark lock of hair that always fell across his forehead. A soft curl framed one eye, and his face bore an imperceptible smile. "Ah, Luna, that was a song I learned so long ago. I was thinking of home."

She opened her mouth to speak, but no words came out. The dark brooding torment he revealed in song compelled her—reaching into her gut and grabbing hold with an invisible hand. In that moment, she felt a potent exchange pass between them. She regretted having to leave him; his distress was palpable. Yet something beyond her consciousness pulled her away. When she tried to stand, she felt rooted to her seat—her body heavy, as if she'd been drugged. It took all her effort to recover and finally say, "I should leave…and let you get on with your day."

On the way home, Luna stopped at the green market and texted Tyler to get a shopping list. Standing in line at the register, she finally felt the fog lifting from her brain. When her phone rang, she saw it was Nico.

"Luna, can you come tomorrow morning? My flight is Monday night. I can really use your help before I leave, and we can fit in a session. I'll give you instructions to keep practicing while I'm gone."

She paused, filling the time with a long "ummm." Knowing she'd agreed to spend the day with Tyler, she finally said, "I suppose so, but I need to check with Tyler because we made plans."

He was silent, and she sensed he had expected a different answer.

She spoke quietly, "Nico? You there? Is everything OK?"

He let out a heavy sigh and replied with tenacious desperation, "Yes, Luna. I just don't understand why you need to check with Tyler when I need your help."

She hurried to reassure him. "I really don't think it will be a problem."

Speaking rapidly, he pleaded, "I'm really stressed out. My mom is sick, and I have to leave my business when it's just taking off. I have a shitload of stuff to do. I'm asking you as a friend. I really need you to help me."

His seemingly desperate need stirred the flameless embers inside her. "Don't worry, Nico. I'll be there tomorrow."

Luna hastily apologized to Tyler, explaining in a rambling chatter that Nico's mother was gravely ill, and since he was leaving the next day, he needed to instruct her in the kriyas she should practice while he was away. Tyler didn't object, but Luna knew he was disappointed. Promising she wouldn't be gone long and they could still go out for dinner, she brushed her lips against his and dashed out.

When she arrived and Nico wasn't in the studio, she called into his apartment from the office door. He called back, "Come on in, bella! I'm in here."

His bedroom was cozy, with a queen-sized bed covered by an Indian bedspread in a sunflower motif. Assorted pillows, some in quilted shams, were piled at the head, and a cranberry comforter was folded at the foot. Above the bed hung a woven tapestry of the Andes Mountains. A professional-looking black and white photo of Nico in a silver frame was displayed on a large, painted dresser. In the picture, he was in Warrior I pose, wearing low-slung sweatpants and no shirt, just a thin, beaded necklace. His hair was, as usual, messy and in his eyes, which glowed even in black and white photography.

Turning her attention to Nico, she could see he was overwhelmed with packing. Piles of clothes were heaped on the bed, and shoes were strewn across the floor. His suitcase was open, but empty. Frustrated, he complained, "I don't know what to bring. I still don't know how long I'll be there."

She walked to the bed, and resting an arm gently on his shoulder, spoke reassuringly, "Let me help. After all, I dress people for a living."

He brightened. "I forgot. That *is* what you do!"

She started sorting through the clothes and he smiled gratefully, making her feel needed.

When she suggested he gather together his toiletries he looked puzzled, so she rattled off a list of items, ending with, "and don't forget that yummy fragrance you wear."

"Artículos de aseo…" he mumbled to himself as he stuffed full-sized bottles into one large plastic bag.

As she worked, he continued, "This morning, my sister said my mother is feeling worse and hasn't eaten in days. I'm very worried." Noticing Luna transferring some of his toiletries out of the big bottles and into smaller ones, he interjected, "Wait, I have a travel size of Aqua di Parma."

Once everything fit neatly, Luna closed the suitcase. With that task complete, Nico's entire body relaxed and his face softened. "I don't want to lose any clients while I'm gone. I e-mailed everyone, and posted a note on my website and the studio's Facebook page. Do you think they'll understand and I won't lose anyone?"

Before Luna could answer, he continued, "Maybe you could line up some new clients for me while I'm away?"

To allay his concern, she assured him, "Of course I will, Nico. I'll ask Tyler, too."

He nodded, seemingly relieved. "Wonderful! Thank you, bella. Now let's go start your session."

A mournful wooden flute echoed hauntingly over a low, resonating chant as they settled in the studio. "What list is this?" Luna asked. "I love your Spotify playlists. The music is really unusual."

Ignoring the question, Nico wasted no time beginning the session. "We're going to practice a heart-warming kriya. Really, this is nothing more than a pelvic tilt. Stand with your feet shoulder width apart and knees softly bent." Placing two fingers on her pelvic bone, he instructed her to inhale while tilting her hips back. Still guiding her with his fingers, he said, "This pulls the energy up toward your heart. When you exhale, tilt forward and tuck the pelvic bone between your legs. Now, repeat the move with the breath. We really want to get this movement fired up, uncoiling the kundalini and moving it through the first two chakras—the root chakra and the sacral chakra. We want our sexual energy to move!"

She was somewhat embarrassed, but mostly enthralled. Nico clearly felt strongly about this subject, and she listened raptly.

"This energy isn't just for sex, but also for healing and vitality. In Kundalini, we connect sexual energy and heart energy. To help you feel it, place one hand on your genitals and the other on your heart. Feel yourself draw energy from your genitals to your heart as you inhale, then let it go back down while exhaling." He placed his hands on his hips and rocked his pelvis back and forth. "Like this," he said. Looking straight at her without blushing, he added, "It's like when you have sex, Luna."

With that, Nico placed his hand on hers, guiding her to pet herself from genitals to heart while tilting her pelvis back on the inhale and tucking forward on the exhale. Luna didn't have time to feel shocked, as he moved their hands in unison continuously up and down the front of her body. "Notice your heart gets warm, and you can feel the energy rising up from the root chakra—the *Muladhara*—where you hold fears and insecurities. Move the energy from there to the second chakra, *Svadisthana*, the sexual energy of water, where you hold your emotions and guilt."

He guided their hands down to her pubic mound, pressing the soft flesh there before moving back up to her heart, where his fingers slipped casually, slightly grazing her breast. As though he hadn't noticed, he kept coaching, "Move the energy up toward the heart, through the solar plexus chakra—the *Manipura*. This is fire energy, where you harbor your anger and shame."

Her head swam. The world seemed to melt away as Nico purred more and more instructions into her ear.

"Feel the fire, Luna. Manipura is the center of your personal power and control over yourself and others. *Use* this fire to expand your possibilities."

She felt his breath warm in her ear. "Manipura can give you the ability to manipulate situations. Feel the energy move to your heart, Luna. Feel the warmth and love move through your body, awakening your divine energy."

Embarrassed, she couldn't look at him and closed her eyes to focus on the sound of his voice. Seemingly oblivious to her unease, he kept coaching, murmuring in a lower tone and volume, saturating her head and her world.

"Move the energy to a higher vibration, Luna. The lower chakras are where we store our experiences, what we've chosen to manifest." He placed his hand on her heart chakra again. "The heart chakra, *Anahata*, is the connection between our higher self and the physical experiences of the lower chakras."

His hand went down low again, making her feel dizzy and flushed all over. Her vagina pulsed and her labia swelled as she breathed heavily and tilted her pelvis back and forth. Was it the kundalini or Nico moving his hand up and down her body, she wondered.

Without betraying any emotion, Nico kept very still, his voice low and breathy as he spoke about meditating on the third eye, the sixth chakra—*Ajna*—our intuition and wisdom. "The third eye is where we understand our purpose. Eliminate confusion and overintellectualizing. Allow yourself to become clairvoyant, clear seeing."

Hearing his hypnotic voice in the back of her mind, Luna let herself float, feeling warm and wet, the pulsing of her vagina taking over. Nico's voice had become a rhythmic melody, and she moved to the music. Keenly aware of his hand stroking her body while she rocked back and forth as if having sex, she reached the edge. Abandoning herself to the pulsing, she climaxed, and wetness flowed out of her.

She was completely overwhelmed by the throbbing of her body and certain Nico was aware of what had just happened. Suddenly, she stopped moving, prompting him to clutch her hand tightly. She stared at the floor until he lifted her chin to gaze deeply into her eyes, where she saw a gleam of knowledge.

He asked sincerely, "Was that the first time you've had a touchless orgasm?"

She nodded silently, and he murmured, "Well, Luna, see the power of kundalini?"

Embarrassed at allowing herself to get to that point, she had trouble looking at him. She should have stopped herself, but like the good student she had always been, she kept following his instructions. Had he known that would happen? Glancing up at him, she felt tears well up in her eyes.

He calmly reassured her, "Ah, bella Luna. No need for tears. You're just feeling the release, and this is a good thing." She saw amusement in his eyes, which made her feel very vulnerable. Intuitively, he quietly said, "Let's go have some tea, bella. Tea always makes things better."

In his apartment, Luna sat at the counter while Nico put the kettle on. He asked if she was hungry, but she still couldn't look directly at him. She heard herself mutter, "I guess."

Pretending not to notice her lingering embarrassment, he went on nonchalantly, "I have a roasted chicken and some kale. Since I'm leaving tomorrow, there's no point in throwing out good food." He pulled ingredients out of cabinets and the fridge. Then, as he began cooking, he said, "You should practice the Sat Nam every day while I'm gone. It's the best daily exercise for moving your energy up. And if you want to do the heart-warming kriya you just learned, most definitely do."

Luna thought she saw a little glint in his eye at that suggestion, but didn't reply.

He continued casually, "Luna, what happened is not unusual. Many women have this experience. They hold a lot back from their sexual expression, so release isn't unexpected." He smiled openly at her, and she was relieved she no longer felt uncomfortable. He made it seem natural, like they were friends and she could trust him.

She watched as he threw some penne pasta into a pot of water he'd set to boil and cut the chicken in quarters, putting it in a pan in the oven with the kale. He wielded the chef's knife with such confidence, it was like an extension of his hand. *He's so sexy in the kitchen*, she thought. Suddenly, the sound of his phone buzzing broke the spell. He picked it up and typed feverishly in a chat with someone. Luna didn't understand why, but she was upset his attention was no longer on her. When the kettle whistled, he stopped texting to finish preparing their lunch.

While they waited for the food to cook, he told her about his dog, Stella. "I'll be so happy to see her and take her running along the river. She has boundless energy and loves going for hikes." Nico got up and moved to a bookshelf, where he picked up a framed photo of himself and a pretty black and white dog with a pink nose. In the picture, Stella was cradled in his arms. Both of them were grinning like it was a big joke for him to carry such a huge dog.

"I rescued her from people who use dogs for fights. Some of them are called bait dogs. They let the fighters attack the bait dogs for practice. Stella was destined to be bait, because she was too sweet." He paused, a troubled look on his face as he remembered the awful destiny awaiting Stella had he not interceded. "Ita feeds her too much, so Stella always sits next to her at the table, begging for scraps." Suddenly exclaiming, "¡Maldita sea!" he flung open the oven door, pulling the chicken out just in time. Filling her plate, he coaxed, "Eat, Luna. You need to eat!"

After lunch, he said, "I need to get some gifts for Ita, my mother, and my sister. Can you come help me pick out some things?" When she said she'd be glad to help, he smiled gratefully. "Remember I saw those vintage bags in your car? Let's go there. Would they have things for me to get that aren't too expensive?"

Luna perked up. "I have a better idea. Let's go to my office. We can look through the items that haven't been selected for the show. I'm sure we can find something for each of them."

"You won't get in trouble for that?" He sounded genuinely concerned.

"No, there's always extra, and at the end of the season it all gets donated anyway."

At the office, Nico browsed through everything like a kid in a candy store, fascinated by all the stuff she had. She had to scold him slightly to slow him down, because although it didn't appear so, everything was tagged and organized.

As he browsed, he fretted. "I always bring them gifts from my travels, but in L.A. everything's so expensive."

She consoled him, "Don't worry, Nico. Remember, this is my job. I'll find something for them that'll be perfect."

At a rack of cashmere sweaters, she selected a cream cardigan with pearl buttons. "Here, Ita can wear this with anything."

Nico touched the sweater gingerly. "She'll really love this. It's so beautiful—and soft."

Thinking of something perfect for his mother, Luna opened a big drawer and pulled out a Pashmina shawl with hand-tied fringe in a paisley of colors reminiscent of Monet's *Water Lilies*.

"Perfecto!" He exclaimed, thrilled at the selection. He stepped out of her way as she quickly moved around him to open a closet filled with clear boxes, where she picked one off the shelf.

She didn't know his younger sister, Lucia, but had gone to her Facebook page and saw that she was very pretty, with Nico's eyes and dark hair. Something a bit trendy would be fun for her, Luna thought, presenting him a necklace of turquoise beads with a silver cross. The look was modern and tribal at the same time. Relieved, he sighed, "You're really good at this, especially without knowing them. These gifts are perfect!"

Luna beamed with delight, proud of herself for solving his dilemma. With gifts in hand, they drove back to Amaru, where they sat in the car in the parking lot for a while, talking about his business.

Expounding on his plans for the future, Nico shared, "I'm going to do a clothing line. Maybe you could help me with the designs and manufacturing?"

She was excited by his ideas. "I'm honored you'd want to include me."

"Ah, Luna. I trust you as a friend, and I respect your talents." After a moment, he reminded her to recommend him to her friends and have Tyler do the same.

Luna was sad he was leaving, but felt selfish because his mother was, after all, very sick. She got out of the car as he walked around to her side to give her the traditional double-cheek kiss. Instead, she wrapped her arms around him in a comforting hug, holding him close. "I'll pray for your mother. Please e-mail me, Nico. Let me know how she's doing." She watched as he walked toward the building, then stopped to turn back and look at her with melancholy, pleading eyes. Thinking how much she would miss him, she drove away, struggling to focus through the tears blurring her vision.

5

It had only been two days since Nico had landed in Buenos Aires, yet he consumed Luna's thoughts. Unable to wait any longer, she messaged him. His quick response provided only the smallest consolation.

> *Luna,*
> *She is not good and won't eat. I just fought with*
> *her because of it. Everyone loves the gifts…thank*
> *you.*

Inseparable from her phone, she anxiously awaited word from him. Finally, when an e-mail arrived, the weight lifted from her chest.

> *Luna*
> *Today a man in a room near my mom died from*
> *a heart attack. It was very sad. Life is so weird some-*
> *times. One minute you are here, and the next you*
> *are not.*

She remembered telling Nico that he would help her and she would help him, and now realized how prescient her comment had been.

Waking before dawn, she felt the distance between them. Reaching to get her phone off the nightstand, she saw the message from Nico.

> *Hi Luna*
> *I feel useless. All I do is go back and forth from the hospital. My head is back in L.A. Is it wrong for me to want to leave? There is nothing I can do to make her better.*
> *I want to leave…*

Luna knew he'd regret leaving without closure, so suggested he stay and make the most of their time together. Taking a book off her shelf, she copied a poem by Jetsun Milarepa, Tibet's great yogi and poet:

> *In horror of death, I took to the mountains—*
> *Again and again I meditated on the uncertainty of the hour of death,*
> *Capturing the fortress of the deathless unending nature of mind.*
> *Now all fear of death is over and done.*

Obsessively clutching her phone and looking at it, she waited.

> *Hi Luna*
> *The poem is very beautiful and very deep… thank you. I think it's just a matter of time now.*
> *Besos, I miss you…*

The next day, she received the message his mom had passed away. As sad as Luna was, she was glad the worst was over. This time when she wrote, it was to his family, and she signed it from herself and Tyler. But she really wished she could hold Nico.

During his stay to handle his mom's estate, he sent pictures from the house, and later, photos of himself at the beach. Hoping she didn't sound audacious, she wrote back admiring his beautiful muscular legs. She studied the photos for perspective on who he was and where he came from. When she opened a photo of him standing with a spear in one hand and an octopus in the other, it took her breath away. His lean, toned body had attained a healthy glow, his hair had grown longer, and he was wearing the Om pendant she had given him.

o   o   o

"Olivia!" Manny's shout pulled her back from her reverie. "What's wrong with you? Pay attention; that table has been waiting!"

Olivia had read Nico's e-mail so many times, she'd memorized it. Having read it yet again, she shoved the phone into her pocket and headed over to the annoyed customers. With each e-mail, Nico flirted more, saying he longed to see her again and was unable to get her out of his mind.

Soon the e-mails became sexually explicit, and Olivia was careful to keep her phone with her. After serving her tables, she darted to the ladies' room and locked the stall door. Pulling her panties down, she sat on the toilet and reread one of the e-mails, following his instructions carefully. As she inserted a finger into her vagina to locate the small mound he said was inside, she realized he didn't suspect her virginity. Curling her finger upward, she felt around until she found the mysterious mound and began pressing slowly, as he described. Quickly, Olivia found herself wet, and the juices from her pussy ran down her finger. She reached her free hand into her bra and fondled the nipple of her right breast, twirling it between her thumb and index finger.

She prayed no one would come in the bathroom, since her breathing was heavy and audible. He had said to hook her finger slightly and curl it back and forth in a come-hither motion, and she felt the mound hardening as she stroked it repeatedly. Unable to sit upright, she gave herself over to her pleasure and leaned back, her legs stiffening as she continued flexing her finger to caress it lovingly. Sliding her finger in and out, she rubbed her slick juices over her pulsing sweet spot as it swelled under her tutelage. Wetness exploded into her hand and her pelvis arched upward in ecstasy as the rolling waves of orgasm consumed her. Completely overwhelmed, she took several moments to recover. She had never had such a long and intense orgasm when masturbating before. In the past, she had only fondled her clitoris until she had a gratifying release. Clutching her phone, she obeyed Nico's directive to reply with a detailed account and how she had felt each step of the way.

Having never experienced anything so thrilling, Olivia rushed home from work that night, eager for the next installment. He had told her to take a feather and lightly tease her clitoris, but she wasn't allowed to touch herself with her hands. Slowly, she tickled her nub with the feather. She'd never used anything other than her hand to play with herself before and the sensation was delectable. A low ache began, and lying comfortably alone in her bed, she gave herself over to the feeling. Dragging the feather back and forth, she moaned, her hips rising and falling as she felt herself drawing closer to orgasm. She pinched her nipple hard, pulling on it as she had done earlier in the bathroom stall. Groaning loudly, she thought she might come undone any second, and in a frenzy of lust she dropped the feather and pushed one finger inside while massaging her clit. The waves of her powerful orgasm crashed around her, sending every muscle in her body into spasms.

Olivia wrote explicit details about her experience, detailing how the feather drove her wild. Deciding the truth was actually most erotic, she admitted to touching herself as she climaxed, describing how she'd screamed out and shoved her fingers into her pussy. Captivated by this bewitching game, she awaited his reply.

Nico's next e-mail said that because she'd broken the rules, she was to be punished. At first she was distressed, thinking he was angry with her. But reading on, she became enthralled.

Reluctant to take the next step in this game, Olivia stared intently at the image of Nico's dark, smoky green eyes to build her nerve. Then, with an open hand, she began to spank her pussy, at first very softly, until she mustered the courage to spank harder several times before plunging her finger back into her now dripping pussy. Squeezing her nipple hard, she spanked herself again, intoxicated by the intense euphoria overpowering her. Curling her finger inside and petting her spot, she came apart, shuddering and crying out Nico's name. She couldn't wait to try out these fantasies in real life.

Grateful for having learned her mother's native language of Spanish, Olivia followed signs to the baggage claim area. She'd received an e-mail from Nico stating he had to stay in Buenos Aires to handle legal affairs. In an unexpected tone distinctly different from his erotic missives, he wrote he was lonely and wanted her to be with him during this mournful period. It had taken some pleading on her part to persuade her mother and Kathy to allow her to go, but she finally succeeded when she told them his grandmother and sister were both there—pouring on the tears and dramatically underscoring how despondent Nico was over the loss his mother. Her performance was, she thought, irresistible.

Exiting security, she scanned the crowd for Nico's familiar face, and when she spotted him, her breath hitched. The tight T-shirt he wore clung delightfully to his sculpted chest, and the well-worn jeans clung to his thighs. He kissed her neck, then embraced her, giving her a deep, passionate kiss, flicking his tongue just slightly around her lips as a prelude to what would soon follow.

As they drove through the narrow streets, she soaked up the sounds and colors of Buenos Aires. Coming from California, she was captivated by the historic architecture. Nestled in the sanctuary of historic Pasaje Santamarina, an interior passageway hidden from the bustling streets of the San Telmo district, Olivia's eyes widened upon passing through the elaborate iron-gated doors. The ceiling towered twenty feet above them, and iron lanterns mounted on the cream colored, dadoed walls cast a soft, yellow glow on the chocolate brown glazed Moroccan tile floor.

She felt she had been magically relocated to the turn of the century, surrounded by opulence reminiscent of one of her beloved operas. Moving through a pair of large dark-green doors, they stepped into a glass-roofed conservatory with tiled floors in a classical arabesque design, complete with bubbling stone fountain in the center. A stout black and white dog with pink nose greeted them excitedly, the entire back half of her body wiggling wildly. Nico bent down to let her lick his face as he grinned. "Olivia, meet my first love, Stella." Stella kept close to him as they continued through the house and he softly explained, "To get from one room to another, you must pass through this patio. So, princesa, you can never get lost!"

Sensing they were alone, Nico gave Olivia a quick and secretive tour the house. Off the patio, double glass doors opened to a formal living room with a French balcony overlooking the courtyard, where a giant palm tree towered over the roof. She felt oddly reassured to see a large flat screen TV hanging on one wall alongside oil paintings. Another set of doors led to a spacious dining room with a large crystal chandelier hanging over an enormous wood pedestal table. Olivia gasped, "This looks like a ballroom!"

Nico laughed, "Well, as a matter of fact, formal dances were held in this room for many generations!" Finally, they sat down at the cozy kitchen island and Nico opened a bottle of the best Malbec he could find in the house. After pouring some into two cut-crystal wine glasses, he tucked the bottle under his arm and whispered, "Let's go, before someone comes home."

Entering his room, he closed the door behind them. "We'll have to be careful how loud we are, cariño," he whispered as he sat down on the bed to take off his shoes. The high carved bed and was styled with a crisp white duvet and embroidered white pillow cases; a colorful Uzbek Suzani was folded at the foot.

Olivia's eyes landed on an oil painting above the marble-topped night table. "What a charming painting. It's quite haunting…but I love it," she remarked. The image was dark and moody—an elderly man wearing a hat played guitar under a street lamp on a misty evening in the Plaza Dorrego, San Telmo's main square.

Nico turned. "Oh, my uncle is a famous Argentine painter. I have a painting he did of Ita in my apartment. You'll see his work throughout the house."

She had barely taken two sips of the Malbec before she felt Nico's arms around her. Gathering her to him, he kissed her gently once. "Ah, Olivia, your lips are sweet." Holding her tightly, he kissed her with short brushes of his lips, coaxing her playfully, teasing her mouth. Melting into him, she tentatively let her hands play in his hair, twirling a long lock around her finger as he nibbled on her upper lip with quick little tugs. She shivered, letting out a soft sigh when he gently sucked on her lower lip, pulling slowly until her mouth relaxed under his persuasion.

Remembering the night in her car, she responded, taking his velvety smooth lips in hers. Slowly Nico worked her mouth open flicking his tongue along the inside of her lower lip. Finding her tongue, he coiled his around hers in a silent dance of exploration. Entwining his fingers in a tangle of her long, brown curls, he held her head and his kisses became more fervent, his mouth devouring hers. With a passion that would have once alarmed her, but now only heightened her arousal, they kissed feverishly. Inflamed by the swelling in his groin, she greedily pressed her body more tightly against him. Nico released a low pleading groan that made her pussy throb in answer to his call. Thrusting her pelvis forward and grinding against his throbbing cock, she felt the wetness grow between her legs; the scent of her desire permeated the room.

Seizing her by the wrist, Nico fingered the front of her T-shirt with his free hand and lifted it over her head. Her panting caused her heaving breasts to spill over the violet lace cups of the Victoria's Secret bra she'd purchased just for this occasion. Gingerly, Nico reached in to cup her firm tit, then lifted it to his lips taking the perfect pink nipple in his mouth—sucking gently until it grew erect. Gasping, Olivia reached for his shirt, desperate to undress him, but Nico stayed her hand. Pulling steadily on her nipple with his lips, he glanced up at her and murmured huskily, "No, I will make you come hard before I let you touch me." Frantic with need, she held her breath while Nico unzipped her jeans and eased them down over her hips. Dropping to his knees before her, he directed her to first lift one foot, then the other as he undressed her. Mesmerized, she silently obeyed his commands.

Olivia dared not speak as he ordered, "Take off your bra."

Sitting up, she reached behind herself to quickly unhook it and let it fall as she gazed at him in anticipation of his next order.

Nico's dark and smoky eyes glowed mysteriously, drinking in the sight of her nude before him. "Oh princesa, your body is perfect and begging for my touch."

Olivia had become transfixed on the huge bulge conspicuously visible beneath his jeans. Following her eyes, his lips twitched entic- ingly. "Would you like to see my cock?"

Meeting his gaze, she nodded.

"You've dreamed about it often, no?"

She nodded again, licking her lips.

"I dreamed about you, too, Olivia. Your sweet lips were wrapped around my hard cock."

She felt her pussy tighten, and she moaned when he unzipped his jeans, releasing his erection. Olivia eagerly eyed him, memorizing every bulging vein, and the thickness and shape as he grabbed hold, stroking with firm pulls.

"I will go slowly," he whispered.

Shyly, she asked, "Is it OK?" She was relieved he knew she was a virgin, but nervous she would disappoint him.

"I'm thrilled I'll be your first."

She murmured, "I did everything exactly as you told me to in your e-mails. I liked it all very, very much."

Looking at the massive wet spot on the bed, he grinned. "Yes, I can see you found my lessons stimulating."

"Watch me get off, Olivia. Later, I'll watch you pleasure yourself. I want to see your fingers pump that sweet, glistening pussy."

His words were so *dirty*—and sexy. Olivia bit her lip in blissful agony.

His voice rasped with short, hot breaths as he worked his erec- tion up and down, nearing climax. As he knelt over her panting, Nico let out a low growl, "I'm going to spurt hot cum all over your virgin pussy." Hearing his thick, throaty voice, heavy breathing, and the slapping sound as he jerked off faster sent Olivia over the edge. She shuddered and the tight coil deep in her belly began unraveling. Nico's eyes burned brightly as he ejected a huge stream of cum over her taut stomach and plump mound. She had never seen a man come before, and it sent her into a spiraling tornado of lust. Her fingers found the slippery cleft between her legs as Nico knelt over her, his dark hair cascading down his face. He watched her closely, their eyes locked. Her breathing hitched as she feverishly rubbed her clitoris and pumped her fingers in and out of her pussy—the wetness running down into her hand. Her legs stiffened as she arched her back, convulsing in a deep, long, undulating climax.

Spent, Olivia rested her head on his chest, almost dozing off while listening to his steady heartbeat. Nico whispered into her ear, "I can't wait to make you come like that on my cock." Glancing down the length of his body, she saw he was no longer limp. Nico followed her gaze.

"Look at what you do to me. I'm getting hard again already."

Kneeling up, he kissed her, his mouth hot and his lips both hard and soft. He trailed kisses along her neck and around her ear, nibbling on the lobe. Her lips were parted, waiting for his, and he raked his tongue along her lower lip before pushing into her mouth, flicking the tip of her tongue. Desperate for his touch between her legs, she squirmed in a frenzy of passion. Working his way down her body, he stopped to lick first one nipple, then the other, before trailing his tongue around her navel. Sliding off the bed, he took hold of her ankles and pulled her toward him.

Feeling his hot breath on her pussy, her whole body ached with longing. Nico looked up from between her legs and held her gaze, his green eyes dancing in delight. Creating a trail of kisses and light tongue licks along her inner thigh, he worked his way toward her pussy. Spreading her legs wider, he parted her plump folds with his tongue and circled the rim to expose the opening, then slowly licked from the mouth of her pussy to her clit, like a cat lapping long-desired milk.

Quivering, her body begged for more, and she arched her hips to meet his tongue, shockwaves pulsing through her entire body in anticipation. She never knew anything could feel as heavenly as when he rolled her tender bud around with the tip of his tongue. Crying his name, her voice pleaded for deliverance as he wrapped his lips around the swollen nub, tugging on it gently the way he had her nipple. When he stopped, she squirmed against his strong hands on her thighs and bucked, letting out a whimpering scream. "Please, Nico. Don't stop!"

Crawling onto the bed, he purred, "Taste yourself," before thrusting his tongue into her mouth. His pulsing hard-on pressed urgently against her inner thigh, and she felt an aching need deep inside her belly, a ravenous hunger for him.

Slowly, he pressed the mushroom tip into the opening of her hot, tight pussy. Moving gently inch by inch deeper inside her, he began fucking her with slow long pulls. Each time he withdrew, Olivia pushed her pelvis up and dug her fingers into the firm muscles of his buttocks, pulling him back into her.

As she clenched tightly around him, he let out a deep sigh and picked up the pace, his movements becoming more powerful and his thrusts deeper, fucking her harder. Feeling her go slick around him, he let out a strangled growl, then quickly pulled out and shot a hot, thick jet of cum over her belly. Finishing himself with one hand, he used his other hand to tweak and rub her clit, making her tremble violently with her release.

Nico fell on the bed and kissed her deeply. They were covered in sweat and cum, and the musky, primal scent of sex hung thickly in the room.

o   o   o

Olivia's heart pounded when Nico took her hand, leading her toward the sounds of lively Spanish. Upon entering the kitchen, a beautiful, raven-haired young woman who looked like a female version of Nico squealed in delight. "There you two are!" she exclaimed in English.

"Oh, Olivia, you are more beautiful even than my brother described!" Lucia blurted, hugging her and giving her a double-cheek kiss.

Blushing, she put her head down. "Eres muy amable."

Ita had invited a few family friends who peppered Olivia with questions about opera and California while the women finished preparing a feast of Argentine meats. Her musical ear picked up on the softer, almost slurred, Argentine pronunciation of Ys and double Ls, and she dropped her proper neutral Spanish as she easily fell into conversation.

Olivia leaned across the kitchen counter for an olive as she intently watched Ita prepare dinner. Her ample cleavage overflowing her push-up bra wasn't lost on Nico, and he quickly pulled her into the pantry for a scolding. Deftly sliding his hand up her skirt and pushing her lace panty to the side, he slipped two fingers into her hot, wet pussy. She let out a small cry as he petted her, feeling her wetness build until it covered his fingers and dripped down her thighs. With Ita only a few steps away, Nico rubbed her clit hard with his thumb while pumping his fingers in and out of her pussy. Unable to control herself and nearing orgasm, she moaned audibly, and he crushed her to his chest, roughly covering her mouth to silence her so no one would hear her cry out. She shuddered as she came hard onto his hand, and Nico whispered in her ear, "You're a naughty girl, Olivia. I'll show you who is in charge. If you tease me, I'll take you by force, regardless of where we are."

Over dinner a few minutes later, he locked his eyes on hers, and with a smoldering intensity in his gaze, licked his fingers not just of juice from the beef they were eating, but of *her* juices, too.

o   o   o

Rummaging through old books as they strolled down the Calle Defensa ten-block long street fair of antique stalls, Olivia spotted a copy of *Love Poems* by Pablo Nerudu and presented it to Nico.

"Princesa, eres mi corazón." His eyes glistened as he peered into hers.

Olivia caressed his face and kissed him. "You are my heart, too." She took his hand and they continued down to the next stall, where she purchased handmade leather sandals for both of them.

At sunset, when the street lights came on, the cobbled streets glowed and the building angles softened. While sharing a bottle of wine at Dorrego Café, Olivia heard the nostalgic quadruple meter of a bandoneón as tango dancers began performing on a portable floor placed over the uneven cobblestones. Olivia was awed by the dancers' fluid movements. The men and some of the women wore ordinary street clothes, while others had flowers in their hair and were dressed in fancy red or black dresses with flounces on the bottom and plunging necklines. As the night progressed, the crowd grew larger. Nico took Olivia in his arms and taught her the tango, holding her very close so she could feel the subtle movements of his body. He was very serious about the dance, as she expected an Argentine to be, so she tried hard to follow, and when she attempted to anticipate his next move, he pulled her closer with his hand on the small of her back, purring, "Olivia, just follow me. I will guide you." Relaxing, she happily allowed him to take control.

o   o   o

Scrutinizing herself in the mirror, Olivia saw only what looked like a preppy California girl. Pulling out her hair tie, she released her long tousled curls. Attempting to look more sophisticated, she smudged her eyes with a bit of brown eyeliner she'd recently bought but hadn't used, then applied lip gloss, liking how her darker eyes contrasted with lightly stained lips. Taking out her pearl stud earrings, she replaced them with silver hoops. Finally accepting that this was the best she could achieve, she headed down to the parlor where Lucia was waiting.

"Olivia, I love your plaid skirt. And I would kill for your hair! I can't wait for you to meet my best friend, Gabriela. She's so cool!"

Great, Olivia thought to herself, *I'm doomed!*

While Nico attended to legal affairs related to his mother's passing, the girls spent the day in Palermo, Buenos Aires' answer to New York City's Soho. As the afternoon wore on, Olivia had too many shopping bags to carry, so Lucia and Gaby carried some for her. When they passed a window display of elegant, modern jewelry designs, something caught Olivia's eye, and she ducked inside to try on a pair of simple, organic design platinum rings. Slipping one ring on her finger, she was admiring it when the girls appeared next to her, chiming together, "Tan buen gusto! Son preciosos!"

"Should I...para mí y Nico? Is it too forward, demasiado rápido?"

Lucia grinned, "Él va encantar!"

Without asking the price, Olivia handed over the credit card Kathy had given her, telling the shopkeeper to wrap them.

Before heading home, the girls collapsed at the colorful Lele de Troya, where they ate salmon ravioli and homemade bread on the vine-covered lemon-yellow patio. Olivia insisted on picking up the tab to thank Lucia and Gaby for being her personal stylists.

Chattering loudly, the three girls walked into the parlor, and Olivia instantly caught Nico looking her up and down. "Wow, baby, come here. Let me feel those skins."

Wearing her new glove leather miniskirt, cropped silk T-shirt, and python skin jacket, Olivia blushed as she sidled up next to him. His hands sliding up her thigh and over her ass, he purred in her ear, "I can't wait to undress you." Excusing themselves, they darted upstairs, where Nico ravished her. As they lay together, he tenderly chided, "See, I said you would have a good time with Lucia. You have to trust me more, Olivia. I'll awaken you and make you more confident."

Kissing his ear and down his neck to his nipple, she whispered, "Yes, Nico."

"My princesa. You will sing in the opera, and I will have a center in Beverly Hills. Everything will come to pass soon…I promise."

Straddling him and taking his hands in hers, she leaned over him, her hair in his face. She kissed his full lips. "Together, my love, we will be stars!"

Deliberately coiling one of her wild tendrils behind her ear, he locked his eyes to hers in a penetrating gaze, "Olivia, ask the rich heiress for the money for the center. It's for us…and we'll be together."

"I don't know, Nico. Do you think she would? I mean, she doesn't even know you."

"Don't be an idiot, Olivia," he snapped. Then, running his thumb along her lower lip, he cooed, "Tell her we're getting married, and you need the money to build our center. I'm a famous healer. It's a good investment; it will make millions."

Thrilled at the prospect of being his wife and both their dreams coming true, she exclaimed, "I'll ask her as soon as I get home. I'm sure she'll give me the money! After all, it's a healing center!"

"That's my princesa!" He kissed her deeply, twining his tongue with hers.

Breaking away, she burst out joyously, "Nico, I almost forgot. I bought something…special. I hope you'll like it." She awkwardly offered the wrapped box to him. Thinking she might pass out from anticipation, she waited for Nico to slowly unwrap it.

When he opened the box, his eyes danced in delight. "Olivia, mi amor, I love this! Matching rings—they're so beautiful."

6

A simple, white, stucco and glass structure, obviously modernized in recent years, the beach house sat high on a cliff with spectacular views of the sea and sand dunes covered in acacias, pampas grass, and, surprisingly, pines. They'd driven down to the Pinamar beach house for Nico to sign papers transferring the title to him. On the way, he told Olivia stories about spear fishing and childhood summers with his mom. She could hear his voice crack, and it made her sad that he had lost her.

After collecting driftwood, Nico built a fire on the beach. Snuggling under a warm blanket, they watched the stars move across the sky, listening to the sound of waves crashing on the shore. Spooning her tightly, his hips began moving as he pressed his hardening cock against her ass. Taking her from behind, with her ass perched high, his hands gripped her hips as he fucked her hard. The sound of her moaning inspired him to record the erotic scene. Secretly turning on the video camera of his iPhone, he filmed his dick withdraw from her pussy and disappear back inside. With his arm held overhead, he captured the roundness of her ass and the sweep of her back and shoulders, her dark curls pendulating back and forth as he pummeled into her. He hoped the audio would pick up the sucking noise his dick made as it thrust in and out of her pussy. Feeling her clench around him, he murmured, "Touch yourself, baby. I'm gonna come!" He liked the sound of his voice directing her.

As she twirled her clit between her fingers, her panting became ragged and she cried out, "Nico!"

When he viewed the video later, hearing her call his name at the end gave him an instant erection. It was so hot, he jerked off, playing it again. Seeing himself and Olivia fucking was far better than commercial porn. When he showed it to her, she was alarmed he'd recorded them without her knowledge, and resisted when he wanted to do it again. But after seeing the video a few more times, she became aroused. Wild with sexual desire, she eagerly followed his instructions when he directed her to masturbate, just like in his e-mails. Olivia had become an expert at all of that, and she didn't restrain herself. Her groans and hitched breathing, culminating in cries of ecstasy, had Nico hard as a rock in seconds. After she climaxed, he continued filming himself jerking off, the veins of his thick shaft bulging and the tip mushrooming as he came on her stomach.

Emboldened by these first videos, Nico then filmed her giving him a blow job. Through trial and error, filming several times, he'd discovered the best angle was on her knees below him with him fucking her open mouth, going deep into her throat. Holding her head with one hand, his fingers laced in her hair, he ordered her to look into his eyes. He took control, pulling her tightly against him as he fucked her mouth long and hard. A low, deep vibration in her throat when she moaned had Nico rocking his hips, pushing harder. He released her when she gagged, saying, "That's good, Olivia. It means you're willing to take me all the way."

When she looked up at him with teary eyes, he said, "You give me so much pleasure, princesa. You have a luscious mouth. Open for me." On command, she blinked back her tears and licked her lips, opening her mouth as Nico went deep into her throat. His breathing became rough and she could feel him twitch, and she groaned low in her throat as he exploded. Desperate to please him, Olivia swallowed once, and catching her breath, swallowed again as Nico jetted into her. Gazing up into his smoldering eyes, she smiled seductively into the camera and licked him clean.

o   o   o

The young handsome waiter was particularly attentive since they were his only patrons. Several times he'd returned to refill their water glasses, and ask if everything was to their satisfaction. Olivia noticed Nico was quieter than normal, not entertaining her with stories the way he usually did. Walking back to the house, he marched ahead of her and she had trouble keeping up. Once inside, he grabbed her arm roughly, shoving her against the kitchen counter.

"What the hell, Nico?" she gasped, stunned by his sudden aggression.

"I saw you, you little slut," he growled, his face very close to hers.

"What are you talking about?" she asked, her voice shaking with fear. She'd never seen this side of Nico.

"The waiter, Olivia. Don't play games with me! Why were you flirting with him? I should never have taught you how to be sexy."

Olivia's pulse raced, but she defended herself. "I wasn't flirting! I was just being friendly. We were his only table, for God's sake. You know, I never said anything to you about the woman at the polo match!" She was referring to a match they'd attended the previous week. "That slut bitch was all over you and rude to me besides!"

A particularly beautiful family friend of Nico's had draped herself all over him in front of Olivia at the polo match. Speaking in Spanish, the woman asked, "When did you take to sleeping with little girls, Nico?" Olivia was mortified when Nico laughed, but at the time, she'd let it go, feeling out of her league. The incident had kept her up all night.

Now, reliving being demeaned at the match, she blasted him. "You think I didn't understand what she said about me? I speak Spanish, too, you know! What a bitch!"

Turning abruptly, Nico raised his hand. Stopping short of striking her, he spoke in a measured, low voice, "Don't you raise your voice at me or insult my friends! I will hurt you. Don't provoke me!"

He stormed out of the house, and suddenly alone, Olivia's anger melted as she burst into tears. For the next several hours, she lay in a ball on the sofa and sobbed, until he finally returned. When he strode through the door, she ran to him. "I'm so sorry, Nico! Please don't be angry, and please don't leave me alone again," she pleaded, relieved when he led her into the bedroom.

Silently, Nico pushed her face down on the bed. Quickly pulling off his leather belt, he deftly tied her hands behind her back. In one swift motion, he pushed her skirt up and ripped her lace thong off.

Olivia's heart raced. Anticipating his next move, she was electrified by his rough urgency, glad he returned and wanted her—however he wanted her. His smoky green eyes turned dark. "Don't speak, Olivia. Don't say a word. Don't even look at me. I will have you the way I want you."

Yanking her to the edge of the bed and kneeling on the floor, he slid his hands over her ass, then parted her cheeks as he lowered his lips to the mouth of her pussy, ready to devour her. She writhed in expectation as she felt his breath near the entrance, and when his tongue flicked over her clit, she shivered uncontrollably. Digging his fingers more firmly into her ass, he spread her pussy lips apart with his mouth, stiffening his tongue to run the tip all the way around the rim before pushing into her. Gasping for air, Olivia groaned, pressing her pussy hard to his mouth. Darting his tongue in and out, he lapped up her flowing juices. She squirmed in rapturous delight, every nerve in her body tingling exquisitely. Her pussy bared to him, he relentlessly fucked her with his tongue, slowly and deliberately lavishing attention on her G-spot, building the tension inside her. Her entire body heaved, edging toward release. Unable to stay silent, she begged, "Please…"

Nico stopped.

Snickering as he leaned back to stroke himself, he warned, "Don't you dare come unless I say so."

Watching him, she moaned in frustration, and he smacked her ass, bringing her to a frenzy. Her pussy, dripping wet, throbbed with thwarted desire.

Admiring his trussed-up prize, Nico spread her thighs apart and rubbed the tip of his massive erection rapidly across her clit. Gripping her hips tightly, he thrust himself into her. She gasped, arching her back, then whined softly and dropped her face back onto the bed. Nico watched his stiff cock plunge inside her, disappearing from view, then emerge again as he drew himself out, entranced by the sight of his fat dick cleaving her open. Olivia heard his breathing become ragged as the flowing wetness from her pussy made erotic sucking sounds. Holding her by the ankles, he leveraged his body into hers, picking up the pace. She let out a strangled cry when he thrust harder, repeatedly ramming his cock into her. Feeling herself close to the edge, she whimpered with each punishing thrust as his groin slapped into her buttocks.

"Don't you dare come," he growled.

Reaching forward, he clutched her by the shoulders and dug his fingers deep into her flesh, his weight pinning her to the bed. Breathing rapidly he murmured huskily, "I love having you this way."

Her face now pressed into the mattress, everything slipped from consciousness except the feeling of Nico's cock rubbing the walls of her pussy, stretching her open. She felt him twitching inside her as he climbed higher. Unable to touch herself, she groaned and bore down to rub her clit against the bed sheets as he powered into her. Shuddering, she exploded violently, convulsing rapidly around him.

Feeling her pulsating, he slapped her butt hard. "You're being punished, Olivia. You're not supposed to enjoy this!" The sting of his harsh words and slaps increased the intensity of her spasms, causing him to erupt, spurting hard into her.

Untying her and turning her over so they faced each other, their sweaty hair intermingling, he kissed her deeply, his tongue circling hers. Running his thumb over her mouth, the yellow flecks in his eyes flared. "I own you, Olivia. You're mine. Do you understand me?"

Free from the bonds, she stretched her limbs and purred blissfully, "And you're mine, Nico, always."

o   o   o

Driving to Amaru, Luna felt her heart racing. She hadn't seen Nico since before he left for Buenos Aires, and found it sweet that he had texted her when he landed. Nearing the studio, she felt that butterfly feeling in her solar plexus. It was very intense, and she wondered if it was from the Kundalini breathing. She had noticed a change already, especially at work, and Googled about the chakras, learning that clearing in the solar plexus removes fears and expands possibilities.

Walking in, she found Nico in his office on the computer. The apartment door was open, which was not typical, but she assumed he was moving back and forth, getting things in order. He bounded toward her like a big, enthusiastic dog and hugged her. "Bella!" He kissed her on both cheeks, which she eagerly returned. "Oh, Luna, your friend Sofia Lombardi e-mailed me, and I've already scheduled her for next week! But I'm sure she told you she was contacting me, right?"

Happy to see him so elated, she chimed, "Yes, she told me she would!"

Nico flitted about, doing a number of things seemingly all at once. "Well, thanks for referring her. Listen, bella, we'll do your session in a little while. But first I need to run some errands. Walk with me."

She eagerly agreed. While he'd been away, her life had returned to normal. Not bad. Just normal. Being around Nico again stirred her soul. She was captivated by his energy. Even accompanying him to the store was exciting. Something out of the ordinary always happened when she was with him.

"Good, we're just going down the street."

Outside the studio, he looped his arm toward Luna and repeated, "Walk with me."

Smiling, she linked her arm in his as they walked the few blocks together.

First they went to Nature's Way, a health food store Luna had never been to. Nico greeted a woman with a double-cheek kiss, then introduced her. "This is Angelina, Luna." The tone in his voice held a certain reverence.

A beautiful woman about Luna's age, Angelina was intriguing, and Luna thought she might be a witch. She wondered if the incredibly attractive streaks of silver in her hair were real or dyed that way. She and Nico appeared to have a secret to which only the two of them were privy.

Nico continued, "Angelina grows and dries her own herbs and sells them here."

Holding up a large paper sack with his name written on it, Angelina said, "Here you are niño."

Realizing she had just called him "child," Luna smiled inwardly.

Angelina continued, "The herbs were ready over the summer, so I prepared your order. Everything you asked for is here."

"Wonderful. I have to get some other things, so I'll pick that up on the way out."

Angelina nodded, and Nico took Luna by the arm again as he grabbed a basket in his other hand. Luna felt the butterflies stir in her belly, for a second uncomfortable it might seem she was more than a friend, but secretly reveling in the idea. Following him as he roamed the store, she noticed he took time to examine the contents of each bottle. He explained he was seeking the freshest of the special oils to be used for ceremonies and massage, and Luna couldn't help fantasizing what it would be like to feel his strong hands on her body, his long fingers kneading her muscles.

Taking the bag from Angelina, Nico double-cheek kissed her again and whispered something into her ear. Smiling knowingly, she nodded her head.

Before heading back to the studio, they strolled the stalls at the local farmer's market. Sunlight filtering through the colorful awnings created kaleidoscopes on their skin as they walked. With her arm linked into his, they leisurely browsed the offerings at most of the vendors. Stopping to sample a goat farmer's cheese, Nico placed a morsel in her mouth, asking if she liked it. The intimate gesture, rather than discomfiting, made her feel she'd known him for years.

Nearing the end of the stalls, a crowd had gathered to watch a boy trying to catch a small bird that was unable to fly. Waving the boy off, Nico got down on his knees and cupped his hands, capturing it easily. Gently stroking its crown, he made soft chirping sounds as they continued along with the bird in hand as if it were an everyday occurrence. Luna asked quietly, "What are you going to do with him?"

"Come, I know where we can free him."

Beside the bank was a small playground, and they waited on a bench until they heard it—a cacophony of birds chirping. Nico set the bird down under a hedge, and the small creature looked up at him, chirped a few times as if to say thank you, then hopped deep into the covering bushes. Luna felt certain Nico was able to communicate intuitively. There was something magical about him that she found enchanting.

When they returned to Amaru, Nico didn't offer to do her session, as she expected. Instead, looking at his desk, he fretted. "Do you mind helping me with this, Luna? The mail piled up while I was away, and the bills are terribly late."

She could imagine feeling overwhelmed by the large pile, and readily agreed. "Of course."

Sighing in relief, Nico put the kettle on, and they settled into side by side chairs. Taking charge, Luna decided the best method would be to sort the mail according to urgency. Showing him what she'd done, she got frustrated when he began methodically looking at each piece of mail, including coupon booklets. This was something she would have sped through, yet for Nico it was like shopping, where every item was given far too much attention. Thinking he should know the difference between what's junk and what's urgent, Luna went into his apartment, found a big garbage bag, and started dumping the junk mail.

"No, no! Luna!" he cried out in panic, snatching the mail from her before she was able to toss it.

"Well, that's not going to work," she announced out loud. Looking at Nico still scrambling to retrieve junk mail from the garbage bag, she suggested, "How about we try something else? This will take all week if you keep up the way you're going."

When Nico looked up at her, she saw his anguish and gave him a gentle hug.

"OK," he replied, looking more hopeful.

Luna sat down and took the entire pile of mail. Then, one by one, she called out the name of each piece, explained what it was, and once he understood, convinced him to throw it away.

Opening the bills, Luna was puzzled, but happy to help, when he asked her how to fill out the checks. But Nico quickly became increasingly distressed. "I can't believe how much money I owe!" he exclaimed in alarm.

Feeling his mounting anxiety, she tried to reassure him. "Don't worry. You're getting a lot of new clients!"

When they could finally see the surface of the desk, he sighed and said, "Thank you, Luna. I don't know what I would've done without you. Why don't you stay? I'll make tuco, Argentine meat sauce."

Behind his magical eyes, Luna saw a sad and lonely boy. Although part of her knew she needed to get home to Tyler, she'd missed Nico terribly when he was away. She trailed him into the apartment, where he reached into a cabinet and brought out a bottle of wine. Seeing her cocked eyebrow, he said, "Yes, I did drink a bit of wine while I was in Argentina. Being home with friends and family, and with the stress…Do you want a glass?" Luna hesitated, but since he was offering and having a glass himself, she accepted.

Saying he didn't want it splattered with oil, Nico took off his shirt and worked bare chested, browning the meat and sautéing onions and peppers. He was so natural in the kitchen; the way he wielded the knife, moving gracefully around the room, laughing and telling stories. Luna had never seen him this relaxed, and she admired the sight of his bronze skin. If he didn't teach yoga, he would surely be a chef. He made ravioli as if it was no effort, rolling out the dough and cutting the shapes, the muscles of his forearms rippling enticingly. He filled them with a mixture of chopped spinach, ricotta, egg, parmesan, and to Luna's surprise, a dash of nutmeg. Setting up a pot of water to boil, he floated them in the water delicately until they were done. She was enthralled by the effortlessness with which he produced a gourmet meal, and they relished every bite, talking and drinking till she was stuffed and could barely move.

With a second bottle of wine in hand, they moved to the seating area, where Nico picked up his guitar and played a gypsy song. Before long he was lost, and Luna watched him close his eyes, hair falling in his face. Seeing the black cord on his muscular neck as he bent over the body of the guitar, she noticed the leather had softened from sweat and salt water; it was clear he hadn't removed the pendant since he'd put it on. She couldn't take her eyes off him, and when he stopped singing he gazed up at her, green eyes smoky and glowing. "Luna, you are very important to me."

Her insides fluttered, and she scooted a bit closer to him, emboldened by the wine.

He continued, "I feel so close to you, and I trust you more than anyone else in my life." He rested the guitar on his lap. Taking a deep breath, he looked up at her, as if unsure he should continue, then finally said, "Luna, I want to tell you something—about my mother."

She waited patiently for him to go on, sensing this was difficult.

"I never told anyone, she died of AIDS."

Astonished, she sensed he was gauging her reaction. "I'm sure that was hard for you. Do you know how she got it?"

"From her boyfriend. He didn't know he had it. Please don't tell anyone…I'm only telling you because I trust you."

"I would never say anything, Nico. I promise."

He nodded, fingering the guitar strings, then stopped. "I'd just finished high school in New York. I guess I was about seventeen. I'll never forget. She was talking to me on the phone, and when we finished, she asked to talk to my father. When he picked up the extension, I didn't hang up. I don't know why…I think I sensed something from her. They talked for a while, and then she told him she was HIV positive. When my dad hung up, he could tell by my face that I'd overheard them."

Luna edged closer and took his hand. "I remember when my father told me that my mother had died. I was eleven. She'd been away in a hospital for a long time…my dad never took me to visit her. I guess he didn't want me to see her so sick. She had leukemia. No one told me, but I just knew she wasn't coming back."

He had tears in his eyes. "That's sad, Luna. You were just a little kid. Well, I had to go back to take care of her and make sure she took her medicine."

Still holding his hand, Luna offered, "That took a lot of courage."

He sniffed, "It was very hard. She was stubborn and I fought with her. After a while, I just couldn't stay…" Putting his head down, he plucked the guitar strings. "That's when I went to Kerala. These friends from Buenos Aires closed their ad agency and opened a spa and yoga retreat there. They invited me to teach yoga, and desperate to get away, I went. I loved my mother, but I was very depressed, and there was really nothing more I could do for her."

Luna consoled him, "You *did* help her. I'm sure she didn't want you to sacrifice your life."

Walking to the bookshelf, Nico picked up the black and white photograph. "Have you ever been to India? Kerala is like paradise.

It's on the southern coast. I fell in love with an Indian girl there and stayed two years." His face changed as memories flooded him. "Nitya…her name was Nitya. She was so beautiful—and sweet."

He returned to the couch and handed the photo to Luna.

"It would have been so easy to stay there in paradise with Nitya. But I wanted to do more with my life than teach yoga at a resort, so I asked her to come with me, but she wouldn't. I said we could go live in New York, but she wouldn't leave India—or her family. She was innocent about the rest of the world. She thought small and wanted me to stay and make a life there instead…it was all she knew. I left."

Fingering the strings of the guitar, he began playing "Spanish Getaway," a song by Yoga Tribe that Luna loved. She'd been listening to Amaru's Spotify playlist at work. But as much as she loved hearing him play, she'd been immersed in his story, and was glad when he continued.

"I went back to Buenos Aires to see my family. I'd heard about tourists going for healing ceremonies with the Q'ero and wanted to take my mom, but she wouldn't go. So I went to learn. I stayed with them, getting my training and bringing tourists up for ceremonies. When I returned home, I did healing on my mom, and it worked for a while…" he trailed off.

She was quiet, then said softly, "I'm honored you shared all this with me. You did a lot to help your mother. You did your best. That must be why you decided to make this your life's work. Do you see how everything happens for a reason?"

He gave a half-hearted nod. "This time, I fooled myself into thinking I could heal her all over again. But she didn't want to make the effort. She simply refused to take her meds." He paused before again pleading, "Luna, please don't tell anyone. I've never told anyone before. You really mean a lot to me. You're the closest person to me right now."

"Of course I won't tell anyone, Nico. You can trust me."

A heaviness had permeated the room. Attempting to lift his spirits, she ventured, "How is Olivia doing? Is she still singing at La Forza?" Luna thought she caught a glimmer of uncertainty in Nico's eyes.

Avoiding eye contact, he hesitated before saying, "We're seeing each other."

He looked up at her sideways, as if to gauge her reaction. When her expression remained impassive, he continued, "She came to visit me in Buenos Aires when she heard my mother died."

Luna's stomach fluttered, but she displayed her bright professional smile. "Oh, how nice, Nico! She's so pretty and has such a beautiful voice."

"She is very beautiful." He enunciated each syllable slowly, then added, almost as a concession, "But very young. She's like a baby."

Luna found the salacious way he said the word "baby" disconcerting, and flushed with embarrassment. She couldn't help feeling jealous, remembering the pictures he'd e-mailed. "Ah, so that must be who took all the great photos of you!"

Nico nodded and his lips curled up in a perceptible smile. "We had a good time, I guess. She took my mind off my mom and all the legal stuff I had to deal with."

He peeked at her through his long eyelashes with what she thought was a flirtatious look. "I'm actually seeing her tonight." He plucked the strings of the guitar still lying across his lap. Speaking slowly and seductively, he continued, "I didn't know when she arrived she was a virgin. Her pussy is so small and pink. She was swollen and wet and opened right up for me—and she had multiple orgasms. Now she can't stop, and begs for me all the time. We made love everywhere. I fucked her for hours. She didn't know what happened when I made her squirt; she didn't know what that was. She came so hard, she shuddered and passed out."

His story caused Luna to blush with embarrassment, and she felt a wetness and throbbing in her sex. The look of amusement in Nico's eyes revealed he knew it, and she wondered what his motive was in telling her these things. Deciding it was no longer worth being coy, she laughed, "Why do you insist on driving me crazy? What am I going to do with you?"

He laughed out loud. "Bella, do I make you nervous? You're so innocent and get embarrassed so easily. Why is that? Should I not tell you these things?"

She realized in an instant that being around him awakened her, stirring the sediment that had long ago settled at the bottom of her well. He made her feel a part of him, of something larger, and somehow more alive.

She decided to answer playfully, encouraging him. "You tell wonderful stories. I enjoy hearing them."

Looking up at the clock, Nico declared, "Oh no. I didn't see what time it is. I have to go." He leaped up and said hastily, "Don't worry, Luna bella. I'll tell you lots of stories."

o   o   o

Nico had been mysterious, saying he had something special planned. Calling out as she walked into the studio, Luna stopped short upon entering the chamber. Her heart pounded in anticipation when she saw he was making preparations for another ceremony.

He explained, "Bella, I've been waiting to do this ceremony with you since I returned from Buenos Aires. I could only get some of the elements I needed there. The ceremony is called San Pedro, after the Catholic saint who is the gatekeeper of Heaven." He paused just long enough to pull her to where he was busy placing items on a soft, white blanket, then continued talking rapidly, "My role tonight, as the maestro curandero, is to make you bloom during the ceremony—to make your subconscious open like a flower, like the night-blooming Huachuma itself. I've been preparing you for this ceremony."

Catching Nico's excitement, she listened intently.

"This ceremony restores balance. It will awaken you to a greater spiritual awareness, helping you see clearly what is holding you back. Then you can remove those obstacles from your path." He paused and looked her in the eyes. "Luna, we've become very close to each other, and I know you trust me."

Thrilled by his declaration, she nodded.

Kneeling on the blanket, Nico gestured to the many objects laid out upon it. "What you see here is called the mesa—the altar. The mesa is divided into the past, the present, and the future. Together, they are the complete universe. On the left of the mesa are the ancestors—our past and the world below."

Soaking up everything he said, Luna looked at the objects on the left and saw an arrangement of bones, antlers, ancient artifacts, stones, leaves, bottles of herbs, and shells.

In the center of the mesa, a sun-shaped iron mirror lay next to a cluster of clear quartz crystals. Nico explained, "There must be a balance between life and death; good and evil; past and present; matter and spirit. The shaman doesn't see these as opposites, but as two halves forming a whole. So the middle of the mesa is the integration of those energies. The crystal channels and clarifies my vision."

When Luna commented that the right side of the mesa had so much Catholic imagery—crosses, images of saints, and a portrait of Jesus, Nico responded, "Santa Maria represents Pachamama, Mother Earth." Picking up the devotional candle, he said, "This stands for The Holy Spirit; the sacred spirit that is in all things." Lastly, picking up the picture of Jesus, he added, "Jesus Christ is the personification of the ideal shaman for all humanity."

In addition to those items, the right side of the mesa held tobacco, sugar, corn, limes, talcum powder, and bottles of wine and perfume. Lined up like a barricade behind the mesa, a row of sticks, posts, and swords stood guard.

Carrying two cups of greenish liquid, he announced, "We're ready to begin. Now, drink this down quickly, bella. It's bitter, so you don't want the taste lingering in your mouth."

She studied the strange liquid, wondering what it was, but she trusted Nico and definitely wanted to share this mysterious and powerful ritual he'd prepared just for her. She drank as instructed.

Nico smiled. "Good, Luna. Now we'll wait. It will take a little while before the magic happens." Picking up a flute, he played softly, and the light notes wafted through the air like perfume.

Luna was content; happy just being in the chamber with him, feeling part of something sacred. Soon, Nico put the flute down and blew into a whistle, making a soft whirring sound. While chanting a prayer, she heard him say her name, making her feel warm inside. Just like in the despacho ceremony, the sounds and artifacts comforted her, like being brought back into the womb of her personal history.

She saw Nico select a staff from the mesa. He recited a chant, focusing his attention on the staff and other objects. Somehow, she knew Nico didn't see these objects as inanimate. He sang to the plants, stones, and shells as though they were living entities who were speaking to him, giving him their secret knowledge. Luna felt tranquil—soothed, in a dream from which she didn't want to awaken.

Thoughts floated in and her mind wandered as she fell under the spell of Nico's dulcet voice singing in the ancient tongue of Quechua. A slight tingling and numbness spread over her legs, then her arms, and she realized she couldn't move her body no matter how hard she commanded it. Unafraid, she let herself slip away while Nico continued chanting and shaking a rattle. Suddenly, she felt his hands on her body, massaging her arms and legs.

Dimly aware of his actions, she wondered if she'd know later that these things had really happened, or if she'd think she dreamed them. Shaking the rattle over her, he blew the whistle before pressing his lips to her skin and gently sucking in exactly the spot where she always felt the fire butterflies—her solar plexus. She felt detached, as if Nico was doing this to someone else while she observed from high above, in the far corner of an enormous room.

Luna was perfectly aware she was with Nico in the safety of the chamber, yet at the same time she was being swept by an invisible current transporting her to an ancient place of rivers and woodland. Back home to the Mohawk tribe of her ancestors. She heard a familiar voice singing to her, but felt no need to locate it. Instead, she looked up. The sky was vast, and she could see billions of stars. Each individual ray of light clearly etched a grid across the sky. A cool breeze and the mist from a waterfall drifting in the night air brushed lightly against her skin as she climbed higher onto the cliffs to touch the stars with her bare hands. She marveled at how she was completely connected to all things, throughout all time, without beginning or end.

Then Nico was there with her, his bare skin radiant in the moonlight. His muscles rippled as he took her by the hand and led her up the precipice beyond the falling water. A rainbow of colors emanated outward from him until they enveloped her as well, and she thrilled at the knowledge she was sharing his aura. She reached out and felt his arms, then gently caressed his face, running her fingers across his lips to feel their softness. Pulling her fingers through his hair, she reveled in the feeling of his energy commingling with her own. Luna realized Nico was there with her in forever time. Gazing into his eyes, she fell into a dark green pool of memories and familiar feelings from long ago. Again, she heard her name in something Nico was chanting.

Luna fell deeper and deeper, spiraling down a funnel of undulating rivers, fragrant pine trees, and the sweet scent of oranges. She felt a flood of understanding and knowledge—that time no longer existed, and there was no self and no other, they were one. Nico reached over and placed a garland of herbs around her neck, then he wrapped them around her wrists, like bracelets. Stroking her hair, he held the staff above her head while chanting her name, and she fell further into the elliptical galaxy of his eyes—right into his soul.

Taking a bottle of fragrance, Nico sprinkled it to all four corners of the mesa, then spilled corn, sugar, and wine as an offering to the holy spirits. She knew he was doing this to connect the past and the future, the light and the dark, the world above to the world below, and the sacred to the profane. She saw everything—through Nico's eyes.

"Luna, you are blooming, flowering—*florecimiento*. This is the moment of your baptism, your transformation into a being of light and pure consciousness."

Luna knew she had been here before, with Nico. This ritual, this ceremony, was symbolic of something they had shared hundreds, if not thousands, of years ago. They had once been together in a sacred space in time, and now they were making a journey from life taking to life giving.

The early morning light slipped quietly through the crack between the window frame and shade, jolting Luna into the present. "Oh my God, I have to go home." The sound of her own voice startled her, and dazed, she sat up asking, "What time is it?" She had been half asleep, her head on Nico's shoulder while he played guitar, lulling her.

"What is it, Luna? Why must you leave now?"

Her heart raced; she didn't know how she would explain this to Tyler. Standing up, she noticed all the colors were brighter and she felt keenly aware of everything around her. Unable to ignore the myriad of sensory experiences, she wasn't sure she could drive.

"Luna, you're panicking for no reason. Just call Tyler. I don't think you should drive. I'll make us breakfast."

She nodded and took out her cell phone, and saw she had a dozen messages from Tyler. Swallowing hard, she dialed home. When Tyler answered, she mustered a conciliatory tone. "Hi, honey."

Before she could say another word, Tyler gushed, "Oh thank God, Luna! I was so worried about you." A second later his tone changed. "So what the fuck? Where are you?"

He was furious, and Luna felt he had every right to be. She turned away from Nico as she replied, "I'm so sorry. Really. I can't explain everything now, but the ceremony was a lot longer than I ever thought it would be. I'll tell you all about it later, OK?"

Tyler sighed. "I guess."

"I'm sorry," Luna repeated. "Really. I'll be home soon, and I'll tell you all about it."

"OK."

"I love you."

Tyler grunted, "Yeah."

Luna hung up feeling guilty about leaving out that the ceremony involved only her and Nico, though she deemed it better left that way. She had never lied to Tyler, but she told herself there was no harm in omitting a small detail.

o   o   o

Tyler didn't look up when Luna walked into the room, which meant he was still angry with her. She sat down in the chair facing his desk. "Honey, I really am sorry."

He glanced up only momentarily before pretending to be busy on his computer again. She continued, "I just had no idea how long the ceremony would take…Our cell phones were off…so I couldn't call or text. This was a ceremony Nico learned in Peru—a very sacred one." She paused to gauge Tyler's mood. Seeing his face still stoic, she implored, "Ummm…Had I known the time, I would have called… But there are no windows in the room. I just didn't know…"

He finally looked up. "I don't know what to say, Luna. I was so worried. That was very inconsiderate of you. I worried all night long, and didn't know if I should start calling hospitals or the police or what."

She hung her head. "I know. I'm so sorry. I don't know what else I can say."

"Well, you could say you'll never do that again."

Looking up, she saw his face had softened. "I promise."

Later, she texted Nico:

> *Everything here is OK. How are you feeling? I feel like a new person is inhabiting my body. It's wonderful. I hope this feeling lasts forever. I'll try to stop by later.*

After a long shower, feeling refreshed and somehow newly reborn, she drove to her office. Though she felt an urgent need to go straight to Nico's, she had work to do.

o   o   o

When she arrived at Amaru later, Nico called out to her from the office, "Luna, thank God. I'm confused about these." He waved a stack of envelopes in the air.

She rolled her eyes. "Oh, Nico. I don't understand why it's so hard for you to stay on top of this stuff."

He chirped, "That's why I have you. To do these things for me. I'm not good at organizing." He patted the chair next to his. "Here, sit and do this with me. It doesn't take so long when you help."

Absentmindedly, she suggested, "Maybe you should hire a book-keeper."

He frowned. "I don't like strangers knowing my business. I trust you."

She sighed to herself, but was pleased to hear him say he trusted her.

Making small talk, she asked casually how things had gone with Sofia.

"I've cured her IBS. We did energy balancing with the yoga. She's all better."

The work with Sofia had taken time away from Luna, and she felt a bit resentful. But at the same time, she was glad he had gotten more business. Congenially, she responded, "That's great about Sofia! And Tyler has a new client for you, too. Her name is Erin Whelan. She's the founding partner of Grey Dog, a big ad agency in Santa Monica. Tyler and she went to college together, and she messaged him on Facebook asking about you. I guess she saw a post of yours that he shared."

Nico put his arm around Luna and pulled her even closer. "That's great! I really need a client like that. Is she going to call me?"

"I'm sure she will. Tyler gave her your phone number."

"When was that?"

"I don't know…I guess about a week ago?"

Nico frowned slightly, but quickly returned to a normal tone. "Well, could you ask Tyler to follow up with her? Maybe encourage her to call me soon?"

Annoyed, Luna scolded, "Nico, don't be pushy! Pressuring people can backfire." Tyler was especially laid back, hated being aggressive, and rarely extended himself. Luna knew getting pushy with Tyler wouldn't work.

Frowning openly, Nico took on a snappy tone himself. "I need high-end clientele like that."

Feeling how stressed he was, Luna dropped the subject. Putting her head on his shoulder, she rubbed his bicep affectionately. "Don't worry, Nico. I'll ask him. I'm always here for you."

He looked up at her from under his thick black lashes and allowed his eyes to get misty. "I'm sorry I snapped at you. I'm under a lot of stress."

Luna warmed inside.

When she'd finished making out the checks and organizing the papers that had been strewn around, Nico suggested they go for a walk. "I need to get to the health food store to get supplements for Sofia."

"Oh? What do you need to get?" Luna asked.

He hesitated. "Nothing, really. Just something for balancing the flora in her stomach." Then, taking Luna's arm in his, he said, "Come, bella. Walk with me."

Strolling in the direction of Angelina's, Nico became noticeably agitated. "Why do you want to know what supplement I'm getting for Sofia?"

Seeing he was descending into a dark mood, Luna attempted to avert the storm. "I was just taking an interest in your work…as a friend. I didn't know it would bother you."

"I just don't want you telling anyone anything you learn from me."

"Oh, Nico. I would never discuss anything about you with any-one!"

"Just please promise me."

She quickly vowed, "I promise."

A steady drizzle started falling, and Luna was getting a chill. He urged her to walk faster, scolding her for not wearing a jacket. They made it to Angelina's just as the heavens opened up into an early autumn thunderstorm.

The rain was falling steadily when they left the store, and while waiting under the awning for it to subside, Luna looped her arm snugly into his, her other hand encircling his bicep. Lulled by the peaceful serenity of rain muffling the city sounds, and the crisp, refreshing scent of the ozone aftermath from lightning, she leaned into him, resting her head on his shoulder. Standing silently, she felt him relax and his ceaseless anxiety dissolved as a calm stillness enveloped them. Cherishing the feeling that there was no one else in the world but the two of them, Luna sighed and said quietly, "I love you, Nico."

Letting that sit for a few beats, he flexed his bicep so it squeezed her hand, then murmured enigmatically, "What exactly do you mean, Luna?"

She hesitated, not knowing how to reply. His tone caused her to question the answer he sought. Finally, she answered, "I feel very close to you. I love spending time with you. You make me feel young and beautiful." She paused before adding, "I'll always be here for you, Nico."

"Luna…you're married. This is wrong."

"No, no, Nico. That's not what I meant. I'm just saying that if things were different, a different time and place…if I were younger and not married, I could see us being together. That's all."

He put his arm around her shoulders. "Are you cold?"

She nodded.

Rubbing her shoulders, he professed, "Luna, I don't see age. It means nothing. I am, in fact, older than you…We're all timeless. Age is something we made up."

She chewed on her lip. "Did I make you uncomfortable telling you that?"

"Not at all, Luna. I feel the same way. But you are still married."

Suddenly, she was the one feeling uncomfortable. "Are we OK?"

"Yes, of course we are."

By then the rain had stopped, and they headed back to the studio.

o o o

Luna eagerly pored over social media, sharing posts on Pinterest and Facebook, adding relevant hashtags like #vintage and #street-style. The style Luna had created for *Going My Way* had become a fashion trend, maybe even a brand. She couldn't wait to tell Nico. Her dreams were unfolding, and she owed this success to him. After all, it was his ceremonies that removed all the obstacles from her path.

On the way to her office, she decided to stop at Coyote Exchange, a favored source of vintage for the industry's costume designers. Every time Luna went into the shop, the owner, Gail, had some new treasure she'd found for Luna, and she was always right on target for the kinds of items Luna looked for.

As Luna walked in, Gail waved her over. "I just received an estate consignment that has a well-curated Native American jewelry collection. You're gonna love this." Gail disappeared into the back room to retrieve a box.

From the box, Luna picked up a heavy, wide, silver cuff stamped with a Navajo design, and a large Zuni inlay ring of a thunderbird. Luna loved old pawn jewelry, mostly Navajo and Zuni pieces from the early part of the twentieth century. Then she spotted a pale stone bear nestled inside. It was a Zuni fetish the size of the palm of her hand. Less traditional and a bit larger than the small fetishes common in trading post shops, this bear was gracefully carved. Luna had become enamored of Zuni fetishes, believed to contain a living power that can help its owner, during her travels to Santa Fe, and she collected them. The bear is considered the healer. Surely this was no coincidence, her stopping *that* day and finding *that* bear fetish, the perfect gift for Nico. She told Gail she would take all three items—the bracelet, the ring, and the bear fetish. Putting on the jewelry, she asked Gail to gift wrap the bear, then headed to the office.

Stepping into the production meeting, she spotted Sofia Lombardi. Though she was sure of the answer, she asked, "What do you think of Nico?"

Sofia blushed. "He's awesome, Luna! Thank you so much. I'm feeling much better already. I just love our sessions."

Before Luna could reply, the showrunner began the meeting, and she took her seat at the table. When the meeting wrapped, Luna hung back, falling into step with Sofia.

She admired Sofia's outfit of skinny black jeans and a Helmut Lang top. Having a keen sense of people, Luna learned a lot about them from their style. To her trained eye, it was obvious Sofia had come to L.A. from New York City. She wore a lot of black and had a chic simplicity. Though petite, and with legs on the thick side, Sofia excelled at camouflaging her less than perfect points. She always wore high heels to elongate her legs and add height. Today she wore buckled high-heeled ankle boots. "Where did you get those delicious boots?" Luna asked.

"Thanks! They're Michael Kors. I actually got them on sale." Sofia was a staff writer, and Luna surmised she got financial help from her family, but admired Sofia's good east coast manner of not flashing money or privilege.

Luna continued, "So tell me how it's going with Nico."

"I don't think you know, but the doctors said I had irritable bowel syndrome and always prescribed pain meds. Nico gave me something he'd concocted from the health food store, and in less than a week, the pain was gone!"

The women had reached the front desk area when Sofia asked, "Hey, are you hungry? Do you want to grab some lunch?"

Luna grinned. "Sounds great. I'm starving!"

They both ordered iced tea, then took a minute to look at the menu. Luna made up her mind before Sofia, and she looked the younger woman over while she waited. Having a keen sense of people, Luna learned a lot about them from their style. Sofia wore her voluminous blonde hair loose, and while giving her order, used her hands to sweep her hair back and push it to one side, creating a golden waterfall around her face. Her eyes were a bright, clear azure-blue. Her only makeup was a red lip stain on her very plump lips.

After they ordered, Sofia opened the conversation. "I really love the looks you've created; even the jewelry and handbags speak volumes!"

Though ingratiating herself, her remark felt well-intentioned, and Luna returned the compliment. "Thank you! Your writing is central to the show. The dialogue is hilarious and poignant all at once."

Sofia blushed a little. "I have to tell you, when I first came on the show, I was so nervous. I just sat at the table listening. But they all wanted my feedback, saying it's because I'm fashionable and from New York. I was so flattered! But since working with Nico, my writing has gotten even better, and I'm being given so much more freedom with the scripts."

Luna nodded. "I'm not surprised to hear that! Nico helped my creativity flow more easily, too."

Sofia laughed, "You know, whatever those strange ceremonies and potions are that he uses, they sure do work!"

She told Luna about an article she was writing about Nico to send to one of her best friends in New York, a publicist. "I think she can get him some national coverage."

"That's fantastic, Nico must be thrilled!"

"Yes, he's pretty pleased at the idea of some good publicity to give the business a boost."

The women chatted amiably over lunch, and after the waiter had picked up the bill, Luna took on a slightly conspiratorial tone. "Do you know who Erin Whelan is?"

Sofia's curiosity piqued. "Yes, of course. Why?"

Luna gossiped, "Well, Erin is a former classmate of Tyler's, and she's signing up for a private program with Nico."

Sofia rolled her eyes. "I guess that's good. But it's also a little scary. I've heard she's a dragon lady!"

They laughed together, forming a bond, then exchanged air kisses and wished each other a good weekend.

o   o   o

Luna stopped at Amaru to give Nico the bear fetish, and noticed a black Jaguar in the parking lot she hadn't seen there before. Just inside the door, she heard laughter coming from the chamber and called out.

Nico answered, "Luna, come in! We're in here."

Walking into the chamber, she explained, "I'm so sorry, I didn't realize you had a client. I should have called first, but I was just driving past."

Nico made introductions. "Luna, do you know Erin Whelan?"

Although Luna had always been an exotic beauty, she felt drab next to Erin. Her jet-black, trendy, chopped hairstyle and Irish porcelain-white skin accentuated grey eyes. Luna guessed trips to the dermatologist were the reason there was not a wrinkle on her face.

When Erin complimented Luna's heavy antique Navajo cuff, she thanked her decorously, then admired Erin's monastic, long, loose, black dress over cigarette pants.

"Céline," Erin stated, matter-of-factly. "I just don't have time to shop, so I have a personal stylist at Maxfield pull together my wardrobe each season. Did you ever work there, Luna? I hear most of the wardrobe girls have worked there at one time or another."

Luna bit her tongue. "No, I began as an assistant costume designer, but it must be a lot of fun to work there."

Seeing she had just been bested, Erin gave Nico a sultry smile, kisses on both checks, and made a sweeping exit, saying she would see him on Saturday at the Foundation Dinner. Luna's heart did a flip flop. *Wow, she sure doesn't waste any time*, she thought. Clearly, no one was off the table for Erin, even a twenty-nine-year-old yoga instructor!

At the door, Erin did a quick over the shoulder good-bye to Luna.

Remembering Erin was a bit older than Tyler, she replied, "Bye, Erin. Oh, wait, I almost forgot. Happy birthday soon. This is the big one, right?"

Erin pushed the door open and hastily marched out.

Hiding her satisfied grin from Nico, Luna was pleased with her good verbal volley and casual jabs. When she finally looked up, he was staring at her with a playfully mischievous look.

"What?"

"You surprise me, bella. I didn't think you could do that."

Luna answered coquettishly, "There's a lot you don't know about me, Nico."

"You really don't like her, do you?"

"I just don't get why some people need to be arrogant and brash to prove they're good at their job."

Nico laughed. "It's the image she wants. It's all an act. She is one tough bitch, though. She doesn't take any bullshit from anyone."

Luna sneered, "So I've heard. Everyone says that."

Nico's lip turned up and his eyes twinkled. "She likes me."

Luna glared. "Yeah…I bet she does. What's this about going to the Foundation Dinner with her?"

He chuckled. "Are you jealous?"

Luna responded too quickly, "No, why would I be jealous?"

"There's no reason to be jealous. You're always number one in my life. Now, come into the office. There's something I need you to help me with, and time is running out."

Placing two chairs side by side at his desk, he pulled up Craig's List. "I've been searching for a motorcycle, and I want you to help me decide."

Luna didn't really know much about bikes, but thought they were sexy. She pictured Nico with his tight jeans, leather jacket, and muscular arms on one, and felt that flutter dancing inside her. Scanning the list, she said, "Look at that gunmetal grey Ducati. It looks brand new."

"Yeah, it's really hot!" Opening the listing to read further, Nico pointed, "It's never been ridden. And the price! They're practically giving it away. Luna, call them."

"Why me?"

"A woman's voice makes a difference. They might go easier on you."

Sighing, she picked up her phone and dialed the number. A woman answered and said her husband had bought the bike, but she refused to let him ride it; she'd posted the ad because she wanted it gone and had priced it to sell fast. All excited, Nico exclaimed, "Tell her we're coming to get it right now!"

Following Nico into the apartment, Luna saw he had camouflaged a safe with a tapestry. Punching in the combination, he opened it and counted out $5,000. Luna wondered how and why Nico had so much money stashed away, but thought it would be awkward to ask.

They got to the address on Coldwater Canyon in less than half an hour, and the woman was so happy to be rid of the motorcycle, she threw in the helmet as a thank you for getting it out of her garage! Back at the studio, Nico acted like a kid who had just robbed a candy store. He said he would buy another helmet so Luna could ride with him. She stirred at the thought of wrapping her arms around his waist and pressing her body against his.

Sensing her thoughts, Nico looked at her squarely, then let his eyes slide down to her cleavage. Seductively, he licked his lips and gazed up through that dark forelock always slightly hiding his luminous green eyes. He uttered flirtatiously, "Luna, you're teasing me again, showing me your tits."

She was addled by his words, but his voice caused a throbbing between her legs. Her pussy ached for him, but not daring to reveal it, she bantered, "I'm not teasing you, Nico. You're teasing me! Besides, I have nothing you desire. You have lovely Olivia. What's going on with her?"

His face and mood darkened. "She's a little slut. I showed up unexpectedly and caught her eating lunch and laughing with one of the waiters. We had a huge fight, and I told her she has to sit and eat alone or with a girl, but not with a man. Do you think I'm too possessive?"

Luna burst out laughing. "Do ya' think?"

He stuttered a bit, but got control of himself and went on in a low, guttural voice. "Olivia is always wet for me—she's insatiable. The other night we went by one of my uncle's bars to do a wine delivery for my father. I pulled her into the back of the van and told her not to make a sound, so no one would hear us. I lifted up her skirt and pulled her tights down just below her knees so she couldn't move. Then I fucked her standing from behind, grabbing her tits with one hand. She came so hard that when I pulled out she fell on the floor."

Luna was speechless, and even with her dark olive skin she was certain her flush was obvious.

His eyes danced with the knowledge he'd aroused her. "Ah, Luna, my bella. You and I would have such a good time together. It's a pity you're married."

In an attempt to diffuse the growing sexual tension in the air, Luna leaned over and bit him hard on his bicep. He let out a yelp and pulled her by the hair just hard enough to cause a frenzy of palpable pulsation in her pussy, upon which she kissed his neck next to the black leather cord of the Om pendant. "You'd better stop all that, Nico, or trouble will start."

Stepping away, she changed the subject. "I have a gift for you." Reaching into her bag, she took out the little box Gail had wrapped.

"Should I open it now?" he asked.

Luna smiled at how adorable and childlike he was whenever she gave him something. The way he held the little box reminded her of when he had held the small bird. "Of course, Nico. I'll explain it to you."

She tried not to fidget while he took his time opening the gift painfully slowly. Wondering if he was that attentive during sex, her pussy began to throb again with desire.

Lifting the lid, he looked up perplexed when he saw the pale green stone bear. "Is this an American Indian thing?"

Luna laughed softly. "Yes. It's called a fetish. American Indians believe animals are imbued with spirit and each animal has a different power…like the crystals in the ceremony. The bear is a powerful healing fetish known for his curative powers, passing on the teachings to the medicine man in the tribe. You are a medicine man, so I thought you should have a bear fetish. The bear is your totem animal, Nico."

Holding the bear in his hands, he closed his eyes as he spoke tenderly, "This is so beautiful." He walked to a shelf. "I will keep the bear here in the chamber where I do ceremonies. This is where he belongs."

Profoundly moved that Nico cherished the bear, she hugged him, then said she had to go because Tyler was waiting for her at home. Nico gently caught her arm to stop her from turning away, adding "Luna, you're a gift from my mother. You helped me through the hardest days of my life, and you'll always be the most important person to me."

He walked her to her car and waited for her to open the Land Rover's door. As she climbed in, she looked into his eyes and saw a heartrending hint of sadness in them, creating a tingling sensation running down her arms and into her fingers. She had stopped being alarmed at these sensations because they happened so frequently.

Turning on Florence and the Machine, Luna headed home singing "Never Let Me Go."

∘   ∘   ∘

It had been almost two weeks since Kathy had surprised Olivia with the news she'd been awarded the San Francisco Opera's Adler Fellowship. Only a few applicants were accepted, and Olivia knew Kathy had used her connections. It was the opportunity of a lifetime—one she couldn't pass up.

Fearing his reaction, Olivia had procrastinated about telling Nico. But she hoped that after his initial disappointment, he'd be happy for her, seeing how good it was for her career and knowing they would see each other on weekends. She only had a few days before she had to commit to the program, and she'd been working up the courage to tell him by rehearsing her speech over and over again in the mirror.

After going to dinner, Nico was driving her car back to the studio when she began her soliloquy. "Nico, I have some good news."

Only partly hearing her, Nico answered, "Huh, what's that?"

She hesitated, gathering her thoughts. "Well, you know how you always say that I *am* an opera singer?"

Nico sensed something unpleasant was coming. "Yeah, and?"

"Well, I've been accepted into a very special program. A fellowship, actually."

Glancing over at her, he gripped the wheel tightly. "What do you mean?"

"Well, Kathy surprised me by sending the demo we made from my performances at La Forza to the board of directors at the San Francisco Opera, and they accepted me. The fellowship is a kind of scholarship and a huge honor."

Nico scowled, but didn't answer. He sped up, taking the curves on Mulholland a bit too fast, frightening her. "Please, Nico, slow down and just tell me what you're thinking," she pleaded.

"What the fuck do you think I'm thinking?" he sneered at her, taking another corner too quickly, this time causing the Mini's tires to squeal. "What about the money for my center? You never asked her for that, did you?"

Olivia grabbed the armrest, leaving nail marks in the leather. She gasped in fear, and suddenly Nico slammed on the brakes and yanked the car into a turnout. Jumping out, he pounded his fist on the hood. She couldn't believe what she was seeing and froze in place, horrified, when Nico picked up a big rock, hurling it full force off the side of the road. She trembled as he paced back and forth cursing in Spanish, his hands pulling at his hair, raging for another few minutes before climbing back into the car.

Olivia yelped when he pulled out without looking and accelerated, speeding faster down Laurel Terrace toward Ventura. He pulled up in front of Amaru Yoga and stormed out, slamming the door behind him. Leaving the car running, she ran after him pleading, "Nico, please! I'll ask her, I promise! I don't want to lose you! I won't go if you don't want me to!"

He turned around to face her, his eyes black pools vacant of emotion—no anger, no sadness.

Tears streaming down her face, she continued begging. "Please, Nico. I don't *want* to leave, but it's a once in a lifetime opportunity! What would I tell my mother? And Kathy? She pulled a lot of strings to get me in."

He eyed her coldly. "Are you leaving me?"

She sobbed, confused. "No!! Not really…Nico, I don't understand! San Francisco isn't far. I'll ask her for the money! I promise! And I'll help you on weekends…"

"I don't want a long distance relationship, Olivia. I want my woman to be here with me." He continued glaring at her.

Olivia cried, "Then I won't go! I'll stay here—with you. I'll get the money for the center." Her heart sank when his demeanor only got colder.

His eyes narrowed to mere slits, but the flashing of the yellow was like bolts of lightning.

Olivia threw her arms around him, sobbing hard. She had trouble getting the words out between breaths. "I'm sorry! I won't leave you. Never…I promise."

His mouth distorted as he tried to form the words, "Olivia…If you loved me you would have already asked for the money. I can't trust you again."

She clung harder, but he peeled her off and she reached out to him, grasping at his shirt. When he pushed her away, she stumbled backward, but caught herself before falling. She pleaded in anguish, "Nico! Please…I don't understand!"

His voice was flat. "You already showed your true self, Olivia. You only used me to sing at La Forza—to make a demo. Without me, you'd still be waitressing across the street. Go away."

Olivia's panic soared and her voice became shrill. "That's not true!"

He snapped back, "You're a using little slut! You just want me because you can't get enough of my dick. I'm the best fuck you'll ever have. Now, get the hell away from me—before I hurt you!"

As he spun on his heels and headed toward the door, she ran after him, crying out, "Why are you saying these things? I don't understand what I did wrong."

He reeled around, his face red and veins in his forehead bulging, eyes cold and dark. Shaking her by the shoulders with both hands, he spit, "Leave me alone." He shook her once more and Olivia fell backward, hitting her tailbone hard on the sidewalk. She cried out in pain.

Ignoring her, Nico turned away and marched inside without looking back, while he texted a message on his phone.

Still sobbing, hiccupping with each breath, Olivia got up and went to sit in her car, believing he would come back out and they would make up. He would apologize and say he overreacted…that he loved her, and knew she loved him, too. Everything would turn out fine. They would exchange sexy e-mails during the week like they did when he was in Buenos Aires and make passionate love on the weekends. She sat in the car with her head against the steering wheel, sobbing. After a few minutes, she texted him:

PLEASE. Come out and talk to me!!!

She waited a minute, then texted again:

I love u and believe in u!!! PLEASE BELIEVE

IN ME! We can make it work!!!

She waited. He didn't answer the text. She called. It went straight to voice mail. She texted again:

> *How could u do this to me??!!! I LOVE YOU!!!! I*
> *WANT US! I shouldn't have to choose between two*
> *things that MAKE ME HAPPY! I thought u would*
> *be happy for me…instead you're KILLING ME!*

She waited. But Nico never answered—and he never came back out.

8

The Wardrobe Department buzzed with talent coming in for fittings, and there were racks of clothes everywhere. Once she had a second to breathe, Luna saw she had missed three calls from Nico, and when he called the fourth time, she felt that familiar flutter. But since she was in the middle of a fitting, she had to let it go to voice mail.

At the end of the day, when she and Sam were the only ones left, Nico called again. Before she could even say hello, he barked at her, "Why haven't you answered, Luna? I called a hundred times!"

"I'm sorry, Nico. It was a madhouse all day. I didn't have a minute alone."

Nico snapped back, "I don't care what you're doing, Luna. When I call, you answer! Is that understood?"

Luna didn't want an argument, so simply answered, "I'll try, Nico."

That wasn't what he wanted to hear, however. "There is no try, Luna. Just do it."

He seemed more agitated than usual, so she asked, "What's wrong?"

"I'm very upset. Olivia's leaving."

"What do you mean leaving?" Luna was surprised.

"Just what I said," he barked. "She got into some bullshit program with the San Francisco Opera—thanks to me getting her that job at La Forza," he added bitterly.

Excusing his irascibility, Luna attempted to console him. "Nico, it's not that far. You can visit her. It's a great opportunity for her. Think of her career."

"You're an idiot! I taught her everything. She's mine, and now she'll go and fuck everyone in San Francisco."

With that, her phone beeped, indicating he was gone. She thought about calling him back, but decided to let him cool down instead.

On her way home from work, she stopped at Amaru to offer Nico some comfort. The door to the apartment was open, and she walked in, calling out his name. He greeted her casually, wearing only a towel wrapped around his waist and a mop of wet hair. Momentarily uncomfortable, Luna turned her back to him. "Oh, sorry. I didn't realize you'd be in the shower."

"Don't be silly. I always want you around."

She was relieved he had, indeed, calmed down and was actually being sweet. Deliberately looking her up and down, his eyes landed on her cleavage. She feigned shyness. "Nico, stop it. You embarrass me!"

He replied flirtatiously, "Do you go to work like that and flash your tits at everyone all day?" Then, without waiting for an answer, he turned, calling over his shoulder, "You want a glass of wine?"

Luna trailed along behind him. "Sure, if you're having one."

Handing her a glass, he raised his in a toast, "Los amigos son como las estrellas. No los ves siempre, pero siempre están allí."

"That sounds beautiful, Nico. What does it mean?"

He translated slowly, gazing deeply into her eyes. "Friends are like stars. You cannot always see them, but they are always there."

Thinking how Olivia was leaving him, Luna whispered, "I won't leave you, Nico, ever. I promise."

After a few glasses of wine, Nico lamented, "She's not who I thought she was. I'll never find anyone who really cares about me."

Luna nodded sympathetically. With nothing to say, she simply took a sip of her wine.

o   o   o

In high spirits, Nico spouted, "Luna, did you see 'LA Social' in *Los Angeles Magazine* today? There's a picture of me with Erin Whelan. They call me the go to yoga guru! My phone has been ringing all day!"

Just the sound of Erin's name made Luna's skin crawl, but it was good news for Nico and a welcome distraction from the break with

Olivia. She mustered some enthusiasm. "That's great, Nico! I'm so happy for you!" She thought to herself that of course his phone was ringing off the hook, anyone who saw what he looked like would want to come to his studio.

"Erin says I need a press kit immediately, and she booked a photo shoot for me. You have to come with me tomorrow." The words tumbled out.

Luna assessed the situation; she wouldn't want to bump into Erin. "Who's the photographer?"

"Let me look, Erin wrote it down. Here it is. Marcus Vander."

Luna wasn't surprised. Marcus was a superstar, but also in Erin's pocket. Certainly, Erin wouldn't actually attend to watch her boy toy posing for the camera. "Sure, Nico. Let me know what time, and I'll pick you up so we can go together. Did she tell you what to wear?"

"She told me to look hot."

She laughed. "Well, that'll be easy!"

When she picked Nico up at seven the next morning, he looked heart stopping. After a few pictures of him in tight jeans and leather jacket with no shirt, the shoot progressed until Nico was practically naked. Luna had expected as much, since Marcus was well known for shooting the world's male and female supermodels as scantily clad as possible.

Later that day, Luna was focused on style boards when she heard a light tap on the door. Looking up, she saw Sofia standing in the doorway and motioned for her to come in.

"Hey. I just stopped in to say hi and let you know that Nico e-mailed me some of the shots from this morning. They're amazing!"

"Great. I figured they would be."

Sofia gushed, "Guess what? Lindsey, my publicist friend in New York, got *Harper's Bazaar* and *LA Magazine* to run the article I wrote about Nico! Isn't that awesome? Now I can send these photos along. He looks so hot!"

"Fantastic. By the way, did you see the shot of Erin and Nico in the social section?"

They both rolled their eyes.

Twisting golden locks around her finger repeatedly, Sofia tentatively asked, "So what do you think is up with them?"

Luna shrugged. "You know Erin's reputation. If she can party with him, then she will. He's a good-looking accessory, but she's old enough to be his mother."

Sofia bit her lower lip. "Yuck. Gross."

They both chuckled, then Sofia brightened. "By the way, I'm having a get together on Sunday. It's at my house in Malibu at two. I'd love for you and Tyler to be there."

"Of course. Sounds great!"

"Don't forget your swimsuits." Then, with a sweet wave of her hand, Sofia disappeared down the hallway.

o o o

Luna chose a white crocheted sundress and nude suede thong sandals, which gave her the appearance of being barefoot—the perfect look for a Sunday pool party in Malibu. Instead of silver hoops, she wore real feather earrings and a collection of beaded bracelets. She'd applied Moroccanoil to her long chestnut-brown hair, and it fell, silky smooth, around her shoulders.

Passing Tyler's desk, she reminded him, "Don't forget, we've got the party at Sofia's today."

He replied grumpily, "I've got a ton of work to do. Do you really need me to go with you?"

She gave him a sideways look. "Yes, please, Tyler. It's important to me. A lot of the crew and my friends will be there."

He grumbled, so she added, "Besides, you know everyone from work loves talking to you."

When he pulled out a pair of traditional khakis and a white polo shirt, Luna directed him to wear a new pair of navy shorts instead. "You have great legs, Ty. You should show them off. Besides, it's a pool party."

By the time they arrived, the beach house was already packed with a diverse group of Sofia's friends and work colleagues. When Luna spotted Nico, she noticed he wore conservative pinstriped swim trunks, although he was bare chested with just the Om pendant laying on his bronzed skin. Greeting Luna with the double-cheek kiss she'd adopted, Sofia complimented her sundress. Handing Sofia a chilled bottle of champagne, Luna admired her Dolce & Gabbana lace corset top paired with white skinny jeans and sky-high white Saint Laurent platforms.

Luna moved quickly toward Nico. His silken voice caressed, "You look lovely today, Luna." Discreetly, his eyes covered her admiringly before he turned his back on her to shake Tyler's hand. "Good to see you, Tyler. Luna tells me you're writing a book; what's it about?"

Tyler shrugged. "It's a textbook…philosophy of religion."

"Not exactly a best seller, huh?"

"No, not exactly. I've written textbooks before; it's expected of me," Tyler responded impassively.

"I'm going to write a book on energy medicine and the healing ceremonies I learned from the paqos."

"Really? That's very interesting."

Nico beamed. "Do you ever think of writing something more mainstream? You know, for the public?"

Warming up, Tyler smiled. "Actually, I've already planned to do that. After this textbook is finished, I'm going to take some of my blog material and write a book about karma and reincarnation."

Intrigued, Nico remarked, "I believe in karma. I'd love to sit and talk with you about that some time. You know, I grew up Catholic, but I lived in India for years."

"I'd like that, and I'd love to hear more about your stay with the Q'ero."

Thrilled by both Nico's erotically suggestive once over and seeing the two men in her life bonding, Luna interrupted, "I'm going to leave you two to chat while I make the rounds." Snatching a glass of champagne from a server, she peeked over her shoulder in time to see Nico's eyes following her as she wove her way through the guests on the pool deck overlooking the ocean. Rumor had it that Sofia's dad, a big New York attorney, represented Italian mobsters, so no one questioned how she could afford this house. Some of the other writers from the show were in the living room, and stopping to speak with them, Luna swapped her empty glass for a full one when a server came by.

Before heading back out to the pool, she needed to find the bathroom and ended up walking through Sofia's bedroom. A four-poster bed of whitewashed wrought iron, with a white French matelassé coverlet and pillow shams, reflected Sofia's simple but elegant style perfectly. Above the bed hung a Longhorn steer skull encrusted with turquoise stones. The bathroom was natural stone with a glass-enclosed walk-in shower and steam room, the outside wall facing the ocean. Luna froze in front of the vanity when she saw Nico's toiletries sitting on the counter. Quickly and quietly closing the bathroom door, she sat down on the toilet with her face against the cool stone wall and cried softly. Then, berating herself, she reasoned Sofia was perfect for him. She was young, smart, and talented. Armed with her new-found knowledge, she dried her eyes and checked herself in the mirror, then headed back out to the pool to find Tyler.

Luna stood alone by the deck railing watching the sinking sun. Tyler was in the house, talking with some other guests he knew from UCLA. Feeling a nice buzz from the champagne—not drunk, but with just a pleasant sensation of well-being—she listened to the sound of the waves blending with Faith Hill's stirring voice singing "Breathe." Somewhere, she faintly heard Nico's voice in the background calling to her. Looking over her shoulder toward the pool, she saw him in the water, propped up on the ledge near her.

"Can you take my sunglasses from me and put them on the chair?" He shook his head and flipped his hair back; a spray of water droplets glistened in the golden late afternoon sunlight.

Luna walked to the edge of the pool and bent down to take the sunglasses from him. As she leaned over, Nico grasped her hand and pulled her in, fully clothed—shoes and all. Tipsy from the champagne, she laughed when she came up for air, her hair plastered to her face.

"Nico!" she squealed, feigning outrage. "How could you!?" Quickly, she glanced around at the guests. Most hadn't noticed, and the few nearby laughed with her. Deciding it was all in fun, she swam with him across the pool, allowing him to playfully sweep her around, holding her tightly. Suddenly, he dove underwater and slid his hands under her dress and up her legs, catching her by surprise.

Grabbing him around his broad shoulders, she pushed him away. "Nico, everyone's looking. Cut it out!" She laughed as she swam to the ladder. Luckily the sun was setting, but a wet white dress was still quite revealing, so she darted into the sauna to dry off.

Following her, Nico parked himself on the hot redwood bench. "You look very sexy all wet. You know that, right?" He smiled at her, the yellow flecks in his eyes glittering. His wet hair clung to his neck, and the wayward lock over his eye was slowly dripping one bead of water at a time past his cheek to land on the ground.

Following one droplet as it fell, Luna saw Nico's wet shorts clinging to his powerful thighs. Still breathless, she gathered herself together and scolded, "Now, just stop it, Nico. Tyler will be looking for me."

Wistfully, Nico tucked a thick strand of wet hair behind her ear, then disappeared back toward the pool.

o   o   o

When Sofia appeared in the doorway, Nico barely looked up from the computer before snapping, "Where have you been? I'm going crazy here! I have too much to do, and this is not how I should be spending my time."

"It's OK, Nico. I'm here now," she said, shifting into calming mode. "Remember, I have to work, too."

He retorted, "No, you don't. You need to help me!"

Since the *Harper's Bazaar* article had come out, Nico had been deluged with e-mails from all over the country. Ignoring his caustic outburst, she threw her arm over his shoulder, and jested, "I guess I never should have gotten you all that publicity, huh?"

Nico flared, "Don't be fresh to me. Of course I needed those articles! People need to know about me."

She'd forgotten how he lost all sense of humor when he was anxious. She reassured him, "I love helping you, Nico. You're amazing, and you helped me so much. My stomach never hurts anymore." She paused and looked closely at him. "Don't you see? I admire you more than anyone."

"Yeah, yeah…enough talk. Just take over this bullshit."

Though he was still snippy, she could hear in his voice that her presence and adoration had pulled him off the ledge. She slid the laptop over to begin answering e-mails and adding appointments to his calendar. These kinds of tasks were easy for her, but he took them as a personal affront. Sitting in the chair next to her, he kept his face in his phone and grumbled in Spanish while texting. Although it was annoying to Sofia, at least he wasn't interfering with the work she was doing. She knew that girl Olivia had upset him. Even though she'd moved to San Francisco, she kept messaging him. Sofia figured she'd work on promoting Nico, do all these tasks to help him, give him the keys to her beach house and car, which he loved, and he'd soon forget all about Olivia.

She had made reservations for a late-night supper at Providence on Melrose, so after finishing his office work, she announced she was taking him out to celebrate.

Nico scowled. "What do I have to celebrate? That *Bazaar* article has been nothing but a pain in the ass. Most of these people writing me aren't even from L.A. Why are they writing?"

"People write to celebrities all the time. They're hoping for an answer."

"Well, that doesn't pay the bills."

"Nico, between *Bazaar* and the nomination for *Going My Way* from the Writers Guild, I think we have a lot to celebrate. Why don't you get dressed while I freshen up? Besides, I haven't eaten all day and I'm starving."

While Nico was changing, she added a fresh coat of red lipstick— the color Taylor Swift wears—and ran her fingers through her lush blonde mane. Nico soon reappeared, looking deliciously hot in black overdyed Diesel jeans and a tight black Armani linen sweater. He ran some product through his hair, pushing it off his face, but allowed that errant coil to fall forward on its own. A five o'clock shadow added more sex appeal to his strong masculine jawline.

Tossing him the keys to her Rhodium Silver Porsche 911 Cabriolet, she said breezily, "You drive."

"That's my Spyder Woman," he purred in delight. "You know how I love driving the Porsche."

Sofia winced. He had nicknamed her Spyder Woman after the infamous Porsche 550 Spyder James Dean had lost his life driving in 1955, even though her Porsche was not a Spyder. It was, in fact, her father's old 911 convertible he'd given her when she moved to L.A. But what really irritated her was how he always mispronounced Porsche. She bit her tongue, but when he asked again how to switch into manual shift mode, the words popped out before she could stop them. "I've shown you this a thousand times, Nico. And it's 'por-sha,' not 'porsh.'"

Offended, Nico's eyes flashed like lightning. Sofia knew she'd pissed him off and tried to smooth things over quickly. "I just mean, you know…you're so perfect driving this car, and people in L.A. are judgmental. I don't want anyone to get snobby with you." She waited, and he softened, but only a tiny bit. They drove to the restaurant in silence.

At Providence, they were greeted warmly, then led to a prominent table with a great view of the restaurant so they could see and be seen by everyone coming and going.

Suddenly charming, Nico told Sofia she looked very nice, but his eyes were everywhere else, taking in all the pretty women in the room. Sofia noticed many of them looked him over as well. To get his attention back on her, she prompted, "You know so much about wine, would you please order a bottle?"

Reviewing the wine list, he looked up at one point to say, "You should get them to order from my father."

"I'll mail a thank you card and include your dad's business card. That would be more professional."

She was aware her last words brought them close to the next blow-up of the evening, and held her breath when he eyed her coolly. But the waiter reappeared, distracting him, and the night moved forward smoothly.

Nico relaxed, entertaining her with stories while they ate and drank a crisp white wine. On the way home, she plugged in her phone and launched Gipsy Kings radio on Spotify, and soon he was breaking out the 911 in full sport mode.

At her house, Nico changed into sweats and a T-shirt, then flopped down on the sofa and turned on the TV. Sofia changed into cotton tap shorts and a tank top, hoping she didn't seem to be trying too hard to get his attention.

Flipping through channels, he landed on an old James Bond movie. She curled up next to him with her head on his chest while he gave running commentary and quoted dialogue. Sofia thought he sounded like a little kid, which she found endearing. Besides, she wasn't really paying attention to the movie, she was feeling the heat of his body against hers and his breath on her face.

She loved his mellow voice, finding the deep, purring tone both arousing and soothing. Tonight, she was aroused. Casually sliding her hand along his hard thigh, she purposefully roamed closer to his cock, clearly outlined beneath his sweat pants. She feigned obliviousness when his dick stirred as her hand casually grazed him. Though he quickly hardened and his breathing altered, he remained focused on the movie.

Pressing his hips against her hand, he closed his eyes and, taking her by the back of her neck, pushed her head down into his lap. With his free hand, he slipped the sweat pants off, revealing his swollen, thick erection twitching for attention. Sofia lightly swirled her tongue around the head, stroking the shaft up and down slowly, but firmly, from the base to the tip.

She looked up and locked her intense blue eyes with his. Nico fixated on watching her perform magic as she teased the head, flicking her tongue along the ridge. Covering him with her saliva, she continued her firm grip, jerking him off while her fingers fondled his balls. He raised his hips up as a strangled groan rumbled from deep within him.

Rocking into her mouth with powerful movements, he growled, "Suck me. Let me fuck your mouth." As she sucked him in deep, he entwined his fingers into her thick blonde hair, holding her head down on his cock while he pumped himself between her lips. Working both her hand and mouth up and down and taking his thick shaft deep into her throat, she felt his muscular thighs tighten and contract as his hips bucked. Her soft humming as he slid along her tongue created vibrations that further tantalized him, driving him over the top. He laid his head back on the sofa with his eyes closed, breathing raggedly, and begged her not to stop. "That's it, baby. That's it. I'm going to fucking cum in your mouth. Swallow it!" he commanded as he exploded, coming hard, his thick, hot cum coating her throat. Sofia swallowed then slowly licked him clean to show him how much she enjoyed pleasing him.

Trailing kisses from the tip of his cock to the hair just below his bellybutton, then to each nipple in turn, she finally kissed him on the lips. Nico returned the kiss, murmuring, "Thank you, baby."

When she leaned over him with her hands on the back of the sofa, he slid his hand into her tap shorts, inserting a finger into her wet pussy. "I like how wet you get when you suck me off." He inserted a second finger into her while his other hand reached under her tank top.

Kissing him, Sofia moaned loudly while she sucked his lip and her tongue danced with his. Taking one very wet finger, Nico slid it back to her ass and inserted it gently, making her moan louder. He raised her tank top over her head so it covered her eyes like a blindfold, then sucked each of her nipples alternately, nipping them with his teeth until they grew long and hard in his mouth. His fingers moved back and forth, slipping deep inside to rub her G-spot.

When she pleaded, "Oh God, Nico. I'm so close!" he rolled his thumb over her clit, stopping just before she came. Panting a protest, she raised herself up and straddled him so that her pussy was closer to his mouth. "Lick me—please!"

Toying with her, he slowly licked her, teasing her clit and poking his tongue inside along with his fingers as she rocked back and forth, grinding down on his hand and face.

Placing his hands on her waist, he guided her wet pussy onto his once again hard cock. Bucking her body up and down, he fucked her hard, rhythmically grinding into her, her clit rubbing against his pelvis. Feeling her orgasm nearing, he cupped her breasts, squeezing her nipples until she shuddered and fell forward onto him.

When her pussy clamped down on his cock, she felt him jerking as he jetted into her. Though his head was buried in her hair, she could make out his words when he softly murmured, "Sofia, Sofia, you are a gift." Pleased, she lay quietly in his arms.

o   o   o

An unidentified motor sound startled Sofia awake. Nico was not in the bed next to her, so she stumbled out of the bedroom, following the strange sound to the kitchen. There, she found him using her slightly ancient industrial juicer, a pile of vegetables and fruit strewn along the counter. "Good morning, Spyder. I'm making us smoothies, then we can go do some yoga on the deck. It's a beautiful day!"

Sofia was happy he was so chipper. For now, at least, she was in his good graces. He was always happier and more easygoing here at the beach house. "That sounds fantastic." She gave him a hug from behind, standing on her tiptoes to kiss his neck. "What a nice way to spend my birthday!"

Nico hesitated. "Yeah. By the way, I ordered your present, but I have to pick it up."

She suspected he'd actually forgotten it was her birthday, but just cocked her head and gave him a crooked smile. "C'mon, let's take our smoothies out on the deck."

Sofia sat on her yoga mat next to Nico, basking in the sunshine and admiring the view of her pool and the ocean beyond. Glancing at him, she admired how good he looked, his chest tanned and bare, the Om pendant dangling below the hollow of his throat. Having such a good-looking man here just made everything that much better.

After their yoga, he joked, "Hey, for your birthday, you have to jump in the pool backward!" But before she knew it, he'd pushed her in, then followed after her.

They were in the pool horsing around when her cell phone buzzed, and she climbed out to look. Seeing it was her father, she answered, "Hey, Daddy!"

"Happy birthday, gorgeous! How'd you like to have dinner with your dad?"

"What do you mean? Are you in L.A.?"

"Yes, I am. I flew in to surprise my princess for her birthday. I made reservations at Mélisse for seven o'clock, but meet me in the bar at six."

"Oh, Daddy, Mélisse. How exciting! Nico and I will see you there."

After hanging up, she effused, "Daddy's in L.A. for my birthday, and he's taking us to Mélisse! He said to meet him at six…what should I wear?"

The look on Nico's face crushed her. "Dinner at six?! That's stupid. I don't eat that early. Besides, I've got a meeting. Meet me at the studio afterward, and don't be out late."

Devastated, she complained, "I can't believe you won't come! It's my birthday!"

Heading into the house, he called over his shoulder, "We'll do something special for your birthday another time. Right now you have to do my laundry. I need my John Varvatos rivet jeans for the meeting. And you're not going anywhere until you write that web copy."

Stunned, Sofia sadly trailed him inside.

As she was folding the laundry, he came into the room and snatched the jeans and a black T-shirt from the basket. A moment later he charged out of the bathroom. "What the hell is this?" he demanded, waving the shirt in her face.

"What?" Sofia asked, annoyed by his outburst.

"This bleach spot!" Nico spat. "You ruined my $300 shirt!"

Incredulous, she informed him, "Nico, we don't even have any bleach!"

He scowled. "You have to buy me another one." Then he stormed off to take a shower. This wasn't the time to remind him she'd bought the T-shirt and jeans for him.

After he left, she was breathing a sigh of relief when her phone rang. It was Nico. "Bring me my motorcycle gloves!"

She hit end call with a hard punch of her finger, then grabbed the gloves.

Taking them from her, he stopped and frowned deeply. "What the hell? Look at this!" He pointed out the tip of one finger on the left glove where the seam had split. "What did you do to it? You broke my glove!"

Caught off guard, she stammered, "But, Nico! I didn't…How could I break your gloves?"

"You fuck everything up," he spat, before climbing on the Ducati and taking off.

Sofia took the quickest shower of her life and blew out her hair. Her dad liked it best when she didn't wear a lot of makeup, so she used only a tinted moisturizer and mascara, sweeping her lips with a warm nude Chanel lip gloss. Ripping through her closet, she pulled out a new tomato-red Herve Leger bandage dress. Before selecting shoes, she eyed herself critically in the full-length mirror. The dress looked fabulous on her shapely body, the color cheerfully delicious—but she deemed it too sexy for dinner with Daddy. Pulling it off, she tossed it onto a chair and selected another new dress she hadn't yet worn—a violet Roland Mouret crepe minidress that was perfectly draped, with a cinched waist and asymmetric hem. The color accentuated her eyes, and it was extremely alluring without being overtly sexy. Placing her cell phone, lip gloss, and ID in a clutch, she then donned an Hermès head scarf and black Chanel sunglasses for the half hour drive along PCH to Santa Monica. The sun would be setting, but with the top down, she would still need her sunglasses for the wind and glare on the winding road. Choosing her most upbeat playlist, Katy Perry's song "Roar" came up first, and she turned up the volume.

Arriving at Mélisse, she spotted her dad's bodyguard and surmised he must have had an earlier meeting with a client. She often thought about his clients and how dangerous it was working with gangsters. As a child, she would ask him a million questions, and he would joke around sometimes in a way that would frighten her, saying in a fake gruff voice, "If I told you…I would have to kill you," before he'd tickle her. It wasn't until she was much older that she realized it may, in fact, have been true. Walking into the restaurant, she saw her father at the bar talking with a tall, relatively younger man with sandy hair, wearing tortoiseshell glasses and dressed in what appeared to be golf attire. He certainly didn't fit the stereotype of mobster, she thought, making a mental note of his appearance. She already had an outline for a screenplay she planned on writing about a mob attorney and his clients, although she never told her parents about it.

Joyfully, she walked up and eagerly threw her arms around her father to kiss him dramatically on the cheek. "Daddy! I'm so glad you came!"

Beaming, he kissed her back. "You look beautiful, princess. I guess L.A. is good for you. You're glowing!"

The bespectacled man turned to Gerald, whose attentions were still on Sofia, and gently interrupted. "It was good to meet you face to face, sir." Then he quickly left the familial scene, seemingly to avoid an introduction.

"What was that all about?" Sofia queried nonchalantly, tossing her hair back.

Pointedly ignoring her, he signaled the bartender. "What are you drinking?"

"I'll have the same as you, a dirty martini. Three olives." She knew better than to press for details, but couldn't resist asking. She had a journalistic mentality—if you don't ask, you definitely won't find out.

They were escorted to a remote table for two in the back, against the plum-colored wall. Sofia discreetly opened her clutch to silence her phone while her father perused the extensive world-class wine list. When the sommelier came to take the order, her father pointed to the 2006 Screaming Eagle Cabernet Sauvignon from Napa Valley, a cult wine with limited production that cost over a thousand dollars a bottle. Nodding, the sommelier returned shortly, presenting it without any fanfare. After the wine was poured, Gerald asked Sofia, "How's the job, and have you made friends?"

"I love it, Daddy! The other writers always ask for my opinion. Oh, and I had a big party at the house and everyone came!"

"Well, I'm glad you're happy. I hated to see you leave home so soon. Now tell me…what is this fellow Nico like? And I want the truth!"

"Oh, Daddy! He's smart and funny—and plays guitar. And he's a brilliant healer! He cured me of all my stomach problems. I just adore him."

The waiter served an appetizer of lobster Bolognese with black truffles and refilled their wine glasses. Sofia ordered the almond crusted Dover sole and her father the aged liberty duck.

"So why didn't Nico come to dinner? It's your birthday! I'm *glad* it's just me and my baby girl, but I would've liked to meet him."

"I know, Daddy. He had to work late today. He's always so busy. Between private sessions, teaching classes, and meetings…he's stressed out. And exhausted. He doesn't even make plans with his friends. Besides, he's kind of shy. He doesn't like to go out very much, even if I'm paying. Did I tell you he's a terrific cook?! Maybe it's because we just started dating, but he prefers to be alone with me."

Gerald cocked an eyebrow, but carefully tempered his response. "Sofia, you're just twenty-three. Are you sure you want to limit yourself like this? Maybe you've jumped into this thing with Nico too quickly."

"Daddy, I love him. He's just very serious about his business and wants to open a center in Beverly Hills. I help him a lot with his office work and writing." Realizing that might not have sounded so good to her father, she hastened to add, "But I love to help him!"

"Hmmm. You always did bring home wounded animals, like birds with broken wings. Your mother still says you should have been a doctor!"

"Yeah, I know," she said wistfully. "But I love writing." She paused, lost in thought. "The show is doing great. I expect to be staying out here." She took a long sip. The wine loosened her, and she sighed, "Daddy, don't worry. Nico loves me. It's normal to be stressed out with your own business. I think he's…" she struggled to find a word that wouldn't alarm her father, and finally just said, "nervous." She peered up with a look of concern. "He has anxiety—I guess that's the best way to describe it."

Gerald had been relishing the lobster Bolognese, but paused, setting his fork down momentarily. Picking up the wine glass instead, he mused, "What do you mean by nervous…anxiety?"

Sofia chewed on her lower lip, a sign of her own nervousness that was not lost on her father. "He gets…impatient. Like when I'm at work and things aren't going his way, he gets angry and calls me names…but I'm sure it's just stress and he doesn't think first. I know he doesn't mean it—and he apologizes."

The waiter arrived with their entrees, and Gerald waited for him to go before continuing. "I know men like that. When they don't get their way, they do bad things and hurt people…without remorse. As long as you're valuable to them, they'll keep you around."

Sofia burst out, "Oh, Daddy! Nico would never hurt anyone!" She continued dismissively, to alleviate his concern. "He's just nervous and hates to be alone. His mother just died a couple of months ago, and he has no one."

"Sofia, that's no excuse to be verbally abusive. He doesn't raise his hand to you, does he?"

"Oh no! He just needs me. Once he feels secure about his business, he'll relax. I shouldn't have said anything to worry you." She paused. Realizing she had said too much, which might cause her father to investigate Nico, she added, "I mean…he's not a gangster, you know."

"I'm sorry about his mother, Sofia. Truly. I just don't want to see you lose yourself getting wrapped up with someone who has emotional problems. You're a beautiful and talented young woman, and could easily attract the kind of man who is controlling and manipulative. The kind who readily targets people who are compassionate… that they can take advantage of. How did you meet him?"

"Someone at work. She said he could cure me, and he did! Daddy, he's a healer. He lived with shamans in Peru and in India teaching yoga. He's very good at his profession."

"Ah! And now you're grateful to him. This is a classic pattern! You think you owe him. But you paid him, right?"

Sofia looked down. She could never lie to her father, and now she was scared to tell him the truth. "Of course I paid him."

"How much did this guy cost you? Or should I say *me*."

Unable to look him in the face, she whispered, "Ten thousand."

She knew her father well enough to know he wouldn't bat an eye-lash—and would certainly never yell at her. He had remarkable self-control. He had to. If his clients sensed weakness or a lack of control, he wouldn't last, literally.

"I see. Well…do you feel better?"

"Yes, Daddy. I feel the best I've ever felt in my life."

"Good. I suppose he knows his job, then." He was quiet while the waiter refilled their wine glasses. "I don't like that he didn't come tonight to meet me. It would have been the polite thing to do. Well, your mother and I will meet him when you come home for Christmas."

"Yes, Daddy, of course! You'll adore him."

"In the meantime, Sofia, please go out more with your friends. You tend to immerse yourself too much in one thing—I suppose that's why you're a good writer. And, please don't let him take advantage of you. Have some boundaries."

They finished their entrees while making small talk about the characters on the show and about what her friends from New York were doing. Gerald insisted she order the caramelized date pudding, and she agreed only if he promised no one would sing happy birthday to her. He ordered the fine cheeses and two glasses of Cockburn's vintage port from 1960. While they were sipping their port, he reached into the inside pocket of his jacket. "I almost forgot. Mom said to give you this for your birthday." He handed her a small gift box.

Opening the box, she exclaimed, "They're gorgeous! Thank you, Daddy!" She picked up one of the earrings nestled inside.

"Don't thank me. I would never know what to buy you," he laughed. "What are they made of, anyway? They look like rocks."

"They're by Kimberly McDonald. She makes organic jewelry. They're 18-karat blackened white gold, and those are reclaimed diamonds around an agate geode. Look…aren't they beautiful?" she exclaimed, holding one out for him to examine while she put the other one in her ear.

As he studied it carefully, he kissed her cheek. "Not as beautiful as you are."

It was past midnight when Sofia drove into the parking lot at Amaru. Bracing herself for Nico's wrath, she went inside. For over an hour, he berated her, pacing back and forth as he rattled off a list of things she hadn't done or had done wrong. She'd come to call that behavior "crazy time." It's what she expected would happen if she left him alone while she went out with her father. But there was no getting around it, since her Daddy had come all this way to see her on her birthday.

When Nico's fury was finally spent, she curled up on the bed, holding him close. "Don't worry, honey. I'll take care of everything first thing tomorrow. I'll call the electric company. OK?"

He nodded sullenly. Sofia kissed him, first on the arm, then on his neck, then tickling his ear with her tongue until he turned to face her. Then she kissed his lips gently, her mouth slightly parted. At first he kept his lips tight, so she dragged her lips down and lightly sucked his lower lip into her mouth. Finally relaxing under her persuasion, he opened his mouth to receive her. Their tongues danced, licking around the inside of each other's lips and twining around each other.

Sofia trailed one hand down the front of Nico's body, stopping at the waistband of his jeans. Continuing to flick her tongue in his mouth, she unbuttoned his waistband, pulled his zipper down, and wriggled his jeans off. Slowly, she teased his cock through his boxer briefs until he got fully hard under her gentle touch. When he sighed and his hips lifted into her hand, she pulled his cock out. Breaking their kiss, she lowered herself down until her head was level with his crotch. She licked her lips and wrapped them tightly around his thick shaft. Looking up at him, she saw his eyes glowed. She flicked her tongue all around the tip, then dragged it up and down the length of his shaft, from the base to the tip. Taking one of his balls into her mouth, she sucked it very softly, enjoying the sound of his breathing becoming increasingly ragged. Raking her tongue along the length, she paused to lock eyes with him before gently dribbling some spittle on the slit of his engorged head.

After sliding him in and out of her mouth to get him nice and wet, she stroked roughly up and down the shaft. Using her hand to control the angle, she pressed the tip along the roof of her mouth. Tantalizingly, she pulled him nearly all the way out, running her thumb firmly along the underside while she traced her tongue around the head, before plunging him back into her mouth and sucking hard, taking him deep into the back of her throat.

Nico reached down, and grabbing fists full of her blonde hair, pulled her head down harder onto his cock. Listening to his breathing, shallow and rapid, she felt his balls tighten and retract slightly, signaling he was on the edge. Sucking hard, her mouth like a vacuum, she moaned softly and hummed, teasing his dick. Picking up the pace, his hips undulated rhythmically, hitting the back of her throat with each thrust as he fucked her mouth. His cock twitched, and his whole body shuddered as he came hard. "Oh fuck," he growled, as he sprayed hot cream down her throat.

Swallowing quickly, she waited for the next jet of cum, and the next.

Nico groaned loudly with the last of his ejaculation, then fell back on the bed.

When he dozed off, he was still dressed except for his cock resting outside his boxer briefs. Sofia sighed with relief and snuggled up next to him, her head on his chest, listening contentedly to the sound of him snoring like a big cat. Smiling to herself, she was quite satisfied to have given him so much pleasure—and just as proud of her ability to deal with his mood swings. She had tamed the lion, and now he slumbered.

When she had first met Nico, his dark, masculine good looks captivated her, and his eyes revealed a pain and sorrow that wrenched her soul. She had fallen under his spell their first session, certain they had a karmic connection and believing she could take away the loneliness she sensed in him. She'd never felt so attached to anyone the way she did with Nico. She was certain destiny had brought them together, and because Nico had given her wings, she would reciprocate by being his angel.

Sofia got up and went to the kitchen for some water. She liked the studio and Nico's cozy apartment in the back. Everything here was personal to him and told her something about him. Still, she

suspected there was much she didn't know and that Nico kept a secret—something troubling. She thought she had succeeded in the
challenge of figuring out this enigmatic man far better than anyone
else could, yet she could not ascertain the roots of his dark side.

The sound of Nico's cell phone vibrating on the table drew her attention, so she glanced at the message that popped up—a text from
Erin Whelan saying:

> *Thanks for the hot yoga, babe…it's always
> steamy.*

Sofia stuck her tongue out at the cell phone. That Erin was really
starting to piss her off.

∘ ∘ ∘

Luna set the coffee table with Limoges luncheon plates she and
Tyler had received as a wedding gift, sterling silver flatware, and
Tiffany flutes, then put a bottle of Veuve Clicquot in a champagne
bucket. Placing the cake on a silver tray, she found a pack of birthday
candles in the kitchen drawer. Finally, she arranged the salmon on an
antique Meisen platter with alternating asparagus spears and lemon
wedges around it.

After much cajoling, she had gotten Nico to agree to come have
lunch on her birthday. When one o'clock came and went, Luna was
dejected. But at 1:30, Nico was at the door bearing a beautifully
wrapped box and a big smile, proud of himself for remembering. As
he often behaved during celebrations, he urged her like a little boy,
"Open the box, Luna!"

Luna concluded Sofia had wrapped it, since it was done so perfectly. She took her time untying the ribbons and undid the paper
carefully. Finally, the box was unwrapped and she peeked inside, seeing a buttery soft suede shoulder bag with long fringe—totally her
bohemian style. She threw her arms around him. "I love it, Nico! It's
perfect, and it reminds me of a vest I had in college."

"I knew you would love it. It reminded me of you."

She saw a flash of something like recognition in his eyes. A flutter rose up inside, and she looked for a distraction. "Come on, let's eat."

They ate sitting on the floor at the coffee table, using oversized throw pillows as cushions. "This is delicious, and you made such a pretty arrangement. Happy birthday, bella." He lifted his champagne glass in toast, and she clinked hers against his.

When they finished lunch, Luna brought out the chocolate cake with the candle on it. Nico lit the candle for her, but before she made her wish, he interrupted, "Wait. Let me take a picture." He got the cell phone camera ready then told Luna to go ahead. She closed her eyes, wishing for a lifetime of days like this, then opened her eyes and blew out the candle. Nico's timing was ideal. He got the shot at the perfect moment, just as the flame went out.

Looking at the photo, she laughed. "You'd better not say my age when you post that!"

He chortled. "Bella, you're so beautiful. No one would ever believe it, anyway."

Luna blushed a little, but inwardly she soaked up his attention like a parched sponge. Encouraging him to talk about himself, she asked how all his projects were progressing, and he began boasting how Erin was pitching him for a designer jeans campaign and hooking him up with a big movie agent.

Although the luncheon invitation had been innocently contrived to spend time with Nico, she began feeling slightly uncomfortable being alone in her apartment with him. During an awkward lull in the conversation, she asked how things were going with Sofia.

Turning serious, Nico confided, "Luna, I care for her, but only as a friend. I know she wants more, and I wish I felt passionately about her, but I just don't feel that attraction—at least not like with Olivia. I *am* very close to Sofia, and she's a great friend to me..." he trailed off.

Luna offered, "Sofia adores you! You know, passion wanes, but a strong friendship, with love and respect, lasts forever."

He sniffed, "You're wrong. Passion is everything! But what do you really know about it?"

Taken aback, Luna gaped.

Nico continued emphatically, "Let me explain to you. You and

Tyler are just good friends. Of course you think that's the best. But you don't have hot sex any more, do you? So how great is that?"

Luna balked. "Right, Nico. Just wait until *you're* married for as long as I've been, then you can talk to me about how great passion is for the long haul." As Nico started to say something, she cut him off, "When Tyler and I first met we had plenty of passion. But a relationship evolves and deepens. At some point it's not just hot sex anymore—like you had with Olivia in the back of the truck. It's much better to build a relationship on trust, friendship, and common interests."

Nico countered, "No, I don't think this way at all. I believe in passion…and chemistry, it's in the smell of a person's skin. I loved Olivia's smell, the way her pussy smelled, too. Sofia does not smell good to me. I don't like fucking her. I try to like it." Nico paused and winked at her, "She does give good blow jobs, though."

Luna relaxed and finally giggled. "So, what do you say to her?"

He replied matter-of-factly, "I thank her, turn over, and go to sleep!"

She shook her head. "Nico, you're impossible!"

o   o   o

Seeing an invitation to Erin's company Christmas party, Sofia gave Nico her best wide-eyed ingénue look and asked, "What should I wear?"

Nico responded dismissively. "Don't start, Sofia. You know I can't bring you. It's business."

She countered saucily, "Really, Nico? Well, I've done a lot for your business. *I've* introduced you to tons of people, gotten you clients, and you won't take me to Erin's party?"

Narrowing his eyes, he snapped back, "Erin is a client. I have to go alone and use the opportunity to see people."

Knowing she'd lost the argument, Sofia turned and walked out of the room.

Much to her surprise, Nico followed, and his tone softened. "You know you're my girlfriend, Spyder. But Erin gets jealous. It wouldn't be comfortable. It's just business. *Really.*"

Sofia fumed, but when he came closer, she allowed him to kiss her and squeeze her breast. She decided to just let it go.

Nico ripped through his closet trying on several pairs of pants before settling on the black DSquared2 jeans and tight-fitting black dress shirt she'd bought him. Holding back her tears, she watched him slide his belt with the silver dragon buckle through the loops. Standing in front of the mirror running product through his hair with his fingers, he looked so hot it made her heart ache and her clit throb at the same time watching him.

Thinking to herself how those jeans and shirt had cost fifteen hundred of her hard-earned dollars, she felt debased, knowing how disappointed her father would be by her fawning behavior. Nico had been talking to her about nonsense, but she hadn't heard a word of it. Wearing his old Schott Perfecto black motorcycle jacket, he picked up his gloves and the keys to the Ducati off the console by the front door. Sofia had bought him a new Burberry Brit leather biker jacket, but Nico insisted on always wearing his dad's beat-up one from the '70s, saying it was good luck. She had to admit, he looked hot.

Looking down, hiding behind the veil of her cascading blonde hair so he wouldn't see the pool of tears in her eyes, she choked up as she suggested, "Honey, please take the 911. I'd feel so much better."

Nico laughed, then patting her on the head as if she were a dog, took on a patronizing tone, "Don't worry, Sofia. I won't be too late."

Dozing off, Sofia woke up every hour, still seeing the bed empty next to her. If he wasn't dead on the highway, she would surely kill him! Late in the morning, she heard the motorcycle pull into the driveway and went out onto the deck.

Exasperated, she asked, "What happened, Nico? Why didn't you call me?"

He snapped at her, "My phone died."

"Why didn't you borrow a phone to call me? I was worried!"

Nico glared at her, brushing past and striding into the house.

She followed closely, asking, "Where did you sleep?" Her heart stuck in her throat. It was a stupid question, and she knew the answer. She just wanted him to say it.

"Erin's. I drank, so I didn't drive. Nothing happened."

Sofia's stomach sank into a knotted, hard pit in her abdomen. She snapped, "Yeah, right!"

His temper flared. "Look, Erin's hooking me up with a lot of people. I met Alexa Morgan, a big studio head, who said I'm 'star quality.' And Erin booked me for the Armani jeans campaign. It's huge. I'll be on billboards and in all the top fashion magazines."

"Right," Sofia dripped sarcasm, "so she can get into your jeans!" She knew full well he'd really been saying Erin had done so much more for him than she had—or could.

Dismissing her, he lowered his voice and said derisively, "Things are exploding for me and you're asking me where I slept?"

"I'm sorry, Nico," she backed down, feeling stupid for her petty jealously when he was making things happen.

"This is why I don't take you with me. You would say something stupid."

Sofia fought back tears. She wanted to scream that she knew he was turning it all around on her. Who wouldn't be distraught about being left home alone, then worried he'd been in an accident, or jealous about him staying at Erin's? He made sure no one knew he had a girlfriend. But instead of prolonging the argument, she walked away.

Nico quickly took one big step and pulled her by her ponytail back to him, causing her to yelp out of fear. "Don't walk away from me!" Then he smiled devilishly and fixed his eyes on hers. "You know you're my woman, Sofia. I don't have to tell the world, just as long as you know it. When I make it big and I'm famous, you'll be the one to share it with me. Now, look." Digging in his backpack, he retrieved a small box and pushed it at her unceremoniously. "I know this is late, but I have your birthday present. I was going to wrap it, but you've made such a fuss…here."

Sofia took the box, biting her lip so she wouldn't say, "Yeah, two months late." Still suspicious about his sudden change from surly to wooing, she opened the box. Her jaw dropped in awe. "Nico, oh my God! An Ippolita bangle! It's beautiful." Throwing her arms around his neck, she kissed him. "How did you know this is my favorite?" Gleefully, she put it on, admiring it, then threw her arms around his neck again. "Nico Romero, you always surprise me."

o　　　o　　　o

Luna was at her desk when she heard the tippity-tap of high heels in the hallway. Looking up, she saw Sofia peeking in the door.

Intently scrolling the Santa Fe website, Luna waved for her to come in and sit down, then looked up to give her full attention. Sofia tossed her golden mane, causing it to cascade over half her face, and brandishing her wrist at Luna, announced, "Look what Nico gave me for my birthday!"

She didn't have to say the bracelet was Ippolita. Being in fashion, the brand was well known to Luna.

"Ooh…the blackened silver. It's one of my favorites."

"Me, too!" Sofia exclaimed. "I'm just so surprised Nico knew what to get me."

Luna smiled, but she knew Erin Whelan's agency had the Ippolita account—and pieces disappeared from photo shoots all the time. At least he had finally gotten something for Sofia!

Glancing back at a picturesque scene of snow-covered mountains on her computer, Luna asked, "What are you guys doing for Christmas? We're heading to Santa Fe."

"Oh, we're going to stay in L.A. and relax," Sofia said as casually as possible. "I just can't handle airport hell this time of year."

Luna wasn't surprised she covered for Nico. He'd complained to her that Sofia had been nagging him about going to New York for Christmas.

With a tiny shrug of her shoulders, Sofia sighed, "But you know how Nico is."

Luna nodded sympathetically, uttering "Yeah…"

"He's always worried about his clients and afraid he'll lose everything. I help him all the time—like the way you used to. But he expects me to do even more…and then berates me. It's like he's not even grateful for all the stuff I do for him." Suddenly, as if she'd been holding back, Sofia's eyes watered, as if the blue sky opened up and began pouring rain.

"I know how much you've helped his career, Sofia. I'm sure he's

127

grateful…" Luna trailed off, thinking how demanding Nico could be.

Choking up, Sofia revealed, "We had a huge fight. He asked me to make some calls for him and made me tell his clients I was his assistant! I was appalled! I'm a writer, not his hired help!"

"Why would you need to call for him?"

"He says it's beneath him…he has more important things to do."

"That's awful. It's an excuse to cover up that he doesn't know how to do things himself. Why don't you tell him to hire an assistant?"

"He won't. Says he can't afford it and he only trusts me. I'm afraid if I stop doing all this work for him, he'll leave me too."

The word "too" ricocheted in Luna's mind. She realized it was a reference to her marginalization by Nico after Sofia had replaced her in his life.

"Sofia, Nico can't be alone, he has huge abandonment issues. It must come from his childhood, being sent away by his mother. And now he's lost her."

"There's something else. But, please, you can never tell him that I told you this! He never offers to pay for *anything*. I invited him to stay with me…after all, we're together. He pays for the studio, but he expects me to pay for everything else; says he's saving for the new center. I feel like he just takes me for granted! He never asks how my day went, or about how I feel. Everything's always about him!"

With that, Sofia burst into tears, saying how much she loved him and couldn't bear the thought of losing him—that she couldn't see her life without him.

Putting her arms around her, Luna consoled, "He's very needy—are you sure you want to be with him? At the very least, I think you should talk to him about these things."

Nodding, Sofia grabbed a tissue and dabbed at her eyes. Even all smeared with eyeliner, they were like staring into a cloudless heaven. A light shone in them as she relayed, "Nico read me the poem you sent him—the one about when someone comes into your life for a reason. It's very beautiful."

Luna was appalled he'd shared something she considered private, but Sofia seemed not to notice. "I know how you feel…how you miss him. And I just want to let you know that he loves you very much."

Luna didn't know what to say in response to Sofia's presumptuous declaration of Nico's feelings. She'd believed she and Nico would remain best friends and taken for granted that the comfort and trust—the intimacy they shared—would be forever. But his work and Sofia had taken him away. Luna had found a poem on Pinterest that perfectly phrased her feelings and sent it to him. It began:

> *When someone is in your life for a reason*
> *It is usually to meet a need you have expressed.*

She'd hesitated to bare her soul to him like that, but needed him to know how much he meant to her. Underneath the poem, she had added:

> *You brought me joy…and you made me cry. You pushed me to my limits and taught me lifetime lessons. They say that love is blind, but friendship is clairvoyant.*

Nico had written back:

> *I love you, and I'm always very close to you. Nothing has changed.*

It was a nice reply, but he still felt absent from her life.

Sofia startled Luna out of her reverie. "I'm so grateful he has you in his life. It means so much to him, even if he doesn't show it or make time for you. I insisted he accept the luncheon invitation for your birthday."

Luna had been quite certain Sofia wrapped the gift, but still hoped it had been Nico's idea to accept her invitation. Still, even though Sofia had encouraged him, if he hadn't wanted to, he wouldn't have come.

People were starting to move around in the hallway, and Sofia stood up to leave. "Luna, you're the only one I can talk to about these things." Taking out her cosmetic bag, she cleaned up her eye makeup and reapplied her red lipstick. Putting on her thousand watt smile, she tossed her blonde hair to one side, hugged Luna and kissed her cheek, then strode out in her Valentino studded heels.

10

Daylight poured into the room from the full wall of windows facing the ocean, waking Sofia. Looking over at Nico, she took in the enticing appearance of his tousled curls spilling onto the pillow and long black eyelashes resting on his high cheekbones. Rejoicing over the long-awaited Christmas hiatus, she decided to wake Nico by going down on him, hoping it would brighten his mood for the day. Pulling the sheets off him, she positioned herself and licked the head as if she were relishing a tasty ice cream cone, twirling her tongue all around the tip. Once his already semi-erect cock was glistening with saliva, she took it fully into her mouth and sucked on it. Quickly, he stirred, and Sofia smiled to herself, knowing Nico was now awake, just silently basking in the moment.

Sofia enjoyed giving Nico blow jobs; she liked having control, and she felt she had some semblance of power when she blew him. Admiring his beautifully formed cock, she watched it grow to its enormous thick, full hard-on size, the head mushrooming and veins bulging with excitement. She often joked with him that he could have been a porn star.

He raised his hips up to her welcoming mouth. She loved deep throating him, believing it would keep him close to her, though she'd had to refine her technique to allow for his length. She'd never been with a man as big as Nico before. At first, she wasn't sure she could take all of him, but love found a way.

Using her hand to firmly control him, she slid him in and out slowly, rubbing the ridge of his head with each thrust. She felt the familiar signal that he was about to come when his balls hardened and retracted from her touch just as he pushed his hips harder and jetted inside her mouth. Gazing up at him, she swallowed his sweet cum, showing her enjoyment by licking him clean.

Now highly aroused herself, she urgently sat on his cock while he was still hard, taking him all the way inside. Moving her hips, she slid up and down, squeezing him tightly with her pussy. Leaning over, she kissed his full lips until they parted, allowing her tongue to slip inside. He awakened to her; but Nico never took very long to come alive again. Without warning, he abruptly rolled her over to take her from behind. "On your knees, you little Spyder," he commanded gutturally.

Digging his hands into her hips, he pumped her hard with his growing erection until he was rock hard again, then he suddenly pulled out of her pussy and slipped his fingers into her. Finding her already very wet, he swept his moistened fingers along her plump, pink folds, working his way around them until he reached her clit. Her throbbing bud, slick with her pussy juice, ached as he added pressure, increasing her feverish desire.

"Oh God, Nico," she panted frantically. "Put that big dick back inside me!"

Instead, dipping his fingers back into her pussy to wet them again, he fingered around her puckered opening, sliding one very wet finger into the tight dark hole, then slowly adding a second, widening the entrance.

Sofia groaned in lustful hunger as he rubbed the tip of his cock just inside her anus, coaxing it open, while his fingers deftly stroked her G-spot, milking it into submission.

She growled in anguished ecstasy when he slowly worked himself deeper into her ass with his fingers wound around her hot spot—the juices flowing down into his hand. Her legs stiffened as the tight coil in her belly unraveled. Picking up the pace, Nico fucked her ass hard. At the sound of his balls slapping wildly against her pussy, Sofia cried out, "Oh God, yes! Fuck me!" Her body convulsed around him.

Leaning over her back, Nico cupped her tits with his hands, pounding harder and faster, his breath becoming rapid and ragged. Unable to hold on, he erupted into her ass. Together, drenched in each other's sweat, they collapsed on the bed, his body covering her.

Resting her head in the crook of his arm, she lay silently, listening to his heartbeat, enjoying the quiet and a peacefully contented Nico for a few minutes. All too soon for Sofia, Nico popped up.

"What's for breakfast?" Looking at her still lying on the bed, he smacked her butt cheek hard. "Come on, woman. I don't have all day!"

"Ow!" She yelped, jumping up, unsure if the smack was meant to be playful. "What are you talking about? What are we doing today?"

"What time is it? I'm going to be late!" He barked his next command, "Get the coffee going! What are you doing?"

Rattled, she asked, "What are you talking about? This is our vacation! I thought we'd have lunch at that cute new place down the beach, since I don't have to go to work." She trailed Nico to the shower, trying to figure out what was going on.

As if she already knew, he chastised, "I have a meeting."

Sofia didn't know whether to be dismayed or furious. She did know this was one fight she couldn't go near, because it involved his business, so she would only come off looking like she wasn't supportive. Swallowing hard and taking a deep breath, she calmly replied, "Take your bike. I need the car."

Stepping out of the shower, Nico wrapped a towel around his waist and went to the kitchen to pour himself a cup of coffee. Annoyed, he called out, "Sofia, why didn't you make coffee? I asked you to make coffee!"

Scurrying to make a pot, she rationalized she wanted some, too.

Nico barked at her the entire time. "You have to work with me, not against me. Erin has people she wants me to meet. I don't have time to lounge around with you. This is for *our* future, remember? Do something useful, follow up with your editor friends and write me another article! I need more publicity."

When he reappeared in the kitchen doorway, she saw he was wearing faded black jeans that were so worn, she could see more than just the outline of his perfectly formed manhood against the zipper. He also wore a tight-fitting T-shirt underneath a crisp, white Diesel shirt with a black dragon embroidered on the shoulder—another gift from Erin. He fished for compliments. "How do I look? Is this dressed up enough for the meeting?"

Though sad her day would be spent without him, she put on her best smile and kissed him. "You look dashing, Nico. Good luck with the meeting, you'll do great."

Grabbing his black leather motorcycle jacket, gloves, and helmet, Nico kissed her on the forehead and strode out. Once Sofia heard the bike go down the drive, she threw herself on the bed and had a good cry.

Through feeling sorry for herself, she decided to make the most of her day without Nico. Setting her priorities in order, she met a couple of her girlfriends in Beverly Hills for a mani-pedi and some shopping. Now, sitting with their feet in the bubbling blue water, they asked her where she had been hiding, and if she was still seeing that hot yoga instructor. Nico discouraged her from seeing her friends, dismissing them as frivolous and a waste of time. She sighed deeply when the woman doing her pedicure pressed her thumbs into the soles of her feet. Listening to the other women take turns bitching about their boyfriends, Sofia, feeling content in the company of her friends, decided against sharing any of her complaints about Nico. Instead, she boasted how he was becoming *the* celebrity guru and getting lots of press—giving herself praise for helping in that area. She beamed talking about him, and the girls tittered when she discreetly whispered about how good he was in bed, boldly sharing some details. Agreeing he was hotness personified, they cautioned her to enjoy him for the ride, but avoid getting too emotionally involved. Sofia wasn't sure if they thought he wasn't rich enough, too arrogant, or both. Regardless, it was much too late for that now.

Walking to her car, she passed the David Yurman boutique on Rodeo Drive. Inexplicably, she felt compelled to go in and was immediately drawn to the black leather and silver bracelets. Admiring one particularly simple but striking design, she chose one for herself that would stack nicely with the Ippolita bangle he had given her for her birthday, then selected one for Nico and asked the salesman to engrave "Love, Spyder" on the inside of the closure. She was not going to win Nico by being bitchy or demanding, so she would have to win him with love.

○   ○   ○

Erin Whelan stood at the head of the conference table, all eyes upon her. Her presentation was going perfectly. She had developed an innovative campaign and her hand-picked, well-paid team hadn't let her down in the execution. She ended her presentation with a clever punch line, causing the room to erupt in applause that made you think you were at a TED Conference; and actually, Erin *had* spoken at several TED conferences over the years.

Erin never competed with her product—whether it was the agency or her client's brand. Today she wore a black Prada jewel neck dress and platform high heels. Just like her design sensibility, the dress was simple. A wide, knit headband held back her black, angular-cut hair, and her makeup consisted of only a soft peach lip gloss and a light application of eyeliner to highlight her distinctive grey eyes. Leaving her team to make social niceties with the client, Erin left the conference room quickly and headed straight to her office, where she grabbed her Céline black trapeze bag holding, among other things, her yoga clothes.

An hour later, Erin pulled her black Jaguar into the Amaru lot on Ventura, parking far at the back. Before stepping out of the car, she checked her eye makeup. The liquid liner was cool, making her appear more youthful. She knew she didn't look anywhere near her age, but Nico was twenty years younger, after all.

Instead of calling out Nico's name, she walked around to locate him. When she found him at his desk in the office, he looked up from his computer, studying her from under his long black eyelashes, and said, "Let me go lock the door." When he returned, she said she'd change in his apartment. He smiled intriguingly at her. "What's the hurry? Let's have a cup of tea first."

Erin caught the drift and grinned. "That sounds just fine to me. I don't have to be back at the office today." Watching him make his special tea, she knew it had more to it than meets the eye, but was never able to discover exactly what, and Nico wouldn't tell. He opened his supplement cabinet, and she watched him pull out a canister of loose leaves slightly larger than bay leaves. When the kettle whistled, he added the leaves to a teapot, then filled it with hot water. Taking a glass bottle down from the shelf, he removed a white capsule, and pulling it apart, poured the contents into the teapot.

Taking their cups over to the sofa, Nico picked up his guitar and Erin kicked off her shoes, letting her bare feet push underneath his thigh to rub along his groin. He eyed her discerningly. "Why don't you take that silly dress off?"

Erin smirked and shook her head. "Nico, this is Prada."

He chuckled. "Prada. Whatever. It's not sexy."

She teased, "You want sexy, mister?" Standing up, she reached around and pulled down the zipper, stepping out of the dress and tossing it on a nearby chair. She was wearing an Agent Provocateur black satin push-up bra and matching thong.

Nico gave her an approving once over. "That's much better. Come here." She strutted over and stood in front of him. He set the guitar down gently on the floor. Kneeling in front of her, he slipped his fingers in her panties, finding her pussy. "I love that you don't wax your pussy. It's so natural, like the animal you are," he growled.

Closing her eyes to half-mast, she leaned forward, resting her hand on the back of the sofa. Purring from his fondling, she saw the outline of his erection inside his jeans, but before she could release it, he took her by the hand and led her to the bedroom. Watching him remove his T-shirt and jeans, she grinned, thinking it extremely hot he wasn't wearing any shorts.

Nico reached over to turn her around, then slid her panties off, bending her forward onto the bed to rub her ass. She yelped when he gave her a hard slap. "Ummm…that's my little wolf," Nico referenced the howling wolf tattoo on her shoulder blade. "Let me hear that again," he murmured while gently fingering her asshole. Then he slapped her ass again, this time harder. She groaned.

Gently massaging her ass cheek where he had spanked her, he slowly reached forward to fondle her tits, which were overflowing the cups of her bra. Reaching inside, he teased her nipples, grabbing onto one and squeezing hard. Moaning, she pushed her ass out at him, and he smacked it hard, making her yelp again. "Baby, I love that howl. You're going to make me come before I even get inside you." Placing the head of his cock on the entrance of her pussy, he worked the tip just inside her.

She pleaded, "I'm just so wet for you, Nico. I need you inside me."

"Easy, wolf. I'll get there," he growled.

She replied with a little mewling sound of stifled desire. By the time Nico pushed himself in, she was open and ready. Desperate to get him deeper, she pushed her ass higher.

"Just wait, baby. There's no hurry, remember?"

Pulling himself out of her pussy, he ran his hand back down between her legs, feeling her juices flowing. Fingering inside her to capture some of the wetness, he rubbed it on the rim of her anus, then inserted his finger in her ass, slowly opening her up.

Begging, she groaned, "Nico…my God. Take me. Please!"

"That's it, baby. Open up for me." Sliding his finger in and out slowly, he felt her muscles relaxing. "That's it, baby." Lost in the sensation of the moment, it was all he could do to not plunge into her ass and explode. Removing his finger, he took his cock and rubbed the opening of her anus with the head. As he lavished attention on her G-spot with his fingers, he pushed his cock deeper into her ass, bringing her to a frenzy. She bucked and rocked her hips, and with each thrust, she quivered with pleasure. Unable to hold off any longer, he gripped her hips with both hands, thrusting himself deep into her ass, readying himself for release.

He panted, "Touch yourself, baby. Make yourself come." Obediently, she reached between her legs and inserted her middle finger deep into her pussy, petting her G-spot while her thumb worked her clit. Pressing his body close to her back, he held her to him and grabbed one of her tits, squeezing the nipple hard until she squealed. He rocked deep inside her ass, his hips slamming against her.

She called out, "Nico, I'm coming, baby…"

Feeling her shudder, coming apart as she melted under him, he hammered her hard until he erupted inside her ass.

Erin was still feeling the buzz from what Nico called his "special brew." Every time she asked what it was he would never say, just calling it a special brew and saying it was healthy. One time, he went so far as to say it contained tea and a supplement for energy, but no more than that. All she knew was it gave her the most intense orgasms—or maybe that was all Nico's doing.

Dressed for his yoga session, Nico emerged from the bathroom. "Let's go, Erin. My class will be arriving any minute."

o   o   o

Nico woke to the tempting aroma of bacon, eggs, and coffee coming from the kitchen. Filling him in during breakfast, Sofia reported, "I talked to Lindsay, and she'll do another piece about you if it has a different spin. She said because the last article in *Bazaar* focused on your yoga practice, this one should focus on energy medicine instead." He looked pleased, so she continued, "She told me to include information about the healing practices of the Q'ero paqos and your experiences living with them. What do you think?"

Excitedly, Nico replied, "That's perfect, Sofia! Erin just said she wants to have a director she works with do a documentary about me. Having a corresponding article would be perfect. You should get on that right away."

When she was cleaning up the breakfast dishes, Nico yelled in, "My dad is back, and says we should come to his house for Christmas."

Not one to give up easily, Sofia had tried unsuccessfully to convince Nico to spend Christmas in New York City with her family. He eventually succeeded in convincing *her* that traveling over the holidays would be a nightmare, and it was too cold in New York in December. He said if anything, they should go to St. Barths. Sofia consoled herself with the fact she'd seen her dad on her birthday. Having been really depressed about missing Christmas with her family, this news thrilled her.

Nico came into the kitchen and sidled up behind her, caressing her butt. "So, Spyder, are you happy now that we have a place to go for Christmas?"

She turned, and wrapping her arms around him, kissed him deeply. "Yes! I'm really looking forward to finally meeting your father, too."

Nico laughed, "He's crazy! We fight all the time. He has no sense sometimes."

Seizing the opportunity, Sofia asked, "Tell me about him. When did he come to L.A.?"

Nico leaned on the counter as she returned to the dishes. "He had his own restaurant in New York with Mario, who owns La Forza. I was a kid then, and that restaurant was a very cool place to hang out—lots of models and rock stars ate there all the time. When the restaurant closed, Mario came out here, and my father got into importing wine from Argentina. Then he moved here, too." Pausing to reflect, he added cheerfully, "We'll have good wine for Christmas!"

Sofia's contentment was soon curtailed by the sound of Nico cursing in Spanish.

"What's wrong?" she asked and was immediately sorry she had.

"Erin's fucking lawyer just sent me a bill for $1,500! She's trying to fuck me over. I know it. Now I have to fight with Erin to make this go away," he ranted.

"Well, what's the bill for?"

Nico scowled. "All she was supposed to do was file my trademark and LLC."

She suggested, "Wait, Nico. Before you jump to any conclusions, first ask what the invoice is for, *then* you can negotiate."

He pounced, "You're such an idiot! You don't know anything. To you, everything is a negotiation. I'm not paying this. These women are all out to fuck me, and they're all whores." He turned and shoved his laptop toward Sofia. "You call this lawyer and tell her you're my assistant. Find out what this is for, and get her to remove this bill!"

Sofia was appalled. "I don't mind doing you favors, but I'm not your assistant. I'm your girlfriend! I want to help you, and I like writing articles about you, but I don't want to call the lawyer!"

His face reddening, he grabbed the nearest phone and shoved it in her face, raging. The veins in his head popped out with fury. "You *will* call her! Right now, Sofia. Now!"

Frightened by Nico's rage, she took the phone from him saying quietly, "OK, but I won't give her my real name."

He snarled, "You can tell her you're the fucking whore of paradise for all I care. Just fix it, Sofia. Fix it!"

Still fearful, but unwilling to let this go, she whimpered, "I didn't create this problem for you, Nico. So don't speak to me that way." Regaining her voice, she provoked him, "Or call your whore Erin to fix it for you!"

Nico's eyes bulged and his face turned dark red. Before she knew what was happening, he had shoved her further back onto the couch and punched her in the arm, just hard enough to make his point. He growled, "Call the lawyer now, Sofia. And shut the fuck up!"

Dialing the number, Sofia was sobbing. When a woman answered, she pulled herself together, and without giving a name, said she was calling regarding an invoice sent to Nico Romero. Steadying her voice, she inquired about the fees.

The lawyer replied, "Oh, those are the fees for filing the trademark, the LLC, and the additional publishing cost. Those have to be done within a set time frame or he'll lose the registration."

"I see," Sofia replied, as professionally as she could muster. "Thank you so much." She hung up and looked at Nico.

He wasn't pleased. "You should have told her I didn't ask for that to be done. That's ridiculous and too much money!"

Feeling less afraid again now, Sofia prodded, "You just told me to find out if it was a legitimate charge. She said it is. It's not *her* fee, it's from the State of California. So you can take it up with them—or ask Erin to pay it!"

Now in a completely horrific mood, Nico hissed his next order, "Get dressed. I need you to follow me to the bike shop. They did something wrong, and now the Ducati isn't running right."

Sofia wished she was at work, where people were polite and appreciated her. Worn down by him, she didn't even care how she dressed, just throwing on jeans, a sweatshirt, and her new motorcycle boots. After dropping Nico off, she'd go shopping for Christmas presents for Roberto and his wife.

Sitting in the car at the bike shop waiting for Nico, her agent called with exciting news. "Sofia, it's not really official yet, but the gossip on the grapevine is *Going My Way* will win The Writers Guild Award for Best New Series!" he squealed.

"I'm so excited!" she shrieked. "That is such great news! Are you sure? I don't want to get my hopes up..." While chatting, she ignored the call waiting beep from Nico.

Just as she hung up, Nico called again. "What the fuck, Sofia! Why the fuck didn't you pick up? I've been calling you," he screamed.

"Sorry, Nico, but I was on the phone with my agent," she apologized.

He fumed, "I don't give a fuck if you were on with the Pope. You answer me when I call you! Do you understand?! **I...come...first**." He spat the words out like miniature fireballs. "Your stupid little writing project means nothing. Now get in here—and bring your credit card!" he hissed.

Tears springing to her eyes, she decided not to tell him about the award. He wouldn't even hear her now, anyway. She'd just wait until she received the award, then maybe he'd appreciate her! But she couldn't wait to tell Daddy—as soon as Nico wasn't around.

After she'd paid the bill in the bike shop, Nico coolly informed her that he had important business to attend to and would text her later. With his inner psycho full blown, she didn't dare ask where he was going.

◦　◦　◦

After luckily finding an open meter on North Camden, Sofia opened the front door of the low brick building with black bell-shaped awnings, and was hit by the delightful aroma of leather. Il Bisonte's décor still adhered to the old world charm of the original workshop in Florence, Italy. She decided to get his dad a classic notebook to use as a wine journal. The leather would develop a fine patina with age, but she couldn't decide between cognac and dark brown. She finally settled on the dark brown, thinking it the most elegant. Nico had never said much about Roberto's wife, Claudia, other than they didn't get along very well. She spotted an old-fashioned French framed coin purse in ruby red. Without even knowing Claudia, Sofia thought it was perfect. Then, at the last minute, she saw a black leather Dopp kit and knew how much Nico would appreciate it, since he usually just threw his toiletries in a Ziploc bag.

Getting home before Nico, Sofia hid the Christmas gifts where he wouldn't find them. After taking a bath in lavender oil, she put on a short, fuchsia slip dress, and new Christian Louboutin metallic high-heeled sandals. Clipping her hair back in a low ponytail, she poured herself a glass of wine, then began pulling out ingredients for her marinara sauce. At about nine o'clock, she finally heard the bike pull into the drive, then Nico's footsteps on the deck stairs. He didn't say anything when he came in. Opting for cheery, she chirped, "Hi, honey. How was your day?"

He replied tersely, "Erin's got some things going on for me. You need to get that article on energy healing done and published right away."

Sofia noticed a new chain around his neck, and glimpsing a pendant, asked, "What's that around your neck?"

Nico responded just as casually, "A Christmas gift from Erin. It's John Hardy."

"Let me see it," she said sweetly. "Did you pick it out? I know you like dragons."

"No, it's a gift."

Stinging from his veneration of Erin, she blurted, "It's cool, Nico. Shame it's stainless instead of sterling."

Seeming to ignore her small dig, he left her to her cooking, announcing he was going to take a shower. That was just as well—Sofia could smell Erin's scent, and she was itching for a fight. There was something about the smell of tobacco and patchouli that grossed her out.

Nico returned from his shower wearing sexy, low-slung lounging pants. Leaning over the pot of bubbling, thick red sauce and seemingly looking for a fight too, he questioned snidely, "What are you doing, Sofia?"

"I'm making my boyfriend a delicious home-cooked dinner. Would you like a glass of wine, honey?" she drawled in a saccharine musical tone.

Nico came over to the counter and took the glass from her, then clipped, "Hmmm. That's not how I do it. You don't know how to cook."

He'd kept his inflection emotionless, but Sofia knew he was starting in with her. "Would you like to take over? I just finished the meatballs," she offered.

"No, you go ahead. Do your thing," he replied nonchalantly.

She poured the box of rigatoni into a large pot of boiling water and set the timer. Lifting a wooden spoon to her mouth, she blew gently to cool the steaming medley of crushed tomatoes, garlic, herbs, and caramelized onions simmering in another pot. She'd begun calling it tomato sauce, but her family still referred to it as gravy, as did most traditional Italians. After tasting it, she added several more pinches of red pepper flakes.

When the pasta was al dente, she drained it, then added some of the gravy and olive oil before cooking it on top of the stove for the last few minutes—serving the meatballs on the side. She invited Nico to sit down at the table, set with her turquoise Old Havana stoneware dishes and etched glass stemware from Anthropologie that her mom had given her. She loved the one-of-a-kind hand-stamped dinner plates, particularly how they picked up on the turquoise accents in the room. The glassware had an old world feel, complementing her "rediscovered" flatware, actually a mix and match collection of patterns reclaimed from old hotels and ocean liners. Placing lace-trimmed white cotton napkins next to their plates, she turned off the lights and lit the candles. Cascading moonlight and flickering flames through the glassware created dancing shadows on the high, white walls.

As he sat, Nico remarked how nice everything looked, leading Sofia to think that maybe his mood had changed for the better. He ate some pasta, then took a bite of a meatball, her Sicilian grandmother's recipe, and made a face. "They're not as good as mine, but they'll do for tonight."

She let him have it. "Nico, you should be nice and appreciate that I made my grandmother's recipe for you. They're delicious; I tasted them myself."

He snapped, "Well you don't have taste buds then. They're no good! I'm telling you—mine are much better!"

Sofia took the bait. "We're not talking about the ones between your legs! You can suck them yourself," she hissed. "Don't eat my food, then. Go back and eat with Erin Whelan, that bitch, and let *her* eat your balls!"

Nico's eyes flashed like lightning, and an appropriately stormy look swept over his face. When he stood up, Sofia was instantly terrified, unsure what he might be getting ready to do. Picking up a meatball, he smashed it on her head. Humiliated, she threw a punch at him, but he caught her before it landed and twisted her arm behind her back. He kept twisting until she couldn't stay on her chair anymore, finally dropping to her knees before him. Glaring darkly into her eyes, he commanded, "YOU suck them."

He hadn't even said her name. Ashamed and frightened, Sofia looked down at the floor. Nico entangled his fingers in her hair, repeating, "Suck them. Now!" He yanked his sweat pants down and kicked them off. Growling in the guttural tone he had when psycho Nico was in control, he ordered, "Now, Sofia!"

Looking up, she saw he was already hard; the fight had stimulated him.

Though she was angry and mortified, she also knew this was the way to win with him—the only way she'd ever found. So she cupped his balls softly in the palm of her hand and half-heartedly took one into her mouth.

"Not like that!" Nico roared. "Lick them like you mean it!"

Frightened, Sofia softly licked first one ball, then the other, taking them in her mouth and gently sucking.

Nico moaned, "Now suck my cock, bitch."

Taking his full length into her mouth, getting him really wet with her saliva, she sucked him, only taking him out of her mouth to flick the head with her tongue. Gripping his cock and sliding her head up and down the shaft, she felt him harden to his full rigidity before moving her hand back down to play with his balls. When she slid her wet finger into his ass, he groaned and pushed his hips up to fuck her mouth harder, grabbing the hair at the back of her head to control her. Sofia had no idea if Erin could pleasure him as well as she did, and she wasn't going to dwell on it. She'd just make sure he called *her* name when he came in her mouth.

When his cock hit the back of her throat, Nico bucked and rolled his hips to meet her as she repeatedly pumped him in and out of her mouth, using her thumb to rub the mushroomed head. His thighs straining, he was practically elevated off the chair, his fingers entwined in her golden mane as he plunged his cock further into her mouth. Soon, Sofia felt him twitching to come, and shoved him all the way in for his climax. He let out a strangled groan and called her name, pulling her head into his groin while she swallowed the hot jets of cum. Afterward he was calm, and she put him on the sofa with a bottle of wine while she went to take a shower and wash her hair. The lion had again been tamed, at least for a little while.

11

Sofia couldn't believe Nico had never had a Christmas tree. This being their first Christmas together, she decided to surprise him with one decorated as beautifully as the ones she'd had at home in New York. Waiting for him to leave for the studio, where he'd be occupied all day, she dawdled around the house before pulling on a pair of skinny jeans and a long-sleeved James Perse top. It was sunny and warm for December, so she wore her new white Belstaff leather motorcycle jacket and put the top down on the Porsche then headed over to Mr. Greentrees in West Hollywood, where all the decorators went. The young man in the lot was more than attentive, and after asking him to drag out at least ten trees for her scrutiny, she selected the fullest tree that would reach to the top of her vaulted ceiling at the far end by the fireplace, in front of the sliding glass doors to the deck.

Telling the delivery guy she needed an hour's head start, Sofia gave him a large tip in advance, ensuring that he'd help wrap the dozens of strands of mini lights she purchased, and put the big star on top. Her next stop was Neiman Marcus, where she bought German blown-glass angels, long glass icicles that reflected the light, handmade birds with real feathers that clip onto the branches, and glitter-encrusted glass moons and stars. Spying a box of delicate gold seahorse ornaments, she smiled, thinking she'd wrap them as a special gift for Nico, knowing how much he loved seahorses. Happily, she found a turquoise velvet tree skirt that coordinated with her décor and a number of white pillar candles to create a romantic ambiance. At the counter, she picked up silver and gold plaid wrapping paper with wide red French wire ribbon, determined to make her first Christmas with Nico special and show him he had a home with her.

Wearing La Perla tap shorts and a lace tank top, she stood back to admire the majestic tree decked out with the lights and sparkling ornaments, just as she heard the Ducati pull into the drive. She poured some wine and lit the candles, trembling with excitement in anticipation of Nico's reaction. Standing by the kitchen counter, out of view, she listened to his footsteps on the stairs. When he came through the door, he froze and just stared, not speaking for at least thirty seconds. When Sofia was about to say something, he murmured in awe, "Sofia, honey. It's so…beautiful…you did all this?"

She replied proudly, "I did it for you, Nico. Your very first Christmas tree." Walking over to him in her Jimmy Choo pumps, she didn't have to stand on tiptoes when she kissed him invitingly. He played with her hair while their tongues danced together. Sofia whispered, "You smell so good, Nico." Happily, she didn't smell Erin's sex. Instead, he smelled like citrus, as if he'd just taken a shower.

"You're so good to me, Sofia. Why are you so good to me?" he murmured sheepishly, his face buried in her neck.

Combing his hair back away from his face with her fingers, she stared deeply into his smoldering eyes; the yellow flecks glinted from the lights of the tree. "You're my angel, Nico. I love you and want to be here for you, to help you fly. I want us to be together. We're a good team."

"I don't deserve you, Sofia," he mumbled.

While Nico changed into his sweats, she put out some guacamole and chips and the rotisserie chicken she'd picked up on the way home. After she poured them each another glass of wine, they sat on the sofa, staring at the tree for a long time. Remembering the seahorse ornaments, Sofia retrieved a beautifully wrapped package. Taking the pretty package, Nico balked, "I can't open this now, it's not Christmas yet!"

Reassuring him, she said, "This is a special, before-Christmas gift. Go ahead, open it!"

Shaking his head, he hesitantly opened the package extremely slowly, first untying the bow. He handed her the ribbon, instructing, "Don't throw that away. It's very beautiful ribbon."

Sofia laughed to herself, thinking, *Yes, I know—I bought it.* Leaning over, she kissed him again on the lips.

Corner by corner, he undid the tape so as not to tear one bit of the wrapping, again saying, "Save the paper. We can use it again."

She nodded, waiting patiently.

With the package finally open, he gazed speechlessly, as if he'd opened a treasure chest of precious jewels, until Sofia lifted his face and saw his eyes were filled with tears.

"Seahorses mean so much to me." His voice was just above a whisper. "When I was a little kid, my mom and I used to find them on the beach. Sofia, you're a gift from my mother."

After hanging each seahorse, Nico stood back to ensure the placements were perfect. Returning to the sofa, he laid his head in Sofia's lap, staring at the shimmering Christmas tree. Eventually, his eyes closed and his breathing quieted. Sofia thought he was asleep. Then he suddenly whispered, "Did you finish the article about me living with the paqos?"

"Yes, I did Nico, and you can read it tomorrow."

"Good," he yawned. "I need that article for Erin to make the documentary about me." Moments later, he fell asleep.

o   o   o

Sofia got up early and began preparing a special Christmas Eve spinach, tomato, and bacon frittata. Nico called it a revuelto, but basically it was the same thing. She opened a bottle of Prosecco, since she had no plans to leave the house other than yoga on the deck followed by a long walk down the beach, even going in the pool if it was warm enough. But for now, because it was Christmas, she went for a sexy Santa's helper look, wearing a cute cranberry cotton Elle Macpherson chemise, sassy Santa hat, and Brian Atwood floral print high-heeled sandals. In contrast to her outfit, Nico shuffled into the kitchen in his Adidas shower slippers and poured himself a mug of coffee, asking groggily, "Can we put the tree lights on again?"

"Of course, Nico. Why not?"

He flicked the lights on, then stared at the tree for a while. Completely ignoring her sexy Santa outfit, he started reading the article she'd written. After putting the frittata in the oven, she poured two glasses of Prosecco and sipped hers while she nervously watched him read, awaiting his approval.

Placing the heavy iron skillet onto a trivet in the center of the table, Sofia served them both generous portions of the savory frittata. Nico ate heartily without complimenting her on the meal, but when he scooped up seconds, she was pleased he was enjoying it.

After breakfast, Nico handed Sofia his comments on the article, then made himself comfortable on the sofa and watched a movie while she revised it. Sensing he was in a mood and it wasn't going to go smoothly, she took off her shoes and the cute Santa hat and poured herself another glass of Prosecco. When she gave the article to him to read again, he got snippy.

"I never said this," he pointed to one phrase. "Why did you say it like that? It's all wrong."

Sofia remained stoic when, handing it back to her, Nico softly said, "Sorry, just make it right, please." When he finally said it was fine and he'd send it to Erin, she was relieved, despite the obliteration of her original plans for a romantic day.

Pouring herself another glass of Prosecco, Sofia plopped into the double-wide white club chair. Propping ikat pillows behind herself, she threw her legs over the arm and called Lindsay. Giggling, they caught up on the latest gossip, and eventually Sofia got down to business. She knew her friend wouldn't let her down after making certain the last article had been picked up by a major publication. After thanking Lindsay for her help with Nico and wishing her a Merry Christmas, they hung up.

Overhearing, Nico quickly chastised her. "Why did you thank her? You're such a moron. She should be thanking me for giving her an article to pitch to those magazines."

Not wanting to get into it with him, Sofia scurried into the kitchen to wash the breakfast dishes.

About a half hour later, Nico came looking for her to tell her that Mario had called from La Forza, inviting him to the restaurant that night. He was preparing a traditional Christmas Eve seafood dinner, and because it was also his friend Paolo's birthday, some of Nico's old friends would be there, too.

Sofia's mind whirled. She'd never met any of his friends, and still hadn't met his family. She waited, but when he didn't say anything more, she suggested, "Nico, it'll be fun. Shouldn't we go?" She noticed he was avoiding looking at her directly.

He resisted. "I would Sofia. I'm just not sure. All my friends will be there with their model girlfriends."

His implication stung, and though she didn't want to react, she felt she had to make a point. Her voice was shrill and taut. "What are you saying, Nico? I'm not good enough because I'm not a model? Is that what's most important to you?" Pausing to take a deep breath, she pointedly declared, "I'm attractive, smart, and talented. I write for one of the hottest TV shows out right now. If dating a model is so important to you, then what are you doing with me?"

Nico remained nonresponsive, angering Sofia, who wasn't going to let it go. She fumed, "I get it, Nico. I have a house in Malibu and a Porsche I let you drive. I do a lot for you—writing articles and getting them published, organizing your paperwork. And I buy you nice things and take us out to dinner. I'm certainly good enough for all that, right?"

Nico stared at the floor, his face sagging slightly. "Sofia, you're my woman. It's just that my friends are rich and flashy and expect me to be that way, too. I have the hottest yoga studio in Los Angeles—shit, in the entire country! They expect me to be with a top model or a hot actress."

Incensed, she sneered, "Oh, they expect you to be with some dumb-ass model instead of a pretty, fashionable, smart, and successful woman?" She paused, staring Nico down, but he continued to avoid eye contact. She finally spat, "Well, Nico, why don't you go without me, then?"

Abruptly, he pulled her to him, grabbing her ass with both hands. Chagrined, he appealed, "We *are* together, Sofia, and we're going to my dad's tomorrow, so let's just stay in as planned tonight. We'll drink that special bottle of wine and admire our beautiful tree, and then go skinny-dipping in the pool."

When Sofia remained icy, he leaned over and kissed her tenderly, nibbling on her ear, then trailed his tongue along her jaw and down her neck. Tightening his grip on her butt, he pulled her to him and squeezed one of her tits.

She let out of deep sigh of acquiescence. Seeing she had defrosted toward him, he amped up the passion, playing with her tits over her chemise to make her nipples harden underneath the satin. Sofia responded by pressing her body into him and rubbing herself on his muscular thigh.

Slipping his tongue into her mouth, he flicked it around the tip of her tongue, then sucked on her lower lip, tugging gently with his teeth. Her nipples pushed against his hands, and he squeezed them hard, taking her just to the point of pain, and she wiggled against his groin. "You want more, Sofia?" he teased.

"Nico," she appealed huskily, "Suck them…please."

"You like when I play with your tits?"

"Oh, yes, Nico. More…please," she gasped.

Sliding the thin strap of the chemise off her shoulder, he lifted her tits and licked each nipple in turn, sucking and pinching them until they were long and hard. "You have such beautiful tits. So round and big."

Arching under his teasing tongue and pretty words, she reached for his fly, feeling him straining at the zipper. His engorged cock now freed, she stroked him, sweeping her fingers playfully around the tip, then slid her hand softly down his shaft toward his balls, where she tantalized him by letting her fingers roam to his anus. He purred into her ear, "Put those shoes back on." He pointed to the sandals in the middle of the room where she had abandoned them.

She purposely bent over with her ass toward him as she slipped the heels back on, and Nico fondled her from behind, murmuring huskily, "Spyder, you can be so hot…and your magnificent tits," he moaned, rubbing against her ass from behind. "Much hotter than those flat models. Walk for me," he commanded, adding instructions. "Walk to the tree and back—and keep your eyes on mine."

Though she knew he was playing her, Sofia couldn't help herself, she still loved the things he was saying. Combing her hands through her hair and pushing it back so it would gain volume, she sashayed toward the tree in her best high-heeled sexy sway. Slowly she turned around, thrusting one hip out to the side and slightly bending one knee to adopt a stance that amplified her luxuriant curves. Raising one arm, she fixed her gaze on him as she voluptuously pushed her lavish mane to one side. Even from across the room she could see the glow in his eyes. He had hold of his cock, tugging on it heartily, his mouth upturned in a hungry grin. Sofia went moist, drinking in the sight of his excitement for her. When his eyes locked onto hers, she felt a magnetic pull from him, and returned, swaying even more seductively than before.

When she was standing in front of him, Nico lifted her by the waist, sitting her on the dining table. He pushed the satin chemise up so he could see her pussy, wet and swollen, waiting for him. His powerful, long-fingered hands caressed her thighs, working slowly up until they reached their destination. Sliding two fingers into her pussy, he felt her wetness. "You are always so ready for me," he softly murmured.

She leaned back, her hair cascading over her shoulders and back. He kissed her neck and clavicle, then planted wandering kisses down her body all the way to her pussy. "Fuck me, Nico. I want you inside me," she gasped.

"Not yet." Sliding his hands underneath her butt, he lifted her to his mouth. His tongue found its way inside her, and he flicked it deep, lapping up the juices. Pushing hard against his mouth, she squirmed as he licked her from the rim of her pussy to her clit, sucking on it until she was close to the edge. Crying out in ecstasy, she arched her body as he pushed his fingers deep inside, rotating them around to open her wider. Inserting a third finger, he pressed them along the slick walls of her pussy, seeking her G-spot. Surging upward, Sofia let out a tiny squeal, fucking his hand while he curled his fingers in a come-hither motion inside her. Panting, she quivered, her juices flowing onto his hand and down his wrist.

Reaching his other hand up, he pinched her nipples between his fingers and pulled on them. An unrelenting need swept over her, making her clit ache. With her nipples on fire, she begged, "Nico, fuck me. I want to come on you."

Mercilessly, he knelt down to lick her clit, and purred, "I'm not done with you yet. In time I'll let you come." Working each finger magically along her hot spot until all his fingers were inside, he slowly maneuvered his hand in up to his wrist. With his fist deep inside her and his mouth nibbling and pulling on her clit, she writhed in bliss from the sensation. Feeling her orgasm build, her legs tightened and her hips lifted off the table. A powerful tension uncoiled, releasing enormous waves of contractions that rippled from deep in her belly, over and over, and she squirted, gushing forcefully, calling out his name. She had never had an orgasm like that before, and utterly spent, collapsed back onto the table. Nico gently removed his fist from her pussy and pulled her toward him, leaving her wide open.

Knowing he couldn't hold back much longer, he wrapped her legs around his waist, digging his fingers into her ass, and plunged relentlessly all the way in. Fucking her with an urgency bordering on desperation, he went harder and faster until he exploded, growling as he jetted intensely inside her. Pulling her ass up and pressing her against him, he relished the feeling of his cock at the back of her pussy through the last pulse of his ejaculation. Exhausted by his release, he collapsed over her. Her legs encircling him and feeling his cock twitching in the aftermath of orgasm, she held him close and entwined her fingers in his damp hair.

o o o

Christmas morning, Sofia woke with Nico wrapped around her body, his breathing heavy on her neck. Gently moving his arm, she slid first one leg, then the other, out from underneath him. Looking at him sleeping peacefully, she thought *like a little lamb*. But a lamb who turns into a maned lion at the drop of a hat. *What was the drop of a hat anyway?* She made mental note to Google that later. But first, Christmas breakfast of blueberry pancakes, made with tart Greek yogurt so that they were fluffy, and real Vermont maple syrup. She still had another bottle of Prosecco, too. As the pancakes were made, she placed them in the warming oven, and when she was just about finished, she went in and kissed Nico on the forehead, whispering, "Merry Christmas. Breakfast is served."

Nico stumbled into the kitchen in long shorts, baggy T-shirt, and Adidas shower slippers, and poured a mug of freshly brewed coffee, black, the way he liked it. Sipping on the hot brew, he tried to swipe a pancake off the top of the stack, but Sofia smacked him with the spatula and told him to sit at the table. He obeyed. The tree lights were on, so Nico sat where he could look at them while he ate. "What time are we expected at your dad's house?" Sofia inquired.

"He didn't say. But we can go early. It's a nice day, and we can look at the houses around there."

Sofia dressed casually in black jeans, a black crew neck, and a Chanel red tweed jacket, perfect for Christmas. While lacing up ankle boots with a short block heel she asked, "Do you know who else will be there?" When Nico replied he hadn't asked, Sofia wasn't surprised, thinking to herself, *Of course not—he wouldn't care.*

Changing his shirt for the third time, Nico asked again if he looked OK, his little show of nervousness cute and endearing to her. Finally, he chose John Varvatos dark wash jeans and a plaid woven shirt she had bought him, over which he put on the black cashmere sweater Luna had given him.

When they'd finished dressing, Sofia said, "Let's open our gifts before we go."

He looked surprised. "I thought the seahorses were my gift! I didn't get a chance to wrap yours—I wanted to wrap it nice with the paper."

Sofia chuckled sweetly. "It's fine, Nico. No big deal, really."

Opening a drawer in the dresser, he pulled out a paper shopping bag with Dior printed on it, then handed it to her. Knowing he absolutely could not afford Dior, Sofia was skeptical. Yet, inside was the quintessential little black dress. Mid-thigh and slightly longer in the back, it was sleeveless, with a round neck. How did he manage to always get it right? She was certain this had come from Erin's office. There was no way he could know what to get her, let alone afford this dress. Knowing better than to say anything that would provoke him, she exclaimed, "Nico, thank you so much! It's perfect! I love it!" Wrapping her arms around his neck, but leaving his perfectly styled hair alone, she kissed him several times on the lips.

Handing him his two gifts, she prayed he wouldn't spend an hour unwrapping, but she knew better. He sat at the table, undoing everything slowly and methodically, as if disarming explosives.

First, he opened the David Yurman bracelet. She didn't have to point out the engraving because he examined the bracelet carefully, and when he saw it, laughed out loud. "Spyder! I love it!"

She clasped it onto his wrist. Next was the Il Bisonte Dopp kit. Unzipping it and looking at the plaid fabric, he fretted, "This is too nice…what if something spills inside?"

Sofia reassured him, "The fabric is water repellent, like an umbrella."

"That's good. I don't want to ruin it," he mumbled. When he acted sweet like he was, as if he thought he wouldn't get any Christmas presents, Sofia wondered what it had been like for him growing up.

Nico was serious about buying a house and having a vineyard with his father. On weekends, he took Sofia with him to look at properties. She loved getting on the back of his bike, holding herself tightly against him and leaning into the turns—feeling content knowing he wanted her in his life. Sofia visualized living in the country, married to Nico and having a family. He'd been asking her if she could get the money from her father to buy a house and start the vineyard. But she was curious why he should want so desperately to share his dreams with his dad, since he had left Nico and his sister as young children. From the stories Nico told, he was ten when he was sent to live with his dad, who owned a trendy Upper East Side restaurant that remained open till dawn catering to an after-hours crowd of celebrities. Nico boasted about pilfering money and cigarettes from the handbags of the endless stream of women who came to the apartment and had sex with Roberto and his friends. Pretending it was cool, Nico would excuse his dad's behavior, saying that was just the way things were back then. Still, with his mom gone, Sofia was glad he was bonding more with his father. Though she wasn't with her family this Christmas, she was excited about spending it with Nico and meeting his dad.

Leaving the house, Sofia handed Nico the car keys. They put the top down, and she wrapped her head with an Hermès scarf, pulling a black Pashmina around her shoulders and donning her big Chanel sunglasses. They made good time, even with Nico sometimes slowing to look at the homes and ranches. Although the countryside was beautiful, Sofia preferred the beach, comforted by the constant rolling of the waves. Walking together along the beach, Nico would first agonize about the future, laying blame on everyone else for his misfortunes, then moments later boast with complete conviction his certainty of being a celebrity guru, while Sofia assured him he was a gifted healer and that she believed in him.

Though some areas of Agoura Hills were covered with mini-mansion subdivisions, Claudia and Roberto's house was modest, sitting on a few acres of land with a barn. When Nico and Sofia arrived, everyone was out on the patio, where his dad manned a large stone fire pit outfitted as a grill. In keeping with Argentine tradition, his dad had prepared a *parilla*, the traditional Argentine barbeque of assorted meats. Lanterns hung from the trees, creating a festive setting. Relieved to see Claudia was also wearing jeans, Sofia followed her into the kitchen to ask where she should put the gifts.

"You didn't need to buy us anything," Claudia warmly admonished. "We're glad you and Nico were able to join us. You can put them by the *pesebre*—the nativity—next to the tree."

As she put the packages down, Sofia noticed their tree had cotton balls hanging on it along with traditional ornaments, and wondered about them. Returning to the kitchen, she offered to help Claudia, who just smiled and handed her serving utensils, saying, "If you don't mind, just set these on the table, and I'll be outside soon."

When dinner was served, and everyone was seated, Roberto placed a huge metal platter of barbequed steak, ribs, and chorizo in the center of the table. On either side, Claudia set down decorative pottery bowls filled with traditional Argentine dipping sauces: chimichurri, a green sauce of olive oil, vinegar, garlic, and herbs; and criolla, a spicy red sauce. Then Claudia held up her glass, "Let's toast the *asador*."

Sitting next to Sofia was Claudia's son, Anthony, who was good-natured and quite chatty, asking how she and Nico had met. Without going into too much detail during dinner, she explained, "I had stomach problems, and a friend at work told me about Nico. So I went to him, and with yoga classes, energy healing, and the supplements he made for me, I was cured! That's something no doctor had ever been able to do."

Anthony perked up. "That's fascinating, Sofia! Being a pharmacist, I've studied all the traditional supplements, as well as the curative powers of herbs like chamomile and peppermint. Both are good for stomach troubles. Do you know if he used one or both of them?"

She quickly swallowed a bite of steak. "I don't know, he doesn't really tell me the specifics. I just know he said we had to combine the supplements with his energy healing and yoga. He does Kundalini Yoga, you know."

Anthony nodded, and she continued, "Oh, and the tea. He makes a special tea that I drink before the energy healing ceremonies."

"A tea?" She shook her head, but before she could answer, Roberto led another rousing toast, "Happy Christmas. Feliz Navidad!"

As the evening air cooled, Sofia pulled her Pashmina tighter around herself as Roberto called jovially, "It's time for fireworks. They're set up at the top of the hill, far from the barn." Winking at Claudia, which Sofia found very endearing, he added, "We wouldn't want the horses to break their stall doors!" Squealing, the children ran ahead with the dogs running alongside.

Finding Nico, Sofia tried to take his hand, but he snatched it away. She frowned. "What's wrong?"

"Why did you wear those fancy boots? You're struggling to walk up the hill," he sniffed.

"I'm not having trouble, Nico. These are short heels. I'm fine."

He shook his head. "You're an idiot."

Hoping no one else had heard him, Sofia flushed with embarrassment. Finally at the top, as Roberto launched the fireworks, she reached for Nico's hand, hoping he wasn't really that angry with her. But when he pulled away again, she stepped back, signaling her displeasure, too. It had been a beautiful dinner, a wonderful traditional Christmas, with children and dogs and fireworks. *Why is Nico such a spoilsport?* she wondered. Why did he have to make her miserable—

or was it that he just couldn't enjoy himself?

Once gathered in the living room, Sofia sat on the floor next to the tree with the children, who eagerly tore the wrapping paper off gifts tagged with their names. While the gifts were passed out, she remembered to ask about the cotton ball ornaments.

Roberto laughed. "That's our snow, Sofia."

Nico and Sofia were thrilled when they were presented with a case of the ambrosial Malbec they'd had at dinner. Roberto, pleased with the journal, said he would paste his favorite labels in it; and Claudia declared that the little red coin purse was as precious as a piece of jewelry. Except for Nico still giving her the cold shoulder, Sofia felt the reassuring warmth of family. After saying good night and Merry Christmas to everyone, they walked to the car, and Sofia benignly suggested, "Let's put the top up."

"It's a nice night. I want the wind to keep me awake."

Great, she thought, *he's drunk and driving us home*. Worried, she offered to drive.

Gruffly, he replied, "Get in, Sofia. I'm fine."

Deciding the air would do her good, too, she wrapped her head in the scarf. They hadn't gotten far when Nico started in again about her shoes. "You're such a stupid fashion victim, Sofia. It's embarrassing to be with you stumbling around like you can't walk, all because you have to show off your expensive shoes."

She countered, "Your jeans cost more than my shoes, and at least I can buy my own stuff!"

The flash of his eyes told Sofia he wasn't done yet; he hadn't even gotten started. "Sofia, I don't ever want you discussing my business with anyone! Especially not Anthony. He's a doctor, and it's not for him to know what I do to cure people. He'll just steal my ideas. You're too stupid to see he was pumping you for information. You're a fool, and you damage my business. It will cost me!"

Sofia was incredulous. "Seriously, Nico? You think Anthony, a pharmacist, is going to become a yoga teacher and steal all your ideas?"

Nico tensed and pressed hard on the accelerator. Looking over at her instead of at the road, he screamed, "I'm not just a yoga teacher!

You're a fucking idiot. A moron! I'm a shaman! I know a thousand times more than that idiot you were talking to! So you keep your mouth shut about my business! Do you hear me, Sofia? You're a fucking asshole!"

She started to panic. "Nico, look at the road, please! Stop yelling at me and watch the road."

He bellowed, "Don't tell me how to drive, you fucking moron! I know how to drive. I'll show you how to drive this fucking car. You drive like the fucking pussy you are!" With that, Nico hit the accelerator harder. Sofia bit her lip as the Porsche's torque surged the car forward, and the speedometer rose to 100, then 110, then 120 miles per hour. Taking the turns on Kanan Dume wildly, Nico barely managed to stay on the road. Still, he kept up his frantic pace, and thankfully, the Porsche held its ground.

Sofia started crying and implored, "Please, Nico. Please slow down. I promise. I'll never speak about your business to anyone, ever! Please, please slow down. I'm scared!"

Ignoring her appeals, he continued accelerating, and Sofia started praying. She prayed that they wouldn't crash. She prayed they wouldn't die. She prayed until they had stopped in the driveway at her house. Then she flung her door open and ran up the stairs without saying a word, slamming the door of the bedroom shut. Not knowing whether to be angry or sad, she threw herself on the bed and sobbed. She was just grateful to be alive.

Nico came in and turned her over to face him. Sitting on top of her to hold her down, he snarled, "Stop your crying! Stop being such a baby. I know how to drive a fucking car, Sofia. Nothing was going to happen!"

Unable to catch her breath between sobs, she replied in a thin and tremulous voice, "You scare me, Nico. I don't know why you had to do that."

He thundered, "I had to prove my point to you, Sofia! You never listen to me—you disrespect me! You damaged my business tonight because you don't think before you open your stupid mouth!"

Still trying to catch her breath between sobs, she stammered, "Nico, we could have been killed. You're crazy. Insane! There was no reason to drive like that!"

Nico's eyes were dark. Still pinning her arms down with his legs, he growled, "I had to teach you a lesson, Sofia. You made me very angry, and you embarrassed me. Now apologize."

Sofia whispered helplessly through her tears, "I'm sorry that I embarrassed you."

Nico shook his head, the darkness on his face growing deeper. "Say it like you mean it, Sofia—and what else?"

She blinked back tears, her voice catching in her throat, "I *am* sorry, Nico. I love you. I'm sorry that I spoke about your business to Anthony. I'm very sorry."

Slowly, his darkness lifted a tiny bit. He grunted, "OK, that's better. Don't let it happen again." He paused, staring her down. "Now blow me." Rolling off of her, he commanded, "Kneel on the floor."

Still weeping, Sofia complied. Towering arrogantly over her, Nico unzipped his fly, and she saw that the wild ride and fight had excited him; he was hard in anticipation. Unexpectedly, Sofia found she was also aroused. After stepping out of his jeans, he looked down at her darkly, the yellow flecks in his eyes flashing like lighting. Being dominant always made him hornier, and he stroked himself as she licked her lips in anticipation. Placing his hands on each side of her face, he ordered, "Open your mouth."

When she parted her lips on command, he pushed into her, sliding his cock along her tongue. As Sofia wrapped her mouth around his stiff shaft, his eyes glazed over. Sucking hard, she ensured he was very wet with saliva before taking hold of him to slide her wet palms over the throbbing head. Rocking his hips and fucking her mouth, he gathered fistfuls of her hair, moaning deeply and plunging punishingly into the back of her throat. Lost in rapturous ecstasy, he didn't speak, just pumped swiftly, only stopping his relentless thrusts long enough for her to stroke the length of him and sweep her tongue around the tip. Holding her head to him, he pumped his hips to meet her mouth as she deep throated him, milking the base of his cock with her hand and sucking him mightily. Making sure her fingers were very wet, she slid a finger to his anus, pressing along the opening. Nico released a guttural groan in anticipation. As if spellbound, he made low growling noises when Sofia explored the opening of his anus. Feeling himself hitting the back of her throat, combined with her patient massaging inside him, he became even more aroused, swearing, "Goddamnit, Sofia. You make me crazy."

Unable to move, she moaned so he would feel the vibration at the back of her throat. He yanked her hair until her scalp stung, but she could feel him twitching and knew he was ready to erupt. To heighten his pleasure, she slid her finger slowly in and out of his anus, fucking him until he ejected hot semen down her throat. She took it all, swallowing each burst as he kept coming while he forcefully held her to his groin. When he released her, she licked every remaining drop, telling him how beautiful he was—how much she loved him—and how much she loved the sweet taste of his cum.

12

Luna felt at home the moment the plane landed in Albuquerque. No matter how often they drove to Santa Fe along the Turquoise Trail, it was always clear to her why New Mexico is called the Land of Enchantment. The snow-covered mountains in the distance were framed by deep red and terracotta colors, accented with green sagebrush against the turquoise sky. In the spring, the crisp air carried the fragrant scent of the ubiquitous lilacs and blooming irises, like the ones painted by Georgia O'Keefe. Now, autumn's light saturated the colors of the cottonwood trees emblazoned in yellow leaves, providing a stark contrast against the cloudless cerulean sky. With native ceremonies and the scent of burning piñon permeating the air, Christmastime was special.

While Tyler was driving, Luna read another diatribe from Sofia about Nico. It was obvious to Luna that she was the only one Sofia could talk to about him—the only one who wouldn't tell her she was crazy—because she loved him, too. Secretly, Luna treasured Sofia's e-mails, which were more like journal entries or confessions. They had become her vicarious connection to Nico. Between his booming business and Sofia monopolizing his time, Luna now only heard from him when he needed something from her.

He had awakened something in her. It wasn't as if she had been unhappy, but rather confined, like never having colored outside the lines. She loved Tyler. He was the perfect husband…and he allowed her to be herself. But Nico was exciting, an adventure, even a bit dangerous. He made her feel more alive and like anything was possible. Re-reading Sofia's dismal letter full of complaints about him made Luna miss him more. Gazing out her window, the red layers of the sheared rock cliffs blurred through her tears. Calling him now in front of Tyler was out of the question, but not because she couldn't. It was that she knew Tyler would feel hurt—dismissed.

Feeling a hot plume of butterflies erupting in her belly, she gripped the phone tightly in her hands, wishing he would call. When it didn't ring, she shut her eyes, hoping to suppress the fire that consumed her. Shoving the phone into her tote bag, she heard that song she'd put on her playlist by Avril Lavigne, "Anything but Ordinary," playing in her head.

Grateful for their arrival in Santa Fe, Luna pulled herself out of her compulsive thoughts. The cute B&B where they were staying was just off the Plaza. A kiva fireplace in the room added to the romantic atmosphere. She intended for this time alone with Tyler, away from their daily routines, to ignite some passion in their relationship and hopefully dampen her obsession with Nico. Luna quickly unpacked while Tyler lit a fire, filling the room with the exotic aroma of piñon. Already feeling the drop in temperature at the 7,000-foot elevation, Luna changed into leggings and a cashmere turtleneck, along with her favorite suede jacket. Pulling on tall, dark brown, distressed leather cowboy boots with cream colored embroidery, she felt ready to dance at El Farol, where they traditionally dined their first night in Santa Fe. After they enjoyed a selection of tapas and a bottle of hearty red wine, Tyler allowed Luna to get him onto the tiny, packed dance floor. With her arms wrapped around his neck, any sadness and longing she held dissipated with the movement of their hips to the spicy salsa rhythm, both laughing when they attempted to follow the merengue danced by the locals.

Christmas morning, Luna woke up thinking about Nico and Sofia. She was happy they were going to his father's, and would be with family. After breakfast at Pasquals, she and Tyler purchased several gifts from the Native artists who sold their wares under the portal at the Palace of the Governors. Christmastime was magical, filled with sacred animal dances and a torchlight procession of the Virgin at Taos Pueblo, followed by the customary *matachina*, a colorful dance in elaborate costumes that had been introduced to the area by Spanish missionaries.

When Luna called Nico to wish him a Merry Christmas, he seemed cheerful. Yet he didn't want her to hang up.

"Wait, Luna…" he interjected.

"Are you OK?" she asked.

"Yes, it's just…you know how Claudia and I don't get along. She doesn't like me."

"I know," Luna sighed. "But Sofia will be there. Just be nice." It was her way of telling him not to start a fight.

"I guess so," he muttered. His silence hung in the air. Feeling connected to him, she didn't want to hang up either, and just listened to him breathing softly. "How is Santa Fe?" he finally asked.

When Luna told him about the sacred dances, he perked up. "Text me pictures, please."

"We're not allowed to take pictures, but there are some cool pictures online. I'll show you when I get back." She noticed Tyler signaling her. "Nico, don't you have to leave?"

"Yeah, I guess…"

"Have a good time, honey…Merry Christmas." She waited for him to hang up first. He didn't like it the other way around. When he didn't, she added, "I love you."

Making the mmmmwhaa sound for blowing kisses, he replied, "I love you, too." After hanging up, she sat on the bench in the Plaza, teary eyed. Something about Nico physically tugged at her heart.

A few days after Christmas, Luna received another e-mail from Sofia:

> *Dear Luna,*
>
> *I am accepting that I cannot change him, and neither can you. I am having the most difficult time facing the fact that I love someone who takes love for granted. HE IS ABUSIVE! He will do anything to get what he wants. He blew up at me on Christmas Day because I talked to Claudia's son, then he nearly killed us on the drive home in my car. He drove over 100 mph all the way and I was crying, begging him to slow down. When he acts like this it scares me!*

Walking up Old Santa Fe Trail, Luna stopped to admire inlaid pocketknives in a shop window. She thought they were like jewelry. Nico would love one, and it would be something he would have forever. Inside the shop, she inquired about the blade. It was not shiny silver, but dark grey with swirls in it. The shop owner told her it was hand-forged Damascus steel, which she thought was very unique and exotic—kind of like Nico. Deciding right away to get him one, she first had to choose from a myriad of inlay combinations. She loved turquoise, but it didn't have the right look and feel. Nico was darker. Finally, she picked out a knife that was black jet, a gemstone derived from decaying wood under extreme pressure, with Apache Gold cabochon, a combination of steatite and golden pyrite. The gold flecks reminded her of the yellow flecks in Nico's eyes. After paying the shopkeeper, she tucked the little box into the zippered compartment of her handbag.

o   o   o

"Nico, what would you like to do for New Year's Eve?" Sofia asked. "I could see who's around, and have a party here," she offered.

After not answering right away, he finally said, "Paolo's throwing a huge party at the club."

Though thinking *uh, oh, déjà vu all over again*, Sofia remained silent. Not impetuous enough to dredge up his insults over the birthday party they didn't attend on Christmas Eve, she ventured, "Sounds great! I'll wear the new Dior dress you gave me!" When he didn't object, she sighed in relief.

On New Year's Eve, Sofia took herself to Beverly Hills for a full pampering treatment. Concerned about how Nico might behave that night, she wanted to be relaxed and confident about her appearance. To ensure she would look and feel gorgeous, her first appointment was for a luxurious massage, manicure, and pedicure. Then she had a full leg and Brazilian bikini wax. She topped it off with an appointment to get her hair done at one of L.A.'s best red carpet specialists.

When she got home, the bike wasn't there. She called Nico, but got no answer. Rather than allowing her imagination to run wild, she busied herself with confirming their reservations at Piccolino for 9:00 p.m. They'd head over to the Emerson Theater after dinner for the countdown, then dancing until 4:00 a.m. He didn't return her call until 7:00 p.m., and it was all Sofia could do to not scream at him. "Where have you been?" she asked through clenched teeth.

"I got hung up," he replied coolly.

"With what, Nico?"

He replied testily, "I told you. I had sessions today."

"You never mentioned that to me. I was worried."

He insisted, "I told you, Sofia. You just never listen. Just get ready and come to the studio."

"Did you pack your clothes for this evening?" she asked, though she knew he hadn't.

After hanging up, she took her time fixing her makeup, then putting on a black lace push-up bra and black lace thong panties. Opting for bare legs, she slipped the little black dress on.

Studying herself in the mirror, she considered shoes. The dress was simple and elegant. Without a doubt, the Manolo Blahnik high-heeled gladiator sandals were perfect, adding just that touch of bondage she was looking for and revealing the beautiful Aruba Blue polish on her toenails. Finally, she put on black sterling silver and diamond hoop earrings, a gift from her father for her twenty-first birthday, and layered one wrist with her two new bracelets, the Ippolita from Nico and the David Yurman leather. The bracelets looked great together, just as she had known they would.

Grabbing their overnight bags, she carefully made her way down the stairs to her car. The drive to the studio was easy, and listening to "Diamond in My Pocket," by Better Than Ezra, put her in a good mood, fantasizing it was Nico singing to her on the chorus.

Impatiently waiting for her, Nico barked, "Do you have my clothes?"

166

Offended he hadn't said anything about how fabulous she looked, Sofia replied dryly, "Bad day, huh?"

"Why do you say that?" he snorted.

"Well, I thought you might notice…" She spun around gracefully.

"Oh, right. You look nice," he said sarcastically, adding, "Is that what you wanted?"

Sofia realized she was becoming numb to his stinging barbs. "Nico, this is the Dior dress you gave me for Christmas," she had purposely not said "bought me." She thrust his overnight bag at him. "Forget it. Here's your bag."

While he dressed, she waited on the sofa, and when he came out he nonchalantly asked, "How do I look?" as if nothing had been said previously.

Smiling sweetly, she bit her lip. "Dashing as always, Nico."

She handed him the keys so he could drive over to Piccolino on North Robertson, where Sofia was a regular with her work colleagues. Even though he was being difficult, she was proud to walk in with him; she'd never dated anyone as good-looking as Nico.

After they were seated, Nico abruptly got up without excusing himself and went to talk with people at another table. To camouflage her discomfort, Sofia busied herself with the menu. She knew he had purposely waited for her to sit down so he wouldn't have to introduce her. What would he say—*this is my assistant?* But not wanting to ruin the evening, when he returned she didn't bother to question him.

He matter-of-factly announced, "That was Alexa Morgan. I had to say hello! But don't turn around, it will look obvious."

Feigning apathy, she coyly remarked, "Oh, I would have liked to meet her. You should have brought me over and introduced me." When he didn't respond, she continued, asking offhandedly, "Is she here with her husband?"

"No," he stated flatly. "She's never been married."

"Oh really?" Sofia arched her brow, adding with dripping sarcasm, "I wonder why?"

Nico tried to be funny, "She looks like a man! And she's crude. I don't care for her, but she knows everyone and said she'll get me a movie. I just met her at Erin's office party, and she's already flirting with me in front of her friends."

Sofia looked up, piercing him with her eyes. "Do you think that's good for your business, Nico? To flirt with your clients?"

He flashed her a warning glare, then snapped, "She isn't a client… yet! Besides, I don't flirt back."

"Ah, Nico, but you do." As soon as she said it, she was sorry. Not that it wasn't true, but she really wanted this evening to go well, and she most certainly didn't want a scene.

Nico was unforgiving. "You're an idiot, Sofia. I'm a perfect gentleman at all times. I would never fuck a client."

She almost reminded him that she had, in fact, been a client, when the waiter arrived to take their order. Nico ordered one of the Argentine wines his father had supplied to the restaurant upon Sofia's introduction.

Alexa stopped by their table as she was leaving. Sofia was sure she'd come by just to check her out, undoubtedly observing that Sofia's dress was Dior, and her jewelry, though understated, was expensive. When Nico didn't make an introduction, Sofia extended her hand. "Sofia Lombardi. Pleased to meet you."

Alexa was curt, but polite. "Alexa Morgan."

Sofia faked a smile while giving her the once over, judging she was overdressed in top to bottom Alexander McQueen, including the knuckle bag. Doing the math quickly in her head, Sofia decided the outfit took her for eight grand. Sofia admired Sarah Burton, the designer for the McQueen label, but this woman couldn't pull off the look—unless she was *trying* to look like a matronly Nazi drill sergeant. Even worse, instead of wearing sexy heels, such as the woven leather and chain sandals shown with the outfit in McQueen's fashion show, she wore practical, low-heeled sling-backs. *Geez…if you're going to do the look, you have to go for it all the way*, Sofia thought, rolling her eyes to herself.

Alexa interrupted Sofia's thoughts. "I hear you're a writer for *Going My Way*."

Sofia remained aloof. "Yes, we're all thrilled. Word has it we're getting the Writers Guild Award."

"Will you stay with the show?"

Though it seemed like a dumb question, she answered confidently, "Sure, I like it here in L.A."

That opened the door for an obvious question. "Where are you from?"

"New York City, so it's been quite a transition."

Alexa fished, "I imagine so. And how did you meet Nico?"

Sofia paused, unsure how he would want her to respond. "We were introduced by Luna Saint Claire, the costume designer on the show." She thought that was safe. It didn't make her sound like a client, and maybe more of a girlfriend. Finally, Alexa shook her hand again, and Nico stood to give her that kiss kiss cheek cheek thing he did with clients. It was his way of getting them close to his skin, and a tactic that always worked for him. Sofia was glad when she finally left.

Looking up at Nico from underneath her lush, long lashes, her bright blue eyes accentuated perfectly by smoky kohl eyeliner, she saw he was staring at her. "Are you pleased with yourself?" he asked accusingly.

"What do you mean by that?" Sofia countered.

"You know what I mean."

"No, I don't, Nico. She was interrogating me. She obviously wanted to know all about me."

Nico stabbed and twisted the blade. "She didn't know you existed, but you certainly let her know."

"Don't be ridiculous. She knew where I worked already."

Nico pondered, "Well, she must have asked someone about you, like the hostess."

"Is that a problem?"

Nico retaliated, "We'll see how big a problem you just made. I want to get this deal, and I'll have to undo the damage you cause me."

o   o   o

Sofia heard the pounding of the bass thundering from the Emerson Theater as soon as she stepped out of the car. There would be a host of celebrity DJs, and Calvin Harris was supposedly going to perform. Being the hottest club in L.A., the Emerson was *the* place to be seen. Though clubbing wasn't something Sofia did much, even in New York, she was excited about tonight because it was New Year's Eve, and she was with Nico Romero. Walking up to the ropes, they didn't have to present an invitation; the doorman just opened the door, greeting Nico professionally with, "Good evening, Mr. Romero."

Hooking her arm into Nico's, she glided in alongside him. The music pulsed through her body, causing her lungs to struggle for breath in time with the beat. Nico wove in and out of the throngs of people until he found their table. Sofia had no idea how the bottle service—she guessed it to be as much as $10,000—was being paid for, but trusted Nico had it under control. He greeted his friends, and one gave him a bear hug and said something in Spanish. Staying glued by Nico's side, Sofia scanned the room for famous faces.

Designed around a 1920s Prohibition theme, the club personnel were appropriately costumed. A flapper girl arrived to open their bottle of tequila and prepare fancy party drinks called Melon Cartels, tequila with honeydew. Above the floor, Sofia took in the burlesque show of girls in brightly colored fishnet stockings, gem-encrusted brassieres, and feather boas, dancing wildly on elevated platforms. Too loud to converse, Sofia didn't get properly introduced to any of Nico's friends or their dates, but they nodded and smiled while sipping their drinks. The girls accompanying Nico's friends were all tall and skinny, dressed in the look du jour of club clothes: tight miniskirts of patent leather, python, or lace; corset or bustier tops; purposely revealed garter belts and stockings; and stiletto heels. Sofia looked refined by comparison, and knew she'd feel cheap and ridiculous dressing in such a tacky style. She noted how they all looked the same—and like they were trying to hook up. A couple of the girls acknowledged her and said their names, but Sofia couldn't really hear them.

When the DJ took over the booth, the group all leaped up to dance, it didn't matter with whom. Sofia looked around for Nico, but couldn't find him anywhere and decided to walk around to see if she recognized anyone. Working her way around the room, a couple of times guys grabbed her hand and tried to pull her close, but she always slipped away gracefully. Looking for the restroom, she saw it just said WC on the door, without any indication of male or female. She tried the handle, but it was locked, so she waited a few minutes until a couple tumbled out. Intending just to fix her lips and toss her hair, she figured she'd better pee while she was in there. As she exited, another couple went in. Back at their table, she saw Nico had returned, and he caught her arm roughly, demanding, "Where were you?"

"The bathroom!"

He clenched his jaw and stared her down. "Alone? You went alone? Don't leave this table! If you need the bathroom, I'll take you."

She nodded her understanding with a silent sigh. Nico pushed his glass toward her. "Here, hold this. But don't drink from it. It's very strong; they made it especially for me."

He promptly strutted away, leaving her standing alone, holding his drink. Sofia sniffed the glass. It smelled normal. Wondering what was so strong about it, she decided to find out and took a small sip, but it tasted normal. She shrugged, then stood there for a long while, scanning the room for Nico, but again not seeing him anywhere. When she finally tired of waiting for him, she took another sip of his drink. She was starting to feel really good.

A few minutes later, the music sounded irresistible to her, and she moved with the song in what must have been a very suggestive way, because one of Nico's friends came up behind her and put his arm around her waist, pressing her butt against his pelvis as they moved their hips to the beat. All of a sudden the music pounded and every-one yelled…10, 9, 8, 7, 6, 5, 4, 3, 2, 1. At "one," the music blared, and the crowd jumped up and down with the cacophonous techno beat. Sofia downed Nico's drink and bounced up and down, too, then danced with abandon. When Nico finally returned, he snatched her away from his friend, shaking his head angrily. Seizing her by the hair, he questioned, "Where's my drink?"

Sofia shrugged her shoulders. "You disappeared. I drank it."

Nico hissed, "I told you it was too strong!"

Sofia bounced up and down. "I feel great. What was in it?"

"It was made special for me."

Though he was pissed, she didn't notice. "Oh. Well, I liked it. I like dancing—dance with me, Nico," she slurred a bit. Draping herself around him, she kissed his neck, working her way to his lips, and rubbed her body against his pelvis, grinding with the beat of the music. Then she felt his cock with her hand.

"Shit, Sofia. Stop. You're making me hard," he growled.

She purred, "That's the idea. I feel very good…and you're making me very wet."

Suddenly, Nico took her by the hand and guided her through the crowd with his hand on her back to steady her. He opened the door to the water closet then locked it from the inside. Whipping out his already engorged erection, he stroked himself to make it fully hard, then turned her around so that she faced the mirror. "Bend over," he commanded, lifting up her short dress and pulling her black lace thong down. Kicking her feet wider apart, he ran his hands over the cheeks of her round butt, sliding his fingers over her anus, then down into her wet pussy.

"Hold onto the sink," he directed, so she wouldn't slip down to the floor in her current state. Spreading her cheeks open, he admired how her pink, wet pussy glistened. Sofia panted as he placed the head of his cock just at the opening of her swollen pussy, rubbing it around the entrance to cover himself with her juices before shoving it in. She gasped with the suddenness of his entry, then let out a sigh, adoring the feeling of his deep penetration. Looking in the mirror, she watched his face while he fucked her, his brow slightly furrowed and his eyes half-mast. Not caring that she'd have bruises in the morning, he dug his fingers hard into her hips while he pumped her slick, velvety pussy, lunging harder and deeper in time with the music.

Sliding his cock out, he admired how it looked covered in her wetness, and took a moment to stroke himself indulgently before plunging back into her. Pulling out his cock again, he slipped his fingers inside to massage her G-spot until she moaned and called his name, begging for him. Slowly, he inserted himself back between her plump folds and gently placed his wet fingers into her ass. Her legs stiffened in anticipation of a massive orgasm, and he could feel her clenching his cock; she was even tighter with his fingers inside her ass. Closing his eyes, he readied for his own release, pounding her harder and deeper, hitting the back of her cervix while his fingers fucked her anus, heightening both their pleasure. Frantic with desire, Sofia reached between her legs to rub her swollen clit.

Convulsing around him, her juices gushed as she went over the edge. She knew from his breathing and low growl that he would come any second, so squeezed him hard, causing a new orgasm to pulse down the walls of her vagina outward, rolling over and over again. Balls deep, he thrust his hips into her and swore out loud as he came, the hot jets of cum squirting repeatedly inside her. Feeling the actual heat of his cum, Sofia realized she felt everything deeper, bigger, and louder than ever before.

When he pulled his fingers slowly out of her anus, then eased his cock out of her pussy, letting their mingled juices drip to the floor, Sofia collapsed over the sink, spent and dizzy. Her own orgasm had been so intense that she was unsteady on her legs. She nearly fell to the floor, but Nico caught her and sat her on the toilet while he wiped himself clean and put it back in his jeans. Helping her to her feet, he prodded, "Come on. We'd better get out of here." Seeing she was in no shape to take care of herself, he pulled up her thong and fixed her dress.

Suddenly feeling very thirsty, and her lips dry, she reapplied her red lipstick as best she could and quickly finger combed her hair. Still wobbly, she held tightly to Nico's arm as they made their way to the exit. The fresh air felt glorious to her, and she leaned on his shoulder while the valet brought their car to the front.

Nico drove all the way to Malibu even though they had planned to stay at the studio, saying he wanted to wake up to the Christmas tree. After the wild ride home from Agoura Hills, Sofia was leery about driving with him, but really couldn't work up enough concern to say anything. Wondering again about what was in that drink at the club, Sofia mused about the scent-laden night air she hadn't noticed before. She had never had an orgasm that strong; it was mind blowing. When they got to the house, she gulped several glasses of water as she undressed, yet still felt parched. Nico sat on the sofa with the guitar he kept at her house and began singing a romantic love song in Spanish. She nestled up next him, closed her eyes, and fell into a mesmerized trance at the sound of his voice.

∘   ∘   ∘

One eye opened first, then the other. Sofia saw it was after noon. She hadn't washed her face before going to sleep, so the pillow case was smudged with black eyeliner, mascara, and red lipstick. *Whoa… how **did** I get into bed?* she wondered. Nico's legs were threaded through hers, and his arm was draped over her hip, but she managed to slip out without waking him. She staggered into the kitchen to pour herself a large glass of orange juice, stirring in an EmergenC. God, she was still so thirsty. What the hell was in that drink?

Stumbling around the kitchen, she managed to make coffee and get some bacon out of the fridge and into a pan. She started cutting up onions and peppers to sauté in the deep iron skillet, only pausing briefly to wonder if wielding a knife was a good idea in her condition. After making it through the onions and peppers with all her fingers intact, she also cut up some asparagus and mushrooms to add to the mix. Starving and assuming Nico would be, too, she scrambled a dozen eggs, adding parmesan cheese and red pepper flakes. Soon the house smelled like the best B&B ever, and Nico emerged. "Wow, what time is it, Spyder?" he mumbled, raking his hands through his hair.

His eyes half open and hair tousled, he looked sexy as ever, wearing low–slung, worn-out yoga pants that did nothing to hide his semi-erect cock. He always woke up like that, and it made her horny for him. "It's after noon, Nico. What a night that was, huh? My ears are still ringing!" She put her arms around him and rubbed up against him playfully.

Sidestepping her, he reached for a mug and poured himself some coffee, snatching a piece of asparagus out of the pan.

"I was going to open Prosecco for New Year's Day, but I don't know if I want any after last night," Sofia giggled.

Nico agreed. "Let's go for a swim in the ocean after breakfast instead," he suggested.

She balked, "Um, it's January, Nico. It'll be cold."

"Yeah, but we can go for a run first, then take off our clothes and step backward into the sea. It's good luck in my country. Actually, we should have done it last night when we got home!"

Sofia wrinkled her nose and squirmed at the thought. "Yeah, right! I couldn't even walk!"

After breakfast, Nico spoke to his sister and Ita, while Sofia called home, then they put on running clothes and headed down to the beach. Inhaling deeply, Sofia was elated by the smell of the briny air and warmth of the sun on her face. With Nico pulling her along when she couldn't keep up, they laughed, being playful with each other as they ran. This was the Nico she adored. On the return trip, as they neared her house, they stripped down to underwear and ran, splashing, into the waves, shrieking with delight.

This was about the happiest Sofia had ever been with Nico. Why couldn't it always be this way? Why did he have to go over to the dark side so often? She thought about getting back to work, the Writers Guild Award coming in the next month, but mostly, she thought about speaking with Luna. She was grateful to have someone to talk to about Nico. Recently, she had shared a Pin with Luna about bipolar disorder, adding an LOL and making a joke about his radical mood swings between hopeless despondency and an unrealistic sense of superiority. Luna responded with an LOL even though it wasn't funny, theorizing it was a reasonable diagnosis and sparking Sofia's curiosity by postulating he had an indelible desolation and fear of abandonment, but she felt there was more.

Emerging from the cold waves, they gathered their clothes and dashed up the steep steps to the deck, then into the house through the sliding glass doors. Sofia went straight to the shower and stepped in, letting the hot water caress her while she gazed out the window overlooking the ocean. She thought about how much she loved her house and how grateful she was for her life at that moment.

Appearing from the bedroom, Nico opened the glass door, embracing her so they both fit under the showerhead. He shampooed his hair, letting soapy bubbles run down his chiseled physique and onto his beautifully formed thighs. Sofia put her soapy hands on his cock, lathering him up, and he leaned against the stone wall to brace himself, his eyes closed as he rocked his hips. Suddenly grabbing her, he turned her around to face away from him, placing her hands on top of the shower door. Pressed against the glass, Sofia was surprised at how sensuous the soapy glass felt against her body. Taking her from behind, he pumped her fast, causing her whole body to rub up and down the glass, her tits leaving streak marks. Slowing down his thrusts, he let her down easily and gently bent her over, positioning himself at the opening to her pussy.

Leaning over her back, he wrapped one arm around her chest, holding her close to him while he fondled her tits, squeezing them and pinching her nipples until they were hard. Playing with herself, she reached back, letting her fingers roam to softly pet his balls before returning to her clit. Contracting around his cock, she could feel him ready to explode and made herself come at exactly the same time. Bracing himself against the wall so they wouldn't fall, he held her tightly as her legs stiffened and her orgasm rolled. He called out as he pumped inside her, his hips pressed deeply against her ass.

After their shower, Nico laid down on the sofa and put on a movie while Sofia took out boxes and began taking down the tree. He commented wistfully, "It's sad we can't leave it up all year."

She nodded her silent agreement. After putting the seahorses back into their little box with compartments, she set it off to the side instead of adding them to the Container Store bin. Handing the ornaments to him later, she said, "You should keep these at your place."

"But what will I do with them?" he asked.

She suggested warmly, "You can hang them up there all year. They're not Santas. They're seahorses."

Nico grinned happily. "Yeah. That's a great idea."

While putting the lights away, she overheard Nico confirming private sessions for the week. Erin had texted him that she wanted to see him right away to begin the New Year, causing Sofia's heart to do a little flip flop, but she didn't comment. And he kept messaging that Alexa woman they'd seen at Piccolino, trying to arrange a meeting. Sofia thought there was something sinister about Alexa and didn't trust her. Having thus been slapped by reality, she began looking forward to getting back to work.

13

Setting aside the Writers Guild press release announcing the show's nomination for Best New Series, Luna thought about the Costume Designers Guild Awards. Following on the heels of *Sex and the City*, Luna had begun secretly wishing for an award. Now, with the nominee announcement so close, she tried hard to temper her anticipation with realism, but somewhere deep inside she was already rehearsing her acceptance speech.

She left work early to drive to Nico's studio, hoping to catch him alone and give him the Christmas gift she'd bought in Santa Fe. She found him in front of the computer in his office, seemingly frustrated. Hugging him, she said, "I missed you. What's wrong, Nico? Talk to me."

He looked up. "Luna, I have so much going on, and Sofia makes mistakes that cost me business."

Rubbing his arm, she offered, "I'm here for you, Nico. Just tell me what you need, and I'll help you."

Gesturing for her to sit down, he seemed to relax, saying, "You're the only one I can count on, Luna."

Pulling a chair up next to him so that their legs were side by side, she saw Nico peering up at her from under his eyelashes, flirting boyishly. Luna put her forehead against his, the way she used to do with her horse. It was a gentle, intimate gesture that she knew soothed him. She'd just settled in when he announced he was late for a meeting. Disappointed he was leaving, she piped up, "Wait, Nico. Before you leave, I have your Christmas gift."

He remarked, "Oh, Luna. I haven't had any time all week. I have something for you, but it isn't here!"

Luna knew how Nico was. She might not see that gift for months, if at all. "Nico, all I want is to be close to you…friends forever. You know that." She took the pretty little box out of the zippered compartment of her bag. She hadn't even gift wrapped it; the box alone was a deep turquoise, the same as the sky in Santa Fe, with the embossed logo of the cutlery shop.

Lifting the lid, he saw the pocketknife resting inside. The flecks of Apache Gold sparkled in the light from his desk lamp, a strong contrast against the jet black inlay. When he looked up, she saw how the knife perfectly mirrored the color of his hair falling over the golden flecks in his smoky green eyes. Luna thought she saw a tear well up, but he looked down quickly and opened the blade, admiring the dark grey swirls in the Damascus steel. "Wow. Luna, it's incredible. You bought this in Mexico?" he asked.

"*New* Mexico, Nico. It reminds me of you—beautiful and can cut you to ribbons."

He laughed out loud. "That's right! Luna, you're so special to me. Thank you."

He reached over, giving her a quick hug. When he did, she kissed the side of his neck, inhaling his intoxicating scent. "I love you so much, Nico," Her words startled even her, and she looked down.

He looked her in the eye. "I'm sorry, Luna. I'll call you later. I'm late." He walked her to the door, but when she turned to wave goodbye, he was already gone. She felt sad. Something she couldn't put her finger on bothered her, but she pushed it away.

o   o   o

Sofia was trying to focus despite her constantly vibrating phone. She did her best to ignore it, but eventually another writer said, "Why don't you tell whoever keeps calling you you'll get back to them later. You're totally distracted, and we have to finish this scene."

Flushing with embarrassment, Sofia reached to turn off the phone and saw ten missed calls from Nico. She texted him to say she was in the room with the writers and would get back to him later. His text back read:

> *Fuck them. When I call, you better pick up! Call
> me right now!*

She excused herself and went to the bathroom to call him.

"Sofia!" he snapped as he answered, "Erin needs my script for the documentary right away. You have to write it and send it to me *now*."

Tearing up, she took a deep breath and forced herself to set boundaries. "Nico, I can't do it right now. I'm working."

He shot back, "Fuck you. I'm done with you. You always damage me and ruin my business." Then he hung up on her. She was shaken, but had to get back to the room. For the rest of the day, she hoped her distraction wasn't too obvious.

o   o   o

Erin's agency, Grey Dog, was conveniently located in Santa Monica, not too far from her beach house and a short drive from Shutters on the Beach. As she got out of the car, she unbuttoned the front of her black jumpsuit so the dragon tattoo just above her right breast would be clearly visible, also revealing a bustier-style bra. As much her personal brand as it was her uniform, Erin was known for being almost anti-fashion—one day looking like a dominatrix and the next like a monk. Her cropped, dyed black hair was spiked out to accentuate an asymmetrical cut. Though she liked the masculine edge and low-maintenance simplicity, she had recently found herself fussing with her hair and applying black eyeliner to accentuate her fierce grey eyes.

Shutters on the Beach, with its casual elegance, was known for Hollywood deal making. It was the perfect venue for meeting with Jacob, the creative director and filmmaker whose work had helped make Grey Dog one of the top branding agencies in the world.

Erin knew Jacob was interested in making a documentary about shamanism. When she'd told him that her yoga instructor, Nico Romero, had been initiated by the Q'ero tribe, describing the mysterious ceremonies and the pranayamas that uncoiled the kundalini, he'd asked Erin to make an introduction.

Jacob and Erin were in agreement that yoga instructors and energy healers were becoming the new breed of therapist, making it cool to have a personal healer, much like a life coach. When Erin had texted Jacob a picture of Nico, he'd enthusiastically stated that Nico was perfect—with his powerful masculinity, Kundalini Yoga, and the magical ingredients of mystical ceremonies, Jacob's film would be a visual feast. Erin concurred, and also believed that with the right platform, he could be a hotter brand than Deepak Chopra.

Jacob Kafka was the epitome of coolness. A burly Algerian in his late forties, with an impressive mustache, dark beard, and a mop of unruly long, curly hair, his soft-spoken teddy bear demeanor concealed a talented, masterful, and prescient creative director. Erin's usual bullying had proved useless with Jacob; if she argued with him, he simply launched into a rambling tirade in a mixture of Arabic and French. After trusting in him had earned her agency several awards, she'd ceased trying to tell him what to do. She admired his talent, but moreover, she respected him—and there weren't many people Erin Whelan respected.

Nico roared up to the front entrance of the hotel on his Ducati. From the lobby, Jacob and Erin watched him dismount the bike and take off his helmet, raking his fingers through his hair. He wore soft, faded blue jeans with a white, tailored shirt unbuttoned at the top and the hem hanging out. Jacob laughed out loud and nudged Erin with a knowing glint in his eye. She sighed; Jacob had known her long enough to know, without her declaring it, that she and Nico were fucking.

Striding confidently into the lobby, Nico greeted Erin with a double-cheek kiss, then gave Jacob a firm handshake. Men and women both always looked Nico up and down, and Jacob noticed the heads turning when Nico walked in—a fact not lost on Nico, either. The group made their way into the Coast restaurant, and were escorted to Erin's regular table where she often conducted business meetings. Erin eyed Nico as he unbuttoned the sleeves of his shirt, revealing beautifully defined forearms and a woven leather bracelet. Even just sitting down, rolling up his sleeves, and picking up a glass of water, Nico was graceful and fluid in his movement.

Jacob and Erin didn't waste time ordering, and Nico glanced at the menu quickly before Erin called over the server. Immediately, Erin began their meeting. "Nico, let me fill you in on Jacob. Jacob's work isn't typical advertising you might see. He makes *films*. Artistic, moody films. We think this film should focus on presenting you as a Kundalini Yoga and energy healing guru."

Nico nodded approvingly. "Sounds great," he flashed his million-dollar smile. "Can I see some of your work?" he addressed Jacob.

Erin replied, "I'll show you some later at my office."

Jacob let Erin speak for him, preferring to observe his subject. She continued, "For now I just wanted you two to meet casually, so Jacob could hear your story and get to know you personally." Just then, their meals and beverages arrived, and as Erin and Jacob began picking at their salads, she asked Nico to tell Jacob about his years living in Peru.

Nico got right down to business. "I lived for many years in the Andes with the Q'ero, learning from them." He didn't look at Erin; for this conversation, Nico wanted to ensure *Jacob* understood the sacredness of what he was going to explain.

After ensuring Jacob's attention was fixed on him, Nico continued, "That was ten years ago, and over time I was initiated by them. Here in the United States, the common term used for what I am is shaman—or sometimes healer or mystic. But the word shaman does not exist in the medicine traditions of the Andes. The healers are called paqos." Battling with the noisy, vibrant environment, Nico lowered his voice and spoke slowly and softly to retain Jacob's attention. He explained, "It is a rigorous apprenticeship. Paqos are masters of working with energy, and they understand techniques for transmuting it. We communicate with the spirits of the elements—coca, maize, even the mountain itself—with the mother spirit, which is sacred and never dies."

Nico's eloquence held Jacob and Erin mesmerized.

Nico was pleased by their attention. "I can hear the leaves speak to me when I'm in a heightened state of consciousness. You have to prepare for this and be able to integrate yourself spiritually before you can heal another soul. We are all sacred. Everything is sacred in its own way. Coca leaves are sacred and were given to us by Pachamama,

Earth Mother, to guide us and heal us. We become more open when we discover the spirit in plants like coca. They're here to help us."

Jacob looked over at Erin, a bit incredulous. Erin nodded at him knowingly, and Jacob turned back to Nico, "Coca leaves—as in cocaine?"

Nico sniffed dismissively. "It's not the same. The leaves are part of a sacred ritual, and they're not processed like a drug sold for recreation. We use these leaves to communicate with powerful spirits and to heal, not to party in a nightclub. It's the same with my initiation to San Pedro, which is mescaline. A San Pedro ceremony is the most magical healing ceremony. The shaman wakes up the spirits of San Pedro, and they allow him to see. You must be humble! Little by little, you begin to understand how things function. But you need to ask the right questions before San Pedro will give you answers."

Nico was really on point, and Jacob sat agape as he listened. "The San Pedro ceremony is very beautiful and involves several processes. First is the invocation to the spirits, then the shaman does a diagnosis and a divination to learn what's wrong with the person. Then the healing begins! We use power objects called 'artes,' placed on the altar of the mesa. Artes may include shells, bones, swords, crystals, mirrors, crosses, and of course the shaman's *seguros*—bottles filled with perfume and plants chosen for healing and spiritual qualities. The arrangement of all of this must be *very* precise. Under the influence of San Pedro, the powers of the seguros are seen and experienced, and the shaman is able to use these forces to diagnose and heal."

Nico stopped speaking. He normally would never explain as much as he just had, preferring to keep his initiation and the teaching private. Silence hung over the table for a long pause, like mist from the moors. Erin spoke first, "Nico, I want to do this ceremony with you! Why haven't we done it?"

Nico answered firmly, "You haven't come to me for healing. Though we certainly do work on moving your prana." He turned to Jacob to explain further, "In the Q'ero language of Quechua, what eastern yoga calls chi is called prana—the living energy—Sami and Hucha. We do not have good or bad energy, but rather light and dense energy. Sami is light and natural from the earth. Hucha is created by human beings when we are out of harmony; it's heavy and dense. We accumulate Hucha, making us out of balance with the natural world. But we can use Kundalini Yoga to cleanse our energy bodies of Hucha and return to balance."

Jacob looked at Erin. "Well, this is even more interesting than I expected."

Erin winked at Nico, then addressed Jacob, "What would you like to do first, Jacob? When can you begin?"

Jacob replied excitedly, "Well, I'll make a rough storyboard. Then let's get together again to work up a production schedule and figure out when and where on the ceremonies. Sound good?"

Erin nodded, but both she and Jacob quickly noticed Nico seemed troubled. "What is it, Nico?" Erin inquired.

Nico looked serious. "We have to be careful about what we show in the ceremonies."

Jacob quickly nodded. "That's fine, Nico. You just tell me what's OK and what isn't. You guide me!"

Nico brightened. "OK. That's good. As long as I have approval over the final film. I must be careful to respect my position."

"Well, that all sounds good, then," Jacob exhaled relief. "Give me about a week," he added, turning to Erin. "I'll get in touch with you when it's all ready."

Erin and Jacob exchanged good-byes, then Erin hung back to talk with Nico. When Jacob was out of earshot, she asked, "Are you excited about the film?"

Nico pushed his hands into his jeans pockets and looked down toward the floor, then up directly into her eyes. "It could be good. Or maybe not, Erin. You never know how it will look to others until it's presented. You know this better than most people."

She nodded in acknowledgment. "Well, let's let Jacob do his thing. He's creative and really has vision. I think he'll do something interesting." She eyed Nico before adding, "Why don't you come over to my house. I'm only two minutes from here, and we can have a drink."

"I'll follow you." Nico got on his bike and waited for the valet to get Erin's car. When the black Jag arrived, he pulled out to follow her.

As they watched the last sliver of sun sink into the ocean, Erin's Tamaskan dog, Blue, came out to say hello, poking his nose at Erin for attention. Normally, this was the time of day she would take him for a walk, but this evening she said, "Go on, Blue. Take yourself for a walk. Go be a good boy."

Erin noticed Nico's interest in her dog. "I usually bring Blue to work, but didn't today because he wasn't allowed in the hotel." The main reason Erin had bought this house on Palisades Beach Road was that it was all open and glass, with a deck right on the beach. It didn't matter to her that the house had cost her four million dollars, almost double what her accountant recommended she spend; she had every confidence her agency would be successful and she would have more money than she ever needed.

She kicked off her loafers, tucking her feet underneath herself as she contemplated Nico's brooding. "Lighten up, Nico. Everything is possible. Isn't that what you teach with Kundalini?"

"Yes. It is all possible—especially with your help," he replied.

"I told you, when we get to Cannes, we'll create more opportunities for you. We're sure to win a Lion for the Armani campaign. You'll see. People will recognize you."

"What should I be doing?" he asked.

"Relax." She rolled her eyes; she loved when Nico was vulnerable. Blue came panting up the steps and nosed Erin so she would get up and feed him. It was getting dark, and the temperature was dropping. "Come in the house," Erin said, moving toward the kitchen. Nico followed her through the large sliding glass doors into the house, which was lit up against the dusky sky. The décor was monochromatic and neutral, in keeping with Erin's style, with a natural stone fireplace.

When the dog was happily eating his dinner, Erin took Nico's hand and led him into her bedroom. "What would you like to play, Nico?" she inquired, dimming the lights. The last glimmer of sunlight reflected off the sea to shine through the glass wall, and the crashing of waves was the only sound they could hear. Bringing a duffel bag out of the closet, she placed it before him on the bed. "Your toys, master," she said submissively, with a slightly wicked smile.

Nico immediately got into character; he loved these dominance games with her. "Take off your clothes, but leave on your bra and panties. And put on those boots I like."

Erin did as she was told. Unzipping the jumpsuit, she let it drop to the floor, where she kicked it away. She now stood wearing only a black bustier and thong. On the top of her left breast Nico saw her detailed, ink-black, fire-breathing dragon tattoo. Erin bent over to put on the high-heeled cage ankle boots that Nico liked. In the waning light, her Irish porcelain skin had a translucent glow contrasted by her shaggy-cut black hair. Her grey eyes gleamed, cool and piercing. She waited obediently for his next command.

Nico stripped the bed of all but the fitted sheet, then took a satin sash from the bag and lashed her wrists behind her back. Kneeling her on the bed, he handcuffed her ankles over the leather of the boots. "I don't think it's wise for you to have bruises on your ankles," he winked.

She laughed in agreement. "Always thinking, Nico. How to play rough while being thoughtful at the same time!"

He took out a silk scarf to use as a gag, which was more for effect, but it would keep her from screaming, which might upset Blue. "So, Erin. Take a few breaths," he spoke in a low, sexy tone. "And we begin."

Erin breathed in deeply and exhaled. Nico positioned her face on the bed, keeping her ass high up in the air. Using the black leather cat-o'-nine-tails whip, he gently struck her ass a few times as a warm-up. Erin groaned lightly with pleasure, and Nico massaged her ass, then slapped her butt cheek with his hand. She let out a muffled yelp. Without warning, he lashed her again with the whip—one, two, three—each slightly harder than the one before. He paused, then struck harder. Erin groaned louder with the increasing strength of the whip. Nico tenderly petted her hair, brushing her lips with his thumb and caressing her cheek. Teasing her, he swept the tails lightly over her ass—then abruptly struck hard, eliciting more struggling and muffled cries.

He reached under and between her legs to slide his fingers inside the thong and feel her wetness. "Nice…you're dripping," he cooed.

The tails tickled as he trailed them slowly and softly over her butt cheeks. Without warning, he lashed her hard. This time she flinched. Rubbing her ass softly, he leaned over to kiss her shoulder on the wolf tattoo. "That's my wolf baby," he whispered. Pushing two fingers inside her wet pussy, he curled them over her G-spot, then trailed them up to the entrance of her anus and pressed over the rim until she moaned, pushing her ass further up to meet his hand.

She tried to look at him, but he pushed her back down. "Keep that ass up for me or you'll be punished. I won't let you come. So stay down for me." With his pocketknife, he cut the sides of her thong, letting it fall away. Kneading her ass firmly with both hands, he inserted three fingers into her pussy while his thumb flirted with her anus. "I love your ass up in the air for me and your pussy so ready," he murmured. Drawing wetness out of her pussy, he gently pressed deeper into her anus with his thumb. "Relax for me."

She exhaled as he stretched her open, penetrating further. "Oh yes, that's good," he purred as he continued relentlessly massaging the walls of her pussy. "Oh yes, your pussy is so wet."

Erin squirmed, grinding onto his hand. But when she lifted her head, he pulled his fingers out and slapped her ass. "Remember what I told you. I'll punish you by not letting you come," he reminded her.

Nico retrieved a bottle of oil, and pouring a liberal amount over her ass, worked some into her anus with his finger. "This is a perfect little butt hole, just begging to be filled." Taking a butt plug from the bag, he slowly slid it in and out of her ass a few times to stretch her, while thrusting his fingers into her pussy. "That's nice, Erin. Now ask me to let you come. What do you want, Erin? Ask me nicely."

Despite her voice being muffled, he could clearly understand. "Please. I beg you. Please let me come."

"That's nice, Erin. OK, we'll see about that." After inserting the butt plug firmly inside her, he turned on a large vibrating dildo and played with her clit until she whined in tortured ecstasy. Tugging off his jeans, he liberally lubricated his granite-hard erection, and thoroughly entranced, gazed intently as he stroked the length of the shaft. Rubbing the tip over the mouth of her pussy he slowly put the head in, then pulled out, teasing the entrance as Erin's moans became more desperate.

Then, holding her by the hips, he slammed his cock deep into her waiting pussy. Slowly he pulled back and slammed in again. Erin yelped and lifted her head. Nico slapped her hard. With the plug inside her she was super tight, her pussy gripping him deliciously. Delaying his gratification, he withdrew, and Erin groaned in frustration. Taking the vibrator, he rubbed it over her clit then slowly slid it into the mouth of her pussy. She was open, wet, and engorged. "I want to see you squirt," he taunted, putting his fingers in deep to feel the ridges of the butt plug against his fingers with the buzz of the vibrator against her clit.

Panting hard like a dog, she was practically barking as she strained against the gag. "Please…Nico…Please…"

Pushing the dildo hard into her, he then thrust it in and out slowly. "What do you say, little wolf?"

Whining, she pleaded, "May I come, please?"

Nico untied her wrists and pressed the vibrator into her hand. Clutching her hips, he pushed back into her and fucked her hard. Pressing the dildo against her clit, she came undone with one long moan, then shuddered and collapsed onto the bed. "What do you say?" he prodded.

"Thank you, Nico," she moaned.

Gently, he rolled her over onto her back, leaning over to kiss the top of her head. He stroked her hair as he removed the gag from her mouth. "Shhhh, don't speak," he commanded. "We're not done, are we?"

Erin shook her head. Nico released the cuffs from her ankles and spread her apart. Removing her bra, he dragged the cat tails over her chest, tickling her. He rubbed each nipple between his fingers, teasing them, then leaned down and sucked first one then the other, softly blowing on her nipples until she squirmed. Dragging the cat tails softly down between her breasts, he lightly swatted her pussy with them, causing her to buck slightly. "You like that, don't you?" he asked sweetly.

Erin whispered her reply, "Yes, Nico."

He swatted her pussy again, harder this time, while he fondled her breasts. Her back arched, reaching for his fingers as he pulled at her nipples. He purred, "Your dragon is breathing, Erin. I can see him breathing fire."

She whispered, "He is hot for you, Nico."

He slid his hands down her belly and rubbed her clit, again swatting her pussy with the cat tails. With each swat, Erin let out a small yelp and a moan.

"I'm going to fuck you hard, Erin. And you're going to come for me again. Isn't that right?"

Her only response was another ecstatic groan. Tugging her to the edge of the bed, he spread her knees so wide they practically touched the mattress on either side of her shoulders. With her pussy wide open for him, he placed his cock at the mouth, slowly letting the tip rub up and down over her clit, then slid into her. Moving slowly, he thrust in and out, relishing the feeling of the ridges of the butt plug and how tight it made her for him. Hearing her breathing quicken, he growled, "Don't you dare come, or I will beat you. You're not allowed to come, Erin. Remember! You ask me before you come, is that right? Answer me!"

Erin panted, "Yes, Nico. I will ask you."

He fucked her hard and deep. He knew his hands were clasped so tightly around her hips they were going to leave imprints, but no one would see those. He could feel her contracting around him. "Are you ready to come again? So soon? That's my girl. You're nice and tight with that plug up your ass." He kept up the teasing, "Do you want to come, Erin? Beg me!"

She whimpered, "Nico, may I come?"

"May I come, what?" he growled.

"May I *please* come, Nico?" she whimpered louder.

"OK. I'll let you come…soon." With his cock still inside her, he teased her clit with the vibrator. He could feel the buzzing, and began to move with her, pulling the vibrator away just as she was about to come. Waiting until her breathing slowed, he again placed the vibrator against her pussy until she was on the verge of exploding. And again he removed it before she came.

She whined, squealed, and begged, "Fuck me, Nico! Fuck me!" Gripping her thighs, he pulled her toward him, fucking her hard. He couldn't hold back much longer, and he could feel her pussy contract, going all liquid as she crashed around him. Groaning loudly, Nico's orgasm built until he erupted into her, thrusting in hard with each hot jet.

o   o   o

Taking a sip of her grande skim latte, Luna was reading the script for the next episode and enjoying the quiet of the early morning in her office when Sofia appeared at the door. "Luna, am I disturbing you?" her voice was a bit shaky.

Luna looked up and saw Sofia's hair was in a ponytail instead of the usual loose, lush golden waterfall. But she still looked chic, in an artsy way that Luna admired, wearing black leggings, black washed silk tunic shirt and fabulous black boots. Luna smiled and waved her in.

Sitting down in the chair near Luna's desk, she stammered, "I'm so sorry I keep bothering you, but you're the only one I can talk to about him." Luna nodded her understanding, and Sofia continued, "I just don't know what to do, Luna. Nico keeps calling me here at work. He gets so mad at me when I don't answer. You know I can't talk. I'm in the room with the writers most of the time. Then he screams…says he's more important than my job!" As she sputtered out this jumble of words and feelings, she began to tear up, shifting around in her chair as she went on, "Yesterday, when I finally called him back, explaining why I couldn't answer earlier, he told me to fuck off and hung up."

Luna was tentative; Nico would be furious with her if he knew she spoke with Sofia—but now Sofia was quietly crying, trying to hide her tears from Luna.

Luna sympathized. "I know… He does that to me too—as if I'm an appendage of his. I think he does it out of frustration. Still, there's no excuse for that behavior."

Dabbing at her eyes, Sofia went on, "He's always yelling at me. It makes me so anxious! Now, Erin's creative director is making a documentary about him, and Nico told me to write a description of ceremonies. First he warns me not to give too much information, then screams they need more information! He makes no sense. Then he calls me an idiot and a moron—blaming me!"

Luna commiserated, "You can't let him talk to you that way, Sofia. That's unacceptable. At times he's called me names, too. I know he doesn't mean it, but that's verbal abuse, and I won't allow it and neither should you."

Sofia blinked back more tears. "I stayed up all night last night writing a description of the despacho ceremony, but now he says it's too late, and I lost him the opportunity. I don't believe that! I'm sure he's exaggerating. Now he says I have to make it all up to him; that I damaged him and cost him business."

Luna was getting uneasy listening to the chronic complaints, especially worried that Nico would find out they commiserated.

Sofia's voice was shrill as she became increasingly agitated. "Oh, did I tell you? He dumped the contents of my handbag out, saying I stole a hundred dollars from him! A hundred dollars? You have to be joking! I've spent thousands on him! Why would I steal a hundred dollars? I swear, Luna, he's just crazy!"

An awkwardly long silence followed before Luna asked, "Have you discussed Nico's behavior with your parents?"

"Well, funny you should ask…my mom called me about my credit card. Like I told you, Nico asks me to pay for a lot of stuff. And I like to buy him presents, so with all that, the card was a lot higher than normal, and she questioned me. I was surprised she'd seen it, 'cause the bill goes to my dad's office, and he never looks at it. At least I thought he didn't. I think he may have asked her to call me. I was trying to explain how I'm helping him for now, that there is so much going on with his business and it's exploding—but he's going to pay me back."

"Did you tell her that he screams at you and calls you names?" Luna wondered just how much Sofia confessed, and what her parents would think, or do, about it.

"Just that he gets, you know, nervous. Of course I didn't tell her about the wild car ride home from his dad's house! That would've

completely freaked her out. I just said he can be difficult at times—
when he needs something. And that he calls me at work…and gets
furious when I don't answer, saying he's more important than my
job. Maybe I shouldn't have told her all that, because she flipped out
and told me to come home. I made her promise not to tell Daddy.
He'd be so disappointed in me for allowing it…and for staying with
Nico."

"Well, I understand…moms are easier to talk to, right?"

"I'm very close with my father, but I'm afraid that he might do
something. I don't know…he's connected to some pretty scary people."

Seeing Sofia was getting more upset, Luna changed the subject
and effused, "What are you wearing to the Awards dinner?"

At the thought of clothes, Sofia managed a half-hearted smile. "I
don't know…I was thinking of wearing a new Herve Leger. What are
you wearing to the Costume Designers Guild Awards?"

"Well, you can certainly pull it off! I'm wearing Roberto Cavalli.
Everyone will wear their jewels, and I'll wear my turquoise and silver!"

Sofia contemplated, "I don't know. Maybe I should go for something more sophisticated. Not as sexy as Leger."

Luna nodded agreement. "It is a very prestigious award."

Luna's staff were trickling in, so they finished up, agreeing not to
tell Nico they'd spoken or e-mailed about any of this. "He would go
crazy for sure," Sofia remarked as she left Luna's office, hurrying to
the writing room to take her place at the table.

Determining the fate of each of the characters, Sofia felt like she
was deciding her own fate at the same time.

14

Sofia's office phone buzzed; Aaron, *Going My Way*'s showrunner, wanted to see her. She showed up in his doorway quickly, and Aaron asked her to sit down.

Choosing his words carefully, he professed, "You're a good writer, and you're fortunate to be part of a terrific team."

Sofia uncrossed and recrossed her legs.

Looking serious, Aaron cleared his throat. "The reason I called you in here…it's obvious you have some personal problems. Boyfriend problems."

Mortified, Sofia nodded without looking up at him, suppressing the tears threatening to fall. If Aaron knew, she wondered if everyone else was gossiping about her, too.

He went on, "I just want to clarify that, despite all those legendary tortured writer stories, they are really in the minority. If you want to earn a living writing, it's not enough to be talented, you have to produce. Sofia, you're talented at putting the right words into a character's mouth. Where they're going, what they're doing, even down to what restaurant they frequent or where they shop—that's what makes these characters believable and current. It's those kinds of details that made this show a success.

Sofia didn't really know what to say, so just replied quietly, "I really love working on the show, and I'm so grateful for the opportunity."

"There's something else…"

She looked down again, anticipating the worst.

"The studio is moving me to New York to work on the pilot for a new show called *The Runway,* about four top runway fashion models, their personal lives, and the fashion industry. It takes place in New

"

York, Milan, and Paris. It's no secret to everyone here how much you love fashion and, more importantly, how much you *know* about it. If the pilot is a success, I'd like you to come work with me. But in the meantime, you've got to focus on your work and forget about this boyfriend. He's a distraction."

Sofia was stunned. She couldn't possibly begin to imagine forgetting about Nico. But she knew being considered for *The Runway* was an enormous compliment and a huge opportunity. She finally looked Aaron directly in the eye. "Thank you, Aaron. I promise."

On the way back to her desk, she stopped in the bathroom and sat down in a stall. Putting her head in her hands, she wept quietly. Then, pulling herself together, she fixed her eye makeup and applied a fresh coat of red lipstick. Looking at herself in the mirror, she ran her fingers through her hair, thinking there was no need to say anything to anyone—yet. Maybe the pilot wouldn't take off or he would change his mind. It was too early to create drama with Nico. In the meantime, she would work hard and not allow Nico to distract her and ruin her chances. It was time to go shopping for the perfect dress for the Writers Guild Awards dinner.

∘   ∘   ∘

On Friday, Sofia texted Luna asking if she could get dressed in the Wardrobe Department where there was more room and full-length mirrors. When Sofia arrived, garment bag over her arm, Luna squealed in delight, "Let me see the dress!"

Sofia unzipped the garment bag, revealing an elegant Dolce & Gabbana ruched black lace dress. Luna gasped, "I *love* it, Sofia! If you weren't such a brilliant writer, I'd recruit you as a costume designer!"

"I wish Nico recognized my talents. To him, I'm good for nothing except paying for things."

Luna cringed. "He really needs straightening out, Sofia," she urged, pouring herself a short glass of Maker's Mark. "Do you want one?" she offered.

"No, I'd better not. I'm not going to drink tonight."

Watching Sofia touch up her makeup and slip the dress on, she thought her elegant—pretty, blonde, and very sexy. Remembering

Nico saying he wasn't in love with the way Sofia smelled, it made her wonder about desire. After ushering Sofia off to the event with a good luck double-cheek kiss, she sat down at her desk and poured herself another glass of bourbon. Feeling the smooth oaky caramel heat glide down her throat, she pondered the notion of pheromones attracting people to each other. Were they enough to impel an enduring love?

∘ ∘ ∘

Being a well-attended industry-only event, Sofia couldn't bring a date to the Awards. Not that Nico would have gone with her anyway, since it wasn't about him. Scanning the room, Sofia recognized the most famous writers of screenplays, documentaries, dramas, comedies, and even video games. She felt like pinching herself. Before the ceremonies began, Aaron escorted her around the room, introducing her to several senior industry writers, who all praised her work on the show and seemed genuinely pleased to meet her. When Aaron remained by her side all evening, it struck Sofia he was being more than just a considerate boss. Now it seemed obvious from the way he placed his hand on the small of her back and looked at her admiringly that he was interested in more. When he turned, checking that she was still by his side, she felt pleased someone as accomplished as Aaron treated her that way. She wished Nico thought she was special and complimented her like Aaron did. She'd never looked at another guy since she had met Nico, but Aaron's attentions flattered her. She wished she could fall for someone like him, someone who respected her.

As the ceremony neared the award for Best New Series, she felt her stomach get jittery. When the emcee announced the winner as *Going My Way*, Aaron gently squeezed her hand and led her to the stage with the other writers. Sofia was glad she hadn't been drinking when she realized that even without liquor everything seemed coated in gauze. At the end of the evening, Aaron asked her if she had plans, but she gracefully begged off, reminding him she had a long drive. Nico wasn't there when she got home, so she texted him. He replied that he was at a dinner meeting and would be home soon. When he did arrive, she was in bed reading on her iPad. He didn't ask her about the Awards, and of course he never saw her glamorous outfit. But she knew she was photographed more than once and hoped to see the shots in *LA Social*—maybe that would make Nico jealous.

She tried to engage him. "You haven't even asked how the Awards ceremony went."

Distracted by his iPhone, he mumbled, "The what?"

Sofia huffed, "The Writers Guild Awards. You didn't even ask if we won." When he didn't look up or respond, she added, "*Going My Way* won Best New Series!"

He still didn't look up and sniped, "So what? You and your idiot friends got an award for writing a stupid show."

Remembering Aaron's advice about the possibilities for the new show, she rolled over and tried to sleep.

o   o   o

Tyler was already griping about going to Nico's party, but Luna insisted, "It's his thirtieth Ty, and he already teased me, asking if we could stay up that late!" But later, as he left for campus to teach a class, he acquiesced, making Luna promise they wouldn't stay out too late. She didn't mention that they wouldn't even be going to Greystone Manor until ten, and would most likely be the first ones there. She had been surprised when Nico said Erin was covering the bottle service for the evening, then, as if an addendum, told her to wear something sexy because the club would be filled with super-models! Luna had thought to herself that at the very least she would look better than Erin.

As she was heading out for a mani-pedi, Nico called her cell phone, announcing he was in the lobby. Hoping nothing was wrong, Luna invited him up, and when she opened the door was stunned to see he held a large box tied with an enormous ribbon. Seeing the look on Nico's face, she exclaimed, "Oh my! What's this?"

Beaming like a little child, he announced, "See, I told you I had a Christmas gift for you. Now is the perfect time to give it to you!"

Stunned and overjoyed, Luna laughed. "Um…it's February, Nico!" Then, taking the box and double-cheek kissing him, she gushed, "Thank you so much, sweetie! How'd you get it here on the bike?"

"Oh, I have Sofia's car."

She gave him a sideways glance. "And where is Sofia?"

He shrugged. "Home. I just told her I needed to run some errands."

Luna didn't want to get into that discussion again with Nico. Nevertheless, he added, "Luna, how many times do I have to tell you, Sofia and I are just friends."

Not wanting to irritate him, she answered benignly, "I know. I just feel kinda sorry for her, that's all."

He brushed off her comment. "Well, don't. She's well taken care of, I assure you!" Then he laughed brightly. "You're just very old-fashioned in your thinking! Now, open your gift!"

Luna untied the wide gold ribbon and took the lid off the box. Carefully, she unwrapped purple tissue paper and lifted out a sexy, stylish, little black dress by Alice + Olivia.

Blown away, she remarked, "Nico, it's fabulous!"

"I hope you'll wear it to my party tonight. You'll be the most beautiful woman there."

Luna bantered, "I highly doubt that! You said there will be supermodels!"

He laughed. "They're young girls, Luna. You're a beautiful woman." He looked her up and down admiringly. "Will you put it on for me now?"

Luna paused, not sure if she should, but Nico persisted. "Come on. I want to see you in it."

She sighed, "OK, Nico. Wait here." Emerging from her bedroom a few minutes later, she twirled for Nico. The sheer lace bodice of the dress accentuated her breasts, and the short skirt was lightly gathered and layered with silk organza for fullness. She'd also slipped on a pair of pretty Nicholas Kirkwood lace mesh sling-back sandals. "This dress is very short, don't you think?" she asked.

Nico's eyes glowed as he watched her walk toward him. "My God, bella. You look gorgeous!"

She could feel his gaze combing her body. She adored his attentions, encouraging them, and he often flirted blatantly with her, ogling her breasts with overt admiration. "Don't get me wrong, bella. I like your Indian hippie look. It's your thing…" Lowering his gaze he smiled wickedly, then looking back up at her he purred, "But you have terrific legs, and you never show them off."

Their eyes locked. "You're sweet, Nico. This dress is lovely. If you're sure I look OK in it. I mean, at my age."

"Wear it, Luna. You look beautiful."

She leaned up to kiss him on the cheek. "OK, thank you. I will. I mean it, Nico. It's a lovely dress."

She thought he blushed just a little, but then he quickly said, "I've got to run now, bella. But I'll see you at the club at eleven. Just tell them to direct you to my table."

She walked him to the elevator, giving a final spin as the elevator door closed. Walking back to the apartment, she wondered how she would explain Nico giving her this expensive dress to Tyler. Of course, she knew Nico hadn't paid for it! Erin must have given him some more Grey Dog client swag.

o   o   o

Luna waited until late in the afternoon to call Nico and thank him for including her and Tyler at his birthday party. Still sounding groggy despite the hour, his voice husky from shouting above the music, he teased her, "You were the most beautiful woman in the room."

Delighted by the compliment, she chided, "Even though everyone probably thought we were your parents."

"Nonsense. You looked hot, Luna."

"Thank you again for the beautiful dress. I have your birthday present. I'll drop it off tomorrow."

"Can you come now? I could use your help."

Luna wrapped his gift with handmade papyrus and tied a forest-green grosgrain ribbon into a perfect bow. Putting the package in the handbag Nico had given her, she headed over to Amaru, wearing faded jeans and a sheer, white, embroidered peasant blouse.

She found Nico at his desk, engrossed and obviously frustrated.

Without looking up, he brusquely asked, "Do you mind straightening up in the apartment for a little bit while I finish here?"

"Sure," she replied automatically. Though ruffled, she quickly dismissed his lack of civility, considering his preoccupation. Kissing the top of his head, she went into the apartment, and was stunned to see an astonishing mess. Assessing the situation, she surmised that Sofia purposely hadn't cleaned so it would be more desirable for Nico to stay in Malibu.

Discounting the fact she had a maid, Luna pulled on rubber gloves, filled a plastic bucket with soapy water, and began cleaning the greasy stove, thinking about the wonderful meals he had cooked for her. When Nico still hadn't appeared, she rolled up her jeans and stepped barefoot into the bathtub, running the water to scrub the walls, thinking how Tyler would be furious if he saw her now. With her back to the door, she didn't hear Nico walk into the room. Turning around, she was startled to see him standing there watching her, a wide grin on his face. With her hair clipped on top of her head, her jeans scrunched up to her knees, and wearing the bright yellow gloves, Luna's face reddened and her mouth fell open. "Luna, bella. You look so sexy like that, I could fuck you right here in the bathroom!"

Embarrassed as she was, she couldn't contain the big smile on her face. Without warning, he walked up to her and squeezed her left tit really hard over the flimsy white fabric. She was speechless, and her nipples immediately hardened. Nico moaned softly, "What have we here?" He reached into the front of the loose-fitting blouse and lifted one breast out of her bra. Then he leaned over, took her nipple between his lips, and sucked it.

Aghast, and feeling suddenly ridiculous standing there in rubber gloves with Comet in one hand and cleaning sponge in the other, she exclaimed, "Nico, my lord!! You're crazy!" She splashed him with water from the tap and they both erupted into uproarious laughter.

Darting out of the bathroom, she called, "Help me strip the bed, and we'll put on clean sheets." Tossing the dirty sheets into the hamper, she kept up the distraction. "Go get some clean ones from the closet." Glancing at his bed, she tried to erase the image in her mind of him making love by making small talk. "Where do you do your laundry?"

"Sofia takes it to her house," he answered matter-of-factly. But he looked at her warmly—somewhat intimately—and she feared he'd read her mind.

"Where did you do your laundry *before* you met Sofia?"

He shrugged his shoulders and replied playfully, "Whatever girl I'm fucking at the time does the laundry."

Luna just shook her head. Though she knew he was trying to be funny, she also knew it was true.

Remembering his gift, she chimed, "I almost forgot. I have your birthday present." She got her handbag and without thinking sat down on the bed, handing him the beautifully wrapped package.

"That's the handbag I gave you. I have good taste, huh?"

Luna gushed, "Yes, I get tons of compliments on it. It's special… mostly because you gave it to me."

Nico's eyes smoldered at her proclamation, and she saw in them something more he didn't dare say, though she wished he would. Instead, he looked down at the gift. "You always wrap so nice." He carefully untied the dark green ribbon and handed it to Luna, saying, as he always did, "Make sure you put it in my desk drawer." Then he paid his usual compulsive attention to the wrapping paper. "I love this paper. What is it?" he asked as he slowly opened each corner, careful not to tear it.

"It's a handmade paper called papyrus." Almost launching into a history of Egyptian papermaking, she paused as he finally unfolded the delicate paper and saw a web of fine sinew contained within a hoop, three feathers dangling. He wondered, wide-eyed, "What is it, Luna? It must be something Indian, like you!"

She giggled. "Yes, it is, Nico. It's a dreamcatcher." He was lost in admiring it, so she explained, "A dreamcatcher is essentially a spider web made to catch any harm that might be in the air…um…like the way a spider's web catches and holds whatever comes in contact with it. American Indians hang these above the bed to protect sleeping people. Good dreams pass through and slide down the feathers to the sleeper. But bad dreams are trapped in the web. They burn up in the light of day."

"It's very beautiful, Luna." The hoop was wrapped in black buckskin, and the web was made from natural sinew. Elegant black and brown feathers, accented by silver, black glass, and tea-dyed bone beads, gracefully hung from the bottom of the web. At the center of the web a small amethyst stone represented the spider Iktomi. Nico asked, "What kind of feathers are these?"

"Well, traditionally the feathers would be from the night seeing bird—the owl—but it's not legal to use owl feathers anymore. These are pheasant."

"Is this a good spot to hang it?" Nico leaned over, his face a breath away from hers, and placed the loop of the dreamcatcher over the arm of a standing lamp next to the bed.

Luna's fire butterflies swarmed as he looked at her for approval. Sitting on the bed next to the lamp, she reached over and fingered the feathers overhanging his pillow, seeing that they swung freely with the slightest breeze. She uttered, "That's perfect," and smiled.

"Luna…you're so different. What you give to me has so much meaning."

Glancing at the clock on the wall, she said she needed to get going. Tyler would be waiting for her because they had dinner plans.

Nico walked over to his desk and picked up a stack of papers in a binder clip. Scowling, he shook his head, "Can you please just take a minute and read this. It's my scenes for the documentary. It's very important and has to be right. You know more about me and my work than anyone. You're the only one I trust."

Luna replied, "But, Nico, I'm not a writer. Sofia's a great writer. I'm sure it's perfect."

Nico shook his head. "She's not smart enough. She may be able to write dialogue for those stupid girls on the show, but she has no idea about the spiritual nature of what I do!"

She sighed, "Of course I'll help you, Nico."

He brightened. "We have to recover this thing. I need to get it to Erin right away. Jacob has been waiting for me to finish this, and it's very late, Luna. Jacob wants to shoot where I lived with the Q'ero, in Peru. Would you like to come?"

She smiled. "I would love to go with you! If I can." Luna felt so attached to him and would happily follow him anywhere.

He replied, "OK, good. Then stay here and help me. Sofia wrote all kinds of bullshit that makes no sense."

Luna sighed again, "All right, Nico. Let me see what she wrote."

Nico pushed a chair close to Luna so that their legs touched as they reviewed the pages together. But while she worked, he got up and paced around the studio. Finally, she couldn't take it. All that unbridled energy flying around unsettled her. "Nico, could you busy yourself with something else so I can concentrate?"

Since practicing yoga, she'd become calmer and more centered, yet he was always so hyperactive. Thankfully, he talked on the phone with his sister and Ita while she worked. By the time he hung up, she was ready to show him what she did, offering up comments, "Sofia did a great job describing the despacho ceremony, but she didn't explain the spiritual meaning."

"That's right, Luna," he chimed back. "That's precisely why I need you!"

Luna continued, "She didn't describe the San Pedro ceremony."

"No, I never did that with her. Only with special people."

He caught her eye and she saw something behind them again, and was almost certain she wasn't reading her own feelings into it. She wished he would share his thoughts, but knew better. "I found the San Pedro to be the most mystical and awakening of the ceremonies. I hope you agree, because I summarized my experience and explained how psychoactive plants have been used for thousands of years in religious and healing ceremonies in many cultures throughout the world."

Nico smiled at her approvingly, sitting down next to her again. Scrolling to the top so he could read, he stopped occasionally to re-word a few things. Even though he had a backward sense of grammar, she did what he asked. It didn't change the meaning, and this "script" was really only a guideline to the scenes to be shot anyway. When they got to the despacho ceremony, Nico asked, "Do you think it explains too much?"

Luna slipped up. "I thought Jacob *needed* more detailed explanation of the ceremonies."

She immediately realized what she'd done and saw that Nico caught her slip, too. He gripped her chin, pulling her face toward him. "How do you know that?" he asked menacingly.

Luna's voice caught in her throat, and for a second she couldn't respond. "I ran into Sofia in the ladies room at work—we only spoke for a minute, Nico."

He turned dark. "Why didn't you tell me before that you'd talked to Sofia?"

She feigned nonchalance, "I didn't think it mattered."

"Tell me the truth."

"I didn't want to upset you."

Relentlessly, Nico pursued, "But you kept a secret from me, Luna. What *other* secrets are you keeping?" He eyed her suspiciously.

Luna went on the defense. "I haven't kept any secrets from you, Nico. I just didn't want you to turn an innocent conversation in the ladies room into a drama—like this."

Nico paced back and forth, making Luna nervous. When he sat down again, she was relieved the incident hadn't escalated. She composed an e-mail to Erin and Jacob explaining the script was late because Nico had been traveling. No credit was given to Luna or Sofia for their assistance, and she realized she still craved Nico's approval. "Let me know if they like it. It's going to be such an outstanding film, and it'll be really good for your business."

Taking a quick look at her cell phone, she realized how late it was and knew Tyler was probably wondering why she'd been gone so long. Nico walked her to her car, and she was glad when he thanked her for the dreamcatcher. But as she got into the Land Rover, Nico cautioned her, "Don't betray me again, Luna."

"Never, Nico. I promise you," she replied.

He returned to the studio and Luna's eyes welled up with tears as she texted Tyler to let him know everything was OK, and she was on her way home.

His reply, *Whatever*, signaled he was clearly pissed off.

When she arrived home, Tyler was dressed and impatient to leave. His lean, athletic body looked great in tight dark grey jeans and a black zip-front knit top. His salt and pepper hair was perfectly tousled, making him look much younger. Darting past him, she called over her shoulder, "I'll only be a couple of minutes, promise." Slipping on a calf-length suede fringed skirt with a fitted black top and python printed sandals, she unfastened her hair from the clip and brushed it out so it fell luxuriously over her shoulders. Then she smudged some black kohl on her eyes and warm nude gloss on her lips, and was ready in less than fifteen minutes.

Tyler smiled. "You look beautiful."

She kissed him and took his hand as they walked to the elevator.

"Luna…I don't mind you helping Nico," Tyler said evenly. "Just remember who you're married to—and that I come first."

Luna was a bit shaken. She squeezed his hand and reassured him. "I know, Ty. I would never cross that line. You always come first."

15

When Luna heard the familiar ringtone "Knockin' on Heaven's Door," she panicked, fearing Nico was calling to cancel her session.

He sounded agitated. "Luna, come to Malibu instead of the studio, OK? I need you. Something's happened and I can't tell you on the phone."

"Is everything all right? Where's Sofia?"

"I just told you, not on the phone. Hurry up."

Thankfully, she had already packed a change of clothes and toiletries in the kilim bag she used for yoga. Trembling, she got in the car and headed to Malibu, wondering what could possibly be wrong. Luckily, there wasn't any traffic so early on Saturday morning.

To steady her nerves, she turned the Land Rover's stereo up and selected a playlist with a mix of Sia, Imagine Dragons, and Florence and the Machine. "Burn the Pages" pumped out of the car's speakers, and she sang along while convincing herself that Nico always exaggerated, and it was probably nothing. Pulling onto Malibu Road, she called his cell just to be sure it would be OK for her to pull into the driveway.

Nico answered, "Where are you? What's taking so long?"

His reply flustered her. "I just got here. Where should I park?"

Abruptly, he snapped, "What do you mean? Park here, in the driveway."

On the deck, the bright sunlight dancing off the pool stirred her memory of the party last September when Nico had pulled her into the water. Feeling fire butterflies surging from her belly down her arms to the tips of her fingers, she caught herself on the railing just as Nico slid open the glass door from the living room, a mug of coffee in his hand.

"Come inside. I have to show you something." She could hear the strain in his voice, and she followed him in, anxious about what he wanted to show her.

"Where's Sofia, Nico?" she asked, worried something had happened to her.

"She told me her sister's in town with some friends. They wanted to go out clubbing, and she said she would stay with them at the hotel, so she wouldn't have to drive home. But when I show you this, you tell me!" He pointed to the coffee table. "I think she lied to me. I think her parents are here, too."

On the coffee table sat three used brandy glasses and an open bottle of brandy. Nico looked back and forth between the table and Luna.

She shook her head and, looking at Nico, asked, "I don't understand. What are you showing me?"

Nico barked, "Luna! This is a message. How do you not know that?"

She looked at him incredulously. "What kind of message?"

"This is a warning sign from her father! He must've sent some of his goombah friends last night to threaten me. I didn't get home till late. They must have been waiting for me, and when I didn't show up, they left."

"You mean they were waiting for you...like to hurt you?" she exclaimed, now alarmed.

He answered sarcastically, "Wake up Luna! Yes, her father, the mob lawyer, called his goombahs to hurt me and scare me away from Sofia, thank you very much. That's exactly what I've been trying to tell you! So glad you finally caught on!"

"Fine, Nico. No need to badger me, please. I'm trying to understand how all this came about so I can help you, or at least be supportive."

"I'm sorry, Luna. It's just very upsetting. Obviously."

"So then, how did this all start?"

"When Sofia told me her sister was in town and that she was going out partying, I fought with her. I don't want her out drinking at clubs. I got a little rough, but nothing serious. She called her mother anyway. I've told her a thousand times not to call her mother every time we have a fight. But she's always crying to her on the phone."

Luna recalled Sofia telling her she had spoken to her mom once about Nico, but hadn't said she cried to her frequently.

Nico bemoaned, "I know she said shit about me to her father when he was here. I warned her. But she's a crybaby, and I can't be with a child. I have to be with a woman. I'm sure her mother told her father some shit, and he sent over his goombahs to threaten me."

"Wow…you think?" Luna wasn't sure what to believe. "That seems pretty extreme. Maybe Sofia left the glasses there? Maybe she and her sister had a drink," she offered.

"Luna, don't piss me off." He glared ominously. "Sofia wasn't here. I got that expensive bottle of brandy as a gift, and I hadn't opened it yet. This was a message, loud and clear."

She shivered. "Wow, Nico. I'm scared. What if he has you hurt? Or killed! This is serious."

"No, I'm not worried about that. They just want to scare me, I'm sure. But Sofia's made me look bad to her parents. That's not right. I've been good to her, and I cured her. She's never been healthier than she has with me. And because she is healthy, she's done her best work and even won that stupid award. All because of me! Now she goes and talks shit to her parents about me, and they want me out of the house and to stay away from her. And she doesn't have the backbone to stand up to them. She's already made excuses to me, saying this house is on loan from her father's client—some mobster—and they don't want me here. So, it's starting. I've been calling her all morning, and she hasn't answered her phone. She's afraid to speak to me, Luna. What am I going to do?"

"Nico, I'm sure everything's fine. She loves you, I know it. You just can't fight like that with her and make her cry. You're right, she never should have complained about you to her parents. They will only worry. I told you that you should've met them, or at least have gone to dinner with her father. Then they would know you."

"Do you think I'm too hard on her?"

"Yes, Nico. You *are* too hard on her. She's a young girl."

Luna didn't dare reveal that Sofia had been confiding in her for months. Instead, she did her best to console Nico. She went to get the bottle of brandy and wash the offending glasses, but he told her to leave them. Pouring herself a cup of coffee and refilling his, she said, "Come, Nico. Let's sit on the deck."

He followed her outside. "Luna, what will I do without Sofia? I love her. I know I'm too hard on her. But she knows I love her! I mean, she's my woman."

Luna thought to remind him he'd always said he loved Sofia only as a friend. And that business about not liking her smell. But she knew he needed Sofia, that she made his life easier and more comfortable. She did a lot for him, and he didn't want to lose that.

Nico's cell phone rang, and he put his finger up to silence Luna. "Sofia!" he said, but then he was silent, listening intently. "What do you mean in the hospital?" he screamed into the phone. "What's wrong with her!?"

He was silent again, listening, but began pacing furiously back and forth from one end of the pool to the other. "Put her on the phone!" he huffed, then barked, "Now, don't play games with me!" Whoever called must have hung up, because Nico made moves as if to throw the phone into the ocean.

"Luna," he called to her. "See what I'm dealing with here?" He walked toward her and sat down on the end of a chaise lounge. "Sofia made a huge scene! That was her sister, telling me Sofia had a breakdown and is in the hospital. They took her phone away and won't let me speak to her! Do you believe this?"

Confused, Luna tried to make sense of the story. First, Sofia and Nico had a fight about her going out dancing with her sister and some friends. Then, it escalated to mobsters coming to the house and leaving "signs." Now Sofia is in the hospital with a breakdown? Luna doubted she would ever know the truth.

Moments later, Nico's cell phone rang again. This time, he made the sign to hush but also signaled for her to listen by leaning his head next to hers. This time, rather than Sofia's sister, it was her mother. Nico mouthed to Luna, "See, her parents *are* here!" Sofia's mother spoke easily but firmly and told Nico he was no longer welcome to stay at the house, and that if Sofia didn't break things off with him herself, they would intervene.

Luna gasped silently, realizing that Nico was right. The used glasses must actually have been a warning sign! In any case, what she had heard was certainly threatening.

Nico began pacing again. "I would never hurt Sofia! She's exaggerating. No, that's not what happened."

Luna could hear Sofia's mother say, "There's no excuse for calling her names. From what Sofia told me, I feel you are verbally abusive to her, and I won't stand for it."

While Sofia's mother was speaking, Nico talked over her, "Sofia's being dramatic. I don't know what she is trying to do, but we love each other, and couples fight sometimes. All I said was that she couldn't go to the club. It's not safe, and she is my woman. I love her, and I do not see a reason for her to be out all night, even with her sister."

Luna nodded her head, encouraging Nico to remain composed while explaining himself. Luna could hear Sofia's mother arguing with someone nearby, but couldn't make out what was said. There was a gap of silence, then Nico repeated, "Hello? Hello?"

A few seconds later, Luna heard Sofia's voice, small and meek. "Why do you yell at me, Nico? You get me upset and make me cry. I just don't know if I can stay with you if it's going to be like this all the time."

Nico was distressed and almost sobbing into the phone, pleaded with her, "You're my woman. You know I love you." Pacing back and forth, he kept talking until Luna could tell things were going his way. After a few minutes, he said, "You tell them you exaggerated and that everything is good." After a pause he continued, "Well you need to tell your father. Otherwise, these guys will come for me."

Another pause, then he said, "No, I don't watch too much television. I know this." After a few minutes, during which Sofia must have been talking, Nico laughed, "Honey…"

Luna loved the way that word floated off his tongue. His accent gave it a rounded, mellow sound. He called her honey, too, as an endearment, not intending it to be too intimate, and she had started calling him honey as well.

He seemed to have quelled the storm, at least for the time being. "I'll be here waiting for you. All right, I'll try to be more in control. Just don't provoke me with your nonsense. No, I'm not starting. Just make sure you tell them you overreacted."

Sofia must have launched into a diatribe, because Nico kept interrupting. "Sofia, let me speak. I don't mean it when I yell at you. I just get frustrated…You never listen…Well, no, I don't want you running around to nightclubs without me. You know shit can happen. No, I don't think I'm overprotective. Someone can give you a drink that's spiked. No, I'm not exaggerating again."

Then Nico put the phone on speaker. Luna could hear Sofia whimpering about how much she loved him and that she was sorry she had caused so much drama. Then she said she would be home later, after her parents left.

When she asked if he still loved her, Nico replied, "Yes, of course I love you. When will you be home?" His voice was calmer knowing she was coming home. "Honey…"

That melting word again.

His voice became a whisper, "Text me when you're on the way. I'll be here. OK. Love you, too."

When Nico hung up the phone, he still paced nervously. Looking squarely at Luna as if she hadn't believed him, he said, "See, I told you they were all there, behind this. She made a big scene, causing me all this trouble."

Luna nodded in agreement.

"This isn't over. I'll have to recover from this. She'll make it up to me for causing all this drama."

Luna didn't comment or ask how Sofia was going to "make it up to him." She could see he was shaken up, yet he poured himself more coffee. But she knew better than to reprove him. When he offered to refill Luna's mug, she shook her head and said it made her jittery, hoping he would apply that logic to himself.

Suddenly, he blurted, "Let's do the session outside. It will relax me."

He was wearing heather lightweight grey running shorts and no shirt. Luna noticed that laying on his chest, bronzed from trips to Mexico, he wore a silver chain with a serpent medallion. "Nico, do you still have the Om pendant I gave you?"

Hesitating, he reached up to finger the chain around his neck, almost as if he wasn't sure what he was wearing. "Yes, of course, bella…"

Luna could see more clearly now that it was a dragon, and asked, "I know you like dragons. Did Sofia buy you that?"

Bluntly, he answered, "No. Erin gave it to me."

Luna exhaled sharply. "I see," she said, then quickly dropped the subject.

Nico excused himself to the bathroom, and Luna followed him into the white-on-white, brightly lit great room that overlooked the ocean. She could certainly understand Nico's desire to live here. She liked the cozy, intimate feel of his studio, with the dark walls and tribal artifacts, but the light, airy space of Sofia's house was starkly serene. He was in the bathroom longer than she expected, and she spent the time looking at the titles on the spines of Sofia's books and her collection of seashells. When Nico reappeared, he stood leaning against the counter and watched Luna attentively. "What, Nico?" she asked coyly.

"Nothing, bella. You look good—very beautiful."

Luna had on black flared yoga pants and a tank top with a graphic image of Ganesha the elephant, remover of obstacles—though he also places obstacles in the path of those who need to be checked. Shaking her head as if to brush off his flirtation, she replied, "You always tease me, Nico. Why do you do that?"

He replied innocently, "I don't know what you mean, Luna."

His hair was significantly longer than the last time Luna had seen him, and she wondered if it was by design or if he'd just been lazy about getting to the salon. Drinking in the sight of him, she observed he hadn't shaved. His scruffy beard made him even more alluring, conjuring up the image of a rogue figure from a romantic novel. Luna began to feel heady and unsure of herself, but, thankfully, a breeze swept in from the ocean through the open glass doors. She peered out at the sea to avoid his penetrating gaze.

"Luna, what is it you're thinking? Is something troubling you?" Nico prompted.

She turned back to face him. His smoky green eyes smoldered. She always felt like he could read her mind, making her uncomfortable. Suddenly she felt uneasy being in Sofia's house, as if her presence was illicit. Pushing her thoughts away, she collected herself. "Everything's fine. Can we do our session outside like you suggested?"

Nico gave a knowing chuckle. "Of course, bella. Let's get to it." He got up and took her hand, escorting her onto the deck. Seeing the mats were already in place, she felt a pang of jealousy, assuming he and Sofia did this together all the time. Sitting on the mat, she followed Nico's lead as they began an hour of yoga kriyas together. Sharing this moment with Nico, revitalized by the rhythmic sound of the waves, the smell of the salt water, and the feel of the ocean breeze through her hair, a peaceful contentment flooded her.

Focused on the kriyas, she drank in the sight of him without inhibition. A lock of his black hair fell over his brow. Guiding her through the mantras, his hypnotic chant mesmerized her. His spine erect in Siddhasana, arms resting elegantly on his knees, he appeared tranquil, his movements graceful and unhurried. Mimicking the asanas and mudras perfectly and synchronizing with his breath in the pranayamas, she felt as if their bodies moved together in a pas de deux. She wished he were always in this state of grace.

When she heard, "Namaste," the sun was high, raising the temperature on the deck. Luna stood up and stripped off her yoga pants and tank top—she was wearing a two-piece swimsuit underneath—and dove in the pool, taking Nico by surprise. But just as she had expected, he dashed in headfirst right after her and playfully swam between her legs. Luna sat on the side of pool, leaving her feet dangling in the water. Sweeping her hair to one side and twisting it around to keep it in place, she watched Nico swim laps, doing a perfect flipturn at each end of the pool. Then he hoisted himself onto the ledge next to her, his wet suit clinging to his thighs and outlining his manhood. Shaking his wet hair like a dog, he splashed Luna, who giggled with delight and pushed her hands against his chest as he laughed. Dispensing with her towel, she lay down next to him on the deck to dry off, basking in the warmth of the wood against her back. Closing her eyes, all sense of time evaporated.

"Come, bella. Let's walk on the beach."

Startled back into the present, she squinted, blocking the sun with one hand. Nico was standing over her. Luna obediently got up without questioning and padded behind him down the stairs in her bare feet. They walked a short distance to where the tide came up, where Luna watched the waves systematically erase each of Nico's footprints in the warm sand. Walking without speaking, she occasionally picked up a shell or small piece of sea glass, then finally said, "Did I tell you I won the Costume Designers Guild Award?"

Nico shook his head. "That's great, Luna! When?"

She looked down as they kept walking. "The awards were at the end of February. It was for best costumes in a Contemporary TV Series, but I doubt I'll get nominated for an Emmy."

"There's always next year," he offered.

Luna shook her head slowly. "No. All the period pieces get nominated. Like *Boardwalk Empire*, *Downton Abbey*, and *Game of Thrones*. I don't know, Nico. I'm getting to the age where Hollywood starts to push you out. I'm probably just about done with my career."

Nico stopped and embraced her. "Luna, bella," he said kindly. "Remember what I say about age—we have made it up. Just because Hollywood might not see your talent and value your wisdom doesn't mean you don't have it anymore."

His physical demonstration took her by surprise. Tearing up, she said quickly, "That's sweet, Nico. You say wise things…"

Taking her hand as they continued walking, he smiled. "I'm sure you were the most beautiful woman there."

They were silent for a while before Nico shared his thoughts. "Luna, I have so much going on. You know I'm going to Cannes in May to promote my film?"

They stopped at a pile of large rocks and sat down. He nervously bounced his leg. Petting his thigh, Luna politely overlooked that he had referred to *Amaru of the Andes* as *his* film. "So, Nico, that's great news. Why are you nervous?"

He confided, "What if the film makes me look like a…" He

couldn't think of the word. "A…cartoon of a shaman?"

Luna asked, "Do you mean a stereotype? Or a caricature of a shaman?"

Nico nodded. "Yes, exactly. Like it's a comedy or something. I want to be taken very seriously, and I want this documentary to help teach people about energy healing—that it's ancient and to be respected. I want to open people up to its power." He paused again. Then he looked at Luna. "Jacob showed me the first cut, and I actually like it a lot. I think I look good, but I want you to see it."

"I'd love to, Nico." They rose and began walking back to the house.

Nico continued sadly, "I have so much going on. I don't know if I'll be able to go home this year. I told Sofia I want her to come with me to meet Ita and Lucia."

Luna caught his hand as they walked. "I'm very glad to hear that, Nico. Does this mean you've finally reconciled that she's your girlfriend? I mean, you seemed pretty upset earlier."

He didn't look at her. "I suppose so. She's very good to me…but it's not passionate—as it should be—as I would like it to be. I just don't feel that way about her, as you know. But we are best friends, and maybe I will take your advice."

Luna winced when he called Sofia his best friend; Luna liked to think she was. Again sensing her feelings, he clasped her hand tighter. "Bella, don't be jealous. You know how much you mean to me. But I remind you again, you're married—and you're holding my hand!" Still, he didn't let go; in fact, he clasped it more firmly in his.

As they walked, he remained unusually quiet, then stopped, turned her to him, and swept her hair in his hands. "You look wild and beautiful here on the beach, Luna. Here with me."

She didn't respond—there was nothing she was brave enough to say. But she saw the wistful sadness in his eyes. She was usually the one to break eye contact, but this time it was Nico who looked down. "Luna! Your foot is bleeding!"

Startled, she looked down and saw that her foot was covered in blood. "Oh my! But it doesn't hurt, Nico. Don't worry." She stuck her foot in the water to clear away the sand and noticed a small cut on her middle toe that must have come from a shell or sea glass. And it was still bleeding.

"Let's walk back, Luna. I'll fix it up for you," Nico reassured her, holding her hand all the way to the house.

The bleeding had subsided, but Luna walked awkwardly through the living room on the way to the master bathroom, careful to not get any blood on the sisal rug.

A large antique sideboard painted a weathered shade of powder blue had been converted into a bathroom vanity by fitting a porcelain sink. It was just as Luna remembered from the party, except that Nico's personal toiletries were no longer visible, and she assumed they must now have a permanent home in the drawers of the vanity. "Sit, Luna," Nico commanded, taking charge as he gently guided her to the ledge surrounding the bathtub.

She watched with fascination as Nico opened one of the brass-handled drawers on the vanity and found a bottle of hydrogen peroxide. Dousing a cotton ball, he gingerly cradled Luna's foot in his hand and cleaned the bloody laceration, carefully examining it to be sure no foreign object remained embedded. Asking if it hurt, he lightly dabbed the wound, then selected the perfect size Band-Aid and gently wrapped her toe. "There, that should do it." He pursed his lips, proudly checking his handiwork. Looking at Luna from under his errant forelock, he asked, "Are you OK?"

Deeply moved by this tender ritual, Luna was speechless and just nodded her head. The intimacy overwhelmed her, and for some reason, made her feel like crying—not because she had cut her toe, and not because she wasn't going with him to Cannes or on trips to Mexico. She felt like crying because it had been a perfect act of love.

o   o   o

Luna looked around the room at the young pretty girls, wannabe actresses, and saw a few familiar faces.

Nico sauntered around the class, watching the students like a lion stalking a herd of antelope. His thin yoga pants and T-shirt clung to his body, revealing every rippling muscle. Passing by her mat near the front of the class, he knelt and adjusted her posture, placing his hand on her belly to feel her breath, his face inches from hers. Approaching the next student, he touched her shoulder with an eye for perfection, and Luna observed her beam in satisfaction at his attention. All eyes were upon him and vying for his attention—even the men.

After class, Luna was getting ready to leave when Nico stopped her. "Where are you going?"

"Home, I guess," she said, somewhat indecisively.

"Why don't you stay and keep me company?"

Skipping the locker room, she collected her things and followed him into his apartment.

He called out from the kitchen, "Would you like a drink?"

"Sure," she called back. He opened a bottle of wine and they moved to the sofa. Though it was dark, he didn't turn on any lights; instead, he lit a candle. Opening his laptop, he played around on YouTube, and soon Luna heard a painfully beautiful song in Spanish.

"Do you know this song?" he asked.

"No." She snuggled close to see the screen.

The video was of Richard Marx on acoustic guitar singing *"Ahora Y Siempre,"* "Now and Forever." Nico sang along, his gaze locked with hers and his eyes glowing, the yellow flecks twinkling in the candlelight. Luna only understood a few of the Spanish words, but it didn't matter. His voice was liquid, and he sang with such passion that her body pulsed with desire. He was so close, she could feel his body heat, and it made her uneasy. Why was he singing this to her? She feared he could sense her struggling with her feelings, but didn't want to look away and break the connection. After a few minutes, she picked up her glass of wine.

"What's wrong, Luna?" he asked cryptically.

"Nothing," she answered, hoping he hadn't noticed the tears pooling in her eyes.

Nico pressed, "Tell me what you're thinking."

Shaking her head, she didn't answer.

Nico continued probing. "Is everything OK with you and Tyler?"

"Yes, certainly! Why do you ask?"

He continued provoking her. "I don't think you love him, at least not the way I believe in love. You're good friends, but there's no passion. I see it in your eyes."

Defensively, she said, "That's not true, Nico. Passion changes over time. Besides, we've had this conversation *before*! I wouldn't change anything. My relationship with Tyler is *loving* and *intimate*."

Nico rolled his eyes, incensing her. "NO, it's not hot sex in the back of a truck—like with Olivia." She was audibly annoyed. "Stop, Nico. Just wait until you've been married as long as I have, then let's see where you are."

Nico shook his head. "I have awakened your sacral chakra, Luna. I'm afraid you *do* want more, but Tyler is not giving you want you want—what you need."

Luna took another sip of wine, then put the glass down and stood up. "I'd better leave. It's getting late." That love song had stirred too many feelings, making her uncomfortable.

Nico trailed behind her. "Luna. I didn't mean to upset you so that you would run away. Please, sit down."

She picked up her handbag.

"Sit down, Luna," he commanded, forcefully. She complied, but tears spilled down her cheeks. "Come here, bella. I'm sorry." He enveloped her in his arms, then looked into her eyes. "We'll work on it together. I will help you, I promise."

When she stopped crying, he clicked on another YouTube video, saying gently, "Look at this."

It was a World Cup soccer match from 1986 with the famous Argentine player Diego Maradona. Nico excitedly announced, "He's the best player who ever lived. Ever!" Then he went on to narrate the plays like one of the announcers, yelling, "Gooooaaaalll," when he scored.

Luna was relieved the love song was over, and she finally relaxed and laughed along with Nico.

When she collected her handbag again later, Nico reluctantly walked her to her car, opened the door for her, and gave her a list of safety instructions. She just nodded her head and smiled. His hand was resting on the window frame and she bent her head and kissed his knuckles, thanking him for a lovely evening. He pouted, "Ahhh, bella Luna. You are my special one. You're the only true friend I have in this world."

Luna whispered almost inaudibly, "I love you, Nico."

He sighed, "I love you too, Luna."

She started the engine, and he stepped away from the car as she pulled away.

o   o   o

Luna debated whether to head home or to the studio to see Nico. Earlier, Sofia had stopped by her office to say she'd told Nico she had accepted the job in New York. In between sobs, she admitted she'd been living a fantasy trying to make the relationship work—change him—make him better. She hated giving up, but knew she couldn't take the abuse anymore. At first, he'd flown into a rage, calling her every name in the book. Then he'd shut down and left—refusing her calls.

Nervous he would be able to tell she already knew, Luna flinched when her phone rang and saw it was Nico. She wasn't sure if she should, or would be able to cover it up.

At first, she didn't recognize his voice, then realized he was crying. "Nico, what's wrong? What happened?"

All she could understand between sobs was, "Can you meet me at the studio? Can you come now, please?"

When she got there, she found Nico in bed curled up in a ball. Sitting on his bed, she placed her hand gently on his shoulder. He shrugged her off, not wanting to be consoled. "What is it, Nico? What happened?" she asked.

His voice was listless. "She's leaving me. Everyone leaves me alone."

"What do you mean, leaving?"

Nico snapped, "Don't play dumb, Luna. Sofia's leaving me. She's going to work on some stupid show in New York."

She just went along, neither acting surprised nor admitting she already knew. "I'm so sorry, Nico. But it's obviously a good opportunity for her. How can she say no to the studio?"

He suddenly raged, "Both of you are such idiots! Why should she go back to New York? It's going backward! All the important people are here in L.A., not in New York! And *I'm* here! I'm a celebrity! If she leaves…I'm done with her."

Luna tried explaining, "Nico, turning it down wouldn't be looked on favorably. She'll come back."

He spat, "Fuck you, Luna. You women are all the same. This is what Olivia did to me, too."

Luna went on the defensive, "Well, Nico, if you love her, you would make it work. But you already told me you don't love Sofia the way you want, that you're not passionate about her. So maybe this is for the best, anyway."

Nico sat up straight. "Did you tell *her* that? Did you tell her to leave me?"

She stared him down. "Absolutely not, Nico! I think she's good for you, she loves you. I was disappointed you didn't feel that strongly for her!"

He didn't let up. With his heightened intuition, he always seemed to know when he was being deceived or if there were secrets or information hidden under the surface. "What did she tell you?" he asked. "Luna, you'd better tell me, and tell me now. Do not protect her. You're *my* friend, not hers."

Luna knew it was useless to try hiding anything from him. Making light of it, she gave an abbreviated version. "Sofia wrote me a couple of e-mails saying how angry you get if she doesn't answer the phone right away. I said you do the same thing to me if I don't answer. That it's. No big deal."

Nico paced around the room, persistently hammering her with questions. "So, what else, Luna? What else did she say? That's not all, is it? I know you! You're a busybody, always inserting yourself in my life, causing trouble."

She was shaken, and tried to steady herself before responding. "She stopped by my office a couple of times when she was upset. She told me you frightened her by driving recklessly on the way home from your dad's at Christmas. Nico, I worry so much about you. That was crazy. You both could've been killed!"

He fumed and yelled, the veins on his brow protruding. "Luna, I'm warning you. You should have told me she wrote to you and came to see you. This is a betrayal of our friendship! You're *my* friend, and you had no right to talk to my girlfriend about me behind my back!"

Luna tensed, feeling the panic rising. He was out of control, and she'd already said too much. Trying to recover, she explained, "Nico, the only reason she told me these things is because she met you through me, and I work on the show with her."

Nico glared at her, his eyes black with rage.

Now frightened, Luna blurted, "She came to my office! I didn't seek her out! I understand what you're saying, but just know that I wanted you two to work out—*not* break up. So anything I said was to help, not hinder! Regardless, I have nothing to do with the other show wanting her. This would be happening anyway!"

Nico wouldn't relent. "She exaggerated a lot. That drive was nothing, and I was completely in control. I just wanted to scare her a little bit. She does things her way, not the way I need them to be done. She fucked up a lot; like almost losing me that documentary with Jacob. She talked about me to Claudia's son and said things she should not have, so I was angry with her and drove fast to scare her. You are stupid. When we got home, I fucked her brains out. She loved it! You don't know her the way I do, and she played you. Now she's playing this game of going to New York. Well, she'll see. I'm not waiting around for her."

Luna started to cry. She was devastated that he was angry and blamed her. But she felt bad for him, knowing how upset he was that Sofia was leaving. "I'm sorry, Nico. I should've told you that she came to speak to me, but I think she just needed a woman to talk to."

He stopped pacing, and she sensed him calming down. Emphatically, in his most stern voice, he said, "Luna, promise me—you will always come to me first. And you will *never* talk to any of my girlfriends without telling me."

"I promise, Nico. I'm very sorry, and I promise to never do that again." She hugged him and kissed his neck, then took his hand and kissed that, too.

Nico shook his head. "You've really betrayed me, Luna. I don't know if I can trust you."

Somewhere between a plea and a pledge, she vowed, "Nico, you can always trust me! I will never leave you. I love you too much."

16

Erin had just returned from a long walk down the beach with Blue and was in her bedroom changing into a white monogrammed terrycloth robe when she heard Nico's Ducati pull into the carport. She brought a matching robe out onto the deck and greeted him with two filled wine glasses when he reached the top of the stairs. The view of the setting sun brought to mind a Turner watercolor, and Nico marveled at the spectacular panoramic vista from Erin's deck. Fascinated when he saw the dog's eyes glowing a silvery blue-grey color in the fading light, he remarked, not for the first time, how much Blue looked like a real wolf.

The days were almost at their longest; the evening air was warm and the tide was high. Bob Marley radio on Spotify played softly through the outdoor speakers. Nico took his wine and gazed out to sea. "I like it here, Erin. It's so peaceful."

"I'm glad you do, Nico." Her robe was open enough to see the tattooed dragon emerging across her chest.

He worried aloud, "Erin, I need to grow my business, not just get more clients and teach more classes. I want a TV show and a book. I need to make more money without more hours. You know what I want..."

She nodded. "I know, Nico. You have all the right ingredients. What we need to do is make you a lifestyle brand, a celebrity."

He extended his hand to stroke the dragon's back with his index finger. He didn't look at her, just thoughtfully petted the dragon in a quiet state of meditation. Erin didn't say anything, not wanting to startle him out of his reverie. When he emerged from his thoughts, she led him to the cushioned sofa facing the sea, where she'd laid out a platter of chips and guacamole. "You look tired, Nico. Is everything all right?"

He sighed. "I *am* tired. Cannes was a long trip. But I'm glad I went, especially since the film won. Now I have a lot of work to do. I have to spin that to get more publicity from it."

"I know."

Nico looked her in the eye. "I need you to hook me up with a deal like the one you have. A TV show, a book deal—that's what I need, Erin."

She laughed lightly, not wanting to offend him. "Nico, I've paid my dues, and now I own one of the top branding agencies in the country! Give yourself a break. You'll get there."

He nipped sarcastically, "Right! Thank you very much!"

She tried to be more playful, "So what's the deal with Alexa Morgan? Did you fuck her?"

Nico glared; the yellow in his eyes becoming lightning bolts shooting through her. "Shut the fuck up, Erin. Besides, you're no different! You fuck me, too!"

"Oh!" She stung from his remark. "I thought we had fun, Nico."

His ire abated. "We do. I didn't mean it like that. You're not like her. We're good friends, and I enjoy being with you. You know that, right?"

Relieved, she smiled. "Well, at least I thought so."

Nico sighed again, "I'm just really burned out." He drank some of his wine and dipped a chip into the guacamole, considered it carefully, then dipped another one. "Did you make this from scratch like I do?"

She chuckled, "Right, me make guacamole from scratch—are you high?" She paused, but when he didn't reply, she continued, "That reminds me." Reaching into the pocket of her robe, she pulled out a clear packet filled with white powder. Nico smiled. Erin took the marble slab from under the bowl of chips and laid out a few lines, producing a straw from the same pocket. They each did a few bumps while they watched the pink and blue colors of the sunset intensify.

Erin rose and opened her robe, walking toward the hot tub. The wolf tattoo on her shoulder blade came to life as she moved. Letting the robe fall to the ground, she stepped in. The bubbling water, illuminated by the lights in the tub, reflected in her grey eyes as she looked at Nico. He walked over and placed his hand in the water to feel the temperature. "Hot," he said, studying her as he removed his shirt and unzipped his jeans.

While he was climbing in, Erin admired the dimples in his perfectly formed buttocks. She noticed the tension fall away from him when he closed his eyes, allowing the heat to penetrate his body. His skin was luminous in the soft light of the hot tub, and she watched his lean muscles flex as he found a comfortable position, like a wildcat settling into a lair. A curled lock of his hair fell in front of his eyes and he cupped the water from the tub into his hands to rake it back.

She quietly floated over to him and wrapped her hands around his buttocks, moving her body against his and rocking her hips gently. As the water sloshed between them, Nico began to stir under her. Pulling her in closer, he ran his hand along the small of her back, caressing her hip and thigh, then slowly along her abdomen until he found her soft mound. With one finger, he gently spread her labia open, probing the rim of her pussy and massaging her clit until she groaned, pressing hard against him. Her breasts floated buoyantly in the water, and he bent his head, his lips teasing first one nipple, then the other. Feeling the euphoria of the drug, the heat, and Nico consume her, Erin closed her eyes. Gently, he pushed in, opening her up using a slow scooping motion along the velvety walls of her pussy. With just the right amount of pressure, he found her G-spot, and she arched her back, letting out a low moan, her breasts heaving upward toward his mouth. He inserted two, then three fingers, sliding them in and out slowly, taking care to pay close attention to her clit, rolling over it and teasing before pushing his fingers back deep inside. Wrapping her arms around his shoulders, she bore down, grinding harder onto his hand as she climbed higher. With the steam rising from the hot tub she felt as if in a dream, awash in sinful sensation.

Even in the water, he could feel her juices running and her pussy clenching his fingers. "That's it, baby. Fuck my hand. Come for me," Nico whispered into her ear.

His words fueling her lust, Erin pushed her hands into his hair, finding more leverage. She could feel his hard cock pressing against her belly when she leaned into him, but he made no move to enter her. She was so near climax—she couldn't stop. As she arched her back, thrusting harder and harder onto him, the water made sucking sounds between them.

He purred, "Come baby. Come for me. I love it when you howl at the moon."

She was breathless, her body straining. The heat of the water, the coolness of the air, the rhythm of the music—everything filled her completely with ecstasy. Crying out, she closed her eyes and bucked with the intensity of her orgasm, lost in the wash of pure pleasure as her world crashed around him.

Melting onto him, she recovered. No one had ever been able to make her come like that. It was a truly holistic experience—feeling the climax intensely in her body, mind, and soul. When she opened her eyes and looked at him, he wore a devilish grin, and the yellow flecks of his eyes glinted in the dim light.

"I hope that was good for you, baby. Now it's my turn," he growled. Pulling himself up to sit on the first step of the tub, he stroked the length of his rock-hard erection. He was beautiful to watch. The lights of the tub illuminated each protruding vein and the perfectly formed head of his cock. Erin just had to stare for a moment. He seemed even larger in the reflected light of the water. His long fingers encircled the thick width of his shaft as he firmly pulled back along the length. She watched his dark, damp hair fall over his face, and he seemed to be in a trance, his dark green eyes flickering mysteriously from under long lashes.

Erin knelt between his legs, and caressed his thighs with both hands. He lay back onto his elbows as she sucked him, taking him into her mouth and placing her hand firmly around his thick, long shaft. She gazed up, locking eyes with him as she twirled her pierced tongue around the head. Decadently sucking the tip between her lips, she pressed the small metal ball of her tongue stud along the rim. He let out a low moan as she teased and licked him. The rising and falling of his hips made waves in the shallow water, and the heat from the hot tub was electrifying. She rubbed the tip along the roof of her mouth, massaging his head with her tongue, the metal stud working its magic. Spreading his thighs apart, she teased his balls, then gently put them in her mouth. The water lapped at her chin and washed over his cock as she fondled him and licked the space between his balls and anus. Gently, but firmly, she ran her finger from the base of his groin to the entrance. His back arched upward and his thighs tightened when she slowly pressed her middle finger inside, causing him to gasp, then moan in supplication.

As she took him deeper, he laced his fingers into her hair, holding her head to him so he could fuck her mouth. His hips bucked upward as he groaned with pleasure, encouraging her to explore further. With each push inward, his thrusts became more urgent. Then he relaxed, and she could feel him open up for her. With his head tipped back and his eyes closed, he rocked his hips. The water slapped against his buttocks and washed over him, his body arching and hips lifting each time she plunged her finger deep into him. Holding her head tightly to him, he grabbed fistfuls of hair. With one powerful thrust, he came hard, pulsing over and over into her throat, calling in a low strangled growl, "Ya acabo!" with a blissful need she'd never heard before.

She looked up, and Nico pulled her up to embrace her tightly. Normally, he was playful, but tonight he was just spent. Not wanting to be an obligation fuck like Alexa, Erin wanted to please him, and judging from his response, she'd done well. When she felt him unwind from the powerful orgasm, she got out of the tub and put on her robe, then held one open for him. He stepped into it and walked over to the table to pour himself another glass of wine. "Hungry?" he asked.

Erin answered, "Come in the kitchen. I'll make some tacos."

o   o   o

When she woke from her dream, Luna buried her face in the pillow and cried. She longed to hear his dulcet voice and listen to him play Spanish love songs on the guitar. In her dream, she was walking and saw Nico on the other side of the street. He was wearing a black and red backpack. She impatiently waited for a break in the traffic,

226

then hurried across. Losing sight of him, she ran to catch up, only to spot his backpack sitting on a low stone wall. She sat down next to it, expecting Nico to return. Though she had a long wait, when he arrived he sat down next to her, and laying his head upon her shoulder, he cried. Luna held him, crying as well, and their tears blended together.

She got up to call his cell phone, and was surprised when he answered. His voice was brusque and detached, "What do you want, Luna? I'm busy." He was always busy now with Alexa, his new rainmaker.

She immediately choked up, unable to speak.

"You betrayed me, remember? Because of you, I'm alone and I have to do everything myself."

Feeling a sharp pain in her chest, she said meekly, "I want to help you. I'm here for you."

"I can't trust you anymore. You went behind my back. I thought you were my friend."

"I *am* your friend."

"After all I've done for you! I gave you your life back. If it wasn't for me, you never would have won that award. Why did you do what you did?"

"I let her speak to me—but Nico, I always wanted you two to work out, to be together. It's not my fault they asked her to join the other show!"

"You'll have to prove yourself. I don't know…you did a bad thing."

"Nico, I miss you. I'm sorry. I *am* your friend…always."

He remained on the line, but was silent. At least he'd answered, she thought. At least he spoke to her. "Nico…?"

"Yes, Luna, I'm busy. I'm working—doing the schedule—I have a lot to do."

"Can I come over?"

"You need to apologize. You still don't admit what you did. When you understand, we'll see about letting you back in my life."

He hung up, and Luna sat staring into space, tears streaming down her cheeks. She was angry with herself for talking to Sofia behind his back. And she *had* apologized to Nico for not telling him.

Clearly, Sofia leaving for a new job wasn't her fault.

She pieced things together in her mind, and recalled Sofia saying she confided in her so that if "anything happened," Luna would know the truth about Nico. She painfully remembered Sofia telling her that Nico had said, "my mother sent you to me," and how that was a stab to Luna's heart, causing a sharp pang of jealousy. Sofia *must* have known that Nico had said the same thing to her. Luna began to think Sofia's using her as a sounding board might have been manipulation, playing into Luna's weakness for connection to Nico, and she wished she could erase her mistake. Somehow, Luna thought, she would have to work her way back into his life and prove her loyalty to him.

She then conceded, if she wanted Nico back in her life, she would have to accept that she was completely at fault.

> *Dear Nico,*
> *You are right. I betrayed you. Sofia knew I missed*
> *you. She began sending me e-mails to involve me*
> *and paint a bad picture of you, so that when she*
> *left you—as she planned to do—you would not*
> *have me, either. Nico, I am so sorry. I know you*
> *will need time to regain trust in me. After realizing*
> *this, I knew if the situation were reversed, I would*
> *feel betrayed as well. I know you can never forget,*
> *but maybe you can find it in your heart to forgive.*
> *Love, Luna.*

Nico called, his tone cool. "Luna, I can't believe you did this to me, but I will give you another chance. I told you she was a snake and she played you."

She whispered, "I know, Nico. I'm so sorry."

He sounded almost sympathetic, saying, "I know. You're too naïve. But I warned you that you couldn't trust her. She's manipulative."

Luna's voice was hushed. "I know. I didn't listen. Again, I'm sorry."

He reminded her, "Instead, you talked behind my back." He was still angry and hurt every time he thought about how Luna had kept a secret from him, and for that he would punish her. "It'll take time for me to trust you again."

Her voice quivered, "I know."

Nico sighed, sounding exhausted. "I'm tired of the day to day. I'm just not getting where I need to be fast enough. You understand what I'm saying, right?"

"Be patient, Nico. You'll get there." His despair wrenched her. The space between them felt too vast. She wished she could hold him.

"You can start by coming over this weekend and helping me. Alexa said she needs a business plan to give these investors who want to put Amaru studios around the world."

Silence. Luna wasn't sure if the call had dropped.

"I need this, Luna…and I know you can do it."

He needed her! Wanting to be part of him again, she agreed. "Of course I'll help you."

∘   ∘   ∘

Erin's house parties were reported to be among the best in L.A., and now the place was decked out for her July 4th celebration in an understated, cool, but sophisticated style, reflecting the taste level expected from Grey Dog.

California Chandon sparkling wine flowed, along with Monkey Paw Brewing Company's pale ale. Erin was never traditional, and tonight was no different. She wore a Vivienne Westwood black, asymmetrical, draped dress with plunging V in front to reveal her dragon tattoo and black and silver stingray four-and-a-half-inch gladiator sandals. She could barely walk, but damn they looked hot.

She'd booked a live cover band with saxophone, keyboard, drums, and guitars to play a varied mix of favorites, rather than having a DJ. She was pleased, knowing her choice for music was ideal. Guests were dancing to the classic R.E.M. song, "Losing My Religion." When Nico arrived, several heads turned, and Erin couldn't help but smile. She hadn't seen him in a while. She'd been away at Cannes Lions, then he'd messaged her a few times from Mexico. He usually wore distressed jeans and a black T-shirt, but tonight he had on aqua-green slim-cut trousers, cuffed slightly at the bottom, with Japanese print espadrilles, a tight, V-neck white T-shirt that showed off his six pack underneath, and a blue-black linen blazer with the sleeves pushed up. A single long strand of Buddha prayer beads hung around his tanned neck. She liked his central-casting European model image choice, complete with appropriately layered silver, woven, and beaded bracelets on both wrists. He had his hair slicked back off his face, accentuating his prominent brow. Erin wondered if he thought he was dressing for the holiday festivities, but nevertheless, he was the hottest-looking guru at the party. Several women greeted him as he made his way to the bar to pick up a glass of Chandon.

When Nico saw Erin, he paused to look her up and down. Then they exchanged the traditional double-cheek kiss. "Erin, you look absolutely daring tonight," he purred.

She replied with a bewitching smile, fingering his long beads. "And you, my dear, look like a GQ ad!"

As if on cue, the band began playing Guns N' Roses' "Sweet Child O' Mine," and, breaking out his air guitar, Nico sang along.

Erin laughed out loud and spun around on her heels with the refrain, *Whoa, oh, oh, oh, sweet child o' mine.* "Let's go mingle, Axl Rose!" she chirped, taking Nico by the hand. Dragging him into the mix of people, she made introductions to some of her powerful friends and clients along the way.

Later, Nico and Ted were discussing the Gold Fountain account, brainstorming ideas for the *Beauty at Any Age* campaign, and Ted's eyes were glazing over as Nico droned on about cleansing Hucha, heavy energy. Thankfully, Jacob Kafka arrived and provided a welcome interruption. Ted reached out his hand to shake Jacob's, saying, "Congratulations, on the award."

Jacob modestly deflected the attention toward Nico. "I see you're speaking to the master of energy medicine."

Jacob embraced Nico warmly, then said, "I hear from Erin the three of us have a new project together for Gold Fountain."

Ted nodded. "Yes. As a matter of fact, Nico was just explaining some concepts to me, but I'm afraid I'm going to need a tutorial!"

Nico laughed. "Then come to Amaru next week, both of you, and I'll conduct a San Pedro ceremony. That will literally blow your mind."

Erin sidled up to Nico, taking his strong bicep between her hands. She gave Jacob a friendly kiss, then pulled Nico away with her apologies. "Nico, I need you to come meet Dr. Patricia Gold, the founder of Gold Fountain. I proposed you be the face in the campaign for *Beauty at Any Age*, but she's the one to impress with your magical, mysterious charm!"

After being introduced, Dr. Gold dove right in, "So, Nico, tell me about yourself."

Erin was pleased at the million-dollar smile Nico flashed as he said, "Well, the most important thing is that, like you, I help people regain their youth and vitality. You do it on the outside, and I do it from the inside!"

Dr. Gold returned the smile, and Nico continued, "I learned about energy healing and shamanism by living with the paqos in the Andes. And I taught yoga in Kerala, India. Combining the two practices gives me an advantage."

Dr. Gold listened intently, asking only a few questions; she was really listening to his velvety voice and the passion he held for his work.

When Nico paused to take a drink, Dr. Gold asked, "How did you decide to combine those two practices?"

He launched right in, "Those two areas aren't really different at all. I'm sure you know, Dr. Gold, that all matter in the universe is connected. With the paqos, I learned to listen to the spirit in all things around us to help me diagnose someone's particular disorder. I use both together to quickly cleanse people of heavy energy and move the *prana*—the life-force—upward through the chakras." Nico held Dr. Gold captivated with his warmth and interesting explanation.

When Erin returned, Dr. Gold turned to her, "Well, Erin, I must say I really like the idea of my company nourishing from the outside while Nico does the same from the inside. Can we have a meeting— all of us," she nodded toward Nico, "next week in your office?"

Erin grinned. "Absolutely. I'll have Melissa call to find a mutually convenient time."

"Fine," Dr. Gold replied. "And now, much as I hate to, I must go. I have another engagement."

She turned to Nico and extended her hand. "Nicolás, it was very nice to meet you. I'm looking forward to seeing you again."

Nico gazed intently into her warm, brown eyes. "Patricia," he purred softly as he kissed the back of her hand, "The pleasure was all mine."

Dr. Gold caught her breath. "Until we meet again."

After she'd left, Erin rolled her eyes. "Nico, be careful with Patricia. She's a smart woman, and she'll know she's being played."

He feigned sincerity. "Why would you think I'm playing her? I was being sweet—for you."

Erin shook her head. "Come dance with me. I love this song!"

The band was playing "Walkin' on the Sun" by Smash Mouth, and Nico burst out laughing when he realized the lyrics. "It figures! This is your song for sure, Erin!" He swiped another glass of bubbly from a passing waiter as they danced their way across the deck.

∘　∘　∘

Nico didn't greet her with the double-cheek kiss she'd come to expect. Instead, pointing to his desk, he gruffly ordered her to straighten up, starting with the mail. "You are going to have to prove yourself, Luna. You betrayed me."

Without contesting, she solemnly sorted the unopened mail and gathered together the crumpled receipts that were strewn all over his desk. Nico was laying on his bed, one eye on the television while texting with someone. Her back was to him. Unfolding the receipts, she ironed them out with her hand and made a separate pile. Several were from Tulum, but she dared not comment. He was in no mood, and she had lost his favor. "Don't be nosy, Luna!" he bellowed from the other room.

She jumped. The callous tone of his voice was alarming, sending a wave of anxiety through her like a charge of electricity. "I'm not. I'm just organizing things nicely for you." Though she attempted to sound unruffled, her voice cracked slightly from suffering the pain of his rude indifference to her.

Luna had initially defended herself, but Nico had made a convincing case that she was jealous, and she began to question her intentions. She *had* missed him a great deal during his relationship with Sofia. However, the Nico she had back now wasn't the same. But he was right about at least one thing—she should never have welcomed Sofia's confessions. Now she was desperately trying to regain his trust and affection.

Stepping into the apartment, she let him know she'd completed her tasks and that she was leaving. His eyes still on the television, he was curt, "Where are you going?"

"Home. I finished."

"Straighten up the apartment."

She felt like bolting, mortified at the thought of what Tyler would say if he saw her obsequiously laboring as Nico's maid and allowing him to treat her with such disrespect. Tears welled in her eyes as feelings of humiliation mixed with sadness and remorse for betraying him overwhelmed her.

While she was cleaning his apartment, she stole glances at him preparing dinner in the kitchen, wielding the chef's knife with skill. He worked intently, his strong neck bent swan-like over the cutting board and hair spilling forward over his eyes.

When she was done, she put her tote bag on her shoulder and said meekly, "I finished, Nico, I'm gonna go…"

"Do you want to stay for dinner?"

Welcoming his sudden congeniality, she didn't hesitate to answer, "Sure."

Still feeling like she was walking on eggshells, she set two places at the coffee table with placemats and cloth napkins, then poured two glasses of wine. He dished up two plates of roasted chicken with rice and beans—her favorite. There was something about his rice and beans that made them more delicious than any restaurant she'd ever been to. Unexpectedly, he lit a candle and sat down next to her on the sofa, leg to leg. Afraid to breach the precarious peace, Luna remained silent as they ate.

Then he surprised her again by saying, "I'm sorry I've been in such a bad mood. Thank you for helping me today."

Luna nodded and smiled, saying nothing for fear of setting him off. He seemed to soften, but she suspected he was testing her. She would have to remain patient, and hopefully he would warm up to her again.

After dinner, he played the guitar. Luna tucked her feet under herself and was listening when she noticed a hardcover picture book on the coffee table and pulled it over to page through. The book was filled with pictures of Nico with Alexa Morgan; so, out of curiosity, she paged back to read the foreword. Written there was a dedication, "To Nico. Love, Alexa." Luna continued paging through, looking at the pictures of them on the beach, on a boat, doing yoga, having cocktails—all in Tulum, Mexico. *What the fuck*? But she pretended it was just an ordinary book and kept looking without commenting. When she got to the end, she looked up at Nico.

"Don't look at me like that," he cautioned. "Alexa is my client, and we went to Tulum on business. All the movie stars go there for Reiki and yoga, and she thinks it's a good idea for me to have a presence there. We met with investors and I had private sessions with celebrities who paid a lot of money. She said I can charge thousands of dollars for the San Pedro and despacho ceremonies."

Luna didn't say anything, just closed the book and pushed it away dismissively, like spoiled food.

His attempt to mollify surprised her. "Luna, don't worry. I'm the busiest I've ever been. All these things are happening for me. I've been using the documentary for promotion and that's going great, and Alexa has guaranteed me a movie part with a big director. She's a client *and* a business partner, like an agent."

Luna nodded, but her displeasure was apparent.

Nico smiled persuasively. "I need you to design a line of yoga clothes to sell at the studio in Tulum and the new center in Beverly Hills. Everything is on track for me to become a celebrity brand."

She put her head on his shoulder the way she always used to, and though she thought he flinched, she stayed close. She wasn't sure how much of what he'd spouted was real and how much was his pipe dreams. But she was encouraging, "I'm so glad for you, Nico. It's all happening, just as you dreamed it would." She paused, then added, "Just be careful what you wish for."

He pulled away, looking at her reproachfully, as if he sensed she didn't entirely believe him. "What do you mean, Luna?"

Remaining calm, she said sweetly, "I mean that people think it's great to be rich and famous—a celebrity. But I work with celebrities every day, and just because they earn millions and have adoring fans doesn't mean they're happy. Money and fame are no guarantee of happiness; that's all I'm saying."

To her relief, Nico nodded in agreement, seeing she was speaking philosophically and not judging him. "I know, Luna. But I'm only one person, here in this little studio in L.A. with a tiny apartment in the back. I want more than this."

Encouraged by his explanation, she went on, "I know you do, Nico, and I understand. But you need to prepare yourself for the pressures that come with celebrity status. Don't think it's easy. An awful lot of people want a piece of you, and you never know who your friends are."

Nico squeezed her thigh. "I know you are my friend."

She returned his smile, and he added, "Just please be here for me and help me. I can handle it if I have your help."

Luna put her head back on his shoulder, and in a soft, consoling voice, said, "I love you, Nico. Of course I'll help you…and be there for you in every way I can."

He couldn't pass up the opportunity to remind her, "Don't ever betray me again, Luna. Next time, I won't forgive you."

17

Sam and two assistants were lining up the wardrobe, and new talent filed in hourly for fittings. Luna left her laptop open so when she had a few minutes she could work on Nico's business plan. She'd been researching the yoga industry, as well as Reiki and energy healing, yet Nico was driving her crazy asking why she hadn't finished yet. Picking up a call from him, she snapped, "Nico, I'm working as quickly as I can. This is a lot of work!"

He sniffed, "Don't exaggerate just to make it seem like a big deal. It should take a couple of hours. You're just bullshitting to waste time."

Infuriated, she barked back, "Well then, would you rather do it yourself?"

Harshly, Nico snapped, "Luna, don't start, or you'll be very sorry."

At her wits' end, she sobbed, "Nico, please don't speak to me that way. I'm working very hard to make this right."

He sighed, "OK. Just keep working on it and keep me posted."

Only a couple of minutes after they'd hung up, he texted her to put in pictures—lots of pictures—of him throughout.

Luna texted back:

We can add them later.

Moments later, her phone rang and bracing herself, she answered. Without pausing for hello, Nico yelled, "Do as I say! I want the pictures in there *now*—so I can see them!"

His obsessive demands were giving Luna a stomachache.

When he then demanded she come by after work so he could

review her progress, she balked, "Nico, I can't stay long. I have plans this evening." But he had already hung up.

At Amaru, after waiting in Nico's office for him to finish a class, Luna poked her head into the room to signal him. He finished chatting with a pretty young student before brushing past her, annoyed. "Don't ever do that jealous number, Luna. I'm working and these are my students. They already think you're blowing me!" he said brusquely.

She gaped, "Nico, that's disgusting! I'm certain they don't think that!"

"Well, Erin and Alexa think so. Erin asked me the other day, 'Is Luna still in love with you?'"

She let his snide comment drop. "I don't have much time; Tyler's waiting for me. Can we please review this project?"

Sitting down, Nico started reading, bouncing his leg rapidly. Luna pushed on his thigh to stop him, as she had done in the past, but this time Nico glared at her. She was taken aback, "What's the matter, Nico? Why are you behaving this way toward me? I'm helping you."

He pushed back. "You're taking too long, and people are waiting for this. It will be your fault if I lose this opportunity. This all should have been done months ago. You think this is a game? Take off your jacket! You aren't going anywhere!"

Luna was incredulous, "What do you mean?" When he didn't reply, she protested, "I have to leave now. You can read this tonight, and I'll come back to review it with you tomorrow morning and I can work all day on Saturday. Tonight I have plans with Tyler."

She moved to stand up, but Nico grabbed her elbow roughly. "Luna! I said you...are...not...going...anywhere!"

Panicking, Luna's voice rose several octaves, "Tyler will be furious. This isn't right! I can do it tomorrow. Why do you always want me in trouble with Tyler?"

Softening his tone a notch, Nico cajoled, "Luna, I'm your friend and I need you. And as a friend, I need you *tonight*, not tomorrow." His voice took on a darker tone. "So you call Tyler and tell him your *friend* needs you tonight." He paused to let her absorb his command. "Besides, you owe me. If it wasn't for me, you never would have won that award. If you don't stay and help me, then walk out that door and never come back."

Luna froze. There had been times in the past when Nico had *persuaded* her to stay, saying he needed her. But this time she was frightened—he wasn't persuading, he was demanding. Squelching her fear, she tried to steady her voice. "Nico, please," she begged, "I promise to come and work tomorrow. I don't want to piss Tyler off."

Nico was cold and uncompromising. "I want you to do it NOW. This project is already late. Are you telling me dinner with friends is more important than my business—and our friendship?" He let the implied threat hang in the air for a few moments. "Because that's what you make it sound like."

Luna trembled, knowing Tyler would be angry. He already resented the amount of time she devoted to Nico. But having almost lost Nico, Luna had to prove herself or risk losing him forever. Relenting, she steadied herself and called Tyler. "Honey, something's come up. Nico needs the proposal I've been working on for a meeting tomorrow. I didn't get a chance to finish and didn't realize it was late. So I really need to stay. I'm so sorry, but can we please cancel our dinner plans?"

She held her breath. Tyler answered in a measured way, "I'll cancel our plans, but I'm not happy. This is wrong, and you have to think about what you're doing to our relationship. Let me know when you're coming home." Then he abruptly hung up.

After just staring at the phone for a moment, she took a breath and turned to Nico. "Let's get this project done. I wouldn't want you to think I don't do enough for you."

By midnight, Luna was starving and parched. Nico hadn't offered her a morsel of food, and she'd been too distraught to even get up for a drink of water. He had punishingly obsessed over every word she wrote. Exhausted, she finally pleaded, "Nico, I'm ready to faint. I'm so hungry and thirsty. I don't feel well."

"Fine. Go home," Nico glowered.

Picking up her bag, Luna ran to her car, bursting into tears as she fled. She had driven about a mile when her phone rang. Seeing it was Nico, she pulled over to side of the road. He spoke softly, sounding a bit remorseful, "Thank you for staying. I'm sorry I was nervous. I'm under a lot of pressure. You know that."

"I'm sorry, too, Nico. I know you are, and I want to help you. I just don't want to upset Tyler."

"I need this, Luna. I'm trying to get to the next level."

"I know. I understand…"

Nico sighed, "So can you please come back tomorrow? We need to finish."

"Of course. I'll be there early. See you tomorrow."

Neither one of them hung up.

After waiting a few seconds, Luna asked, "Are you still there?"

"Yes," he replied quietly.

She whispered, "I love you, Nico."

"I love you, too."

Tears welled up in her eyes, and she blinked to clear her vision before resuming the drive home.

o   o   o

Pulling on a pair of boho style printed pants and a T-shirt, Luna went to the kitchen to make breakfast and read the paper with Tyler—something they enjoyed doing together almost ritually. After the stressful night before with Nico, she appreciated the comfort of being home, in her secure, safe haven with Tyler.

When Tyler suggested a movie, she hesitated, thinking how important the business plan was to Nico. Shaking her head, she replied apologetically, "I didn't finish last night. I was thoroughly exhausted and couldn't see straight. I promised Nico I'd finish today, but he hasn't answered the phone. I'm worried."

Tyler shrugged. "I don't know, Luna…you do so much for him and he just keeps taking. Enough is enough, don't you think?"

She grew annoyed that her day had been left up in the air. She would much rather do something with Tyler, but Nico would flip out if he finally called and she wasn't available.

Embarrassed by Tyler's on-target assessment, she nonetheless didn't want to lose Nico. When she thought she had lost him, she'd been miserable. "He doesn't have anyone else to help him. He needs me. We can go to the movies tomorrow…"

"I know he's your project Luna—and you like feeling needed. But you drop everything for him. No matter how much you do for him, it will never be enough. He *uses* you, and I hate to see you being taken advantage of."

Feeling defensive, she replied, "I'm not. Nico's helped me, too. I'm feeling so much better about myself. Besides, we're friends."

"I'm not so sure, Luna. Just be careful."

o   o   o

Around 4:00 p.m., Nico answered his phone, groggy, "I just woke up."

"Did you go out?" Luna asked the seemingly obvious.

"Yeah, I got bored and was lonely, so I went out," he replied casually. "Can you come over now?"

"Sure, I'll be there in a few minutes." She surmised the reason he hadn't wanted her to leave and made her stay the night before was because he was lonely. It wasn't the urgency of the business plan! It was that he couldn't stand to be alone.

Luna changed into distressed boyfriend jeans, threw a poncho sweater over her T-shirt, and with car keys in hand, found Tyler at his desk. Wrapping her arms around him, she gave him a warm, lingering kiss on the lips. "I'll miss you today, honey. I would so much rather just cuddle with you and watch a movie here."

He returned the kiss. "Yeah, until something else comes up." The terse reply revealed his hidden anguish that she was, yet again, putting Nico first.

"I won't be long—promise."

"Yeah, yeah," Tyler replied, without looking up.

o   o   o

The door to Amaru was unlocked, and when Luna didn't see Nico in the studio, she became alarmed. Walking quickly to his apartment, she found him asleep. Sitting on the edge of the bed, she gazed upon his tranquil countenance. Seeing his long eyelashes resting on his high cheekbone, his full lips relaxed, and his black hair tumbling across the pillow, she almost couldn't resist the urge to lay down next to him. Instead, she bent over and pressed her lips to his forehead, whispering, "Nico, I'm here."

His eyes fluttered open and he looked up with sexy, beckoning eyes. She wondered if he did that on purpose. "Why are you looking at me like that? Do you want me to climb on top of you?" she teased.

"Yes, Luna, I do. Come here," he purred, catching her hand and pulling him to her, his lips turned up in a wicked smile.

Giving him an admonishing look, she sat up and gently squeezed his shoulder. "Get up. We have work to do, and it's late. Go get in the shower."

Playfully, Nico reached both hands under the covers and pretended to jerk off, making an exaggerated moaning sound.

Luna giggled, shaking her head. "Stop fooling around!" she jested.

When he got up, Luna could see he was semi-erect, and her body instinctively responded with a twinge in her sex. He padded to the bathroom and closed the door. She heard him pee, then turn on the shower. In a few minutes, he emerged with a towel wrapped around his waist, his wet hair clinging to his neck. She had already cleaned up the kitchen and loaded the dishwasher, but knew better than to attempt making coffee because he would say she didn't do it right—in that way he was a lot like Tyler.

When he asked if she wanted eggs, she answered, "Nico, I had eggs almost nine hours ago!"

"What time is it?" he asked.

"Five thirty!"

Nico looked at her in disbelief, and she just shook her head in amusement. Opening the laptop, she started working on the business plan and after a few minutes he sidled up to her with a second mug of coffee, reading and making comments.

When she made ready to leave, Nico reached for her hand. "Luna, you're the only one I have in my life now."

"Nico, that's not true, you have lots of friends. And you have Erin and Alexa." She tried not to sound jealous when she said their names.

"They're *clients*. I want a *girlfriend*…but I have no one."

Luna bit her tongue about them being more than clients. She felt certain he fucked them, although he would never admit it. "Nico, you'll find the right girl. I know it."

There was sadness in his voice, "Yeah, but I don't have anyone right now. Can't you please stay and watch a movie with me?"

Feeling him pull on her heart, she relented and texted Tyler that she would be home in a few hours, promising to spend all day Sunday with him.

Like a puppy who had exhausted itself, Nico curled up on one end of the sofa with Luna on the opposite end and they watched *The Fifth Element* with Bruce Willis and Mila Jovovich, one of his favorites. At the most memorable bits of dialogue, Nico would say the lines out loud. After watching with him many times, there were some phrases even Luna knew by heart. She liked the movie and never tired of the costumes. When the opera scene came up, she poked his leg with her foot. "Shhh. Just listen how gorgeous this is." After the movie, Luna said with more conviction that she had to go.

Nico pouted. "Here it is, Saturday night, and I'm all alone." But he didn't resist when Luna hugged him a bit too long. The Aqua di Parma scent still lingered, and she couldn't resist pressing her lips to the side of his warm neck.

o   o   o

Nico's eyes landed on a very striking woman in his class. She had a killer body, lean and muscular, with flawless dark skin and thick, straight, jet-black hair. She reminded him of the women he'd known in Peru, descendants of the Inca. This wasn't the first time he had noticed her. He had seen her several times over the past few weeks, but every time he looked for her after class, she was gone before he had a chance to speak with her. He walked up and down the aisles of mats, pausing a few times to adjust a posture or coach the Breath of Fire. At the exotic woman's mat, he stopped and observed her breathing—it was perfect. He stayed there to address the class about the next exercise. Before moving on, he touched her long black hair softly, allowing his hand to lightly skim her spine all the way down. "Speak to me after class," he whispered cryptically.

A short while later, the class said "Namaste," in unison after him.

Maya rolled up her mat and waited in the back for Nico. As he walked toward her, she noticed his gait was fluid and graceful. Traveling up her body, his eyes glowed yellow in the darkness of the studio as they traveled up her body, reminding her of a jaguar. For a moment, she was mesmerized. Then suddenly, he was standing right in front of her. Suppressing the urge to break her gaze from his, she held eye contact. Being a trained fighter, she knew that even the slightest change in her demeanor would be telling to someone like Nico. She had been studying him just as much as he had been studying her.

He ran his hand through his hair, pushing it off his face, and she was surprised to see he appeared a little nervous. Yet he was direct when he spoke. "We haven't had a chance to meet. I'm Nico, of course."

"Pleased to meet you, Nicolás." Her voice was soft and smooth, and for some reason it seemed natural for her to use his full Christian name. "I'm Maya Balam. I registered online. Did you get my payment? "

"Oh, yes. I can tell you have taken yoga."

When he paused, Maya interjected, "I like yoga for the breathing." She took it for granted he knew she meant using the breath to move prana, the Sanskrit word for "life-force," but felt her response sounded too pat.

Sensing her discomfort, Nico probed further, "What brings you to Amaru?

Maya paused. Though she wasn't surprised he had asked, she wasn't sure she wanted to tell him.

Intrigued by her silence, he quickly offered, "Will you stay for some tea?"

Maya hesitated—her call time wasn't until later in the afternoon. "Would you mind if I took a shower first?"

Nico smiled broadly, an overjoyed little boy smile. "Not at all. Come into my office and find me when you're done."

He watched as she walked away—her butt was perfect, round and high, and her legs were long and lean. He couldn't help thinking how much he would like to fuck that ass.

Returning from her shower, Maya called out his name, "Nicolás?" Her voice wasn't tentative and girlish, it was full and clear.

"Tea is in the kitchen. Come, we can sit more comfortably in there."

She followed him in and sat at the counter while he poured two cups.

"Is this your first experience with Kundalini?" Though he suspected it wasn't, he hoped to get her talking about herself. "You said earlier you like it for the breath…"

Though always reluctant to open up, Maya found him charming and figured sharing some things wouldn't hurt—especially since she was taking his classes. "I've taken Hatha and hot yoga like Bikram. They all raise awareness, but I like Kundalini Yoga best to unblock spirit energy using Breath of Fire and because it's less focused on physical alignment."

He liked that she called him Nicolás. Her lips were full and dark and her eyes black, mysterious, and exotic. He continued probing, "Is there something specific you're working on?"

"I use the force in my profession," she replied, expecting that would provoke more questioning.

Nico nodded, taking another sip of tea and waiting to see if she would continue. When she didn't, he asked, "What do you do, Maya?"

She sipped her tea and gazed at him over the rim of the mug. She loved watching people's reactions. "I'm a stunt performer."

For some reason, Nico wasn't surprised. He nodded and raked his hair again, a gesture she found charming in its reflexive innocence. "Ah. Well, you have a great body, muscle tone, and graceful movement, along with perfect breathing. I should've guessed."

She smiled and chuckled out loud. He'd surprised her with his easy, charming explanation.

He asked, "What are your specialties?"

"I do mostly fight scenes."

"Cool! What movies would I have seen you in?"

"Right now, I'm in a vampire movie. It's pretty intense, with a lot of sword fighting. But I can handle it. I'm trained in Muay Thai and

244

Brazilian Jiu Jitsu."

Suddenly, Nico blurted, "I just did a screen test."

She smiled, glad for the end of the interrogation about her. His proclamation didn't surprise her; he was hot and this was L.A., after all—everyone is a wannabe actor. "What movie?"

He shrugged, feigning indifference. "I forgot the name. My client is a studio head and she asked me to do it." Nico made a mental note to press Alexa on that, then returned to querying Maya, "How long have you been in the business?"

The tea must have relaxed her, or she would have bolted by then because there'd been too many questions already. Instead, she answered, "For about ten years now."

As if he'd read her mind, he asked, "Have you been injured much?"

She wondered about the tea. Was it some kind of truth serum brew? The sound of the explosion, and the heat of the flames flashed in front of her. She had narrowly escaped before the fire engulfed the helicopter. "Yes, there was a fire…" she said quietly, the traumatic memory still vivid in her mind.

He asked perceptively, "Is fear holding you back?"

Taking a deep breath, she gazed at him while contemplating, then proceeded, "There are scenes where there is fire. I'm afraid I'll freeze up."

Nico nodded, his eyes glinting enigmatically. With a hint of a smile, his words melodically tumbled out, "I can help you with that Maya Balam." He said her name slowly, enunciating each syllable. "What does your last name mean? I know that word, but can't place it."

"In the Mayan language, it means jaguar."

With no answer, he peered into her black eyes, an inscrutable smile on his lips.

o   o   o

Luna read the Amaru news flash that the studio was closed and was astounded. Shooting a movie?

If he *was* shooting a movie, then he was with Alexa Morgan. Hurt that she was informed along with the masses, Luna's imagination ran away with her.

When he called her a couple of days later, she couldn't decide whether to be happy or indignant.

Right away, he said, "I'm in Tulum looking at spaces for the center here."

Inadvertently, she came off as aloof. "Oh, you'd posted you were shooting a movie. Is everything going well?"

"Not really. I'm with Alexa." Obviously preoccupied and self-absorbed, he had either ignored or hadn't heard the irascible tone of her voice. "She never does things the way I want her to do them. She set up a meeting with the investors and real estate people, and they want to open Amaru centers in several cities around the world."

"That's great! So what's the problem?"

"Ugh. She's rude and undermines me! She dismisses me in front of people, taking charge like it's her project!"

Luna wasn't surprised. "Nico, I think that's just her personality. So let her know how you feel. It's *your* business!"

"It's more than that. She's driving me crazy. I was at the pool and there were so many beautiful girls flirting with me, so I was having some fun. Then the bitch humiliated me. She showed up at the pool and made like she was *with* me. You know what I mean. What a buzz kill! She wouldn't let me have fun and party with the girls; she was acting like she's my wife or something! It's so weird."

Though delighting in his dilemma, she still emphatically counseled, "That's bad for your reputation. It makes you look like a gigolo! You must tell her to stop it!"

He let out an exasperated sigh. "I tried and she made a huge fight with me." He paused, then anxiously added, "She's calling me now. I'm sure she's on her way. I'll call you back later," then hung up.

o   o   o

Embarrassed when her phone blared during the production meeting, Luna silenced it, letting the call go to voice mail. At the end of the meeting, Luna headed back to Wardrobe and checking her missed call list, found Nico had called six times. Attempting to thwart his rage, she apologized as soon as he picked up, "Nico, I'm so sorry. I was in a meeting."

Rabidly screaming into the phone in the iciest tone he could muster, he replied, "That's exactly why I pushed you out of my life, Luna. I can't count on you when I need you!"

"Nico, please. I'm always here for you. I was in a meeting. Besides, it was only a few minutes. What do you need?"

Outraged, he huffed, "I was in a meeting with the investor, and he wanted the business plan. I needed you to e-mail it right then, but you didn't answer. Now it's too late."

His outburst triggered a wave of panic. It was as if he did it on purpose. Overreacting, Luna could hear the shrillness in her voice escalate with each sentence. "Nico, I'm sure it can wait an hour. Besides, why can't *you* e-mail it? I gave it to you in Word *and* as a PDF. I even gave you a flash drive that you can keep in your pocket!"

"Leave me alone, Luna. You're not there for me when I need you." He hung up.

Later, when she thought he might have cooled off, she e-mailed him to apologize, blaming Alexa for his dark mood.

> *Dear Nico,*
> *You know I love you. I'm sorry you think I let you*
> *down. It hurts me so much when you lash out at*
> *me and cut me out of your life. This business with*
> *Alexa is destroying you. You don't have to have sex*
> *with her to get what you want. You are not an*
> *object to be purchased!*
> *xoxo Luna.*

18

Placing her yoga mat near the back of the class, far from her favored spot at the front, Luna was nervous about seeing Nico, since he hadn't replied to her e-mail. Walking around the room with his rehearsed swagger, he gently adjusted postures as he passed. All eyes were on him as he called out kriyas, and Luna watched him carefully as he unconsciously pushed his hair back, his eyes gleaming brightly in the dim light of the studio. She waited for him to look over at her, but he never did.

After class, she went up and asked how he was doing. Avoiding eye contact, he replied curtly, "I'm busy, Luna. Things are exploding. I have meetings and dinners and events piling up."

"Are they all with Alexa?" she asked, her jealously palpable.

Nico looked away, "I'm sorry, Luna. I'm late. I'll call you later."

Her e-mail asserting he was using his sexuality to gain Alexa's favor had obviously touched a raw nerve. Kicking herself for her resentful remark, she held back her tears long enough to escape to her car.

When he called a few days later, she was relieved and did her best to reconcile.

"Luna, I have a big event coming up and they want a video of me with several of my clients. I need you to be interviewed."

Relieved to still be a part of him, she responded, "Sure, Nico. When and where?"

"On Saturday, at Alexa's house. Be there at one o'clock."

Luna's stomach did a flip flop. Then, thinking she'd outshine that bitch, she asked snidely, "Where does she live?"

Nico was strictly business. "I'll text you the address. She's on Coldwater Canyon."

Regretting her snippy mouth, she asked sweetly, "What should I wear?"

In the past, he would have teased her playfully and said she was beautiful. But this time he stayed detached. "Wear something nice, and bring a yoga outfit. We'll be doing some kriyas by the pool at sunset."

On the verge of tears, her voice cracked, "OK, Nico. Sounds interesting."

Though she hadn't meant it sarcastically, Nico went on the defensive. "What does that mean? Don't be jealous."

Without thinking, she griped, "OK, Nico. Don't worry, I won't tell her to stop robbing the cradle."

"You'd better behave yourself, Luna. Don't fuck this up, OK?" he scolded.

Trying to be playful, she chided, "Don't worry, Nico. I was just joking with you."

"You're not joking, Luna. That's the problem. I know you mean it. I'm just saying to be careful with Alexa. She's a snake."

Luna hung up thinking, *Great, another snake! Maybe he never should have named the studio Amaru—it seems to be coming back to bite him.*

o   o   o

Luna took her time driving up Coldwater Canyon and through the open wrought iron gate framing the driveway to Alexa's house. Pulling into the turnaround in front of the Spanish style stucco house, she recognized the white Mercedes.

Luna had on a vintage off-the-shoulder tomato-red brocade dress that she had altered herself, hemming it to mid-thigh after Nico had admired her legs in the black dress he'd given her. She wore several sterling silver necklaces of different lengths, accentuating her graceful long neck and defined, tan shoulders. The dress flared out so that it swished playfully as she walked, and she amped up the effect by wearing black, high-heeled Gucci sandals. Other than at his birthday party, Nico had never seen her dressed this sexy. She was always in a yoga outfit, leggings, or jeans, coming from work.

The door was answered by a young Asian man, obviously the housekeeper, who escorted Luna to the back veranda overlooking a natural stone pool with a waterfall. She took in the elegant, yet serene, setting. Several seating areas were woven within lush gardens of ornamental trees and flowering shrubs. She stood on the veranda until Nico, feeling her presence, gazed up from the pool level below. He stared for a moment before smiling, his smoky green eyes emitting a warm glow. Luna could see he was stunned by her appearance, and if not for her distinctive long, flowing chestnut-brown hair, wouldn't have recognized her.

He raked his hair back as he walked toward the stairs as she gracefully descended the stone steps, greeting her warmly with a double-cheek kiss. He whispered near her ear, "You look very beautiful, Luna." His eyes seared into hers, and she squeezed his hand without speaking. She made no expression, but observed that Alexa never took her eyes off them.

Nico introduced the two women. "Nice to meet you," Luna greeted Alexa with cool detachment. "So nice of you to host this event in your lovely home."

Alexa replied with the same formality, "Thank you for coming. I understand from Nico that you work in the Wardrobe Department on *Going My Way*."

Ignoring the subtle dig, Luna emphatically asserted, "Yes, I'm the head costume designer on the show." Instantly, she regretted not underscoring she'd won the Costume Designers Guild Award.

A pretty, curly haired young woman Luna recognized from class approached. "Are you Luna Saint Claire?"

Taken aback, Luna answered, "Yes, I am. And you are?"

Smiling broadly, the girl extended her hand. "I'm Heidi Marks. I took Tyler's philosophy class at UCLA. I was reading his blog last month on Hinduism, and at the bottom he mentioned Amaru. I'd been looking for a yoga studio, so I took it as a sign!"

Luna laughed, "Yep, that would be like Tyler. How long have you been going?"

Heidi released a torrent of dark brown ringlets from her hair tie, accentuating the sexy wild woman appearance she was blessed with, thanks to her curvy figure and ample breasts. Despite all that, she had a sensual earth mother demeanor, making her seem nonthreatening to everyone.

"Just a few weeks. Nico is awesome. I'm learning so much."

Luna saw a flicker in her eye. Luna had long ago learned that everyone crushed on Nico.

When Luna looked curiously at her, Heidi continued, "Oh, sorry. I'm a makeup artist. Nico asked me to do him a favor today. And I'll be joining you all for the filming of the kriyas later." Luna wasn't surprised. Nico would recruit everyone he could to his cause. Glancing over at Alexa, Heidi added, "You ladies look fabulous."

Luna took the opening to compliment Alexa, referring to Alexa's watercolor print silk organza dress. "I love your dress. Stella McCartney did such a fabulous spring collection, didn't she?" Privately, Luna thought Alexa should hire a better stylist, because the tissue weight sheer dress wasn't flattering to her thick figure. The racer back really accentuated her flabby arms and back fat.

Before Alexa could respond, Nico pulled her away, and the two walked to a secluded area in the garden. Luna could tell he was nervous from his body language. Alexa was holding his arm, and Luna heard her telling him not to worry. She could hear just enough to understand he was telling her what he wanted her to say, something about opening up her blockages. Then she heard him say, "Lower your voice."

Suddenly, he walked away in a huff, heading toward Luna. He stopped and signaled for her to come speak to him. When Luna was close, Nico quietly said, "Look, Luna, this is what I need you to say. Talk about how you came to me to awaken your creativity. Explain how the despacho ceremony and Kundalini Yoga kriyas moved the prana and opened up your possibilities."

In his addled state, he rambled, but Luna knew he was looking for assurance that everyone would say the right thing to make him look good—and powerful. Luna agreed, comforting him, "Yes, of course, Nico. I'll say how I'm more open, relaxed, and creative, and that I've allowed myself to flourish in my personal and professional life. OK?"

Nico smiled and calmed down. "Perfect, Luna. I knew you would say all the right things in a beautiful way! Alexa is being difficult. She doesn't want to say what I want her to. I just want her to say how I was able to unblock that anger with yoga and the healing ceremonies."

Luna understood why he would be upset. He'd invested a lot of time with Alexa.

The crew was setting up the camera to film Alexa sitting in front of the pool. Slipping on a pair of nude patent leather Jimmy Choo pumps, she was trying to get Nico's attention. "Baby, can you come here please? I need to ask you something."

Luna was incredulous she would call him "baby" in front of everyone. But that would actually be the point, after all.

Nico turned his head in her direction. So he was accustomed to being called "baby" by her! Luna could tell he was embarrassed, and rolled her eyes at him. He sauntered over to find out what Alexa needed, then stopped to speak to the videographer. Luna went to stand next to Heidi and watched as the director called action.

Heidi had apparently seen other such interactions between Nico and Alexa, and made a comment about their volatile relationship.

"Relationship?" Luna inquired.

"I should say so!" said Heidi. "I was doing her hair and makeup in her master suite, and she told me he's her boyfriend. I'm sure she was letting me know in case I thought I had a chance with him," Heidi laughed.

Luna was speechless.

Heidi continued, "He does flirt with me, and I have to say I was intrigued. He's hot. But she sure let me know in no uncertain terms he's off limits. And this was while I was covering up her bruises with makeup!"

Luna steadied herself, hoping she had concealed any reaction. "Bruises? What do you mean?"

Heidi leaned in to whisper, "She has a bruise on her left cheekbone, and on her arms, as well. I'm sure he's laid hands on her. She made some lame excuse about a cabinet door jumping out at her! And when I did his makeup for a segment of the *Morning Show*, he had a split lip! I didn't dare ask him about it. Whatever. I just covered them up."

Luna was agog as Heidi continued happily dishing away. "But I know it when I see it. And I see it more often than I would like. Of course Nico wants her for money and connections. I mean, look around! But when she makes too many demands, like wanting public displays of affection, he gets angry. He told me that himself."

Luna took it all in, letting Heidi fill the air with more information. "The bruises on her arms are fingerprints, probably from him grabbing her and trying to control himself from punching her in the face!" Heidi sure wasn't holding back!

Watching the shoot, she began mocking Alexa under her breath so no one except Luna could hear, "Look at her posing! Just look at her making a fool of herself. Or maybe not. I guess she has him right where she wants him, doesn't she?"

Luna stayed quiet, better not to say anything than too much was her motto. "I guess…" Luna's voice trailed off.

Alexa spoke briefly, and though adept at not using the anger word, she still got the point across. Soon, Luna realized she was up next.

They placed Luna in a secluded alcove in the garden against a long, limestone dining table shaded by a grape vine-covered pergola. Leaning casually with one hand on the table, she let her hair fall to the side. Her tomato-red dress with black intarsia was striking against the stone, accented by the light playing off the three crystal chandeliers hanging above the table, creating a picturesque fantasy setting. Luna was naturally expressive when she talked, often using her hands as she spoke. She animatedly wove a visual of her experience with the despacho ceremony, describing all the objects and their meaning, creating a magical tale of healing and the flowering of her creativity.

Then she continued with her yoga training, "Nico taught me the Breath of Fire and how to arouse and unwind the tightly coiled serpent—the kundalini—at the base of my spine. He showed me how the kundalini travels upward through the chakras, and the energy opens the fire in your body, moving it up from the root chakra, which is the center of our physical reality and where we feel nurtured, to the sacral chakra, which is the connection to our emotions. As a designer, I needed to awaken this chakra to create effortlessly and without any blockage. I remember when Nico showed me how to move this energy, in a private session. At first I was uncomfortable. But as I trusted him, I was able to accomplish this kriya, and soon I felt as if I could fly. As prana, Sanskrit for life-force, moves through the seven chakras, it opens up our potential. Everything becomes possible! I learned what happens when each chakra is opened up for a free flow of energy. The solar plexus activates our passion for life, turning fear into love, anger into action, and sadness into joy. The heart chakra allows us the experience of unity and nonjudgmental universal love. The throat chakra, our voice, allows us to be heard and understood. It's also a vibrational connection to the universe. The third eye," Luna pointed gracefully to the spot just above the bridge of her nose, "gives us clarity and a focused mind. We can access the essence of our inner knowledge. As the ancient teachings say, know thyself, and the crown chakra brings the experience of the transcendental meaning of life—oneness and bliss."

She was really at her best, the words flowing effortlessly as if directly from some universal consciousness. "My work with Nico has allowed me to experience so much more of life, with more grace and peace than I ever could have imagined." She looked at Nico just off camera, and placing her hands in prayer position, bowed her head, "Nico, namaste. I bow to you." After she ended her monologue, no one said a word—and the videographer let the camera run as Luna walked out of view.

o   o   o

When class was over, Luna didn't want Heidi to know she was staying to talk to Nico. She went to the locker room and took a shower, then put on her signature bohemian look of distressed jeans and a paisley printed cotton gauze top.

Taking her time, she fixed her makeup, applying only a touch of bronzer and lip gloss. When she removed the elastic tie securing her hair atop her head, a lush chocolate brown curtain cascaded over her shoulders. Carefully, she clasped large turquoise beads around her neck, replaced the silver cuffs and rings she'd removed before class, and went in search of Nico.

"Oh, Luna. You're still here? I thought you'd left."

She reminded him, "No, Nico. You and I made plans. Remember? We were going to hang out and talk."

Nico replied simply, "Well, then help me. Can you sort the mail?"

Happy to be allowed to help him, she chuckled, "I don't know, Nico. What will you do if I die?"

He grinned and gave his standard reply, "Bella, you can't die. I need you too much!"

She waited until she felt the timing was right—not that it could ever be right—to bring up what Heidi had said at Alexa's house. "Nico…" she faltered.

"Luna. Stop flirting," he quipped.

Luna got serious. "I'm not flirting. I'm concerned about something I heard."

He shrugged her head off his shoulder. "What did you hear, Luna?"

She took a breath. "Well, Alexa told Heidi that you're her boyfriend."

Nico laughed, not the response she had expected. "Well, bella, that's a lie. Alexa is sick in the head. You do know that, right?"

Luna had known he would deny it, but added, "I just wanted you to know people are talking. It's not good for your reputation."

He continued his defense, "Either Heidi is lying, or Alexa told her that to keep Heidi away from me. Heidi has been flirting with me! Everyone flirts with me Luna—even you!"

She punched him gently in the arm. "You flirt with *me* all the time! So I flirt back. But we're just friends. These other women want you; they want to fuck you and be with you!"

He laughed out loud again. "Yeah, right—and so do you. So stop gossiping!"

She wouldn't give up. "It makes you look slutty." She couldn't help sounding bitter.

He wasn't concerned. "Don't worry. I have them under control. They're friends, that's all. They're all helping me because I cured them."

Luna still wasn't convinced, and pushed harder. "I think it's bad for your business to let the world think you're for sale."

Sounding annoyed, he snapped, "What, you think I can't handle a bunch of middle-aged women with a crush on me?" Then, before she could get a word in edgewise, he barked, "That was over the line. Enough! You're just jealous!"

Seeing he was getting irritated, Luna dropped the subject.

But he was now paranoid, and probed further. "Do you believe that I'm fucking Alexa? Are you spreading these rumors?"

Luna pounced. "Nico! I most certainly am not! I would *never* say something like that. I'm trying to protect you."

"Don't worry, Luna. This is my business."

"I always worry, Nico. You tell me not to, but I can't help but worry about you."

"I have it under control, I promise. I need Alexa to do things for me. She's a business associate, nothing more."

She just sighed, "Uh huh."

Nico didn't look up, and just kept paging through a catalog from Dick's Sporting Goods. He went on, "She's getting me investors, and we're talking to a network about my own show. You better get started designing my line of yoga clothes right away!"

She didn't want to push her luck, and simply said, "OK, Nico. Just be careful of the rumors. Protect your reputation at all costs." She wasn't convinced Alexa would come through for him. And though she knew she needed to stop nagging him, she found it hard to do. They would never see eye to eye.

This time, he looked up at her from under that lock of hair over his eyes. "I will, Luna. Thank you for caring about me. But please, be supportive and not so judgmental. Can you do that?"

She squeezed his arm and said, "Yes, I can do that."

"Good. Come. I'll open a bottle of wine."

Following him into the apartment she remembered, "Tyler and I are going to Santa Fe for Indian Market in a few days. Are you going to visit Ita and your sister?"

Her question put him on edge. "I don't know what I'm doing, Luna. I don't even know what month it is. I haven't even had time to cut my toenails."

She laughed to herself; she loved that expression of his. "But you always go in August, when it's slow here…"

Instead of answering the question, he asked, "When will you be back?"

"We're back on the eighteenth." She continued, "I'll bring you a present, like I did at Christmas."

He smiled. "I like when you bring me Indian things."

"Nico, let me know that you have everything you need before I go, all right?"

He mumbled OK, but she knew he hadn't given it any thought. If he needed something, he would call in the middle of a panic attack.

"Nico?" she tried to get his attention.

"What?" He had his head buried in his iPhone, so Luna waited quietly while he finished texting. She thought it was Alexa, but kept that to herself. Finally Nico looked up and asked, "What, Luna?"

She saw his eyes were troubled. "I just want to say that we never lit a candle for your mom on Mother's Day. I want us to go to church together when I get back."

He seemed surprised. "I'd like that. We missed Mother's Day? When was it?"

She chuckled. "Yes, Nico, we did. But it's OK. In the States it's in May, but in Argentina Mother's Day is in October."

"Really? I had no idea."

She sighed. "Of course, Nico. Why am I not surprised?" Laughing, she added, "So actually, it really doesn't matter when we go. It just matters *that* we go."

He smiled, and the light in his eyes returned. "Yes, it just matters that we go, together, and light a candle for my mom."

While Nico opened the wine, Luna picked the Tulum book up off the coffee table. "So, how is it going with opening a studio in Tulum?"

He filled their glasses as he replied, "They love me. All these things I'm doing give me more exposure. It's all good to show the investors that I'm a brand and have a platform."

He took a sip of his wine, then went on, "I need you to help me get more celebrity clients."

"Well, Tyler has gotten you several clients. Heidi Marks is a high-profile client, isn't she? She's a top makeup artist."

He shrugged. "I've asked her to bring me celebrities for private sessions. She says she will, but hasn't brought anyone yet. She just wants to get into my pants. You know that!"

Luna laughed. "I know. I shouldn't laugh. It's a big problem being so handsome and sexy…come on, Nico, you promised to show me the video…" She eagerly plopped herself down on the sofa in front of the TV as Nico cued up the video. Luna knew she'd done a good job, and that was why Nico was finally rewarding her with his affection again, but she cringed when she saw Alexa. They watched the entire piece and when it was over, Luna clapped her hands happily like a child. "It's wonderful, Nico. Everyone says great things about you, and you look gorgeous!"

Smiling at her approval, Nico picked up his guitar and flirtatiously sang Damien Rice's "The Box"—a song about interior conflict and ambivalence toward fame. Luna had turned him onto the Irish artist, thinking the music would resonate with him. Nico gazed at her longingly as he crooned the words. His buttery accent gave the melody a Spanish flair, and when the notes got high, his voice sounded even sexier, cracking slightly as he passionately emphasized the painfully beautiful lyrics about longing to live wild and free.

He seemed the most happy he'd been since Sofia left. Finishing the song, he peered into her eyes from under his dark lashes, giving her his most winsome smile. "Luna, are you sure he's Irish?"

"Yes, of course, why?"

"He writes songs like a Latin…triste…I mean, sorrowful."

Luna gently patted his thigh. His eyes glowed, then he pushed her hand off and scolded, "Stop flirting with me. I'm having a hard time, and you're asking for trouble."

She got defensive. "I'm not flirting, Nico. I'm showing my affection for you because I care. I'm just being comforting."

He leaned in, eyeing her in his lustful way that made her want to kiss him. "Really? Come here, Luna." He pulled her close, grabbing her T-shirt in the front and looking down her shirt at her cleavage. "Why are you always showing me your tits?"

She huffed, "Nico, I have no idea what you mean. You groped me just now!" She gave him a faux disapproving look, and he couldn't help grinning impishly, causing them to erupt into bawdy laughter.

"I'm starving. Let's make dinner. Come." She took her place on one of the stools while he cooked. Then they toasted each other—*amigos para siempre*, friends forever.

After dinner, they sat on the sofa while he played guitar and sang loudly. Luna laughed in delight and sang along on each chorus, having learned most of his repertoire by heart. She looked at the man-child in front of her. He was so complicated; arrogant and demanding at times, yet at other times insecure and sweet. She felt so connected to him. He was part of her, like a tattoo. And all she knew was she would never let him go.

Putting down the guitar, Nico opened a small box on the table and pulled out a half-smoked joint. "Would you like some, Luna?"

"I haven't smoked a joint in years!" she declared. "Will I be able to drive?"

"I think so. Just smoke a little. Besides, you can always sleep here with me if you want."

She smirked, "Very funny, Nico. That would go over really well with Tyler!" She took one hit and held it in. Soon the room was hot and she felt very high. She exclaimed, "Wow, they sure do make it stronger these days."

Leaning back into the corner of the sofa, she stretched out her legs so her feet pressed into the side of his thigh. *God*, she thought, *he has such great thighs*.

He turned and studied her face, then drawled in a honeyed tone, "Luna, you're so beautiful. Come over here."

She dared not move, and even held her breath. "Just play another song, Nico."

After maintaining their seductive eye contact for a few beats longer, he shrugged and messed around with some chords, singing "Bella Luna…bella Luna!" boisterously and off key, making them both collapse into fits of giggles.

Abruptly, Luna sat up and put her shoes on, but when she stood, her legs wobbled. Nonetheless, she said, "I'd better go."

He eyed her seductively. "Are you sure? You can sleep here…"

Mustering all her self-control, she shook her head and quickly made her way to the front door, leaving without kissing him good-bye. She didn't dare get that close, fearing what might happen if she did.

o   o   o

Sitting on the plane, Luna texted Nico again. He hadn't responded to any of her messages, and she'd been trying for days. They had begun a tradition of texting each other whenever either was on a plane. The unwritten message was a prayer for safety. Nico would never admit his fear of flying, and Luna had given him a little warrior totem they'd nicknamed the traveling man. Nico kept it on his dresser, always taking the totem with him when he traveled, for good luck.

Though her vacation had been needed and she always had a great time in Santa Fe, Luna was eager to get home—and to see Nico. She thought things between them were good now, so when he didn't even reply to her traditional "wheels up" from the plane, she was crushed. She'd been back for days, and still his phone went straight to voice mail. When he finally answered, she found him in a bad mood. "I tried calling you from Santa Fe. I've been worried. Where were you?" she asked.

Nico grumbled, "I was away."

"Well…where were you?" she pressed.

"Why do you need to know that?"

"Because I worry about you, Nico! So of course I need to know."

He mumbled, "Deià."

Incredulous, she replied, "Deià? I thought you would've gone to see your grandmother. Why Deià?"

"Don't ask, Luna. You have no idea what a dragon that woman is. I hate her!"

Luna let out an exasperated breath, "Oh, I see. Alexa. So are you still doing the event at The Rails?"

Nico groused, "I guess…"

Somehow, Nico had convinced Alexa to stage a promotional event in honor of the documentary *Amaru of the Andes,* in combination with the opening of a studio in Tulum, Mexico. Luna knew from Nico that as of yet, there was no signed contract for a studio. But he was boasting that it would open at the end of October, and Luna wondered if he had actually convinced himself or was just saying that to generate buzz.

"Then why are you upset? It's one of the biggest galleries in the world. The whole event is to promote you!"

Nico snapped, "Luna, are you being coy with me? You know exactly! Don't make me say it. She acts like she's my girlfriend in public. It's fucking embarrassing. How am I going to invite my friends and clients when she does that?"

Not wanting to say I told you so, Luna sighed. "Nico, just tell her it doesn't look good. Won't she understand?"

He sulked. "No, Luna, she doesn't understand." After a pause, he added, "No, I misspoke—she doesn't care!"

"Well then, you'll just have to make it really clear and stand firm."

He barked, "Luna, you're such an idiot. Sometimes I just want to kill you."

Losing patience, she raised her voice, "Why? What's wrong with that suggestion, Nico?"

"Let me see, where should I begin?"

He was getting nasty and sarcastic and she wasn't getting anywhere, so she backed down. "I'm sorry, Nico."

He sounded defeated, "She won't hire a caterer, and she won't pay for me to print T-shirts to hand out. You know, the goody bag."

"Is that something she's supposed to do?"

Nico again snapped, "Of course! She knows I can't afford that. She should help me. She's the one producing the event!"

"If she's putting on the event for you, then yes, she should handle all of that. But did you ask her?"

"Yes, I asked her. And she said I should pay for that myself."

"Can you ask Mario to help you with the food and your dad for the wine. And I'll see who I know who can screen print the shirts for you."

Relieved, Nico replied, "Yes, Mario's going to help out. I suppose

I could ask my dad. See what you can do about the shirts."

"Wait, don't hang up yet," Luna added. "I brought you something from Santa Fe that I think you'll love."

"Great, thank you. I'd better go, I have a lot of work and a client on the way."

Luna said quietly, "OK. Don't forget, we're going to the church tomorrow. It's Sunday…remember?"

She heard him sigh.

"I'll call you in the morning…"

"OK, bye." He hung up too quickly.

That fucking Alexa…she fretted.

19

"Good morning, Starshine," she chirped, using a favorite endearment.

He answered sleepily, "Luna, what?"

"It's a beautiful day and we're going to church. I also have a gift for you." She mentioned the gift as an enticement.

His husky voice was sexy. "Can we go to the Spanish church we always go to?"

Luna shook her head. *Just like a little kid,* she thought. "Yes, of course, Nico. It's Sunday, so we should try to get there between services."

He sounded more awake. "I'll pick you up in an hour on the bike."

Luna agreed, even though she was petrified. After telling Tyler she was going to church with Nico, leaving out the part about the motorcycle, she put on thigh-hugging print bells, an indigo embroidered prairie top, her favorite suede fringed jacket and her well-worn Rag & Bone black ankle boots.

She had bought him a hand-beaded arrow trimmed with colorful feathers from a gift shop that carried handmade American Indian shields and weaponry. The arrow was more decorative than would actually have been used to kill a buffalo, but it was just symbolic, anyway. Wrapping it carefully in craft paper, she tied it up with raffia.

She'd selected the card very deliberately—a native woman dancing the shawl dance in front of a mountain. Inside, she carefully wrote: *Let loose the arrow…let thy aim be the good of all and then carry on thy task in life.* This was a message spoken by Lord Krishna to his disciples in the Bhagavad Gita. The quote begins:

Nico loved it when she wrote him poetry and sent him inspirational quotations. She put the arrow in her vintage Ralph Lauren cross body bag, angling the point to the side.

When she got downstairs, Nico was already out front standing next to the bike. He teased, "What took you so long? You women are slow!"

Seeing him made her heart tumble. He looked like a modern day Latino James Dean in his dad's beat-up old motorcycle jacket. Greeting her with the double-cheek kiss she'd long ago become accustomed to, he gently pushed her hair back off her shoulders, letting his hand linger on her back. "Bella, why do you wear hoop earrings when you know you have to wear a helmet?"

She nodded and carefully removed the earrings, putting them into the zippered compartment of her handbag.

"And what is this dangerous stick you have in there?"

"Um, that's your gift. We'll do that later," she scolded. "I'll be careful, just drive slowly please. You know I'm terrified of this machine!"

Nico carefully secured the helmet on her head, buckling it under her chin. Straddling the bike, he signaled for her to do the same as the engine roared to life. Reluctantly, she climbed on behind him. When he revved the engine, Luna squeezed him tightly, pressing her body against his back and yelling for him to go slowly. Hearing his muffled laugh, she realized he'd done it purposely to toy with her. Weaving around the traffic, she tried to lean into the turns. Nico tapped her thigh at a stop light, telling her to sit back and relax, she was too tense. When they pulled up outside *Nuestra Señora Reina de Los Angeles*—Our Lady Queen of Angels—in the Plaza of the historic Olvera Street neighborhood, Luna leaped off the bike before he turned off the engine. Nico had to quickly catch his balance before the bike toppled over. Taking off his helmet, he shook his head at her.

"Luna, you have to get over your fear."

The morning mass had just ended, so the pews were empty, making it feel like their private sanctuary. After they had crossed themselves with holy water from the marble font by the door, Nico went first to the votive candles. Lighting one, he knelt and bowed his head, reciting softly in Spanish. Sliding into a pew, they knelt together in silent prayer. Nico's head was lowered, his black hair falling into his eyes, shielding them from Luna's gaze. Sitting back in the pew in the cool darkness, Nico bemoaned, "You're the only person I trust. Even though you hurt me with Sofia, you're the only one in my life."

Luna held his hand in silence. Then he began to speak from a place deep inside; thoughts he held in reserve until they were here, in what he called "our church."

"I hate her. And I don't trust her. You know she's an addict—oxycodone." Luna knew he meant Alexa. "She won't let me date. We stayed at Richard Branson's hotel in Deià, and all these supermodels were there! We were all partying. Then they invited me to a party, so I left with them. I didn't tell Alexa because I knew if I said anything, she wouldn't let me go. When I got back in the morning, she was a raging bitch. But I'm not her boyfriend! What does she expect? I'm half her age! She makes me miserable, and I'm alone. I want a girlfriend to share my life, but she'll never let me do that. She wants to have a baby with me! Imagine—these are the things she says to me!"

Luna offered, "Nico, if she has a crush on you, that's *her* problem. If you give the impression that more of you is available for a price, then that's *you* prostituting yourself."

He asserted, "It's not like that, Luna! Why do you assume I'm fucking her?"

She cautioned him, "Because, Nico, I keep telling you, it doesn't matter whether you are or you aren't if everyone *thinks* you are. So you may as well fuck her and get what you want out of it!"

He glared at her incredulously. "I can't believe you're saying that, Luna! Is that what you really think I should do?"

She coolly insisted, "No, Nico! *I* would walk away from her. But since *you* won't, you have to do her bidding instead."

He sat silently for a minute. "I've done my part and invested a lot of time in her—she owes me. I can't keep doing what I'm doing every day. I should be like Deepak Chopra and Dr. Oz, with a platform that reaches millions. What am I going to do, Luna?"

She tried to reason with him. "Nico, walk away. Cut your losses."

"What are you, crazy? I can't do that, she *owes* me!"

She insisted. "You enrolled her in your life and career, and what she wants in return is what you're not willing to give. What do you expect when you travel with her? Mexico…Deià…"

He argued, "I do what I have to. Even then, you see, she sabotages and embarrasses me in front of people I should be impressing!"

"Look, Nico, you're a talented healer—charming and sexy. Those are wonderful assets, but they're only part of who you are. Somehow, you mix those traits up with how you value yourself. They become part of the equation, part of the payment. It's like you think you won't get love unless you use sex."

He pouted. "So you're saying this is all my fault?"

"You're her healer and teacher, and that shouldn't get mixed up with being her boyfriend."

"I agree with that. But she wants more. I keep telling her that we're just friends and she's my agent, a business partner. Yet she seems to sabotage things instead. Investors want the Centers booked solid, but they won't be unless I'm famous, so I need more publicity. Alexa is getting *Vanity Fair* to publish an article about how she sees a shaman for healing. But watch, this article is going to be all about her. You just wait and see."

Luna pondered his predicament. "What about Erin? Can't she help?"

"Yeah, Erin helps. When it suits her. She says I need a bigger platform first. It's always this issue, a bigger platform. She got me the Armani and Gold Fountain campaigns, but they're just glorified modeling jobs. The documentary is, you know, intellectual—no big mass appeal. I need something that makes me *explode*."

Despite the risk of raising his ire, she said, "Fucking your yoga instructor is such a cliché! Your reputation is at stake. Nico—get a girlfriend, even a friend with benefits, so people will know you're not

Alexa's boy toy."

He shifted in the pew, interlacing his fingers on his lap and hanging his head. Although Luna knew he'd heard her, she also knew he was determined to get his way—he wasn't done with Alexa.

They crossed themselves on the way out, and Luna got on the back of his bike again, thankful she'd said a quick prayer they get home alive.

Nico hadn't asked her, but she soon realized they were headed toward the studio and she felt happy he wanted to extend their time together. When they arrived Nico began pulling ingredients out of the fridge.

"What are you going to make?" Luna asked, leaning over his shoulder.

"*Ruqru*. That's Quechua for what you call stew." He made fun of the word by emphasizing the eewww. "Why is it called steeewww?" He laughed. Handing her a knife, hilt first, he asked, "You want to help me?"

"Of course!" She chimed, taking the knife from him. "What should I do first?"

"Here." He handed her the cutting board. "You start cutting up the onions and I'll peel these potatoes."

They worked side by side in the kitchen, and Luna couldn't have been happier. There were some things he reserved just for her, and this was one.

In short order, the pot was bubbling. He uncorked a bottle of Malbec and they sat on the sofa, where Luna handed him his gift and card. "Open the gift first! I *know* you always open the card first, but not this time."

He did as she instructed and slowly unwound the raffia, giving her a frustrated look when he saw that the paper was all taped. She just laughed. Painstakingly, he proceeded to remove the tape and unroll the paper.

Anyone other than Nico would not have understood receiving an arrow as a gift. But Nico gathered Luna to him and hugged her. "Bella, you amaze me. An arrow! I love this. It's perfect!"

He opened the card and very slowly read the message aloud, " 'Let loose the arrow. Let thy aim be the good of all and then carry on thy task in life.' Wow…that's beautiful." He read it over again, then got up, fetched a large black marker, and climbed onto the sofa.

Luna screeched, "Nico! What in the world are you doing?"

Holding the marker poised to the wall, he instructed, "Read it to me, Luna."

As she read, he printed in very large letters on the wall above the sofa. "How do you spell 'loose?' With two Os, right?"

Luna giggled. "Yes, two Os." When he was done, she was surprised how the combination of print and script handwriting looked very artistic on the red walls.

"There. I'll always remember to take aim and do good. Thank you, bella. You're my spirit guide."

Grinning, Luna admired his handiwork. "It looks great, Nico. I love it!"

He went to the stove to check on the locro, with Luna following. As he stirred the pot, she said, "You're wonderful, Nico. And you'll be fine. I just know it." She wrapped her arms around him from behind and kissed the back of his neck, deeply inhaling the intoxicating mix of the natural scent of his body and the alluring fragrance of Aqua di Parma. But she felt his body tense as her lips brushed his skin, and feeling guilty for her boldness, she quickly released him and went to set the table.

Carrying over two bowls filled to the brim, he remarked, "You always make things look so nice, Luna, with napkins and candles. When you're not here, I just eat in front of the TV."

Luna considered what he'd said. "Nico, every act is sacred. Even the small things we do every day are rituals, reminding us to honor everything and be grateful. Especially for food. An animal died for this food, and it's important to express our gratitude."

Nico refilled the wine glasses and before picking up his fork, looked at Luna and said softly, "Gracias Dios por los alimentos que nos has dado, and especially for you, Luna." He blew her a kiss across the table.

Luna blushed and looked down, and Nico asked, "Do I embarrass you, bella?"

She nodded. "Sometimes. But it's OK…"

"Ah, Luna. If only you were free to be with me, we would have a good time. If we fucked, you'd never be the same, you could never be with anyone else. You know this, right?"

"I've heard your stories—more than I need to know."

He was trying to look serious, but his eyes twinkled. "Have you ever squirted, Luna?"

She was ashamed to ask, "I don't know, Nico? What is that?"

He laughed out loud. "What is squirting? Oh! You'd know if you had." Purposely embarrassing her, he continued teasing. "I make a woman squirt and have the deepest, most intense multiple orgasms."

Luna didn't have an answer. She sipped her wine and looked down at her plate.

Nico was deadpan. "How many times do you come when you and Tyler fuck?"

Mortified, Luna responded almost inaudibly. "I don't know, Nico. You're embarrassing me. We make love. He makes me come, then he comes. It's very nice…"

He put his fork down. "That's it? *You* come…*he* comes…that's all?"

She defended herself. "Yes, Nico, that's all. It's *fine*."

He shook his head. "I feel sorry for you, Luna. You deserve more. You should get more pleasure than that."

He saw she was on the verge of tears. "I'm sorry, bella. I was only teasing with you."

She replied quietly, "It's OK, Nico. You didn't mean it. It's just the way things are, that's all. Leave it alone. I'm happy."

She hadn't meant to lead him into further conversation, but Nico continued, "Luna, you're not happy. You've just accepted things the way they are. I've been trying to get you to see that you and Tyler are just friends. You're a vibrant, sexual woman. You need passion! Maybe we can try to open up Tyler, get him to awaken his sexual energy."

Luna perked up. "Is that possible? That would be wonderful."

"We can try. See if you can get him to come to a class with you."

"OK, I'll try."

Quietly, they savored the locro, cleaning their plates with bread.

Contented, Luna finally broke the silence, "Nico, about me and Tyler…"

He looked up at her and steadied his gaze. He could see she was serious and on the verge of tears. "What, bella? You know you can talk to me about anything."

Certain he wasn't mocking her and was genuinely listening, she opened up. "Well, I know we have awakened the kundalini. I'm feeling more sexually…vibrant?" There was no one except Nico she could tell; still, she was self-conscious about admitting she'd become lustful…horny. Struggling to find the right words, she inhaled sharply, and her eyes glazed over with unspent tears. "We are having sex more often, and it's definitely a lot better." As much as she wished she had the courage to tell Nico that she fantasized about him while having sex with Tyler, she knew she would regret it. Instead, she just frankly stated, "I wish Tyler was more passionate. More…I don't know… spontaneous."

Nico's eyes glimmered, but he didn't tease her the way he normally would. "Bella, don't be shy. I know what you're saying, and it's normal. You want him to ravish you. You want him to feel the extreme desire that has been asleep within you for many years and is now awake."

She swiped away the tears that hung on her cheeks. "I'm sorry, Nico. I shouldn't trouble you with my problems…I'll talk to Tyler about coming to class." Changing topics to mask her embarrassment, she added, "Thank you, Nico. The locro was delicious."

He winked at her, his eyes flickering in the candlelight. "Thank you, Luna, for bringing me to church—and for the arrow."

o   o   o

Luna was having a difficult time convincing Tyler to come with her to the gallery, so she tried several angles. "Heidi will be there. It'll be an opportunity to see her."

Tyler groused, "OK, I'll go. I'll go because *you* want me to go."

Delighted, she gave him a kiss. "Thanks, Tyler. I appreciate it. Still, I know people want to meet you. They always ask me where you are."

Luna wore a black Donna Karan dress with a sweeping asymmetric hem, cutout back, and plunging neckline. Gazing at herself in the full-length mirror, she admired her slim and toned body. As Nico promised, she looked and felt twenty years younger. She put on a chunky turquoise statement necklace, large silver hoop earrings, and her heavy silver Navajo cuff, then slipped on high-heeled suede sandals to emphasize her long, lean figure. Why not show it off? Of course Alexa would be there—and maybe Erin—though she wasn't sure Nico would have both of them at the same event.

Arriving at The Rails, Luna immediately saw Nico pacing about frantically, setting up the bar with his father. Holding Tyler's hand, she approached the two men, greeting them with double-cheek kisses. As always, Roberto flirtatiously winked, giving Luna the once over. "Beautiful bella!" he commented playfully, so not to offend Tyler.

Nico, sweating at the brow, rushed over to Luna and implored her to prepare the goody bags.

Once Nico was out of ear shot, Tyler protested, "Why are you charged with this task instead of Alexa?"

"He asked me." She shrugged. "Apparently, this is beneath Alexa. I would rather help than have him stress out any more than he already is." Luna hoped it would somehow prove that Alexa was just a bitch.

Tyler's answer was typical. "Whatever..." he said, shaking his head disapprovingly.

While Luna was stuffing an Amaru logo T-shirt and the new issue of *LA Magazine* with the article Sofia had written into a yoga bag, Heidi and another girl from class walked up to say hello, and Heidi questioned provocatively, "Why are *you* doing that?"

Blushing with humiliation, Luna threw down the T-shirt she was holding in her hand and tapped one of the young servers to finish up for her.

Heidi said she had gotten there early to do hair and makeup for Nico and Alexa, telling Luna that they were being interviewed for a morning show spot and then photographed for some press Alexa had set up. Heidi made no bones about it, saying, "That Alexa is milking this for all she can."

Luna seethed inside. "I managed to get all the T-shirts and bags printed practically overnight. What the hell?!"

With perfect timing, Tyler arrived holding a couple of glasses of chardonnay.

"Luna, there's something else strange about this whole situation," Heidi hinted.

"What do you mean?" Luna pressed for more.

Heidi mulled, "It's just strange. I don't like Alexa one bit. She's pulling him around by the balls, controlling him with her power and money. Still, it's pretty clear Nico is playing *her* for everything *he* can get. My mother was a narcissist—I know one when I see one."

Luna wondered what she meant, but didn't ask.

Nico and Alexa were working the room, and Luna tried not to follow them with her eyes, instead intently watching the big screen above the bar where the testimonial video was playing. The music was loud, making the film inaudible, but eventually she saw herself being interviewed as the loop continued.

Seeing Roberto alone at the bar, Luna meandered over for another glass of wine.

"Ah, bella. What do you think of this?" He rolled his eyes.

"I hope Nico gets some good press. He deserves it," she replied diplomatically.

Maybe Roberto had a few glasses of wine, because he became a bit chatty. "Well, bella, do you think Nico is sleeping with her?"

Stunned by his bluntness, she shook her head pensively. "I don't know…what do you think?"

He immediately quipped, "I think they go off to Mexico to his hidden love nest, where he fucks her. He should grow the business slowly himself. I don't think this is a smart way, it will only bring trouble." He shook his head as if forewarning. "She has her claws into him and won't do anything out of the goodness of her heart."

Luna exhaled sharply. "Why don't you tell me what you really think?" she laughed heartily. So, it was obvious to his father and to Heidi—who else knew? Luna suggested, "I think you should tell him how you feel. Maybe he'll listen to you."

He laughed. "Ah, bella. I thought you knew Nico better!"

All night, Nico was constantly at Alexa's side and made no effort to come over and speak to them. So when Tyler asked if she wanted to say good-bye, Luna's feelings of anger and humiliation surfaced. "I'd rather not disturb them. Let's just go."

Later that evening, Nico called. "Luna, where did you go? Come to La Forza, we're all here."

She felt guilty. Maybe she shouldn't have left. He sounded let down. "We're already in bed, Nico. And I have to be at work early tomorrow."

Nico pleaded, but there was no way Luna was getting out of bed and trucking over to La Forza…not after the way she felt she had been treated. "Please, Luna. I need you to come."

She asked remotely, "Is Alexa there?"

"Yes, of course."

"Well then, I'm absolutely not coming."

"Why, Luna? What did she do to you?"

"She could have made a point—or at least *you* could have—of coming to say hello and maybe thanking me for helping you with the event!"

"Luna, you're being jealous. We were working the room for business. You're not business to her."

"Well, have fun then. Is Heidi there?"

"No…and what did you say to her? She was going to come here, but then she was weird and bailed."

"Nothing, Nico. I said good night to her and told her that I had to get up early."

"I don't believe you. You must have said something to her."

"No, Nico…I didn't. Have a good time, Nico. Good night."

o   o   o

Luna was at home eating dinner and watching TV with Tyler. Weary from the previous night's drama combined with a stressful day at work, she vowed to focus on *her* life—*her* job and Tyler.

When her cell rang and she saw it was Nico, she felt a wave of anxiety. Apprehensive, she picked up only because she knew he would keep calling until she answered.

"Luna, I'm very upset with you. You've lost me clients. You must've said something to them. I want to know what you said."

Panicking, Luna shrilled defensively, "Nico, what do you mean? Tyler and I chatted with Heidi and that other girl from class that falls over you, then we left early."

Badgering her, Nico spat, "Did you tell them that I was fucking Alexa? Did you spread this lie because you're jealous?"

She cried out, "Nico, you're crazy. No, I never said that, I didn't *have* to! How many times do I have to tell you it was *Heidi* who told *me* that you're fucking Alexa? Think about it, Nico. Didn't Heidi do her makeup again at the gallery? I guess she must have told her more!"

Luna went into the living room and laid down on the sofa in the dark. Distraught, she broke down crying. "I can't do it any more, Nico. I can't stand this relationship between you and Alexa. If this is what you need to do to advance your career, then I'm sorry, I don't want to be friends."

He spoke softly and slowly, with a hint of desperation. "Luna, I love you very much. You're important to me. I need you in my life. What you're saying isn't fair." He then continued, "Friends play different roles, and I love each person differently. I need Alexa right now. I need her to do what she promised, then it will be done. *You'll* always be in my life, so please, for now I need you to be patient... and help me."

Luna choked up. She felt like she couldn't breathe; she hadn't expected him to plead with her. "Nico, I helped you with this event only to be ignored all evening. I hadn't heard from you for weeks until you needed me to make the T-shirts. I feel like you only call me when you need something. I don't like the way I'm used, and Alexa gets all your attention—and affection. She buys you things, takes you on trips, and throws you events. I can't do those things for you." She was sobbing then and trying to keep her voice down. "So you don't pay attention to me, and I never see you anymore."

In his most convincing voice, Nico said, "I don't see any of my friends right now. I'm too busy. I'm on a mission. This all has to get done—fast. If I don't do it now, I'll lose this opportunity. Luna, do you understand what I'm saying?"

She whispered yes in between sobs. She knew Nico meant that if he didn't appease Alexa, she wouldn't deliver.

"Right now I need you to be helping me, not upsetting me like this. Just wait, please. I'll have more time and more money. We can spend time together then. Right now I need you to be my friend and help me."

Luna felt the tears come hot down her cheeks. "I love you, Nico. Of course I want to help you. Just please be nicer to me and spend more time with me. That bitch didn't even say hello to me. And I was such an idiot, stuffing T-shirts into the yoga bags like a slave. She should have thanked me!"

Nico tried to pacify her. "I know, Luna."

She was choked up with frustration. "Nico, I just can't do it otherwise."

"OK, Luna. I'll see you tomorrow. We'll hang out. I promise."

o   o   o

When Maya arrived at Amaru, music was playing in the studio—music that sounded like it came from heaven—liquid and transcending. She called out Nico's name tentatively, and his soft reply led her to the studio, where he was sitting in the comfortable Perfect Pose, Siddhasana, his hands in Guyan Mudra, softly droning the Aum mantra.

Maya didn't want to tell her fight supervisor that she was having nightmares. She knew he would put her on leave if she told him the truth. When he'd asked if she was good to go, she'd said yes. But if she didn't get herself together quickly, he would surely see any hesitation on her part—and replace her.

She hoped she hadn't disturbed Nico and waited tentatively. He didn't move, but said her name, "Maya Balam, come in and sit next to me."

Maya walked up to the front of the room where he sat. She had noticed when she first walked in that his eyes were only slightly open, gazing upward in Shambhavi Mudra toward his third eye—the divine eye, or vision chakra, called Ajna. Maya recognized this meditation. She knew it was powerful, known to develop great insight into the future and the power of intuition, opening up one's psychic powers and abilities. More than that, she had read it bestows eloquent speech, making one charismatic and magnetic, even allowing for nonverbal communication. Believing in the power of kundalini, she had sought a teacher who could help her. The meditation Nico was doing confirmed her expectations.

"Come, Maya…sit next to me."

Quietly, she sat next to him and folded her legs to match his, resting her hands on her knees.

"Follow along, Maya, and breathe as I do. Then we will begin the kriya for overcoming fear. When Nico moved onto his knees, in table position, she followed suit precisely as he cooed his approval. "That's right, bring your head down, chin toward your chest, as you arch your back up like a cat, pulling in your stomach. In Kundalini Yoga, we use this kriya as an excellent practice for emotional balance and overcoming our greatest fears, including the fear of death. This will clear your emotional garbage, and strengthen your nervous system. You may begin to panic during the exhale phase because of breath deprivation, but you also fight the fear and build great courage."

His voice soothed Maya, and she felt as if everything he said would come effortlessly simply because he said so.

Students had begun arriving for class, rolling their mats out in the studio. Nico wrapped up their session. "Let's not overdo this today. You'll quickly be able to execute the pump phase longer each time, you'll see."

Maya relaxed, but felt a bit light headed from the strenuous breathing exercise and swayed as if she might fall over.

"Maya, are you OK? Would you rather skip class?" he asked.

She shook her head. "No, I'll be fine. I'll drink some water, and I have an energy bar in my bag."

After moving her mat to her regular spot near the back of the room, she headed off to the locker room.

Nico watched her as she retreated. *What an amazing ass,* he thought. More than that, he admired her tenacity.

After class, Maya thanked him for teaching her the fearlessness kriya. He smiled and took her hand into his, then stroked her palm.

"Maya," he purred, "That's such a beautiful name. We are all imperfect beings, limited in our ability to perceive and understand." His words were almost a meditation in themselves, and she stood silently as he continued. "We form our own reality using whatever means of reasoning we have at our disposal. It's not false. It's just not the absolute truth. It's only for us…and only at this time. It is…Maya."

Abruptly, Nico snapped out of it, gave her a double-cheek kiss and said, "See you tomorrow, Maya. Come early…before class."

20

That night, for the first time since the accident, Maya didn't have a nightmare. Was it possible that after only one session with Nico, the terrifying dreams had ceased to plague her? Instead, she dreamed about him. They were in the jungle, walking naked along a river and holding hands. It was dark, though the sky was filled with stars. But their path was illuminated by his eyes, beaming like a flashlight in the blackness. They walked endlessly, until they came upon a snake, and Nico knelt down, putting his ear near the serpent's head. He spoke to the creature in a language she assumed was Quechua. The snake became their guide, and Nico said, "Do not be afraid. He will show us the way."

When Maya woke from the dream, she felt rested and surprisingly serene. She sensed the dream was significant, and she thought about Nico. More than handsome, he was exotic and sexy in a captivating way. All the girls talked about him in the locker room. But Maya thought he was more than that—she thought he was beautiful. The way he walked—and the way he spoke poetically about the meaning of her name. He was confident, and believing he possessed a power within that was connected to the life-force, she wanted to share that with him.

After her private session, she believed in him. She could feel the energy inside her move, and she felt alive—more alive than ever before. Now, lying in bed recalling her dream and thinking about Nico, she felt the energy in her belly stir and a mild tingling sensation in her extremities. She could feel a fire inside her, burning. She closed her eyes again, hugging herself with her arms while she pictured him. Her hands moved down from her abdomen to the space between her legs. She could feel the fire there as she pressed her finger inside, where it was warm and wet. She slid her finger out and rubbed the slick wetness on her clitoris, feeling it stir to her touch. Putting her finger back inside, she continued teasing herself until her body was writhing, the wetness spilling out of her. In a matter of seconds, she fell apart. That was Nico—he'd reached across space and time to pleasure her—she was sure of it.

o   o   o

When she got to the studio, she looked for him in the classroom to see if he was doing the same meditation as the day before, but he wasn't there. Calling out his name, she heard him from beyond the office, "Maya, come in here!"

Walking in, she saw him standing at the counter in the kitchen eating rice and beans.

"I didn't eat all day. Are you hungry?"

Maya nodded and Nico dished up a plate of rice and beans for her. Taking a forkful, she smiled. "It's delicious! What's the herb I taste? It's so fragrant."

Nico answered, "Oregano. Other than that, it's just garlic and onions with the red beans."

"Well, I'm impressed, you're a guru and a chef!"

Her eyes quickly scanned the confines of his inner sanctum and landed on the guitar. "You play guitar?"

"Yes, I do…mostly for myself."

"Will you play something for me?" she asked flirtatiously.

"After you finish your plate," he teased back.

"Well then, I'll hurry," she countered. When Maya finished, she unconsciously licked her lips, then noticed Nico was still watching her.

"So, do you like my cooking?" He grinned invitingly.

"Very much!" She peered up from under her black lashes. "Now will you play for me?"

Nico paused and locked eyes with her, lowering his voice to a serious purr, "Maya, I'm glad you came early. I like you. I'd like to know you better."

She froze, looking into the radiant green pools of his eyes. "Me too," she whispered; the words almost didn't come out.

He picked up the guitar. "We don't have much time, so I'll just do a short song. You may know it." He began singing a traditional Argentine folk song, and when he got to the chorus, he was pleased that Maya sang along with him.

They both laughed when he shook his head and repeated the same verse a few times, not remembering the lyrics of all the verses. Maya chimed in with the refrain *Amor salvaje*, "Wild love," which they both sang louder each time. When the song was over, he leaned in and kissed her quickly and softly on the lips—a kiss driven more by joy than passion. He stood up and placed the guitar against the side of the sofa. "Come, we're going to be late for my class. It's good you're already dressed."

Nico took his place on the mat at the front, sitting cross-legged in a comfortable pose and resting his hands on his knees while he closed his eyes and meditated quietly. When he sensed the time was right and everyone was settled, he opened his eyes and said, "Namaste," which the class repeated back to him.

He began, "We'll start by waking up kundalini. Using Rapid Breath of Fire, move the prana up to your heart—and third eye. This is a basic exercise we've been doing all along to clear toxins out of the body, raise our frequency, stretch our lungs, and oxygenate our blood. Now, let's start by placing our hands together and repeat the guru mantra to elevate the spirit. It means "The ecstasy of consciousness is my beloved." Then he began to chant, "Wahe guru, wahe guru…"

Maya listened to him intently, his voice stirring something deep inside that she could not explain. She followed along with the class as each kriya was performed, easily matching the rapid breathing technique that went along with the exercises. As much as she could, she watched Nico, and her mind wandered repeatedly to the quick, gentle kiss he'd placed on her lips.

Just as Maya thought the class was ending, Nico surprised everyone by teaching another meditation. She thought the kriya may actually have been for her personally, and that he was teaching the class along with her.

"Shabd Kriya builds mental focus, concentration, and helps regenerate the body. Follow my instructions." Nico sat in a cross-legged posture, resting his hands in Cosmic Mudra with thumb tips meeting. He continued, "This kriya uses Nasikagra Drishti—nose tip gazing. Look down at the tip of your nose, and if you get uncomfortable, rest your eyes for a moment, then resume. I'll join in with you at first, then walk the room and observe. Continue this meditation until I say 'Namaste,' for the class to be over."

Maya gazed at the tip of her nose while she did the pranayama, but she really wanted to follow Nico with her eyes as he meandered silently down the aisles. After about ten minutes, she heard him say "Namaste." The class replied, and everyone slowly rose and rolled up their mats.

Maya waited for Nico to look at her, giving some signal she should come over to him, but he didn't. Instead, he began talking to another student. Disappointed, she went into the locker room. She showered quickly and put on a pair of black cut-off denim shorts, with a semi-sheer slouchy T-shirt and her Frye boots. She fastened the Pamela Love bronze dagger necklace that she always wore for good luck around her neck, then shoved her yoga gear into her Proenza Schouler bag. The large PS1 black leather satchel was a gift from an Oscar winning action star who always did his own stunts and had taken Maya under his wing. He'd overheard her tell one of the Wardrobe girls that it was a really cool bag, but with a $2,000 price tag, one she would never buy for herself. When he heard she'd been injured, he surprised her by bringing it to her filled with snacks, magazines, and fancy toiletries to take the focus off the price.

Walking out of the locker room, she was startled to see Nico standing outside the door, waiting for her. "You women take forever to get ready. Come, we're going to be late."

His eyes took in her long, lean, toned body, made slightly taller by the heels of the boots. Her legs were tanned on top of her naturally dark olive complexion. He smiled when his eyes finally rested on her face.

"Where are we going?" she asked, mystified.

"I need to go look at this space where I want to open a larger studio. You took so long, I'm going to be late. Do you want to come or not? I have to lock the door."

"Sure," she answered, a bit flustered by his brusqueness.

At his motorcycle, she put on the helmet and remained silent as Nico explained how to hold onto him and where to place her hands when they braked. She didn't want to interrupt him and announce that, as a stunt actor, she drove bikes in movies at speeds well over one hundred miles per hour. She hoped he wouldn't attempt to show off for her. That's when accidents happen.

They headed south on Laurel Canyon and down Melrose, turning left onto North Robertson. It was about a thirty minute ride, and Maya liked having her arms around Nico, feeling his taut muscles under her bare hands when she held him tighter on twisty Laurel Canyon going over the hill. Nico pulled over in front of a pretty building near Tagine, Ryan Gosling's trendy Moroccan restaurant. Peeking in, Nico texted the realtor, and in a matter of minutes the agent pulled up and escorted them inside. Nico walked around the space with a sense of importance that Maya hadn't expected, very unlike the gentle spirit she felt at Amaru. When the realtor left, Nico suggested they walk a few blocks along Wilshire to check out a space above the G-Star Raw men's clothing store, saying, "That place is expensive…but I need to move to a better location and a bigger space."

After they left, Nico rattled off the pluses and minuses of each location. Finally, as if an afterthought, he asked Maya's opinion, and she paused to think about it.

"I think I prefer the Robertson space."

This piqued Nico's curiosity and he asked, "Why? Isn't Wilshire more prestigious?"

"No," she responded matter-of-factly. "I actually think Robertson is trendier, and Wilshire is more commercial. I mean, you have a BMW dealership, offices, and banks. But Robertson has Tagine. See what I mean? It's a little more low-key, yet very chic."

Nico nodded and said, "Yes, I see what you mean. You're right, and the rent is less!"

"Nico, why do you feel you need to move from Studio City? I

love your place, it's so warm and comfortable. I love the chamber and your office—and your apartment is cozy and so convenient for the time in between sessions, to cook and play guitar."

"It's comfortable, but the location isn't suitable for my high-profile clientele." He became boastful, "Did you see the photo in *LA Social* of me in Cannes? When the magazine interviewed me, they were surprised I'm located in Studio City. They expected me to have a Beverly Hills address. Do you understand?" He took her hand as they walked back toward the bike. "I need you to help me. I want you to promote me to your colleagues. Tell the actors, directors—everyone you work with to come to Amaru for private yoga and energy healing."

Maya asked tentatively, "Well, how much are private sessions?"

Nico was firm. "I don't discuss that in advance. I have to meet with the client and see what they need."

That seemed fair, Maya thought, like a doctor's consultation.

When they got to the bike, he put the helmet on her head, pushing her hair back behind her ears as he did so, then clipping it carefully under her chin. All the while he stared into her black eyes. "Your eyes are so dark. Are you sure you can see at night?"

She laughed. "I think so."

Nico laughed and kissed her again sweetly on the lips. "Come, we'll go back to my little studio that you like so much and I'll make dinner."

Maya's legs pressed gently against his thighs as they made their way back up Laurel Canyon. Nico pulled into the parking lot of the Vons supermarket. Handing her his helmet, he marched ahead, calling over his shoulder, "Get a cart." Placing her bag in the front, she hurried to catch up to him. Maya followed him up and down each aisle before Nico stopped at a jar of Nutella. "Do you know what this is?"

Laughing she said, "Of course! It's delicious! But I dare not eat it often; it's very fattening."

Examining the jar, he read the ingredients and thankfully put it back on the shelf. "Come. Let's get a steak," he announced and headed for the meat case. "The steak here is passable, but nothing like at home in Argentina," he asserted, while carefully examining each one.

As soon as they got back to the apartment, Nico got out the grill pan for the steak and began basting it with a green sauce.

"What's this?" she asked, bravely dipping her pinky in the bowl.

"It's chimichurri. I make my Ita's recipe, and I put it on everything!"

Maya watched him moving around the kitchen as he placed the steak on the pan. While it was searing he sliced the long baguette in half-inch thick slices. When the steak was done, he cut long strips, putting them on top of the baguette slices. Dunking one into the bowl of chimichurri sauce, he said, "Here, try this," as he hand fed her the steak.

Bits of green herbs stuck to the corner of her mouth, and he leaned in to lick it off with his tongue, causing a ripple of excitement up her spine. She boldly picked one up, dunked it into the sauce, and fed him.

They sipped their wine and continued feeding each other for a while before Maya spoke. "Tell me about living with the Q'ero," she inquired casually.

Nico regaled her with stories from his past and then boasted about the documentary. When they finished eating, she took charge and washed the dishes while Nico scrolled through Netflix to find a movie. "Maya, did you see *Skyfall*?" he called out to her.

"I know some of the stunt performers on that movie," she called over to him. When she was finished in the kitchen she joined him on the sofa, taking off her boots and tucking her legs up underneath herself.

Watching the film, Nico peppered her with questions, as if he didn't believe she knew them. When she commented about one of her friend's stunts, he asked, "Really? So who's a better fighter?"

Maya laughed. "Of course, she's a terrific fighter. She was in *Tomb Raider*, and then a big job on *Die Another Day*."

"So those hot babes didn't do their own fights?" he asked, incredulous.

Maya laughed. "Nope!"

Nico smiled at her. "Come here." He pulled her close to him as he murmured, "My fighting jaguar."

This time he kissed her hard on the mouth—burning, needy. His tongue sought hers and they played with each other, swirling and teasing, until she grasped his hair, fiercely pulling him harder to her. Letting her hands roam through his hair, she then slid them down the length of his body to pull his T-shirt over his head, tossing it aside. She ran her hands over his hard biceps and onto his chest; she'd dreamed of this moment.

Nico pulled on her bottom lip, biting just a little. In response, her nipples hardened under the sheer T-shirt. First kissing her neck, his tongue then teased at her ear as he reached for the hem of her shirt, pulling it over her head. He unhooked her bra, letting it fall away, kissing her shoulder as his fingertips found her erect nipples and gently squeezed them, teasing her. Writhing under his touch, her fingers tugged at his hair as he nipped at each nipple with his mouth, pulling and licking them gently.

"You like me sucking your tits?" he purred.

She moaned in reply.

He worked each nipple slowly, sucking and licking them. Arching her back, he sucked hard until she pleadingly cried, "Nico…"

Her hands reached for his crotch, feeling for his erection. Unbuttoning the top button, she slowly pulled the zipper down, sliding her hand over the length of his cock.

He quickly pulled off his jeans as she unzipped her shorts, sliding them down her hips.

Kneeling on the floor, he turned her to face him. "Lean back," he ordered, grabbing her legs and pushing her thighs apart, hungry for the taste of her. As desperate as he was to be inside her—he wanted to hear her scream—he kissed his way up her thigh, then lifted her legs until her knees were almost to her chest, exposing her wet and glistening hot, pink pussy. Running his fingers along the rim, up and over her clitoris, he gently opened the mouth of her pussy for his finger to explore inside, feeling the tightness close around him. When he stroked her G-spot, she moaned loudly, "Nico, Please. Oh my God."

He finger-fucked her rapidly, pressing over the special swollen spot—feeling the wetness grow—then stopped abruptly, slipping the juices over her clit and massaging it. Letting out a small cry, she begged, "Don't stop....please..."

With the heat of her pussy in his mouth, he stiffened his tongue, and fucked her rapidly with it. Breathless, she writhed beneath him, pleading for release, the tight coil in her belly slowly unraveling. He gently nibbled and pulled her clit with his lips, then assiduously licked softly from her anus to the top of her clit. Panting, she pleaded, her clit aching and twitching with desire. She was spread wide open, and the pink folds of her swollen pussy glistened.

"Nico...please," she cried, arching up, unable to contain herself. "I need you now..." Consumed by her tameless tellurian needs, she lifted her pussy up to him, wanting him to fill her inside. His serpentine tongue flicked deep into her, lapping up her savory juices like a kitten.

His cock throbbed, ready to explode, and he raised up and crept close to her. Holding himself just at the opening of her pussy, he rubbed around the entrance.

Maya was mad with desire. "Stop teasing me, Nico. Take me, please."

Holding her hips, he thrust his cock into her, and she let out a cry of relief. Teasing her, he pulled all the way out before easing his way back in. Then, as he picked up the pace, his movements became more powerful. Moaning, she thrust her hips frantically, spurring him to fuck her harder and faster, until she began to squirt, the warm liquid ejaculating over his cock.

"Oh baby. You squirted for me, oh yes..." Fervently, Nico sped up his thrusts, the hotness of her juices exciting him wildly.

Wrapping her legs around his waist, she held him into her. Hands in his hair, she pulled his face to hers, kissing him feverishly, their tongues matching the movements of their hips as they met each other over and over. Clenching around him as he pumped in and out, she shuddered and let out an anguished cry as she came.

Unable to hold back any longer, he erupted into her as they came together in pulsating waves.

Not wanting to let him go, she held him to her, her hands caressing his shoulders and back.

Nico kissed her mouth, her nose, her forehead, and then, gazing deeply into her eyes, murmured, "Maya…I've fallen under the spell of the jaguar."

Untangling themselves, he brought her into his bathroom and they showered. Lathering each other's hair, Maya felt an unexpected familiarity with Nico, as if she had known him a long time. She didn't always feel that way the first time she hooked up with someone. After drying off, Nico pulled on a pair of grey boxer briefs, leaving his chest bare, and Maya slipped on her pink bikini bottoms and slouchy tee. Returning to the sofa, he opened another bottle of wine, hit the remote, and *Skyfall* resumed playing. They collapsed together, Nico resting his head in Maya's lap. She casually played with his hair, at first tentatively, not sure he would like it.

To her surprise, he whispered, "I love you playing with my hair. My mom used to do that when I was little…"

Watching the movie they'd both seen before, Nico commented on the action, scene by scene. Maya laughed, delighted by his playful disposition, interjecting her own tales of behind-the-scenes drama. When the movie ended, she was sleepy from the wine, and sat up to put on her shorts and boots.

"Where are you going?" he asked, sounding disturbed. His mood had changed quickly.

"I'd better be getting home."

"Why? Do you want to leave?" he asked, agitated.

"No, not really…but I don't even have a toothbrush!"

He shook his head, and managed a small laugh. "Do you need a toothbrush? You can use mine!"

Seeing he was relaxing again, she laughed along and shrugged. "I don't have an early call…just a rehearsal for one scene, late in the day." Playfully, she added, "I'll stay if you promise we can do the fearlessness kriya together in the morning."

"So, are you bribing me?" he teased. "Well, I'll go along with it just this one time. But you'll pay for it!"

In the bedroom, Maya asked, "Can I borrow a T-shirt to sleep in?"

Instead of replying, Nico quickly pulled her T-shirt off, playfully pushing her down on the bed so she was propped up against a pile of his kilim pillows. Removing his shorts, he climbed on top of her, straddling her hips as he teased, "I'll give you a shirt later. Right now, I want to play with you again. You're so hot, baby. I need more of you before I'll be able to sleep." He leaned back a bit and stroked his semi-erect cock. "Look, I'm already hard just watching you sit on my bed."

She smiled up at him. Her black eyes were like bottomless pools into which he could dive.

"You're a beast," she said, referring to his enormous size.

Brandishing his cock, he pursed his lips, considering the compliment. "I've been called many things, but never a beast."

She gazed up into his compelling eyes that seemed to always be slightly hidden by that sexy lock of hair. As if on cue, he raked it back with his hand. Then he leaned forward to kiss her, and their tongues met immediately in a dance. Sitting up, he continued stroking the length of his erection. Maya licked her lips in anticipation as he grew harder.

Leaning over her, he angled his body so that the tip of his cock pressed against her lips. He groaned, low and anguished, when she took him firmly into her hands. Intently, she began sucking the head of his cock while rubbing her thumb along the base of the tip. He growled, "Yes, baby, those are the sweetest lips."

Eager to be inside her mouth, he pushed in and she took the whole of him, wrapping her hands firmly around the thick, rigid shaft. She encircled him with both hands, now wet with her saliva, teasing the head and pulling on the tip with her full lips and squeezed him firmly while he fucked her mouth, using her hands to control his speed and depth. Her hands traveled to the base of his cock, where she gently fondled his balls, allowing her fingers to trail back toward his anus. He moaned and fucked her mouth harder as she gently inserted a wet finger and slipped it in and out, driving him wild. Holding her head tightly into his groin, he fucked her mouth harder, pushing his cock against the back of her throat, and tilting her head back so he could go even deeper.

She moaned, sending him into a frenzy. "That's it, baby. All the way. I love it when you moan."

Thrusting harder and faster, he wrapped his fingers into her long black hair to control her. "Take me in all the way, baby. I love fucking that beautiful mouth."

With him leaning over her she had no control and allowed him to guide his cock back in all the way as he fucked her mouth harder and faster. "So good, baby." Just then, he released his hold on her hair and pulled himself out of her mouth without coming. "Not yet," he murmured.

Maya looked up at him. His eyes were glazed over, like smoldering coals.

"You look so beautiful," he rasped. His cock was pulsing, hard and wet, the veins bulging.

Holding her legs, he roughly flipped her over so she was face down, her cheek resting on a pillow, the pulled her hips up. "Keep your ass up for me, baby. I want your hot ass."

Taking a jar of coconut oil off the night stand, he slowly applied it to her ass, pressing his thumb into her anus. Moaning, she lifted her ass higher, begging him for more. Gliding his fingers easily inside her, she pushed back at him. "You like this, baby? You like me playing in your ass, don't you?"

She moaned, "Yes," unable to speak more.

Anointing himself with the oil, he then pressed the tip of his cock into her. Holding her hips tightly, he slowly pushed in. Feeling her tighten around him, he held still for a moment. "That's it, baby. Relax," he coaxed before moving slowly and rhythmically. "Oh baby, you're so tight. Play with yourself," he commanded.

Moving with him, she eagerly inserted first one, then two fingers into her wet pussy, circling her clit with her thumb, and feeling the tightness of him inside.

"Your ass is so beautiful." His words came raggedly…exciting her further while she fucked herself. Pumping herself harder and massaging her clit, her breathing became ragged as she tightened, nearing climax. As she got closer, he fucked her faster, holding her hips and thrusting harder. "You feel so good, baby. I'm going to come inside your hot little ass."

She felt the first hot burst of cum inside her, and then rolling, one after another, he jetted into her. Holding himself tight against her as the final waves of his climax concluded, he massaged her butt and thrust into her again and again. "Come for me, baby," the sound of his voice consumed her.

Coming apart under him, her body quaked as she cried out and collapsed onto the bed, unable to hold herself up. Nico collapsed on top of her, burying his head in her neck, damp with her heat. He stayed inside her, not willing to move. Content, they lay there exhausted. As his cock slowly retracted, she held onto it, not wanting to let it slip from her.

Reluctantly, Nico went into the bathroom to wash up. On the way back to the bed, he stopped at his dresser and opened a drawer. "Here, baby. T-shirt, as promised."

Climbing under the covers, he tapped the space next to him for her to join him, and she pulled on the T-shirt before climbing in. Snuggling into him, her head on his chest, she fell fast asleep.

21

Luna had been expecting Nico to call any day, since she figured he was back from St. Barths. When her cell phone rang, she silently cursed that she was stuck in a damn meeting, letting it go to voice mail. Now Nico would be angry, but there was nothing she could do about it.

Nico hadn't needed to tell Luna where he was going for the holidays. She saw pictures on Facebook that she recognized as St. Barths, the summer camp for wealthy, well-known business tycoons, pop stars, and Hollywood celebrities. The location tag showed they were staying at the exclusive Eden Rock overlooking St. Jean Bay.

It was evident to Luna why Nico chose to go there instead of home to Buenos Aires for Christmas. With Alexa's connections and Nico's good looks, they would be bumping elbows with movie stars and the power elite. Even though Nico complained these weren't "his people," that's still what he chose to do for Christmas and to bring in the New Year.

Luna called him back in less than an hour's time, but as expected, he berated her for not answering instantly. Though she had expected it, it still upset her, and she always ended up apologizing. Nico was speaking so quickly, she told him to slow down. "I met a publisher in St. Barths who wants me to write a book about my life. About how I lived in Kerala and then with the Q'ero; a memoir about how I became a healer. He wants to publish *my story!*" he rattled.

Luna finally registered what he was saying, "That's so great, Nico!" she squealed with delight.

He continued excitedly, "Luna, this is the perfect platform that I need. You and I will write this together. You're the only one I trust to help me!"

Without too much hesitation, she replied, "I'd love to help you, Nico, but you have to be the one to write it. I can *help* you."

"Come over right after work. We need to get started right away."

"All right, Nico," she agreed. "I have your Christmas present. It's been sitting in my car for a week."

In his usual frenzy, he blurted, "I haven't had time to wrap yours!"

She laughed, certain he hadn't remembered to get her anything. Though one never knew what to expect from Nico.

When Luna got to his studio, she went straight back to the apartment and found Nico cooking, music blasting, and his suitcase open in the middle of the floor, clothes spilling out.

"Nico, why didn't you unpack?"

Before he could answer, his phone rang, and he put his finger up to his lips, signaling her not to speak so the caller wouldn't know he had company. Luna hated that, finding it offensive.

Using the spurious sexy voice he reserved for Alexa, he cooed, "OK, of course. You already know that." Luna couldn't discern the intent of the call. He continued talking on the phone, "Look, I'm cooking, and it's going to burn. I'll call you back later." Then, "Well, I do have to eat. I'm making some pasta. OK, you too. ¡Chau!" Nico hung up and looked at Luna, who was picking his clothes up off the floor.

"Bella." He reached out beseechingly.

She looked up at him, letting her hair hide half her face.

"Stop being jealous!" he chided her somewhat playfully.

Luna just took a deep breath and sighed loudly, "I'm not jealous, Nico. You know exactly how I feel. Here I am, picking up your clothes. And I'm going to help you write a book. But she gets to stand in the sun."

Nico had been chopping onions and garlic for the tomato sauce while the chopped meat cooked on the stove. When he just stood looking at her instead of replying, Luna called out, "Forget it, Nico. The meat is burning!"

He turned around to lower the flame, and added some olive oil to the pan. Then he said, "Luna, it's all coming together, just like I said it would. So everyone needs to do their part. She does hers, and you do yours, OK? You want a glass of wine? We can relax."

Luna relented a little and smiled. "Of course. And here's your Christmas gift." She handed him the package, wrapped in traditional Christmas wrapping paper of Santa Claus with his reindeer flying across a night sky, tied up in a wide, metallic gold French ribbon.

Luna had found a hinged box in the Wardrobe Department and decided to decoupage it with a collection of photos—images of Nico, yoga poses, chakra symbols, and inspirational quotations. The process was in itself a meditation to him, taking her three weeks to apply the dozens of layers of school glue creating the lacquered finish. For the top of the box, she'd chosen a photo of Nico taken at Soul & Surf in Kerala. In the photograph, his eyes shone, and that persistent, unruly lock of hair was in his face as it always seemed to be. Only recently had Luna learned that the word kundalini is derived from the Sanskrit word *kundal,* which means "the curl of the lock of hair from the beloved." The uncoiling of the hair represents the awakening of the kundalini. The resemblance to Nico himself in the definition had startled, but not surprised, her.

Nico put the chef's knife down and turned off the flame under the meat. Taking the gift, he began his ritual of slowly unwrapping. In due time, he uncovered the box and studied the collage of photos in disbelief, not understanding at first what it took to create the layers of imagery.

"Nico, do you like it?"

He was speechless, but finally managed, "Luna—this is the most incredible gift I have ever received. It is…the most special thing anyone has *ever* given me—I love it."

Thinking him completely sincere, she said softly, "I'm so glad you like it, Nico."

"These pictures…" he studied the image of himself on the beach in Kerala. Concentrating, he read aloud, "Let loose the arrow." He murmured, "Sat Nam…Sat Nam…Sat Nam," while reading the sides as he turned the box. "You even put the words to the song!" She knew he meant "Knockin' on Heaven's Door." "Where did you get all the pictures?"

Proudly, she recited, "I collected them. I printed them. Some I found on the internet, others in magazines."

Incredulously, he asked, "How did you get a picture of me with the paqos?"

Luna laughed. "Silly, I took it with my phone, from the one on the wall in the chamber."

"Luna?" he murmured hesitantly.

"Yes, Nico?"

"Thank you." He hugged her somewhat awkwardly, as if unsure how intimate he should be.

She put her forehead against his. "Nico. I can't buy you expensive things…or take you on trips. This is all I can do. I won't compete with them."

Nico scolded her, "Luna, you have to stop with that. It's not a competition."

She replied sadly, "That's how I feel, Nico, 'cause you don't spend time with me. I haven't seen you in over a month."

He refilled their wine glasses before putting the onions and garlic into the sauce and adding more spices to the meat. He checked the pasta, and shook his hand off after scalding it in the water. "¡Ay, caramba! The pasta is ready. Go sit down and we'll eat and talk about my book."

o   o   o

When Luna saw the newsletter in her inbox from Kristi Fisher, something compelled her to open it right away. Kristi had worked as an intern for Luna several years earlier, and they'd hit it off. Luna had discovered Kristi's ability to heal when she'd tripped while wearing flip-flops in the wardrobe truck, stubbing her toe so badly that the nail had almost ripped off. Luna had been in excruciating pain, and Kristi had placed her hand lightly over Luna's toe, barely touching her. Luna felt heat penetrate her foot, and when Kristi removed her hand, the pain had subsided and her toenail was back in place. She'd heard later that Kristi had completed a five year program in Chinese Medicine and acupuncture. The newsletter prompted her to call Kristi for an appointment.

Kristi's practice was in a shared suite of medical professionals in a new office building not far from Luna's condo on Wilshire. Despite not having been in contact for so long, they immediately began catching up, and Luna filled her in on *Going My Way*.

Kristi chuckled. "Luna, I watched the complete first season of *Going My Way*. It's the next *Sex and the City*! Your career is doing great. What else is going on?"

Even though Kristi wasn't a close personal friend, Luna felt the warmth and compassion she emanated, and began sharing her anxiety over turning fifty. "I know this sounds shallow…but people no longer say how beautiful I am—only how beautiful I *was*. I'm embarrassed to admit how much that bothers me."

Kristi closed her eyes and inhaled deeply before responding. "What you're describing isn't uncommon with attractive people, like you, who have relied upon their external appearance for validation. You have to learn to draw from a deeper well."

Luna sighed, and the words tumbled out effortlessly, "I began seeing a yoga instructor. He also practices energy medicine—and it was a huge benefit. We did kriyas to open up my possibilities and creativity, and sure enough, I won the Guild Award. On top of that, I'm thinner, more toned, and I feel healthier. And…I'm not sure how to explain it…but I think you will get it…I feel younger and more alive, you know?"

Luna had a feeling Kristi didn't need to ask, but did anyway, "So what's the problem?"

Luna hesitated before admitting, "I feel a strong attachment to my yoga instructor…to Nico. It's disrupting my life, and my relationship with Tyler."

Kristi's eyebrows went up and Luna quickly interjected, "Nothing happened! It's not a sexual relationship, but I'm obsessed with him. I crave his attention, and his approval. I need to be around him to feel good—like a drug. It's hard to explain…but I need him in my life."

Luna noticed a look of recognition on Kristi's face. "So, how long has this been going on?"

Luna recounted Sofia's problems with Nico and how, after Sofia left, Luna had seen a different side of him. "When Nico cut me out of his life, saying I betrayed him, I couldn't breathe. I was literally suffering from that loss. That's when I realized I had a problem. But he let me back into his life," she paused, then added, "telling me I could make it up to him. That was a year ago, and things have never been the same. He's different. He's very needy and demanding—and Tyler says it's wrong that I often put Nico ahead of him."

Kristi's eyes brightened with awareness. "I have a hunch, but before I tell you, I'd like to check something. Would you let me do Reiki on you?" she asked.

Luna had never had Reiki, but was familiar with the therapy, which passes energy from the practitioner's hands to the recipient, bringing about healing on the physical, mental, emotional, and spiritual levels. In fact, it was what Kristi had done on Luna's toe all those years ago, before she was trained professionally.

The irony wasn't lost on Luna that Nico, an energy healer, was her reason for seeking Kristi's help.

Luna lay down on the table and immediately felt the heat from Kristi's hands as she placed them on either side of her head. This was the first time she had told anyone the truth about Nico. Maybe, she thought, there was even more to how she felt, and she hadn't been completely honest with herself.

Kristi was breathing softly and Luna could tell she had moved into a different state of consciousness. She'd said the Reiki—spirit energy—is intelligent, and knows where to heal, so Luna prayed she would find the source of her attachment to Nico.

Suddenly, a crushing sadness overcame her. Assuring Luna that the feeling was normal, Kristi moved alongside her, placing her hands on her solar plexus. Luna was about to say that was the spot where she felt a constant flutter inside, but Kristi shushed her and said not to worry. Then she remained in motionless trance for over twenty minutes, with her hands on Luna's solar plexus and her breathing soft and shallow.

Sitting across from each other later in the treatment room, Kristi spoke softly yet confidently, "I wasn't going to alarm you until I was certain." Luna took a deep breath, but remained silent, waiting for Kristi to continue. "Have you heard the expression *corded?*"

Luna shook her head and said, "No, but when you had your hands on my solar plexus, I was about to say that's where I have this constant warm fluttering, I call them fire butterflies. They began soon after I started practicing yoga with Nico."

Kristi placed her hand on her own solar plexus. "Up here, right?"

Luna nodded. "Exactly there."

Kristi looked her in the eyes, and not wanting to frighten her, said calmly, "Luna, I can see it."

Luna's eyes widened, "What do you mean you can see it? See what?"

Kristi replied matter-of-factly, "It looks exactly like a real cord." She paused before adding, "It connects you to him."

Luna exclaimed, "I knew it. I could feel it!"

Kristi evenly explained, "A psychic cord is natural between a mother and a child. It's like an umbilical cord, providing life support until the child is energetically independent." She went on, "But Luna, some people are like vampires, and the cord allows them to suck life-force. Don't confuse this with a connection like love, which has a higher vibration of light, allowing sharing, but not depletion."

"I know I have a connection to Nico…he needs me. I'm so grateful to him…I love him." Luna hesitated, then rushed to add, "Like a mother or a friend. How can he be a vampire?"

Kristi reminded her, "From what you told me, you're grateful for his healing. He makes you feel good. You said you've never felt better—like you're thirty again. He compliments you, and you crave his approval. He needs you, and demands your attention, even when it's inconvenient, to the point of upsetting Tyler. You've given him permission to cross over boundaries. When you try to draw a line by withholding your energy—your time and services—he gets angry and punishes you, because he's being deprived. Do you understand what I'm saying?" Kristi implored, wanting to ensure Luna grasped the magnitude of the situation.

Luna was shaken, and her voice trembled. "Yes, I completely understand the vampire analogy!"

"Ah, but Luna…it's more than an analogy! The cord is *real*, you just don't see it in this plane. Nico *is* a vampire. It's not blood he craves, it's life-force. It's no wonder he's a yoga master with the ability to control prana."

Luna was enthralled, and exhaled sharply. "Kristi, what am I going to do?"

"Women are victims of cording more often than men because they're naturally nurturing. You see this as a way to be needed and to repay him for how he helped you. You've been too generous in this relationship, and he's draining you."

Kristi took her hand and Luna braced herself, realizing she hadn't finished, "Luna, this cord is very dark. I believe it's more than just crossing boundaries. It feels to me like a psychic attack."

Luna's eyes filled with tears, not understanding how this could be true. Kristi handed her a tissue and reassured her, "Now, I don't believe he wishes you harm. But this cord *was* attached purposely, in shamanic tradition—and Nico *is* a shaman. It was put there to control you. It's his feeding tube for what he needs from you. I would venture to say he's corded other people, too. What you don't supply, he gets from them. I can break this cord, but only if you work with me, and it will *not* be easy—he *will* want to reconnect. You're a valuable source of supply for what he requires from you. You've been a willing provider until now, but when you sever the cord he will be denied. You have to truly *want* to sever the cord and heal the wound."

Luna panicked as tears came quickly to her eyes, and words spilled out uncontrollably, "I don't know if I can! I love him. I need him— he means everything to me."

Kristi was compassionate, but firm. "Luna, it's going to ruin you. I think you know it, or you wouldn't be here."

Luna nodded, dismayed. "I know, Kristi, I can't keep the cord. He takes too much from me. It's like I'm on call twenty-four hours. If I say no, he punishes me. Sometimes he frightens me!" Pausing to collect herself, she added, "It's painful! Tyler knows all of this. I haven't kept anything from him. It hurts him and he doesn't understand what's wrong with me, why I take this abuse. Lately, it's also really begun to affect my job. I know I have to cut the cord, but it's only when I think clearly that I'm willing to. When I don't see him, when he's not in my life, I can't stop thinking about him."

Nothing Luna said surprised Kristi. She continued, this time more insistently, "I can help you because my power, along with your willingness to sever the cord, is stronger than his power. But if you let him back, he *will* reconnect it." Taking Luna's hand and looking her squarely in the eyes, she asked, "Do you want to cut the cord, Luna?"

Putting her head in her hands, then wiping the tears away, she gazed back up at Kristi. Taking a deep lungful of air, she exhaled sharply, then answered clearly, "Yes, I do."

Kristi directed Luna to close her eyes. "Visualize the cord. It's a thick black tube, like at the gas station, entering your solar plexus, the third chakra. Now, Luna, picture cutting the cord and command Nico to let you go. Think about why you allowed this cord. What is your payoff in letting him cord you?"

Luna considered all the reasons she had given earlier. "I feel as if I owe him my life, in a way."

Kristi admonished her gently, "That's not exactly how you put it earlier. You said he makes you feel younger and that you need his approval."

Luna concurred, "You're right. What's the difference?"

Kristi clarified, "You don't need his approval. You have to feel beautiful and young without him. He's made you dependent on him for something you have the power to give yourself. You have to find that without him, or you'll allow him to reattach the cord every time you need a compliment. This cord is going in both directions—unless *you* no longer want it." Kristi shook her head. "Luna, only you can decide. Your reason for the cord is a misplaced desire, feeding your own vanity. It's doing you more harm than good. He feeds you what you think you need and want, so *he* gets what he needs from you." Kristi explained what Luna needed to do next, "A raw stub is left behind, like a wound. You need to protect yourself by visualizing a color like red or blue as a protective salve over the wound. If you see or speak to Nico, he'll sense the cord is missing, and reattach it immediately."

Leaving Kristi's office, Luna felt so much lighter and clearer, like a fog she hadn't known was there had been lifted. She was startled by how vivid and bright everything was, and by how good she felt.

Walking to her car, her phone rang and she fished into her bag to retrieve it.

It was Nico.

Luna hesitated. She held the phone in her hand, staring at Nico's picture as the ringtone "Knockin' on Heaven's Door" played.

Nervous and unsure what to do, she answered.

"Bella…where are you?" he purred sweetly.

"I'm running some errands," Luna lied. She couldn't very well say where she'd been. Her mind raced with questions. How did he know to call at exactly that moment? Did he sense the cord was no longer attached? Luna was freaked out. She could actually feel his magnetic pull.

Tentatively, he enticed, "Can you come over for a little bit?"

That's what Nico always asked when he was lonely and wanted her company. Luna's head was spinning. If Kristi cleared the cord, why do I still feel the pull? Why do I still want to see him? If I go, he'll surely reattach the cord—won't he? Kristi must have expected he would call and want to see me—it couldn't be that simple! Luna knew she shouldn't go over, but how could she tell him she was ending their relationship and never speaking to him again? She would miss him too much, he was a part of her. And Nico knew this as much as she did.

"Sure, Nico. I'm just getting to my car now. I should be there in a few minutes."

He sighed, relieved. "Good, bella. I miss you. I'll cook and we can watch a movie."

o   o   o

Luna's visit with Kristi had left her feeling troubled and confused. Torn between her attachment to Nico and Kristi's perception (or was it recognition) that he was a dark entity, Luna was shaken to the core. When she told Tyler about being corded and about Nico being a vampire sucking her life-force, Tyler hadn't been the least bit surprised. To her astonishment, he'd further elucidated that the true meaning of vampirism *is* the taking of life-force—and stories of the undead sucking blood were a metaphor. Her heart pounding in her throat, the panic had been palpable in her voice when she snapped, "Why do you let me see him? What are you thinking? Aren't you supposed to protect me?"

Sounding like the philosopher he was, he'd replied solemnly, "I would never try to control you, Luna. That would make me no better than Nico. Besides, you would only get angry."

"I need help, Tyler. I'm addicted to him in some weird way. Like a drug. Will you help me?"

"I wish I could help you, but only you can take your life back. Only you have control, Luna. It's like telling an alcoholic to stop drinking."

They were in the den watching television when Luna's cell phone rang. With each ring, her nerves frayed further. Holding the phone up so Tyler could see it was Nico, she declared, "I need to talk to him…explain things. I'll take it in the other room."

Tyler shrugged, "Do what you want, Luna."

She could see the disappointment in his eyes, but more than that, she saw sadness and that pained her. Part of her wished he were more controlling and would forbid her to see Nico. She longed for Tyler to be passionate and sexually commanding, the way she imagined Nico to be. She felt guilty that she thrilled in Nico's artificial lustful admiration of her, when Tyler truly loved her and genuinely praised her inner beauty and wisdom.

In the living room, she sat in a down-stuffed Bergere. They hadn't spoken in over a week. He didn't need to tell her he'd been in Mexico with Alexa. Luna had figured that out by herself. His voice was a whisper, and he sounded half asleep. "Are you all right, Nico? You're so quiet, I can hardly hear you."

He spoke up, "Luna, it's because you're deaf."

She chuckled, relieved he sounded more like himself, always teasing her about her hearing. "It's because I'm old. Remember?"

He relayed the usual litany of complaints. "I'm tired. She's killing me. It's always a fucking drama with her." He paused to take a breath, "If I don't stay on top of her and spend time with her, she won't do anything for me—everything goes dead. She makes a scene about everything instead of doing things the way I say to do them.”

Luna had to bite her tongue to not say *I told you so*. “Nico, you said things are happening and you've been so busy working and traveling. You're exhausted, maybe you just need to rest.”

“Luna, bella. You're the only one I feel close to.”

She sighed; any barrier she'd attempted to construct dissolved with his words.

Suddenly exuberant, he asked, “Do you want to go see the Gipsy Kings with me?”

Without hesitation she replied, “Sure! When?”

He blurted, “Right *now*! And we can get dinner!”

Astounded, she asked, “What do you mean see the Gipsies right now? Where?”

“They're at my uncle's restaurant. He's friends with them. I almost forgot they are there tonight—unannounced, of course.” By uncle he meant one of Roberto's friends who buys wine from him.

“Yes, Nico! You know how much I love them!”

Quickly, he instructed, “I'll pick you up on the bike in forty-five minutes. Be downstairs!”

Luna hung up and ran to tell Tyler, announcing exuberantly, “Ty! You won't believe this…Nico asked me to go see the Gipsy Kings with him. They're jamming right now at his friend's bistro. You know I love the Gipsy Kings!”

Tyler shook his head, giving her a judgmental look, and scowled, “What happened to the work you did with Kristi?”

“Ty, I want to go see them play, and dance…it will be fun! Nico is picking me up.”

“Be careful. I *hate* when you go on that bike,” he said, clearly disappointed.

Luna put her arms around him and kissed him on the lips. “I know—he'll be careful.”

Not having much time, she chose something she felt looked young and hip—a black jersey ruched miniskirt with a fitted black tank top. The outfit was sexy and she hoped it didn't look like she was trying too hard. She topped it off with a classic ACNE Studios black leather motorcycle jacket and ankle boots she could dance in.

In less than an hour, Nico pulled up in front of her building. Handing her a helmet, he opened the visor and looked her up and down. "Wow! Bella. You look really hot!"

It was exactly what she wanted—needed—to hear. Climbing on the bike behind him, she hugged him hard. Nico joked, "Stop pressing your tits against me, I'll get a hard-on!"

She laughed, knowing he couldn't feel anything except the thick black leather and metal hardware of the jacket. Before she knew it, Luna was swaying to the music of the Gipsy Kings playing to a small room of locals. A half dozen couples danced where tables had been pushed away for the occasion.

When they launched into "Bamboleo," Nico captured her by the waist, pulling her into his arms. Even though she'd never danced with him, Nico was a strong leader and she was able to keep up, swiveling her hips as he moved her around the floor.

He whispered in her ear, "You're a very sexy woman, Luna. Be careful, I may seduce you tonight."

She just shook her head and smiled at him. She knew he was just playing her—and it was fine—she took pleasure in the game.

Near midnight, the waiters started putting chairs up on the tables. Luna was feeling tipsy, realizing they'd polished off two bottles of wine, and she'd eaten almost nothing.

Climbing onto the bike, Luna even forgot to be afraid, and a few minutes later they pulled up in front of Emerson Theater.

"Bella, why should we end this magical evening so early? The night is young," Nico urged.

"Nico, it's after midnight. I should go home. Tyler will be worried."

"Text him you'll be home soon."

Truth be told, Luna didn't want to go home. She wanted to do what young people did—party all night and go to a club that ordinary people can't get into. When Nico approached the velvet rope, the doorman waved them in and opened the door. She and Nico were whisked inside.

The music was so loud you could literally feel the beats inside your body. Calvin Harris's "Let's Go" was playing and everyone was jumping up, fists in the air, bouncing to the beat. "Stay here, don't move. If I lose you, I'll text you. Keep your phone in your hand."

Before she could respond, Nico disappeared, leaving her standing there alone. She kept dancing along with everyone else who didn't seem to have a partner. She was relieved when Nico wasn't gone long. He had two drinks in hand—she didn't need more to drink, but she took it.

"Be careful, they're very strong," he warned her, yelling over the music.

"I Need Your Love" began and the crowd went wild, raising their hands up high.

Luna yelled to Nico, "I love this song!"

Looking around the club, Luna suddenly felt awkward, being obviously the oldest person in the room. But she kept drinking and dancing like everyone else. Soon, though, she was wiped out, and her ears were ringing. She knew it was time for her to leave and asked Nico to get her a cab because she didn't want to go on the bike. Taking her by the waist, he led her through the packed crowd.

"Nico, I have to use the ladies' room. Where is it?"

He squeezed her hand reassuringly, "I'll take you, bella. Just stay close to me."

They made it off the dance floor, and as they neared the exit, Luna saw him ask the coat check person for a key, which Nico used to unlock the private wash room door. He held it open for her, and she walked in. He followed.

"Oh, Nico…it's only a one-person room!" she exclaimed, expecting him to leave.

"I know, Luna. Don't worry. I just don't want you to pass out and hit your head."

"Oh, OK," she complied, hoisting her skirt up to sit on the toilet and draping it over her lap decorously.

Waiting by the sink, Nico ran his fingers through his hair while looking in the mirror.

Dizzy and sleepy, Luna couldn't tell when she was finished peeing.

"Luna, are you OK?"

Luna hadn't noticed, but Nico now stood in front of her.

She looked up at him, her head spinning; he wasn't quite in focus.

Placing his hands behind her head, Nico pulled her face into his groin. She felt his cock straining beneath the zipper. Pulling her head away, she looked at him quizzically.

He unzipped his fly, and taking his semi-erect cock in his hand, stroked it in front of her mouth.

Startled, Luna sprung up, pulling up her panties and yanking her skirt down, straightening it.

She blurted, "Nico, what are you doing?"

His eyes smoldered like hot coals, and Luna was so drunk she couldn't read him. He appeared possessed, not sure who she was. Taking her around the waist, he pushed her against the tile wall, pressing his body against hers. He grasped both her wrists together, holding them above her head, "You're so hot, my bella. I want you… right here…right now."

Kissing her hard on the mouth, his free hand slid underneath her skirt and into her panties, fingering her pussy. He murmured huskily, "You're so wet."

Luna felt she was no longer in her own body. "Nico," she said breathlessly, feeling she would fall down if he were not pressed against her.

She desired him…the feel of his hard muscular body against her was so powerful…his hot lips devouring hers…his firm hands willfully caressing her. Her mind raced. *The drink. What was in the drink?* She could hear her ears ringing, the music pounding. Or was it her heart, about to burst?

His touch fueled the fires of her lust. He was rough, breathing hard. His hands, hot on her flesh, tore at her panties. Her breath hitched, and a tormented moan escaped her lips. Was this really happening, or was she dreaming? When the bathroom door opened, Nico jumped. The sudden intrusion was as deafening as unexpected thunder cracking through a breathless, humid night; a collision of two worlds that shattered Luna's nebulous reality. What had really been only a few moments had felt like an eternity. The harsh glare of the fluorescent lights jolted them into awareness. Holding her from falling, Nico gently persuaded, "Come Luna, I'll get you into a cab."

He took her hand as they bolted from the bathroom. The exit door was only steps away, and there was a line of cabs waiting. Nico opened the car door and helped her in, giving the driver the address, adding, "See that she gets inside." Then he turned to Luna, "Text me as soon as you get home." He closed the door of the cab and headed back into the club.

Luna was in a state of shock on the ride home. Had she imagined what happened? She felt certain Nico wouldn't remember, and the incident was the result of too much alcohol, and whatever else was in the drink. In the elevator, she texted Nico:

Home.

The bedroom was dark. Tyler was asleep, and she went into the bathroom to undress, wash her face, and brush her teeth. Looking in the mirror, she thought, *Who are you?* She looked younger and felt changed—more alive, like she would explode inside. Was it possible that Nico actually found her attractive, and that under the influence of drugs and wine could not control himself?

Luna crawled into bed and Tyler stirred, mumbling, "What time is it?"

"It's 3:00 a.m.," she whispered.

"It's late, Luna."

"I know." She knew that typical club guests partied till dawn, leaving with a hookup. She was happy to be safely at home, in her bed with Tyler. She was uncomfortable with what had happened, but part of her was gratified—it was a fantasy come true—even if Nico wouldn't remember it.

22

As she was drinking her third cup of ginger tea, Luna's phone rang out, *"Knock, knock, knockin' on heaven's door,"* and she picked it up.

"Good morning, Nico." The sound of her voice reverberated through her hangover.

"Why don't you come over and finish what we started," he purred.

Luna hesitated, part of her glad he remembered. "What are you doing?" she heard herself ask, not sure why.

"I'm lying here playing with myself," he replied in the deep, husky voice he used when flirting.

She quipped, "Nico, I'm at work. I don't know what you're talking about."

"Yes you do, Luna. You danced and threw your tits at me, like you always do."

Luna laughed. It was his routine flirt, nothing more. Still, she bantered back, "Don't be ridiculous, Nico. I most certainly did not. We danced. And got too drunk, that's all."

Nico sounded disappointed. "Oh, OK. If you're gonna be that way about it. Well, never mind. Can you come over later and help me with stuff around here?"

"Sure. I'll come by after work. Do you have a class?"

"Yes, from six to seven."

"OK, honey. See you later."

He didn't hang up and Luna could hear him breathing. "Nico?"

"Yes, Luna?"

"Are you OK?" she asked softly.

"No. I'm sad."

"Why?" she whispered.

"I need a real girlfriend, someone to love—who loves me."

She wanted to say, "But *I* love you." She knew it was unrealistic—a crazy fantasy. She would never trade the enduring love she had with Tyler for Nico. Nico was that dark entity that compelled her, and used her for his purposes. Still, it hurt her that Nico didn't think of her that way. She simply said, "Someone will turn up, when you're ready."

"I think I found someone, but I don't know yet," he said haltingly, unsure of himself.

"Are you talking about Maya?" Luna asked cautiously, careful not to spook him.

"Well, you said to find someone who I trust and would be a friend and help me, as well as being my lover. You called it a friend with benefits."

Luna laughed, shaking her head even though he couldn't see her. "That's not exactly what I meant, Nico! I said a girlfriend should also be a best friend. You kind of twisted that around."

He chuckled at her falling for his prank. "Ha ha. I know what you meant, Luna bella. I'm just teasing with you."

She snipped back, confessing, "Well, I *did* say that if you can't find a girlfriend who is your soul mate, or someone you would marry, at least find one age appropriate, who you like to fuck and have as a friend. So, yes, a *friend with benefits*."

o　o　o

Arriving at Amaru, Luna was surprised there weren't the normal number of cars in the parking lot. A hand scribbled note reading Class Canceled was taped to the front door. Before ringing the bell, she tested the door and found it open. Tentatively wandering in, she checked the studio, then the office before poking her head into the apartment and calling his name. She heard him mumble, "In here." He was stretched out in bed, watching TV.

She perched on the edge of the bed and began playing with his hair the way he liked, partitioning it into segments, as if she was getting ready to weave them together. "What's wrong? Why did you cancel class?"

"I was too tired. I didn't get home until after sunrise. Did you lock the door?"

"Yes, of course I did."

She got up to go into the kitchen, but he caught her hand. "Don't leave…just sit here with me."

"OK, Nico. I'm here."

Tapping the space next to him on the bed, he invited her to lay down with him, saying, "Let's watch a movie."

She kicked off her shoes and climbed in beside him. They watched *Taken* with Liam Neeson, about a man whose daughter gets kidnapped. Having already seen the movie together, Nico began chatting and brought up Alexa again. "Things aren't moving the way they should be, Luna."

Luna was careful to tread lightly. "Things take time, Nico."

"But it's taking too much time. Alexa is bullshit. She wants to know where I am every minute."

"Nico, you're letting her coerce you!"

"Luna, she owes me! And I won't let her get away with it."

She changed the subject, hoping he would lighten up. "So, tell me more about Maya."

He smiled and reached for his phone. "She's a famous stunt woman! She's sweet, and we have fun. You'll be happy to know I took your advice and she helps me around the apartment, cleaning up. Oh, and she makes great rice and beans!"

Leaping up, he opened a closet door. "Look!" he blurted, showing Luna his T-shirts neatly folded on a shelf in color-coordinated rows.

Luna laughed. "Oh my God, it looks like The Gap!"

He laughed too, grabbing his phone and flopping back on the bed. He scrolled through the pictures on his phone, stopping at shots he'd taken of a very pretty, exotic, dark-haired girl. "Luna, look. She's hot right?" He showed Luna a picture of Maya looking up at the camera with his fully engorged cock in her mouth, then scrolled to another shot of her laying on the bed, wearing a red lace bra, with Nico fisting her. "She'll do anything for me," he boasted.

Knowing what he wanted to hear, she agreed. "Yeah, she sure is hot!"

Nico's erotic tales used to make her blush, but she'd become accustomed to photos of his huge erection and his suggestive comments. There seemed to be an endless number of photos of women giving him a blow job and of him fucking them doggie style. Luna couldn't fathom why these women allowed him to take such compromising pictures.

They finished watching the movie, her head on his shoulder, occasionally petting his hand. When it was over he bolted up, announcing, "I'm hungry! Let's eat!"

Warily, Luna said, "Nico, I have to leave. It's date night and Tyler's making dinner. He won't appreciate it if I don't show up."

Nico pouted, but surprised her by saying, "It's OK, Luna. Thanks for keeping me company. You can leave."

She hugged him hard, kissing his neck, and thanked him, heading out the door before he could change his mind.

o   o   o

On the weekends, Tyler often made his trademark yogurt pancakes with wild blueberries. Luna was sitting at the breakfast bar reading the paper and slowly savoring each bite, the real Vermont maple syrup deliciously clinging to the plump berries. Preferring not to be disturbed on a Saturday morning, she'd purposely left her cell phone charging in the bedroom, and when the house phone rang, she ignored it, not recognizing the caller ID.

"Aren't you gonna get it?" Tyler asked, flipping another batch of pancakes.

"I'm so sick of answering that phone, it's always just a telemarketer. I'm seriously considering getting rid of that number."

Unable to ignore it, Tyler picked up. It wasn't a recording, and he repeated hello several times before there was a response. It was Nico, crying and saying he'd just been mugged and the thief had stolen his iPhone.

Between choked sobs, he said, "Luna didn't answer her cell. But I really need to speak to you. Will you call my number and see who answers? It would be better if a man calls."

Reluctantly, Tyler agreed, and a man answered the phone stipulating brusquely that when Nico paid him five hundred dollars, he would return the phone.

Tyler relayed the message. "The man said you'd know who to pay." Hanging up with Nico, he looked over at Luna critically. "He's mixed up in something shady. I don't like it, Luna. This is getting out of hand."

Always more sympathetic to Nico's cause, Luna said, "Tyler, I'm sure the phone was stolen, maybe at a bar or nightclub, and the thief is just asking for money to get it back. Why assume more than that?"

Tyler looked at her incredulously. "Luna, Nico most likely received some type of service—either it was a hooker or drugs—and he tried to get off without paying."

Luna raised her eyebrows skeptically. "Really, Tyler? I wouldn't have thought that."

Tyler said confidently, "That's because you're blinded by him! Open your eyes, Luna."

Expecting Nico to call again on her cell, she retrieved the phone. There was always a sense of urgency in Nico's voice, but this time she heard panic. "Please come over. I don't want to be alone."

She didn't hesitate, "I'll be right there, Nico."

He quickly added, "Ring the bell. The door is locked."

Tyler caught her arm as she made for the bedroom to change. "Luna, I'm concerned. This could be dangerous…just watch yourself."

"I will, I just can't leave him alone. He's really freaked out."

Tyler was uncharacteristically agitated. "Luna, your relationship with Nico is troubling, at best. You dismissed all the work you did with Kristi and totally ignored the cord cutting! Then you stay out all night. Are you in love with Nico? Because I'm not going to stand for this anymore!"

Luna froze, not knowing how to respond. "Tyler…I love you! I don't want to *be* with Nico—not that way." The truth was she did fantasize about him—and once, in a joking way, she had told Tyler that. But she'd not considered that Tyler would be upset. "I would never jeopardize what we have, Tyler. Please understand, he needs me. He has no one!"

Tyler sighed in exasperation. "Just promise you'll stay in touch with me. And don't do anything stupid."

Luna quickly pulled on boyfriend jeans, an ivory lace-trimmed cotton top, and grey flip-flops.

Picking up her car keys from the pewter dish by the door, she hurried out, assuring Tyler she would report back.

She didn't bother to put on the radio. Her mind raced with all kinds of scenarios of what could have possibly happened. She kept thinking about what Tyler had said with such absolute certainty. A prostitute? Drugs? Luna never talked on the phone when she drove, but when Nico, called she answered, and he kept her on, making small talk, until she pulled into the parking lot. He greeted her at the door wearing sweat pants and a loose T-shirt; his hair was dirty and matted. Usually he looked bedroom sexy, with his face unshaven, but now it was obvious he hadn't slept, and he was pale and drawn. He had a long scratch down his face and a deep gash on his neck. Frantic and scared, he paced around the room. Luna put on the tea kettle, and sitting him down, asked for a detailed description of exactly what had happened.

"I went out last night, Luna. You went home and I was alone and depressed, so I went to the club. I was in the private VIP room, and someone gave me a number to text, saying the girl was hot. I knew it was stupid, but I was drunk and didn't want to be alone. She was already waiting in the parking lot when I got to the studio. It was dark when I brought her into the apartment, and before I knew it, we were getting into it on the sofa. All of a sudden she went at me and tried to steal my laptop. I chased her all the way to the door, where she started hitting me, but I got the laptop back. I didn't realize she'd managed to steal my phone until she was gone."

Fretting, Nico prattled on, "That phone has all my client contact information and e-mails. And it's got all *those* photos!"

"Just move on, Nico. Buy a new phone and forget about it. You're not giving them five hundred dollars—that's ridiculous! Besides, they probably wiped the phone already, and sold it on the black market."

Nico still agonized fearfully, "Are you sure they won't publish those photos on the internet?"

Luna calmly assured him, "No. They want money, not your photos or contacts. You're not a politician, you know! Those are the people they'd seriously blackmail! None of the photos are of celebrities. There's nothing that's of any value."

Nico persisted, "What if they don't know that and put them up anyway!"

Luna had to get him off this obsessive train of thought. "Look, Nico, they've probably already wiped it, and the phone is on its way to a third world country. These people don't care about some unknown girl giving you a blow job! They were just trying to get a few bucks out of you."

She took charge and got Nico to take a shower and get dressed. She had scrambled eggs, toast with jam, and a cup of tea waiting for him when he came out of the bathroom. Finally allaying his fears, Luna convinced him to go to the store to buy a new phone, pushing him out the door and into her car.

Still worried, he yammered, "I don't care about the girls in the bathroom at the club, but do you think I need to tell Maya that the phone got stolen?"

Luna stated emphatically, "Absolutely not!"

Nico exhaled, relieved. "Good, she would be very upset. She is a movie star. Do you think they would publish her photo?"

Frustrated, Luna repeated, "No, they're selling your phone, not blackmailing you. Do you think this could've been a misunderstanding about money? Am I right?"

When Nico didn't answer, she continued, "I think your hookup was a prostitute, and you didn't know that. When you refused to pay, she fought with you. Am I right?"

He stared at her, then looked down and mumbled, "Yes, I didn't know. I was stupid. I thought it was just a girl who wanted to party with me, and when she wanted money, I laughed and said, 'I don't pay for sex.' Then she went at me…and took me by surprise. She was really strong!"

Luna was now convinced Tyler was right that Nico hadn't wanted to pay, and the girl had freaked out. She couldn't leave empty-handed, or her pimp would have beaten her up.

Luna asked Nico, "Who gave you this number? Why would you text a stranger for sex?"

Nico relayed, "This guy at the club—I'd seen him there before in the VIP Lounge—he showed me some pictures on his phone. The girl was hot, and he asked if I wanted to hook up with her and party. I said sure and texted her. When she came over, we fooled around."

"Doing what exactly?"

Nico laughed. "You like when I tell you these stories, don't you, Luna?"

She smiled. "Yes, Nico, it turns me on," she made a point of sounding facetious. "I just want to know how this could happen to you. You're not *that* naïve, Nico!"

"She was blowing me and I was naked. She was dressed."

Luna nodded, she'd figured he'd be getting a blow job.

Nico continued, "I wanted to fuck, but she asked for money before she would get undressed. I asked 'Why? I thought you were here to party.' Then I said, 'I don't pay for sex.'"

Luna knew there was something else to the story; the word *party* implied more. Maybe drugs, like cocaine, were involved. She delicately asked, "So, you really didn't know it was a hooker you called? Not until she asked for money?"

Nico was adamant, "I swear to you. I didn't."

Luna played dumb. "So then, why did you think a strange girl would just come over to have sex with you? And no payment of any sort was implied?"

Nico looked down, at a loss for words. He muttered, "Well, I thought she was a party girl, looking for a good time."

"Nico, what does that mean?" Suddenly something dawned on her. "Nico, do you think it was a transvestite? Maybe that's why he didn't want to take off his clothes."

Nico looked at her squarely, to ensure she wasn't being judgmental and that the question was sincere. He paused, then his mouth dropped open. "Ahhh…that could be, Luna! That's why she was so strong. It could've been a man."

Figuring that was probably all the truth she'd get from him, they walked into the phone store and began looking at new phones.

While Nico worked with a technician, Luna stepped outside to call Tyler to let him know she was fine, "Tyler, you were right. I'm certain he texted a hooker, and didn't want to pay. And…I think it may have been a transvestite. I'll fill you in when I get home, but long story short, Nico won't admit calling a prostitute, which leads me to think he's either really naïve, or was trading something else as payment—like you thought, maybe drugs. The girl, or guy, as it may be, flipped, and gashed him on the face and neck."

Tyler sighed. "When will you be home?"

"I think I'm going to spend some time with him. He's pretty shaken up."

Walking back to the car, Luna asked, "Have you eaten anything, Nico?"

"No, and I'm starving. Let's go for a burger." They went to Stout Burgers and Beer, a cute place near the studio on Ventura.

Now that he was in better spirits, Luna teased him, "Nico, stop with these pictures on the phone, OK?"

He conceded, "You're right, Luna. I shouldn't do that."

She chided, "That poor girl Maya! And it's a good thing that your face wasn't in any shots. You're becoming a celebrity, remember? So take this as a warning, and stop documenting your dick!"

Nico laughed and said sweetly, "Luna, thanks so much. I really needed you today."

"And you'll stop with the pictures?"

He looked up at her from under the coil of black hair covering his eye, and like a little boy caught teasing his baby sister, whispered, "OK. I promise."

o   o   o

Luna spotted her friend perusing Plato Picante's vast menu at a table on the veranda. As she walked toward her, Emily looked up and her eyes widened. Standing to hug Luna, she exclaimed cheerfully, "My God! You look fantastic! Like a rock star!" Luna wore a new black lace miniskirt with an embellished, distressed denim jacket over a T-shirt, and vintage western boots she'd bought in Santa Fe.

Stepping back to inspect her further, Emily went on, "And twenty years younger!" Then, realizing how that might sound, she stumbled over her words as she added, "I mean…not that you don't always look great—and fashionable. I mean…"

Luna laughed and hugged her harder. "I know, Em. I guess you could say I've been transformed. I *feel* much younger, too, and I'll tell you all about it!"

Over the course of several margaritas, Luna opened up about her feelings for Nico, expressing her concern about just how close they were. Her friend acknowledged it might be good for her ego, but dangerous for her marriage.

Luna insisted it was harmless fun, and that she and Tyler still had their date nights, so all was well at home. Laughing, she ordered another round of margaritas. When she finally checked her phone, she realized she had missed several calls and texts from both Tyler and Nico. Quickly texting Tyler she was on her way home, she and her friend said their good-byes.

Sitting in her car and looking across the street at the Amaru Yoga sign, Luna returned the call from Nico. "Hi, you called me?"

"Where are you? Why didn't you pick up?"

"Funny, Nico. I'm across the street at Plato Picante. I just had a few drinks with an old friend of mine from New York."

"Come over here, I need you," Nico urged her.

"I can't, Nico. Ty is expecting me home," she replied.

"Just for a minute. Please. Besides, you shouldn't drive home if you've been drinking," he argued convincingly.

She went across the street and straight into the apartment, where he was playing guitar. He seemed fine, but she figured something was up when he asked her to have a drink with him. She replied, "I drank too much already."

"Sit down. Stay for a while," he countered.

Luna insisted, "I really need to go home, Nico, but I'll see you Sunday. You're coming to Easter, right?"

Nico had accepted Luna's invitation to Easter dinner at her brother's house again this year. But when she suggested he bring Maya, he'd declined, saying, "Well, she already invited me to her friend's wedding, and I turned that down because I don't want her to think we're that serious."

"At some point, you'll have to get to know her family if you're serious." Luna had observed he never met the family of anyone he was dating. Yet he had enjoyed himself the year before at her brother's house and even got the kids involved making pizza. There had been flour dusting every surface, and the kids had been enthralled watching him spin the dough.

Nico proclaimed proudly, "Look! I made an Easter basket for the kids, see?"

Just like a little kid, she thought.

He added, "And a bottle of Tikal for your brother."

Plopping back on the sofa, he picked up his guitar and began playing a romantic ballad while Luna listened attentively.

Before long, she realized another hour had passed and jumped up. "Oh my. I'm so late. Tyler's going to kill me!"

o   o   o

When Luna walked in, Tyler erupted, "I expected you hours ago. You know what? You can go to your brother's with Nico. I'm not going!"

"That's such an extreme reaction, Tyler! I lost track of time. That's all!" She could hear the shrillness in her voice.

"You're so wrapped up in Nico, you have no consideration for me! I was waiting for you, and you didn't even call. I'm done." He didn't raise his voice, but she could hear the tension, and more importantly, the disappointment.

Luna apologized profusely and pleaded her case, "Honey, I'm so sorry…really, I am. I felt a bit tipsy and waited at Nico's until I sobered up some…"

Seeing her attempt at justification wasn't having any effect, she simply mumbled, "I'm sorry," and went into the bedroom. When Tyler was this angry, Luna knew better than to continue making excuses. She just hoped his anger would dissipate by Sunday, but the next morning she could tell he was still bristling. Maybe, she thought, inviting Nico wasn't such a great idea. As much as she dreaded it, she called Nico and nervously told him why Tyler was angry with her.

"I texted from Plato Picante that I was on my way home, but then didn't show up for hours. I explained I stopped off there to sober up before driving, but he was furious. Now he's refusing to go to Easter dinner—and says we should just go without him!"

Getting more upset than she anticipated, Nico blew up at her. "I can't believe you let him manipulate you like that, Luna! After all I've done for you!"

"He'll calm down. I'm sure of it. But right now, he says he's not going. I can't exactly show up with you and not Tyler, can I?" She waited for Nico to say something, knowing he would be disappointed.

He pushed back at her harder than she anticipated. "Luna, Tyler's trying to control you and our friendship. I'm your friend! Why would you cave in to him like this? He's a jealous idiot. I could have taken you from him any time. He should thank me! I returned him a beautiful wife. So what, you were late getting home. You two are always together. I needed you! Not Tyler! You're a grown woman and you were out with your friend, then visited me for a few minutes! He's angry like a baby for nothing!"

Stunned, Luna tried to explain, "Look, Nico, I'm sure Ty will let it go. I think you're overreacting."

"Fuck you both! You were nothing before me. I gave you back your life, and this is the thanks I get!"

"I'm sorry, Nico, I shouldn't have said anything. He was just pissed off at me for being inconsiderate and not calling."

Nico ranted, "Forget it! I don't want to go. I'll go out with my friends. I was only coming for your sake anyway. I bought that Easter basket for the kids, but forget it!" Suddenly the line went dead. She thought about calling him back, but decided to wait, hoping both Nico and Tyler would calm down.

Luna was devastated. She felt that Nico was right. She was sure Tyler had been jealous since the time they went dancing. Getting home late was just the straw that broke the camel's back.

Sunday morning, Luna called Nico to say Tyler had calmed down, and to please come with them. But his phone went directly to voice mail.

She had breakfast, took a shower, then tried him again—again it went straight to voice mail. It was possible he'd gone to a club and stayed out all night, so she waited a bit longer before trying again—still voice mail. Though she felt guilty, they left for her brother's house without him. Hours later, he finally answered, and mumbled almost incoherently, "I don't feel well. I'm not coming. I just want to stay in bed."

Luna begged, "Why, Nico? Please just get on the bike and come, it's only Santa Monica. You'll feel better."

Blaming her, he replied, "You didn't want me to come—and you canceled me."

She argued, "That's not true. Of course I want you."

Nico dismissed her. "Well it's too late now. It's an afterthought. You should've thought of this when you had the fight with Tyler. You're not my friend, Luna."

Luna was sobbing and didn't want anyone to see her, so she walked out into the yard. She whimpered, "I'm sorry, Nico. I truly am. I let Tyler dictate, and I *always* let you down."

Brushing her off, he replied, "Have a nice time, Luna," and hung up.

She didn't call back—there wasn't anything she could say to make it right. Tyler got pissed off at her for being inconsiderate, so she had pushed Nico aside. Now, in hindsight, she realized she had been squeezed between Nico and Tyler, and the clash had been inevitable. This time, Tyler had found the perfect opportunity to place a wedge between them.

23

Luna sat at a table in Pizza Rev on Ventura near Nico's studio, waiting for him. When he walked in and his eyes met hers, she felt the familiar fire butterflies in her solar plexus. It made no difference that she now knew it was because of the cord that attached them.

Stopping at the counter to order, he called out, "Want anything?"

She just shook her head no and pretended to text on her phone. Waiting at the counter for the pizza, he kept looking over at her, shaking his head and scowling. He was wearing his clingy black yoga pants, a T-shirt with a trendy skull design on the front, and classic black suede Pumas. Again, he looked unkempt, his hair matted and his face unshaven, like he's just crawled out of bed. She had an urge to get up and hug him, but she was nailed to her seat, unable to move. He walked over to her table with the pizza and a bottle of water. Sitting down, he looked at her suspiciously from under his lock of hair. Then, disregarding her, he picked up a slice, folding it in half as he took a bite. She looked down, waiting for him to say something.

Breaking the silence, he nudged, "Go on. Take a slice. I know you want one."

Looking up, she saw he had a string of cheese clinging to his lower lip, and reached across the table to wipe it away. He tried to act annoyed at her intimate gesture, but she saw his eyes soften.

"Luna, you really hurt me. You blew me off. I didn't get out of bed all weekend."

"I'm sorry, Nico." Though it sounded hollow, she really meant it. She looked down at the pizza, deciding to take a slice.

"You know I can't resist pizza," she said, trying to make him smile.

"Luna, I'm all alone, I have no one. I thought you were my friend, and you left me. It really hurt."

Her eyes welled up with tears. She hadn't meant to hurt him, but it seemed she always disappointed him. "Nico, I love you so much. I'm so sorry. Tyler was furious with me. I had no choice."

Nico glared. "Of course you had a choice—but you didn't make the right one."

She wiped away her tears. "You're right." She reached for his hand and for a moment he let her hold it, then slid it away. "What are we going to do, Nico? I want you in my life, forever—you know that I don't want to lose you." Looking for the right words, she paused. Unable to find them, she wondered aloud, "Why is it so hard for me to have both of you?"

Nico raised his eyes to meet hers and they penetrated to her soul. "What do you mean?"

Luna hesitated. Struggling, she mused, "Nico, we're a part of each other. I just need to know that we'll always be in each other's lives."

Recalling his words, "I could have taken you from him any time," Luna wished he would echo her feelings. When he said nothing, she inquired, "Do you feel the same way, Nico? Am I imagining things? I don't want to even *think* about what almost happened at the club."

"Luna, don't think anything. We're just friends."

"I hope we're friends forever, Nico, but why don't you want me? Why everyone but me?"

Alarmed, he looked up. His glare burned into her. "Would you want it to go further, Luna?"

She picked at the cheese on her now cold slice of pizza. "Well, it would ruin everything. I know you—if it ever went any further, you wouldn't want to be friends anymore."

Unable to hold his gaze, she looked down, embarrassed and regretting what she'd said. She sensed it was awkward for both of them.

"Look, I have to get to the bank before my sessions. I'll talk to you later."

He stood abruptly, and she blurted out, "Are we OK?" hoping he didn't detect the panic in her voice.

"Yes. Of course we are."

Nico's face was red and puffy. Erin was scheduled to meet with Deepak Chopra and Nico had tasked Luna with preparing his book proposal and sample chapters of his memoir. "Erin said she'd hand it right to him," he said emphatically. Lately, he exploded over the smallest things and the veins in his forehead bulged, frightening her.

Walking on egg shells, Luna felt she had no choice. "I'll get it done, but let's not upset Tyler. He's been saying I give you too much of my time."

Nico sighed and looked at her scornfully. "You'd better not let me down again, Luna."

As hard as Luna tried, things remained strained between them.

Agitated, Nico couldn't be still, first sitting in his chair with his leg bouncing, then getting up and pacing—all the while dictating to Luna. When she complained that his sentences weren't correct, he blew up at her, calling her a moron. Frustrated, she got up. "I can't take it, Nico…"

"No, Luna! You can't leave until *I* say you can leave. You owe me! I gave you your life back!"

He'd done this before—petrifying her. She pleaded, "Nico, I want to go home. You're scaring me. I can't work like this!"

His eyes remained dark. "Luna, don't fuck with me. I'll tell Tyler that you beg to have sex with me, and that you're always throwing yourself at me."

She was incredulous. "That's not true, Nico! Why would you say that?"

Nico's face was stony, his eyes black holes and his voice tight. "Because you propositioned me in the pizza place, and I recorded you with my phone."

Mortified, she shrieked, "What?! You recorded me? That's disgusting! You can go to hell, Nico!"

"I'll go over to your house and play it for Tyler. Don't you believe me?"

Her mind raced, replaying the conversation in her head…trying to remember exactly what she'd said. Certainly, she had no recollection of saying anything close to that. Nico stood frozen, waiting for her next move.

"I didn't say anything I'm ashamed of, so if you want, go tell Tyler. But we're through!" Furious, Luna grabbed her tote bag and made for the door. "I could never trust you again. A *friend* would never do such a thing!" she screamed.

Grappling for her bag, he missed, and his nails gouged the skin on her arm.

Crying out, Luna hurled the bag at his head in self-defense. Blocking the attack, Nico snatched it away from her. Dumping the contents on the floor, he found her phone and threw it. "You're not going anywhere, Luna. Sit back down!"

"Nico!" she wailed as the phone made contact. The sound of it hitting the wall was deafening, not so much from the impact, but from its finality. Picking it up, she screamed at him, "You fucking broke my phone!" Sobbing, she fell to her knees to collect her things, shoving them back into her bag. "I'm leaving, and I never want to see you again!"

"Fuck you, Luna. You're not my friend. You're just like everyone else…"

At the door, Luna whipped around, assailing him, "It's not true. I never said that, Nico!" she sobbed, unable to catch her breath. "And if you cause a problem with Tyler, just remember, we can never be friends again. He would *never* allow it. And not because I may fantasize about you—but because you're *evil*."

Luna's heart raced as the fear rose within her. What if he'd altered the recording, taking what she's said out of context? She did say she *fantasized* about him. She would *never* cheat on Tyler. Finding her words from beneath the waves of dread gripping her, she asked gravely, "Why do you feel the need to blackmail me, Nico. What have I done to deserve that?"

He snickered. "Luna, you've been spiteful and disloyal, and you betrayed me. It's your fault. *You* have pushed me away. I've given you everything…your youth…that award. Without me, you're nothing."

Hurt and broken, she said, "Nico, you've really crossed the line. I'm leaving. And by all means, go ahead and call Tyler."

Before he could stop her, she bolted out the door and into the parking lot. Feeling Nico hot on her heels, she was terrified he might hurt her. The screen was cracked and the case broken, but the home screen opened. Hoping the phone still worked, she speed dialed Tyler. Relieved he picked up on the first ring, she tried to steady her voice, knowing Nico could hear her. "Hi, honey. I just want to let you know I'm on my way, and I have to speak with you when I get home. It's important."

Tyler asked if everything was OK, and she replied, "Yes, I just need to talk to you. I'll be right home."

Blocking the car door, Nico wore a fake smile that looked more like a sneer and chuckled. "Luna, calm down. I was only joking with you."

She pushed him to move aside, but he stood his ground.

She huffed, "Nico, don't worry about telling Tyler. I will tell him myself when I get home."

Nico just stared at her smugly.

She spat vehemently, "He *knows* we flirt. He *knows* I love you, but there's a big difference between what I may fantasize about and what I would do. He'll be incensed when I tell him that you blackmailed me." Luna shook uncontrollably, not sure if she was angry or sad.

Nico cajoled, "I can't believe you're this upset!" He chuckled and attempted to put his arms around her.

Luna punched him hard in the chest. She had exhausted herself. "Nico, it's not funny. You said you recorded me—without my knowledge. Then you threatened me, and blackmailed me. Now you stand here and say you made it all up? Does that sound like a *friend* to you?" she insisted strenuously.

Holding both her arms and forcing her to look him in the eye, he pacified, "Look at me, Luna. I was upset. You've betrayed me—then abandoned me. You promise to help me, then you leave. I need you, but you come and go on a whim. You're not dependable. I wanted to test you, and I played a game on you."

Luna shook her head, and wiping at her tears, said, "That was disgusting, Nico! I'm horrified." She pushed him away from her car, and this time he moved, clearly shaken by her mixture of anger, sadness, and disgust.

His voice softened. "I'm sorry, Luna. I didn't realize you would be this upset. I was really hurt, and I wanted to hurt you back."

Looking at him, Luna saw regret in his eyes and implored, "Nico, you can't threaten me like that. I'm so close to you. I tell you my feelings, then you use them against me. Don't you see how hurtful that is?"

Nico took her hand. "You hurt me, too."

She rested her head on his shoulder and sobbed, worn down. This had taken everything out of her. "Nico, we have to be nicer to each other. I'm so sorry that I disappoint you, but I would never intentionally hurt you. You *wanted* to hurt me by telling Tyler a lie."

Nico petted her hair, his fingers trailing lightly down her back as she lay against his chest. "No, Luna. I would never say that to Tyler. I just wanted to get back at you and teach you a lesson."

∘   ∘   ∘

When she arrived home, Tyler was seated at his desk. Still shaken, Luna sat down across from him and conceded things had gotten out of hand with Nico. It seemed formal, but it felt like the most appropriate setting for her confession. Tyler must have felt the import of the moment, because he turned off the computer screen and focused his attention on her, waiting for her to begin.

Clearing her throat, she began slowly. "Tyler, I don't know myself anymore. You've been more than patient—letting me spend so much time with Nico. I can't imagine what you must think…but I want to thank you for trusting me." Tyler began to look concerned, and Luna rushed to clarify, "I assure you, nothing inappropriate happened… but I have welcomed and even encouraged his flirtations. I crave his attention…his validation…all to gratify my ego—and it's wrong. I completely understand the vampire analogy. He stirs my desire in order to compel me and bind me to him. I should be above that sort of manipulation. Tonight, he insisted that I stay to work on his book proposal. When I said I needed to leave, he blackmailed me, threatening to tell you that I've tried seducing him…which is a lie!" Again, she hurried to explain, "Yes, I've flirted with him, innocently. But it was all in fun. I thought we were friends. Of course he apologized and said he was just kidding, but I'm horrified he would do such a thing! I just wanted you to know what happened and why I called you."

Tyler had listened intently, but wasn't shocked. Emphatically, he explained, "I hope now you see that you are nothing to him except an object he can use. For God's sake, Luna, it's like blaming a snake for having fangs. I hope you will finally disentangle yourself from him."

"I wish it was that simple…," she mumbled.

Getting up, she walked around to Tyler's chair. "I love you so much, Tyler. Please believe me that I never wanted it to get this way."

Tyler stood up and pulled Luna to his chest. "He's coming between us Luna—and he's using you. He manipulates and controls by acting out of control. But he feels nothing inside except incessant pain. He's damaged. If you don't serve him, he will toss you away like a dirty tissue."

Luna nodded. Burying her face in Tyler's neck, she hugged him tightly.

o　o　o

Nervously trying to attach the backs onto her long silver feather earrings, Luna prayed Nico wouldn't call her during tea with Liliane. She knew Liliane would be turned out fabulously in European couture, but Luna's style was trendier. She opted to wear a Navajo-inspired Etro print wrap dress with nude strappy sandals and draped several strands of natural heishi beads around her neck.

Liliane was now a senior executive at the largest luxury fashion holding company in Europe. Although the two women had taken completely different career paths, they remained close friends.

When Luna had told Tyler she had plans with Liliane, he'd blurted perceptively, "Don't cancel for Nico!"

"I'm really looking forward to seeing her, don't worry." Though a few weeks had passed since Nico had threatened her, the sound of Tyler invoking his name pierced her heart. With that, she silenced her new phone, putting it in the zippered compartment of her bag.

Pulling her Land Rover up to The Grill on the Alley just off Rodeo Drive, Luna handed the keys to the valet and waved to Liliane, who was standing near the door talking on her cell phone.

Greeting Luna with a double-cheek kiss, she effused, "Luna, you look gorgeous! Not a day older than you did in college and just as stylish! If I didn't know you better, I would ask who does your work!"

Luna beamed, delighting in the flattery. She hadn't yet indulged in the Botox and fillers that all her friends considered de rigueur.

Instead of tea, they opted for champagne and oysters, spending a luxurious two hours chatting nonstop. She'd forgotten how much fun it was spending time with her girlfriends, and had been so absorbed, she hadn't checked her phone once.

When they said their good-byes outside the restaurant, she counted the missed calls from Nico. Luna felt guilty blowing him off, but if she called him now, she feared he would persuade her to cancel her dinner plans with Tyler. Dropping the phone into her bag, she headed home for date night and to celebrate their anniversary.

Plopping into the down-filled club chair near Tyler's desk, Luna told him about lunch with Liliane, including what she wore, what they ate, and even about the men Liliane was dating.

Tyler smiled. "Luna, I'm glad you had such a good time. I haven't seen you this animated and happy in ages. You should go out with friends more often."

His remark wasn't lost on her. In the two years since she'd met Nico, without realizing it, she had seen less and less of her friends. As she showered and dried her hair, she thought a lot about the time she had devoted to him—seeking his favor and craving his attention. Still feeling a slight buzz from the champagne, she massaged lavender body lotion on her chest and thighs, then put on a lingerie-inspired lace-trimmed slip dress, a look she favored from her younger days, when she would pick up pieces in vintage stores. Her naturally tanned legs looked silky smooth as she slipped on four-inch high black suede pumps, perfect with the simple slip dress. Automatically reaching for her silver hoops, she paused, then chose the antique amethyst drops Tyler had bought her for their first anniversary, calling on the power of the gems for emotional stability and inner strength.

She lightly sprayed Chanel No. 5, Tyler's favorite, on her neck, and went to find him in his home office. He was watching soccer on his computer, and she snuck up behind him, kissing his neck. "Where are we going tonight?"

He chided, "I was going to surprise you. I made a reservation at Osteria Mozza on Melrose. I know we like to sit at the bar, but I booked a table. Is that OK?"

"Absolutely, that's more romantic. I'm so glad you booked Mozza, we haven't been in a long time." For a second, La Forza crossed her mind, remembering that's where she'd met Nico, but she didn't want to think about him. Playfully, she suggested, "It's early, do you want to have a drink here and dance?"

Tyler put the blues rock station on Spotify. "Sure, I'll open a bottle of wine."

Dimming the lights in the living room, Luna lit the sage green pillar candles. Mike Bloomfield's guitar was wailing a slithering lick from "Albert's Shuffle" off the *Super Session* album. After pouring the wine, she clinked glasses with Tyler before taking a sip of the rich cabernet sauvignon. The cozy, dark room had the feel of a library. Luna's books on Native American art and culture, and Tyler's on philosophy lined the walls, interspersed with their collection of American Indian pottery and antique baskets. She never tired of the original Edward S. Curtis prints of Native Americans hung over a wheat-colored, down-stuffed sofa strewn with kilim pillows. In the center of the farmhouse coffee table was a Yanomami Indian basket containing a deer antler, a nautilus shell, and a deerskin medicine bundle decorated with turquoise and feathers. Taking in her surroundings, she felt at peace, blessed with her life, and silently acknowledged she was in a sacred space she cherished. With her arms draped around Tyler's neck, their bodies melded as they swayed to the sexy blues melody. Luna kissed him deeply, her tongue pirouetting around his in a dance of exploration, and he responded with more passion than he had in as long as she could remember. She felt a warm pulsing in her sex as her body awakened to his touch. Languorously, she sinuated against him, moving with the sultry pleading of the saxophone.

"You smell wonderful, Luna," Tyler whispered, entwining his fingers in her long hair. Then sliding his hand over her buttocks, he held her tightly against him. She felt him growing hard, and when the song ended, he laced his fingers through hers and walked her silently to the bedroom.

Lifting the black silk dress over her head, he tossed it onto a nearby chair and guided her onto the bed. Lying next to her, he kissed her deeply and gently began playing with her nipples while his tongue swirled around hers. He moved his hand down over her belly to the inside of her thigh and she opened her legs wider, inviting him in. His fingers explored her warm plump folds and Luna moaned in anticipation. He took his time awakening her to him—kissing her and fingering the velvet wall of her pussy as she grew wetter. Lifting her hips up to him, she took hold of his erect cock and began stroking him firmly. Responding ardently, he moved over her, pushing her thighs apart with his knee, and began working his way inside. His hands in her hair, he deepened his kisses as he thrust into her. As her response grew more fervent and her moans grew louder, he released into her, crying out. As they lay together in the aftermath, Tyler's lips brushed hers tenderly as he murmured, "I love you so much, Luna. We should do this more often."

She playfully rolled over and straddled him, taking his face between her hands as she kissed him. "I agree. And if you like, I will remind you!"

Luna freshened up, then reapplied a fresh coat of burgundy lip gloss and retouched the black kohl liner on her eyes. It had been a while since she'd felt that impassioned and satisfied. Chuckling to herself, she thought next time she would encourage him to have sex on the sofa, to try something a bit less conventional. But she was thrilled Tyler had initiated; at least she was making progress. She picked up her black Pashmina and walked back into the living room. Tyler had put on a charcoal grey Ralph Lauren sport jacket over black jeans and a knit shirt.

Kissing her on the cheek, he smiled, saying, "You're beautiful, Luna. Happy Anniversary."

o   o   o

Luna lay in bed watching the shadows shift along the ceiling. Tossing and turning, sleep evaded her. She felt guilty for neglecting

Nico and ignoring his calls. His text messages were at first desperate, then switched to angry and threatening. Now she stressed over the punishment she would receive. Picking up the phone from the night table where it lay charging, she texted him:

> *Nico, I'm sorry about today. I was so busy I didn't even know you called.*

He texted back:

> *Bullshit. We're done. Don't ever contact me again. I warn you.*

Luna went through all the same explanations:

> *I was in a meeting. You need to understand that I have a job. Besides, you had everything you needed to give to Erin.*

Nico answered:

> *Erin needed something more, and now it's too late. You lost me this.*

She replied:

> *That's not so. What I gave you was perfect.*

His answer was terse:

> *Leave me alone. I don't want you in my life.*

Assuming he would cool down, she texted again:

> *Nico, I'm sorry I wasn't available today. You know I love you, and I'm here for you.*

But Nico didn't answer.

24

It had been over two months since Luna had been in contact with Nico. Left to her own wild imaginings, she tortured herself over his whereabouts. Clicking on the Twitter icon, she typed Erin Whelan in the search box. Scrolling through recent tweets, she landed on a photo of fireworks above the spires of a familiar castle. The hashtags #CinderellaCastle and #DisneyWorld were accompanied by the tweet, "Wishes with my guru @NicoRomero." Luna was certain Nico would not appreciate that tweet. He never allowed anyone to tag him or post anything about him. He was a control freak about his image. Luna also knew he wouldn't risk Alexa finding out he was away with Erin. He kept everyone apart—separate from each other—so no one could compare notes. After some Googling, she learned that there had been a Digital Media conference in Orlando, and Erin, as owner of Grey Dog, had been a keynote speaker. Combing Erin's Twitter timeline, she found another tweet, "@NicoRomero courting giraffes!"

Luna gasped, thinking how derogatory that sounded. The following tweet was "Watching @NicoRomero swim like a dolphin." Luna knew Nico had opened a Twitter account, but never used it, so would most likely never see these tweets. And he most assuredly wouldn't want anyone *else* to see them. This wasn't the social media attention Nico would want.

With that in mind, Luna was on a mission to uncover any other lurking tweets, and decided to scroll back further. She had a feeling that maybe this wasn't the first time Erin had tweeted something about Nico. As she suspected, she found a bare-chested photo of him that Luna could tell was at Erin's house in Santa Monica. Looking seductively at the camera, messy wet hair falling in his face, Luna saw a devilish look in the way his dark green eyes glowed. He was buzzed for sure.

The suggestive tweet read, "Loving my life with Argentines, wolves, and feminine tricks."

Luna was paralyzed by the implication, and saw there were more from the same day: "@NicoRomero Dreaming of Tango in Argentina!" Luna thought for sure Nico would be mortified and had no idea Erin was tweeting all this to her followers.

After dinner and a few glasses of wine, Luna was in the bedroom surfing social media. Like most nights, Tyler was in his office writing his blog before coming to bed. Feeling bold, she wrote an e-mail to Nico informing him of her discovery, describing the photos and quoting the tweets, and emphasizing that Erin had over a million followers who'd seen all of it. She wrote that she wanted to let him know because she knew he would disapprove.

Soon after sending the e-mail and feeling proud of herself for her good deed, Tyler stormed into the room. Although he spoke in a soft, measured tone, Luna could tell he was furious when he said, "Nico e-mailed me. He said, *Please tell your wife to stop stalking me.*' What is this all about?"

At once humiliated and angry, Luna stumbled to explain. "Erin was tweeting all kinds of shit about him…"

Interrupting, Tyler pronounced, "Luna…enough! If you ever have contact with him again, we are through! Do you understand? I hope to God I've made myself clear. I don't want to hear his name!"

Luna was distraught. Here she actually thought she was doing Nico a favor, protecting him. *Stalking?* She had every right to follow Erin's Twitter. Surely, unwilling to unleash his wrath on Erin, Nico had deflected the blame by contacting Tyler and making Luna sound like a jealous girlfriend. *Argentines and fucking Erin's feminine tricks! What was that all about? And a photo where he was probably naked— you couldn't see whether he had pants on or not!* Luna was devastated. This time she vowed to stop e-mailing him and leave him alone for as long as it took for *him* to contact *her* again.

o   o   o

As soon as they wrapped, Maya left the set and headed for Nico's studio, bypassing the freeway to avoid traffic. After receiving accolades for her performance in *Blood Wars,* she had landed a sweet position as head choreographer for the fight scenes on a new series. It had been a long day, not made easier by Nico calling several times in a frenzy. Scheduled to leave the next day for Abu Dhabi, he was flipping out, insisting she pack for him and rattling off a long to-do list. She pleaded with him to delay the trip by a week. She would have time off, and he could attend her family's Thanksgiving feast. Having declined every previous opportunity to meet her family, she hoped he would finally accept this invitation. This past Easter, they had all just sat down for dinner when he'd called her from bed lamenting, "Everyone leaves me." Telling her mom Nico wasn't feeling well, she'd filled a large Pyrex dish with food and rushed to his side.

Looking back, it had been around then, in the early days of spring when Nico had first laid out several lines of cocaine on a tray, asking if she'd ever tried it. Stunned, she'd studied him incredulously when he held out a straw. "A friend of mine gave it to me as a gift. I've never tried it before, but he said to do it with my girl."

Maya had shaken her head. "Nico, I don't do drugs. I can't believe you want to."

She'd grown up in a neighborhood where the dealers ruled the streets and she'd had to literally fight her way out. Even children were recruited by gang leaders, and turf wars claimed many lives. She recalled trembling in fear at the first sound of gunshots—taking her younger siblings and hiding in the closet.

Nico had cavalierly brushed off the enormity of his request. "Come on. Let's have fun tonight. Why let it go to waste?"

Knowing it was wrong, she'd felt anxious. "You go ahead, Nico. You do it, but I don't want to."

"Look, Maya, I'm exhausted. It's just a little pick-me-up, you know. And I'll be able to go longer and pleasure you more."

"I thought the stuff keeps you from getting hard. That's what I heard."

"It can…so I've been told. So I also have this," he'd shown her a blue pill in the palm of his hand, then popped it into his mouth and swallowed it. Since she hadn't taken the straw, he'd bent his head over the tray and snorted up a few lines at once.

Maya had scowled. "Viagra? And coke? Are you looking for a heart attack?"

He'd held the straw out again for her. "Come on, baby. It's just this one time. What can happen?"

Upset, Maya finally stood up and grabbed her jacket and bag. "Look, Nico, I have an early call tomorrow, so let's just call it a night."

Nico had seized her firmly by the arm. "No way. You're not leaving."

"Ow, that hurt!" She broke away, automatically using a fight maneuver. Pissed off, she then yelled, "What's wrong with you?"

"Maya, baby. Look, I just snorted it and took the pill so we can have a good time. You can't leave now. I'll be up all night alone. Or I'd have to text a girl."

"Oh, that's just wonderful. Great. I can't believe you! Fuck it!"

Nico's badgering was incessant, and it had been easier to give in than to argue with him. Taking the straw, she'd done one of the three lines remaining on the tray. "OK? You satisfied?"

Nico had leaned over, running his tongue over her lower lip before sucking on it. Maya could tell by his mannerisms—the way he laid out the lines, the way he held the straw and sniffed the water up his nose—that was not his first time snorting coke. "Beautiful. Now get in the bedroom," he'd murmured.

As promised, he had pleasured her slowly, licking her pussy and fucking her with his fingers and tongue, teasing her until she clenched the sheets, pleading for him to let her come. Each time he brought her to the point of release, he stopped and pulled on his cock. Then, taking his time, he brought her back again, until he finally let her come, and she shuddered with a wracking orgasm, pulling his hair and crying his name.

Wildly, with an insatiable hunger, he pulled her to the edge of the bed, spreading her legs wide before plunging relentlessly into her. When he didn't come, Maya got on top, and moving over him, brought herself to another orgasm, expecting him to climax with her as he often did. Pushing her head down, he lifted her tantalizing ass the way he liked, admiring it as he ceremoniously lavished coconut oil upon it. Enraptured, he fucked her from behind, his hands planted firmly on her hips. He kept forcefully powering into her, causing her to whimper, until she finally begged him to stop. Moving from the bed, she knelt on the floor under him and lustily sucked his cock, taking him all the way to the back of her throat. He had insisted he was holding back, basking in the euphoria, but Maya knew it was the drugs. The Viagra had kept him hard, and the coke heightened his pleasure but delayed his gratification. Playing with his balls, her fingers gingerly penetrated his anus while she deep throated him, and he finally bucked his hips, groaning as he jetted into the back of her throat.

Her hair was plastered down her back, and Nico was drenched in sweat. They had been at it for hours. She went to the kitchen and returned with two bottles of water, then lying next to him, she nestled into his body and fell asleep.

o o o

Pulling into the parking lot, Maya realized how the drive to Amaru every day after work had become part of her routine. Sitting in her car, she thought about Nico being away for a month. As much as she would miss him, she knew she needed this time to focus on herself and detox. Colleagues had begun to comment on her weight loss, and she also realized she didn't look as healthy as she used to, either. When she walked into his office, she found him frantically looking for his passport. He pulled out file boxes and haphazardly rummaged around in them, then opened drawers and dumped out the contents. It looked like burglars had tossed the joint. Calling out to her, he scolded, "What took you so long? Where is my passport?"

Maya dropped her bag and quickly stripped off her jacket. "I don't know. Where do you keep it?" Not looking at him, she started picking up the drawers from the floor, putting the contents back in. Nico stopped in his tracks and glared at her until she looked met his gaze.

"Are you serious?" he asked snidely. "I asked you a question! Don't fuck with me. I need my passport! Help me find it!"

Maya didn't dare reproach him. She could see he was exceedingly agitated and finding the passport was a priority. She continued to pick things up off the floor and put them away while also carefully looking for the passport. "When did you last see it? Just try visualizing."

"Um, it's in a dark red leather case that Luna gave me." He went to a letter holder on his desk and began flipping through the papers, finding the passport case with the passport inside. "Got it! I was looking for a blue plastic jacket. I forgot."

Relieved, Maya put the drawers back in the desk. Just then, his phone pinged, and he huffed and texted a quick response while he barked orders. "I have a thousand things I need you to do. Just start packing for me. What's the weather in Abu Dhabi? I need dress clothes, too!"

Googling the weather on her phone, she called out, "Average temp in December is in the seventies, but it can get down to sixty at night." Maya got busy laying out piles of clothes.

"And here," he tossed her a Lululemon shopping bag from near the desk, "I have some new yoga clothes. Pack them all."

As she removed the contents from the shopping bag, Maya asked intrepidly, "Did you try them on?" Then, surmising he hadn't bought the items for himself, quickly added, "Should I cut the tags off?"

"Let me see these things." Stripping off his well-worn sweatpants, he put on the black stretch pants.

Cutting the tags off, she silently tallied the items before packing them into the Louis Vuitton suitcase, another gift from Alexa, who adored all things LV. The grand total was over one thousand dollars. Commenting would only provoke him, so she kept quiet.

Handing her a new shoebox, he casually instructed, "Here, pack these, too." Catching her peeking at the $275 price tag, he quipped snidely, "Don't be so nosy, Maya. You're just like Luna. In Abu Dhabi, everyone is a billionaire. Alexa got me some new things, and believe me, I wish she hadn't. Because I *will* have to pay for it, one way or another. Nothing is free, you know."

"Sorry..." In a way, she knew he was right. The half million dollars he'd just received from the sheikh in the Emirates was through Alexa's contacts, and that meant he owed her.

Nico hovered, asking her a million times if she had packed his charger, his razor, his dress shoes, and a dozen other items. Remaining composed, she checked again as he watched her, even though she knew she had packed them. Once more, he asked if the wire transfer had come through to his account, and she again showed him that the $500,000 had been posted to his account in US dollars. "When I get back, we'll put in an offer on the place in Temecula. Don't forget to call the realtor and tell him I want that cabin with the five acres. We can plant a vineyard."

Maya smiled, promising she would call first thing in the morning. Watching him, she saw he was skittish and his nerves were frayed. She assumed he was high, but asking would only antagonize him. As if reading her mind, he said aloud, "I assure you, there is no way for me to take drugs there. In Abu Dhabi…I would never risk it."

She was counting on him returning clean—of getting her old Nico back. Reflecting back over the past eight months, she concluded he had lied last spring when he'd claimed it was his first time snorting coke. But she was confounded how he'd hidden it from her until then. In spite of her vociferous objections and better judgment, he'd kept pressuring her to do coke with him. Not wanting to lose him, and knowing he would find someone else to party with if she refused, she'd given in.

Hugging him, she cooed, "Nico, why are you nervous? You've been paid a lot of money to teach a powerful kriya. You should be thrilled." She could feel him trembling.

"Maya, you don't understand. I'm under a lot of pressure."

"You'll do great, baby." His business had exploded, and still he worried it would collapse around him at any moment. Maya knew he had close to a million dollars in his bank account—and that was before the wire transfer. But if she questioned him, he got angry and paranoid.

Showering him with praise, she consoled, "I know it's far away, but we can Skype every day."

At the sound of his cell phone ringing, he rolled his eyes at Maya, putting his finger to his lips to remind her to be quiet. "What, Alexa? I'm packing. I have a million things to do."

Maya could make out most of Alexa's side of the conversation because she had such a loud voice. "I want to see you before you leave. Are you coming over?" she whined.

"I just told you. I'm swamped, and I don't even have time to cut my toenails."

"…gone for so long…miss you…," Maya picked out enough to get the gist of it. She would have liked to put two fingers in her mouth, the sign for gagging, but knew it would piss him off, so she restrained the urge.

"Don't cry. I can't deal with this right now. I'm only going for a month. I'll Skype you."

"…call me…you get there." Maya couldn't make out her words, since she was obviously crying.

"Yes, I promise. OK. Let me go."

"…love you…miss you…," Maya heard Alexa's pleading voice, and Nico rolled his eyes in disgust, hanging up without replying with a similar sentiment.

But he must have felt the need to say something to Maya, quickly blurting, "These women are infatuated with me. They are crazy in the head from menopause."

Maya had been jealous, unsure what their relationship was until she realized Alexa was in love with Nico and he used that to get what he wanted. When Maya had seen bruises on Nico, she'd remarked about them and he'd told her that Alexa was crazy and had tried to stab him. Then Nico told her how Alexa had gone off the deep end. She'd torn her hair out, punched herself, and cut her arms with a razor in front of him, as if that would get him to love her back. Maya began to feel sorry for her. She hadn't cut an artery, but Nico had freaked out anyway and taken her to Mexico. There, the drugs were cheap and plentiful and he could make her happy, at least temporarily. It was as if doing it in Mexico negated the reality for him.

After making his favorite roasted chicken, her mom's recipe with rice and beans, and sharing a bottle of red wine, they watched *Elysium* on Netflix. She was relieved when he didn't bring out any cocaine. Nico soon fell asleep on the sofa with his head in her lap. Reluctantly, she nudged him to bed, happy when he fell right back to sleep. Spooning him, with her arm draped around his waist, it hit her hard how much she was going to miss him. Nico had made her stronger by giving her tools to overcome fear. He had changed her forever—she just wasn't sure it was for the better.

o   o   o

Luna stood before the full-length mirror in the waning afternoon light, modeling the buttery soft midriff halter-top she'd just completed for one of the stars on *Going My Way*. Constructing it by herself instead of assigning it to one of the seamstresses had been good therapy. It fit perfectly, revealing just enough cleavage and accentuating her beautifully defined shoulders. Her full breasts appeared ample above the bra, and her arms, long and thin, were still graceful from years of ballet. Contemplating keeping this one for herself and making another for the actress, she headed to the fabric room for more suede.

A carton stuffed with multi-colored suede scraps had prompted her to sew a patchwork version, like those handbags from the '60s. She was selecting beads and feathers from one of the clear bins when inspiration struck her to make Nico a medicine bundle.

It had been six months since the incident with Erin's tweets, and she hadn't heard from him, other than the newsletter saying he would be on a special assignment in Abu Dhabi till January. She'd joined an exclusive chakra healing center in May, shortly after she and Nico had their final falling out. Working through her kriyas, she envisioned wading into the deep pools of his eyes and touching the serpent's coil of his hair, moving through her addiction to Nico by facing it. As Thanksgiving and her birthday drew near, not a day passed that she hadn't felt the fire butterflies connecting them to each other. Although Tyler's voice had been measured when he demanded she have no contact with Nico, Luna still visualized the hurt and disappointment on his face. His message was clear—he would not tolerate her obsession any longer. So far, she'd kept her promise, but that hadn't prevented her from fixating on a photo of she'd found on the internet of Nico flanked by glamourous women wearing Zuhair Murad gowns, standing in front of a white Maybach.

Digging around in the bins, she found an arrowhead and a horse hair tassel that had once been attached to a handbag. Shamans' medicine bundles, considered holy, often contained items like hair and bones used in rituals for protection and healing. Taking apart an African ankle bracelet, she collected the cowry shells, adding them to the pile of objects along with tobacco from a pack of cigarettes that had been shoved into a drawer. Studying her treasure, she realized the items were reminiscent of the ceremonies she'd done with Nico. Sprinkling in some sweet-smelling pine needles from a sachet, she stitched the soft honey-colored leather bundle closed, adorning it with feathers and sprigs of white sage and attaching the arrowhead as a final flourish. In the center of the leather pouch she carefully drew the Ouroboros, a pictograph of a serpent eating its own tail, representing kundalini energy. Surely, she thought, he would grasp the meaning of the Ouroboros. After all, he'd named his studio Amaru, the sacred serpent—so the teachings would not be obscure to him. In Tantric Buddhism, the concept of the wheel of time, known as Kalachakra, expresses the idea of an endless cycle of existence and knowledge, as does the wheel of life in Native culture. Certainly, he must know their bond transcended time.

o   o   o

Luna was grateful when Tyler suggested Santa Fe again for the holidays. The Inn of the Anasazi, just off the Plaza, was perfectly romantic, with a kiva fireplace in the room. The sky was a cloudless turquoise, and the aroma of burning piñon hung in the air. Snow drifted down as they drove up the winding Canyon Road to Geronimo. The elegant restaurant, with its thick white adobe walls, exposed beams, and large fireplace adorned with enormous elk antlers, had been the original Borrego House, built in 1756. They sat at the bar while awaiting their table, playfully guessing where they thought people were from based on their outfits. Tyler ordered a hearty red zinfandel with dinner, and they shared the wasabi Caesar salad and elk tenderloin with applewood smoked bacon. Luna purposely did not mention Nico throughout dinner, and was dismayed when they were walking to the car and Tyler casually asked, "Are you getting Nico a Christmas gift this year?"

The year before, Tyler couldn't conceal his distress over the attention she'd devoted to Nico's Christmas gift. He'd commented sarcastically, "A gift composed of photographs and imagery devoted to Nico is perfect for a narcissist."

Unable to ignore the tone in his voice, she'd asked if it bothered him, and he'd answered, "No, what bothers me is that he doesn't appreciate you. Your lack of self-respect hurts me the most, Luna. Not that you do so much for him and care so much, but that he disrespects you." That was Tyler—to a T.

Linking arms with him, she snuggled into his winter coat and without hesitation answered, "No, we haven't spoken in seven months, Tyler. You know that. And after that stunt in July when he accused me of stalking, I'm really trying to disconnect…" As an afterthought, even though it may have sounded hollow, she added, "And not think about him."

The sound of country music was pouring out of El Farol, an old stagecoach stop near Geronimo. "It's early, Luna, do you want to go in?" Tyler suggested.

Delighted, she exclaimed, "I'd love to!" It wasn't very late, but normally Tyler would have gone straight back to the hotel. Pulling off her hat and gloves, Luna asked the bartender for their best brandy straight up, and Tyler seconded her. Luna knew Tyler didn't like talking about Nico, but she felt she needed to say something, "I'm sorry, Tyler. I know it hasn't been easy. I'm going to end this thing—whatever it is—that binds me to him. I love you so much, you know that. And no one would put up with what you have. I'm lucky you understand how he manipulated—compelled—me, and I want to break it."

Tyler shrugged. "OK. Enough. I'm done talking about him. I don't want to ruin our time here."

Luna almost said something, but then saw the look in Tyler's eye. He was still pained. It had been too many years of Luna running to Nico every time he needed her. Tyler picked up his glass of

Gran Duque Spanish brandy. Luna picked up hers as well, and they clinked glasses. Sipping the warm, golden liquid, Luna showed Tyler a picture on her phone. "Look, Ty, the six of us at this bar. It must be at least fifteen years ago, right? We look so young! Our first trip here…it was in October. Remember how cold it was?! I bought that camel four-ply cashmere sweater at Santa Fe Dry Goods and I never took it off!"

Tyler chuckled, finding Luna's attempt at a distracting conversation charming. "I love you, Luna. You know I would never try to control you. You have to do it—for yourself—not just for us."

Leaning in, her hand on the back of his neck, she kissed him softly on the lips. "I know, Tyler. I love you so much. I don't want anyone but you—ever."

25

Maya was thrilled when after Nico first got to Abu Dhabi he suggested having virtual sex using Skype. She set the stage by wearing a Victoria's Secret leopard print push-up bra and sheer black stockings with sky-high Jeffrey Campbell black stilettos. Positioning a chair in front of the camera, she lit candles to create a dramatic backdrop for her solo performance. Nico coached her striptease, encouraging her to be more seductive. She made her entrance wearing a robe, her back to the camera, with her long black hair hanging down. His voice low and husky, he instructed her to let the robe slip down off her shoulders and fall to the ground. When she slowly turned, he groaned softly, seeing she was wearing the red lipstick he liked. He purred, "You look lovely tonight, Maya, my jaguar. Put one foot up on the chair, I want to see your beautiful legs." When she obediently lifted one leg, he uttered, "Oh…those sexy shoes! Let me look at you, but don't speak. I only want to hear the sounds of you pleasuring yourself and calling my name when you come."

Maya slowly swept her fingers along the length of her leg, starting at her foot, then sliding provocatively up along the inside of her thigh until she reached her crotch—all the while looking at him on the screen. She could tell from the movement that he was jerking himself off, though he didn't have the camera aimed that low. She wanted to ask him to show her, but he had said not to speak.

He cooed, "Take off your panties, Maya…slowly. Use both hands and pull them slowly over your hips. And wiggle when you step out of them. Push your hair over your shoulders."

She did exactly as he instructed, letting her hair fall to the side so it didn't hide her face as she carefully removed her underwear.

"Now sit down and spread your legs," he murmured,

When she had seated herself in the chair, he went on. "Wider. Spread yourself open for me. Let me see that perfect pink pussy." His breathing was becoming ragged, and she could hear the sound of him jerking off harder. "Bring the chair closer to the camera until I tell you to stop. I want to see both your face and hot pussy." Maya slid the chair a bit closer and brought a candle forward, placing it on the floor so it illuminated her.

"Very good. Keep those legs spread wide. Are you wet?" he asked.

She nodded, and he continued, "Play with yourself. Spread yourself open so I can see how wet you are. Run your finger all around the lips of your pussy. Then show me that clit, and rub it for me."

Maya tentatively parted the pink folds of her pussy, opening them up. She teased the opening, trailing her finger in a slow circular motion to widen the entrance. Then she slowly dragged her finger up and over her clit, pressing the tender nub. Moaning softly, she rubbed her clit harder. As the blissful sensation coursed through her, a shiver ran down her spine and she lifted her butt off the chair, offering up her pussy to the camera.

"Oh, baby," he growled. She focused in on the sound of his hand on his cock, moving faster again. "I love how turned on you are. You love touching yourself, don't you?" The sound of his strangled voice intoxicated her. Sliding her ass toward the edge of the chair, she let her head fall against the back. The soft lighting in the room cast a shadow over her face, illuminating her décolletage.

Nico continued his tutelage. "Fuck yourself with your fingers. I want to hear that sound and see your juices flowing."

Maya inserted first one finger, then another, into her swollen pussy, plunging them in and out until she could hear the sucking sound. Finding her hot spot, she caressed it, applying just the right amount of pressure as she glided through the wetness.

"That's it, baby," Nico panted. She could tell he was very close to coming. Drowning in lustful pleasure, she rocked her hips off the chair, fucking herself harder and moaning as she brought herself close to the edge.

Nico's voice was tight, and he panted heavily between words.

"Oh, God, yes. Lick your fingers. Show me how much you love how sweet you taste."

Obeying his command, she let out a soft whimper as she removed her fingers and provocatively inserted them between the moist red lips of her mouth as she gazed directly into the camera.

"You're so fucking hot, baby. Keep looking at the camera. I'm gonna come." His eyes glazed over as he watched her frantically plunge her fingers back into her pussy. Fucking herself hard and fast, she felt her slick juices running down her fingers into her hand. She curled her fingers around her hot spot and stroked it repeatedly while her thumb swirled over her clit, the rigid tension building inside her.

Nico rasped, "Come for me." His face contorted in ecstasy as cum sprayed from his cock. With each pulsing jet, he emitted a guttural growl, his burning eyes riveted on her.

His release fueled her fire, and a loud moan escaped her lips as she writhed in urgent need. Her breathing hitched as her back arched, and her legs stiffened when the tightness in her belly snapped loose with the rolling waves of her orgasm. Slick, glistening wetness gushed out of her as she convulsed and cried out his name. Neither of them spoke as Maya lifted her hand back to her mouth and slowly sucked the juices off each of her fingers, one by one.

Their rousing Skype sessions were short lived, and though disappointed, she couldn't fault Nico for going out and meeting people. But by the second week, his lusty calls were replaced by text messages instructing her to check the mail, pay the utility bill, and deal with his bank account. She dutifully attended to his demands, knowing how important it was to help him with his business.

o   o   o

The moment Élodie's plane touched the tarmac at LAX, she tapped Nico's profile picture on her phone to call him. It had only been two weeks since she'd met him at Etoiles, the glamorous upscale nightclub at Emirates Palace in Abu Dhabi. Two of her best girlfriends had flown from Paris to visit, and Élodie treated them to a late-night supper of edamame fried rice and crispy duck salad at the acclaimed chic Cantonese restaurant Hakkasan. Instead of wine, they'd ordered exotic cocktails. Élodie couldn't resist the ingredients of The Hakka, a brew of Belvedere vodka, sake, lychee juice, lime, coconut, and passion fruit, while her friends ordered The Kumquatcha, a blend of kumquat, lime, Campari, and Cachaça. After dinner, her friends had been intent on dancing. Etoiles was filled with fashionable Europeans, celebrities, and wealthy locals. Élodie wasn't much for the loud music, preferring conversation to fist pumping, but they'd spurred her on, teasing that she was single and only thirty years old and insisting she act her age and have some fun. Élodie didn't see how being pressed against drunk, sweaty strangers who couldn't hear a word you said was fun, but she'd gone along, trying to act enthusiastic.

Nico picked up on the second ring. "Baby, where are you? You're late. I've been waiting for you."

When Élodie heard the lulling purr of his voice, she instantly felt a warm throbbing between her legs. "The plane has just landed. I only have a carry-on bag, so it should be fast."

"Come here to the studio. I want you to see it."

"Of course, baby. I want to see the studio…and you."

Élodie had never felt such a powerful connection to any man, and she met many wealthy, influential men through her business. She received expensive gifts and invitations to accompany them on private jets to homes around the world, but there had never been anyone she felt magnetically connected to, who made her lose herself, until Nico. When she first set eyes on him, she felt her pulse race; and when he kissed her, she gave herself up to him, completely.

She and her friends had found their way to a bottle service table of wealthy Russians. A tall, lanky man was breathing down her neck while Élodie politely tried not to yell as she answered his questions. He had poured her another glass of champagne, even though she'd kept asking him to please get her a bottle of water. Élodie had been wearing a short black off-the-shoulder dress by Georges Chakra, a Lebanese designer who dressed several celebrities, and whom she had met in Beirut the prior year. The heat emanating from the bodies on the dance floor was oppressive and she'd run her hands underneath her long honey-colored hair that hung loose around her shoulders, lifting it from her damp neck. Tossing it back, she'd caught the flicker of his eyes—bright yellow headlights that peered into hers. He was leaning casually against the end of the bar, holding a tall cocktail. Their eyes had locked, and although it was rude to the man who kept trying to engage her, she couldn't tear her eyes away. Leaning over the bar, he spoke to the bartender, then made his way over to her. Ignoring the Russian, he'd come between them and handed her a bottle of water. He didn't raise his voice above the din, and Élodie was unsure how she'd been able to hear him clearly when he said, "You must be very thirsty."

Breaking the seal on the water bottle, she'd mouthed, "Thank you," and in a very unladylike manner tipped her head back, drinking the entire bottle at once.

Nico had laughed, watching her with delight. When she finished, he took the empty bottle from her, placing it on the table. Putting one arm around her waist, he put his lips to her ear and purred softly, "Let's get out of here."

He was poised and self-assured, yet with a gentle manner, and Élodie was intrigued by this handsome mystery man. In the din of Etoiles, she couldn't hear herself think. All she knew was she needed to know more. Without hesitation, she'd walked out of Etoiles with the stranger. Holding her hand, he wove them through the crowd at a pace she found difficult to match. Her feet burned from standing in skyscraper Christian Louboutin heels, and she would have preferred taking his arm. And when they reached the door, he did extend his arm to her, and she'd smiled at him, relieved. Once outside the club, the thumping sounds of the music receded and they'd exchanged names and made small talk. Nico escorted her through the ornate colonnade and out to the Las Brisas, illuminated pools landscaped with tall palm trees. The Arabian night breeze brought relief, and Élodie relaxed while she walked quietly with the enigmatic man. After learning she was also a guest at the hotel, he asked why she was in Abu Dhabi. Speaking in English, Élodie shared she was an art consultant advising the new Louvre museum on its collection of modern art.

Intrigued, Nico asked, "What does that mean, art consultant?"

She explained, "I'm sorry, my English is not as good as my Arabic. I help people who collect art…for investment."

Nico gazed at her intently. "I didn't know that people did that. Where do you live?"

"My home is in Monaco, but my work is all over the world. Where do you live?"

"I'm from Argentina, but I live in L.A."

Élodie listened intently as Nico boasted that he was a Kundalini Yoga master and shaman proficient in ancient healing ceremonies, and that he had been summoned to teach a particularly powerful kriya to a sheikh. Fascinated, she asked him to explain. He divulged that this specific meditation increases one's psychic abilities and heightens awareness. Then, somewhat modestly, as if it were commonplace, he confided he had been paid a half a million dollars. Élodie smiled admiringly. She wasn't all that surprised by the amount. By normal standards it would seem a lot, but money flowed in this region of the world more readily than water.

Quite certain Nico would have been sworn to secrecy, she still couldn't resist asking the sheikh's name, apologizing when Nico quickly recoiled, stating he was unable to say. To soften her presumptuous inquiry, she admitted, "Ah, yes. I too am not able to share names of my clients. But how did the mysterious sheikh find you?"

Nico touted, "I get a lot of press, and many clients are celebrities. I have centers in Tulum, Kerala, and Beverly Hills."

Accustomed to notable, arrogant men, Élodie found his bravado charming and his confidence sexy. Certainly, making it to Abu Dhabi as a yoga instructor to a sheikh was extraordinary.

They strolled, her arm woven into his, slowly over a wooden foot bridge spanning a narrow neck of the underlit pool. Élodie, still wearing the Louboutins, was grateful when they neared the entrance to the beach and took the opportunity to sit on a white lounge bed facing the sea. Slipping her shoes off, she tucked her feet up under herself. The full moon hanging over the Persian Gulf was almost surreal, and they both gazed at it in awe. Élodie spoke in almost a whisper, not wishing to break the spell, "No matter how often I come here, this place is magical."

Seemingly without thinking, Nico took her hand and stroked it with his thumb. "Yes, magic…and tribal. I am drawn to ancient civilizations, like the Q'ero. There are powerful spirits in the mountains, known as Apus. This is something completely alien to me. Here is this vast, barren desert just beyond the city," Nico pointed away from the sea. "And then this modern city, with glass and steel architecture, like from a science fiction movie!"

Élodie laughed. "I know what you mean. I come from an old European city."

Nico looked at the Emirates Palace. "I mean, this is made to look old, but it's brand new! I went to see the Grand Mosque, and it's magnificent. You think it is ancient, right? But it's not even ten years old. And the chandelier has millions of crystals! When I do a despacho ceremony to make an offering to Pachamama, the Mother Earth, I give her gifts like hair, blood, sage, and candy. It's all so simple. Sure, I grew up Catholic, and there are beautiful old churches in Buenos Aires. They're majestic, with stained glass and gold. Don't get me wrong. I find this juxtaposition of ultra-modern and antiquity, the desert and this sublime body of water…this is awesome…it takes my breath away."

Élodie watched Nico's childlike wonder with delight and admiration. "They have built great beauty from sand, and it is very opulent. Most people see only this. But, you know, they gave over two billion dollars for vaccines for children." She stopped short and blushed, seeing Nico look at her with amusement.

Élodie knew she was always defending this place—it had so much wealth and ostentation—a playground for the richest people in the world. Nico sat pensively staring at the huge full moon growing larger as it sank closer to the horizon. As she watched him, a slight shudder ran up her spine. Nico must have sensed it, because he put his arm around her and pulled her close to him. Resting her head on his shoulder, she sighed as they gazed out over the Persian Gulf.

As the moon set and darkness overtook them, Nico began idly coiling a tendril of her hair around his finger. In anticipation, Élodie involuntarily trembled under his touch. Nuzzling his face into her neck, Nico moved against her, closing the space between them. Lifting her chin, he pressed his lips to hers in a warm, soft, lingering kiss. Tentatively, he nibbled provocatively at her lips, gently teasing out kisses. Cupping her face with his hands, he slowly pulled on her lower lip, coaxing her mouth open. Then, running the tip of his tongue lightly over her lips, he pulled her closer to his chest, entwining his fingers into her hair. Melting into him while his tongue swept slowly over the inside of her lower lip, Élodie's breath quickened, as she became awash in sensation. Slipping his tongue into her mouth, he swiveled it around hers in a devilish dance with deeper and harder strokes until she was breathless. She had never been kissed that passionately before, sending tremors throughout her body. Hungrily, he devoured her mouth, then kissed her jaw, running his teeth along it as he moved his lips down her neck, his tongue flicking the sensitive hollow in her clavicle. Purring, he murmured, "So beautiful."

Élodie gasped, letting out a little cry, somewhere between pain and ecstasy. Nico trailed his hands down over her breasts. Her hard nipples grew longer as they strained under the tissue-thin fabric. Panting, her full breasts heaved over the décolletage of the lace dress as he kissed a trail down to the space between them. Enraptured, Élodie sighed and breathed his name, "Nico…"

He tore his mouth from hers and Élodie cried out in near agony.

"Come with me." Nico's eyes locked with hers.

She had no ability or desire to refuse his command. Her body craved his, and even her soul was compelled. Picking up her sandals by the ankle strap, she held Nico's hand as they moved quickly back to the hotel and into the elevator.

Nico was in the Pearl Room, with a terrace overlooking the tropical gardens, swimming pools, and the beach where they had just been sitting. He turned on the lamp at the writing desk and opened the sliding door to the terrace, allowing the warm night air in.

"Élodie," he exhaled her name with a long sigh. "Even your name intoxicates me. Come here. The smell of you makes me drunk with desire."

Élodie walked over to him, and sliding his arm around her waist, he pressed her body to his and kissed her deeply. His hands swept through her hair, then down her back as he pushed his hips into her. Finding the zipper on the back of her dress, he tugged it down with one hand while his free hand held her close. Maneuvering the dress off her shoulders, Élodie encircled his neck with her arms and helped by wriggling her hips, then stepped out of the dress. Standing in her bare feet she was just the right height, and Nico's mouth fell onto her neck, kissing down to the top of her black lace demi-cup bra as he cupped her buttocks.

His hands covered her masterfully. There wasn't a part of her he didn't touch. Nuzzling his nose to her breast, he inhaled her, then gently lifted one breast from inside the cup of her bra. "Your skin smells sweet, like a flower. This tit is a precious jewel."

He took her nipple into his mouth and sucked it until it grew long and hard. Looking up at her, he said sweetly, "You are perfect, Élodie."

Gazing into his eyes, Élodie was captivated by the glinting yellow flecks. Unable to break his gaze, she tentatively reached up to sweep the lock of hair from his eyes, then slowly unbuttoned his white shirt. His sleeves were rolled up to his elbows, a stainless steel Breitling Navitimer chronograph on one wrist and braided leather and beaded bracelets covering the other. Shrugging the shirt off, he undid his pants. Stepping out of them, he tossed them onto the desk chair. His erection bulged under his grey boxer briefs, and he tore them off, releasing his hard-on. Élodie gasped slightly at the sight of his thick, ridged length.

Nico pulled the plush golden bedspread off the king size bed, letting it spill to the floor, and guided Élodie, still wearing her bra and black lace thong, to the edge of the bed, then knelt on the floor in front of her. Leaning in, he kissed a path from her left knee up her thigh, to the top of her mound, then playfully flicked his tongue around and into her navel. She reached out for him, cupping his head in her hands in an attempt to bring his head back up. Refusing her, he ordered, almost gruffly, "Relax, Élodie, while I taste your sweetness."

Restless, Élodie leaned back on her elbows and tried to breathe normally as she felt her heart racing, ready to explode.

Kissing his way around her abdomen, he trailed his tongue down the inside of her right thigh. Her wetness growing, she squirmed and moaned in frustration. Taking his exploration of her very seriously, Nico massaged her pussy over the top of her thong, sweeping over her clit with his thumb to feel her heat.

Élodie arched her back, letting out a whimper.

Lifting the thong, he slipped one finger inside, pressing into the opening of her pussy, "Ah…you are dripping wet. I'm going to lap up all of your juices." He tugged the obstructing garment off, and placing his hands on her knees, spread them apart, splaying her open to him. Smiling, he commented admiringly, "I love to see a natural woman. It is very sexy. Not like a little girl." Her pubic hair framed the glistening pink flesh. Bowing his head, he leaned into her, licking a path to the mouth of her pussy, then running his tongue around her velvet folds and along the seam to the opening. When he probed the entrance with his tongue, Élodie's breath hitched, and groaning, she rose up to meet him as he darted his tongue in and out.

He plunged his tongue deeper into her, hooking it upward to lap her juices as they flowed. Feeling her tension grow and her legs stiffening, he tore his mouth from her. Crying out, she reached up and laced his hair in her hands, trying to hold him to her. "Ne cessez pas! Please…don't stop," she begged.

Cupping her buttocks in his hands, he nuzzled into her. "Shhh-hhh, baby. Shhhhhh." The warmth of his breath so close to her pussy had her squirming.

Élodie inhaled deeply, then let out a sigh and a small whimper. Nico flicked his tongue over her clitoris, then licked it tautly, sending shock waves through her body. Placing his mouth over the tender nub, he began sucking, pulling it between his lips. Arching up, she cried out his name. Never had she been tortured and ravaged in this way. As he nibbled and sucked on her nub, he inserted two fingers into her swollen, dripping pussy and began to fuck her, curling them upward and moving them in a come-hither motion over her G-spot. The juices ran down his fingers as he licked and sucked her clit. Her hips bucked and he felt her tightening—climbing higher. Panting, she begged, "Nico…please don't stop."

"I love the way you taste, Élodie. You are a feast that I cannot get enough of."

He couldn't wait much longer, and began sucking harder at her clit while his fingers worked their magic deep inside her pussy. He felt her go rigid, then shudder. She cried out, squirting into his hand as she came undone.

"Ah, baby. I knew you would squirt for me. You were so ready."

The intensity of her climax was beyond anything she had ever experienced. Never had she squirted while coming. She hadn't known it was possible.

He knelt down in front of her. Spent, Élodie watched him take hold of his cock—his eyes dark, green pools that glowed from within as if projecting moonlight. Enrapt, he pulled his hand down toward the root and back over the tip, his fingers wrapped tightly around his width, until the head mushroomed and the veins were bulging.

Her breath increased, and she could feel a tightening coil in her belly as he readied himself. Leaning up, he pressed the head of his dick to the entrance of her pussy, steadying her with his hands on her hips. She laced her arms around his shoulders, bracing for him. Slowly, but forcefully, he plunged into her glistening, wet pussy. Wrapping her legs tightly around him, she gasped as he hit the back of her. Still feeling the hypersensitivity from her orgasm, her pussy quivered as he filled her. Burying his head into her hair, his breath became ragged as he fucked her with a frenzied desire she had never felt before. Plunging over and over, he drove harder and deeper into her, growling in agony. Each time he hit that same swollen sensitive spot inside, her body quaked repeatedly, sending her rocketing up to meet him. She adored being possessed by this man as he powered into her with a fevered passion, claiming all of her. He grabbed her hair as he dove into her, and her eyes locked on his as she felt the rippling waves of another orgasm overtake her, watching the pain and pleasure on his face when he ejected hot jets of semen into her.

Nico collapsed and lay with his dick inside her. She kept her legs wrapped tightly around him, holding him to her as their breathing slowly returned to normal. Feeling his cock twitch, she clenched the muscles of her pussy to keep him inside. Fiddling with his hair, she wound the dark locks around her finger contentedly.

Nico nuzzled his face into her neck. "I could stay inside you forever."

Élodie wasn't sure how long they lay there together. Partially awake, she felt him move inside her. Then his lips found hers and their tongues clashed, pirouetting around each other. Élodie couldn't take her eyes off of his.

"I can't get enough of you. I don't ever want to let you go, Élodie," he purred.

They made love again—slowly, with much less urgency. Stroking her hair, he kissed her eyes, then her neck, down to her shoulders, as he moved his body in harmony with hers. They climaxed together; this time an endless, deep, pulsating unraveling within her. He did things to her body she had never felt before, and that she knew she would never find with anyone but Nico.

In the morning, they stood on the terrace looking out over the lush gardens and blue water. Nico spoke sadly. "I only have a few more days here. I have to go back to L.A."

Élodie leaned her head on his shoulder. "I know, baby. But I will come there next week. I have many clients in L.A. We can be together often, and you can meet me in Paris and Monaco."

"I don't want you to see anyone else, Élodie. I want us to be together. "

"Nico, I don't have anyone else. There is no one. I have never felt this way, and I have no need for anyone but you." Élodie couldn't believe her own words, but as she said them, she knew she spoke the truth to herself, and to Nico.

"I can't stand the thought of not having you every day, touching your skin. And your smell…the way your pussy smells to me…it's intoxicating. You're like a drug that I must have every day. Come with me, Élodie. I can't leave you behind."

"Nico, I will follow you. I have to go back to Monaco and finish up some business. Then I will come to L.A. in just a few days. You'll see."

She turned to walk back into the room, and Nico caught her by the hand, drawing her to him in a lingering kiss.

"I have to shower," Élodie murmured. "See," she said, pointing east, "I have to get over to the museum on Saadiyat Island for a meeting, and you are making me late." She laughed softly, reaching up to push his hair back off his face. "Don't you have someplace important to be?"

Nico huffed, "I do…" but he left his destination unspoken. "A car is picking me up soon. So, yes, let's shower. And I will try to keep my hands off you!"

Élodie cleared her throat mockingly, knowing neither of them would be able to control themselves.

o   o   o

The traffic from LAX had been torturous, and the privately owned black Escalade finally pulled up in front of Amaru Yoga, "Voici!" The uniformed driver retrieved her luggage from the back of the SUV and opened the back door, helping Élodie out.

"Oui, bien. Merci."

The driver offered to wait, but Élodie thanked him, assuring him she would be fine. Nonetheless, he waited until she stepped inside before he drove away.

She called out to Nico, her suitcase click-clicking as she rolled it across the polished wooden floors. Hearing her voice, he emerged from the back room. "You're so late, I've been waiting for you." He was barefoot, wearing black yoga pants and no shirt.

"That's OK. I knew you were here. I told the driver to go."

Nico stood looking at her as if she were an apparition. "I can't believe you are finally here." He looked her up and down and smiled. "You look beautiful." Taking her in his arms, he kissed her softly, twirling her hair that hung in a long ponytail. Taking the handle of her suitcase, he guided her. "Come, let's get you some tea. Are you hungry?"

Élodie followed him. "I'm feeling a little *sous le temps*. How do you say…under the weather. Maybe *décalage horaire*—jetlag. I'm sorry. I am too tired to speak English!"

Nico nuzzled her, kissing her neck.

"I will make you some of my special tea. Come."

Élodie looked around the dimly lit studio. Ethereal music played softly, making her feel as if she had stepped into a different world. Passing by, she peeked into a small room with a low slate-topped table, the walls covered with photographs and shelves filled with pottery and glass jars. She would have stopped to look inside, but Nico was steps ahead of her as they walked through his office and into his apartment. He left her suitcase near the door and escorted her to his seating area. "Relax. I will make you tea and something to eat."

Élodie excused herself. "May I?" she asked, pointing to what she hoped was the bathroom.

Nico apologized. "Oh, of course. Take your time. Do you want to take a shower?"

"Not just yet. The tea sounds good."

Nico put the water on to boil, taking down two mugs from the shelf. He added ingredients to the black iron tea pot on the counter—sassafras root, eleuthero ginseng, shaved ginger, a few drops of Echinacea, a scoop of loose peppermint tea, and what looked like several fresh green bay leaves. Carefully measuring out a powder from a small canister, he tapped it into the pot. Crushing vitamin C tablets with a mortar and pestle, he also added them, along with some açai berries. When the kettle boiled, he added the water, letting it steep.

Élodie emerged from the bathroom and stepped out of her classic Fendi pumps. Hanging her Balmain blazer with satin lapels and gold buttons on the back of a chair, she opened her suitcase. Slipping off her pants and cream silk blouse, she changed into a pair of comfortable black leggings and a white Chanel logo T-shirt. Then she huddled on the sofa, wrapping herself in a throw blanket that had been draped over the side. Nico poured the tea concoction into two mugs and carried them over to the coffee table, along with a plate of empanadas. "I made these today while I was waiting for you."

Élodie looked at him incredulously. "Really? You made these?"

"Yes, of course. Mine are the best. They're still warm."

Élodie picked one up, taking a bite. "What's inside?"

"Seasoned beef. It's simple. I cook onions and add cumin and paprika. Here, drink the tea. It will restore you," he said, handing her the mug.

Nico sipped the tea along with her. Élodie shivered, and he nuzzled her, rubbing her shoulders. He followed her eyes as she looked around the room. When she spotted the guitar, she asked, "Do you play?"

"Drink your tea. I will play something." He picked up the guitar. "This is a well-known *vals criolla*. "La Flor de la Canela," cinnamon flower. It is the unofficial anthem of Lima. It's been covered a lot."

He began playing tentatively. It was a simple waltz, and he fingered the chords as he strummed in a one, two, three; one, two, three waltz tempo. His singing was soft and restrained. His neck arched gracefully as he leaned over the guitar, his thick dark hair falling forward over his face and a soft curl framing one of his smoky green eyes. Élodie swayed to the rhythm of the waltz, watching him closely. Peering up at her from under the errant lock of hair, he played more fervently and his serenade became more impassioned. His voice, deep and husky, cracked slightly when he hit the high notes.

When he finished the song, she clapped delightedly. Nico put the guitar down and hugged her to him, his hand sliding up her thigh as he drew her onto his lap. "How are you feeling? Any better?"

Élodie felt blissfully contented. "Yes, I feel a comforting warmth in my body," she cooed, "What is in this tea you made?"

Nico chuckled softly. "Now if I told you, it wouldn't be my secret." Pulling her down so that she straddled him, he looked into her eyes. His hands in her hair as he kissed her, he pulled on her lip playfully. "I missed you, Élodie—my princess."

"Why do say that? Princess…"

Running his tongue along her lips, he whispered in between tantalizing kisses, "Um…I think I will change it to queen—my Arabian queen of the desert. There, is that better? We met in the desert. I can see it now, can't you? The big moon and the desert?"

"Yes," she answered dreamily, clearly envisioning the round moon hanging low over the desert landscape. "I can see it." She pulled her hands through his hair and kissed his ear and neck, fingering the silver chain with the dragon pendant that lay across his bare chest. "You always wear this, yes?" Her voice had a lilting melody.

"Yes, I suppose. I forget to take it off."

She began to suck on one of his nipples. "Mmm…you taste salty, like the sea. I like this." Moving to the other nipple, she licked it as well, meandering around it with her tongue.

Nico squirmed. "You're making me hard."

"That's good." She kissed his chest, then kissed down his body until she reached his navel, teasing it with her tongue. Her hands found his erection under the soft black yoga pants, then her lips found the perfectly formed head peeking out the top of the waistband.

"Hmm, look what I found. Come out to play with me." Lifting the waistband, she peeked playfully. "Bonjour, tortue!" She kissed the tip sweetly, as if it were a child she was putting to bed. Slipping it gently into her mouth, she suckled it lovingly between her lips.

His hips bucked as she teased him, leaving his thick shaft under cover of the fleece, petting him with her palm until Nico, unable to withstand any longer, lifted his hips and pulled down the pants, releasing the full length of his erection. "Play with me, baby," he murmured.

Crawling down off the sofa, she knelt next to him. Locking eyes with his, she wrapped her fingers around his width and stroked him as her tongue traced a path around the head of his cock. Sucking him, she slowly took him deeper, his hips rising and falling as she slid him in and out of her mouth, her thumb rolling over the ridge when her hand passed over the tip.

"God…Élodie." He laced his fingers in her hair, pulling her down hard. His cock hit the back of her throat and she groaned, sending vibrations down around his shaft. "Fuck, baby. You feel so good."

"Can I sit on you?" she asked before holding him firmly, sucking the head and brushing it along her lips playfully.

"Ride me, baby. I'm all yours."

Élodie tore off her T-shirt and leggings. Standing, she slipped off her champagne lace thong and unhooked the matching push-up bra, letting it fall to the floor. Then, straddling him, she held his cock in her hand and rubbed it against the entrance to her pussy while she rocked back and forth over him. Positioning him at the opening, she lifted herself up and came down on him, plunging him inside. She exhaled hard as Nico called out, "God, baby. You're so tight!"

Leaning over him, her hair falling into his face, she clasped his wrists with her hands, pinning his arms over his head. The feeling of her pussy clutching around him like a fist had her drowning in ecstasy. Taking complete control, she rode him, lavishly moving her body up and down until only the tip remained just inside her pussy before sinking down, taking his full length back inside her.

He watched, mesmerized, as his dick appeared and then disappeared into her, filling her completely. His hands glided along her hips and thighs, her skin moving under his touch like watery silk flowing in an ocean breeze.

Entranced, she held him deep inside, her soft moans musical as she ground down, kneading her clit against him. Leaning forward, her eyes transfixed on his, she positioned her tit at his mouth and he sucked hungrily at her nipple. It grew long, hardening, until it was on fire, and her cries became an agonizing toll of elation.

Awash in desire, they moved together for what seemed like hours. Élodie bent down, breathless, and kissed his lips, slowly pushing her tongue into his mouth, envisioning them in an exquisite dance, whirling around each other. Sitting up, she gazed down, watching his expression. His eyes fixed on hers and he cupped her breasts, then slid his hands down along her waist. "So beautiful," his voice was low and raspy. Grabbing her hips with both hands, he surged upward, his dick filling her over and over again, and she cried out as her swollen clit pressed along his pelvis. His eyes glowed brightly as he purred, "So beautiful. You feel incredible. Come for me, baby. I want to watch you."

Enchanted by his hypnotic voice, she cupped and caressed her breasts, squeezing her nipples as her body spasmed, her clit throbbing as she convulsed around him. "Oh mon Dieu!"

When she collapsed over him, he dug his fingers into her ass, pulling her down to keep her tight on his cock while his fingers lightly traced designs on her back until her breathing normalized.

He gently moved her off and got up, returning with two glasses of water. "Here, drink this," he coaxed.

She took the water from him and drank it all down. "Thank you, I am very thirsty," she confessed. "I am very…enchante…our love making…so paradise. You made something with the tea?"

"The tea made you feel better. It's a special potion to restore you, yes—and make you feel very good."

"It is a love potion. I feel it."

"Come with me," Nico helped her up and they went to his bed. Taking out a bottle of coconut oil, he poured some into his hand and began pleasuring himself. Élodie sat on the side of the bed watching him intently. His eyes remained fixed on hers as he slowly tugged his cock, coaxing it back to its full hard length. "Give me your ass, baby."

Élodie turned over and positioned herself on all fours at the edge of the bed, her head resting on a pillow. Nico warmed the coconut oil in his hands and massaged her back and ass. She sighed, relishing the feeling of his hands covering her body. Trailing his finger down her spine and along her cleft he then slowly teased around her anus,

"Your ass is so beautiful." Adding more lubricant, he gently inserted his finger to open her up. Positioning himself in line with her anus, he swiped his cock along the inside of her crack. She pushed back, welcoming him. "I'm going to love fucking your ass, baby," Nico murmured happily.

Élodie whimpered. Wanting him, she lifted her ass higher. Leaning over her, he slowly palmed her back with one hand, gripping her hip with the other. Then he pushed into her. She gasped.

"Are you OK, baby?" His voice was strangled.

"Yes. I want you."

He pushed the tip of his cock into her opening and waited, feeling the tight muscle clench around him. When he thrust into her, she exhaled hard, letting out another cry.

Nico stroked her back. "Relax, baby. Let me in." Holding her tightly, he powered back in, this time more forcefully, until he was balls deep. Leaning over with his body pressed against hers, he moved slowly, as if they were one. Releasing his hand from her hip, he fingered her pussy and lightly teased her clit with his thumb.

Élodie wiggled her ass, letting out a gasp when he slid his finger into her wet pussy. With his cock in her ass and his fingers probing her hot spot, a feeling of overwhelming fullness took possession of her and she moved in synch with him. She was completely his, every inch of her body controlled by him.

He covered her with kisses from her spine to her shoulder blades, his fingers tangled in her hair. He breathed into her ear, "God, baby. I love you."

His words sent tremors through her body. "Dieu, mon amour," she cried out hoarsely as she came apart under him. The waves crashed in, one after another. Her body shuddered, but he held her tightly to him, possessing her.

He fucked her feverishly, one forceful thrust after another, until he exploded into her ass with a strangled, agonized growl. He kept pumping her until he collapsed onto her back. As he lay on her, still deep in her ass, he rubbed her arms, his face buried in her hair. Kissing her neck, he purred, "So beautiful. You're mine, baby. Forever."

She could feel his dick still twitching in her ass as the wetness spilled from her. Unable to move, she cherished the feeling of him possessing her, his chest against her back, his face in her neck. "Je suis à vous. I belong to you." She had never felt so completely one with another person. What was this potion? Certainly, it must be the elixir of love.

26

Nico greeted her wearing his well-worn yoga pants, with a bare chest and wet hair, obviously fresh from a shower. Looking her up and down, the corners of his mouth curled up in a mischievous grin. Maya's long, black hair framed her face. She'd applied red lipstick and a slight smudge of black eyeliner to accentuate her dark eyes. "Damn, I forgot just how hot you are," he purred, ogling her.

"You don't look so bad yourself." She smiled at him, admiring his wet hair falling over his luminous green eyes. He looked as if he had put a few pounds on his normally lanky cat-like body. No wonder, with an all-expenses paid gig, he could eat and drink at every five-star Michelin rated restaurant. Depositing bags of groceries on the kitchen counter, Maya wrapped her arms around his neck, pressing her pelvis into him as their lips locked. His hand cupped her buttocks as he reciprocated, playfully pulling on her bottom lip. "Get dinner ready, I have to finish doing something."

Maya looked at him quizzically, but he made for the bedroom.

She had brought the guitar case from her car and now laid it on the coffee table. Since it was too big to wrap, she'd just stuck one big red bow on top. She had bought him a handmade Cordoba C9 with a European spruce top and solid mahogany back and sides that produced sweet, warm tones. The hand-inlaid mother-of-pearl rosette had a vintage elegance. The shop owner had assured her it was a beautiful sounding guitar, and a bargain at only eight hundred dollars.

Opening the wine, she poured two glasses, put the tortilla chips into a wooden bowl, and served up the guacamole in a Talavera bowl he'd brought back from Mexico. When Nico didn't return right away, she went in search of him, finding him engrossed in checking the contents of the safe he kept hidden under an Indian tapestry. Hearing her behind him, he held up two packets of cocaine. "I was hoping I still had these."

"Nico, I told you, I'm not doing that stuff anymore. And you said you weren't going to, either."

"It's been over a month. I didn't do any in Abu Dhabi. Don't you want to celebrate my return?"

Maya turned away from him, heading back to the living room area where she had laid out the food. "Come on, Nico. Let's eat and have some wine. You promised you were going to quit that shit."

He followed closely behind her after locking the safe, but keeping the packets with him. Seeing the guitar case, he asked, perplexed, "What's this?"

"It's your Christmas present," she said coyly.

He studied the case, then slowly opened it. Removing the guitar, he placed it across his lap and fingered the strings. Then he played "Cavatina," a beautiful heart-wrenching tune. Maya sat frozen—the sound coming from the guitar was sublime. She was certain she saw tears in his eyes when he looked up at her from under his hair and smiled. When he finished, he leaned over and kissed her gently on the lips—a sweet kiss that felt intimate and full of gratitude. His voice just above a whisper, he said, "Thank you. It's beautiful."

After dinner, Maya hoped he would play more songs and then they could make love and watch a movie, falling asleep in each other's arms. Instead, ignoring her earlier renunciation, he laid out several lines of coke on a mirrored tray that he kept on the bookshelf and held up a straw. Shaking her head in disapproval, she nevertheless took the straw from him, quickly snorting only one line. She knew he would continue to badger her, and it was easier to just give in and do it. Besides, if she didn't, she feared he would find someone else. There was no shortage of pretty girls who would love to party with Nico.

◦　　◦　　◦

At first glance, Luna thought it was another e-mail blast about the studio. It was only two sentences. "What is this? Is this some kind of voodoo thing, Luna?" Reading the message, she hadn't grasped its meaning. Then she remembered.

She sighed and typed back, "No, Nico. It's a Native American medicine bundle for your protection. All shamans have bundles that they make for themselves, or that are passed down to them. You can add other elements if you want, like in the despacho ceremony."

He messaged back, "Thank you. It's good then?"

"Yes, Nico. It's good."

o   o   o

Soon after accepting Luna's peace offering, Nico sent a curious e-mail that she surmised was a test to see if she still cared about him. "I met the woman of my dreams. I'm engaged!" She couldn't just ignore his happy message, full of excitement and promise. Without thinking, she hit reply. "I am so happy for you! When can I meet her?"

He messaged back instantly. "I have a meeting with my banker in an hour. Meet us there. I bought her a very expensive diamond ring!"

Luna pulled her green Land Rover into the parking lot, and after checking her makeup in the mirror, she smudged a bit more kohl pencil under her eyes and added a touch more berry red lip gloss. She hadn't planned on seeing Nico, and was glad she was wearing a cute Isabel Marant dress. She grabbed the handbag that Nico had given her, knowing he would notice she still carried it even though they hadn't seen each other in eight months. When she spotted Nico through the glass doors, she felt the rush of fire butterflies in her solar plexus. It was overwhelming, and she paused a moment with her hand on the door to steady herself. Before she entered, Nico intuitively raised his head up from the document he was reading and their eyes met. He kept them locked on hers as she gracefully walked toward him. She didn't smile, but was sure her eyes lit up when she saw him. As she neared the desk where he was sitting, she took in the demeanor of a lean, elegantly dressed woman with honey-colored hair pulled up in a loose bun, tendrils softly falling across her face. She sat impassively listening to the banker speak to Nico, whose attention had turned to Luna.

Luna waited for Nico to make an introduction to the stunning-
ly beautiful woman with clear cornflower-blue eyes, who gazed up
expectantly at her. The distinctive sweet narcotic notes of jasmine
wafted between them. In the seconds that flashed by, Luna wondered
if he had failed to mention she was stopping by to see them. Pulling
up a chair for Luna, Nico motioned for her to sit as he turned his
attention back to his banker. With still no introduction, Luna felt
awkward and extended her hand, introducing herself. "How do you
do, I'm Luna Saint Claire."

Fixing her eyes on Luna, the woman smiled inquisitively. "Élodie
Chauvin." The voluptuous syllables blended together, mellow and
musical. Luna was taken aback for a split second. Nico hadn't mentioned she was French.

Luna unobtrusively took in the stylish, vibrantly printed blue
minidress that she wore with platform sandals. "It's so nice to meet
you. I love your fragrance…What are you wearing?"

"Thank you. It's Joie de Jean Patou." She pronounced in French.
Then quickly amended, "Joy."

Waiting for Nico to make conversation, she looked back and forth
between them. When he didn't say anything, Luna made small talk.
"How long are you staying in L.A.?" she asked, thinking it was a safe,
obvious question.

Nico chimed in quickly, "Élodie is my fiancé. She'll be coming to
live with me in L.A. soon."

Luna feigned surprise. "Congratulations! Where did the two of
you meet?" Another obvious question that, for reasons unknown,
made Nico uncomfortable.

Again, he answered for Élodie. "We met in Abu Dhabi, I told
you…"

He hadn't told her, although she had assumed as much. "Oh, that's
nice." She tried to think of something benign. "Do you work there?"

Élodie tried to answer, but again Nico spoke for her. "She makes
investments. In art."

Luna watched Élodie's expression change, obviously uncomfortable with the way he touted her business. She added, "I advise private
clients and museums with their art investments." Élodie's English

was infused with a heavy French accent. She made her point slowly.

Intrigued, Luna probed further, "Do you live in Abu Dhabi?"

Élodie replied easily, before Nico could answer. "No, I live in Monaco, and come to L.A. frequently. I have several clients here who collect modern art. They want to know who will be the next Basquiat!"

Luna laughed, "That's understandable! Where do you stay? I mean, before you met Nico."

Élodie paused before answering. "I have a client who keeps a bungalow at the Beverly Hills Hotel. I prefer privacy, and they treat me very well."

"Yes, I can see how you would like the Mediterranean character, and there is so much history. Did Nico tell you he had a marvelous event at The Rails Gallery?"

Élodie looked over at Nico. "What is this?" she asked him.

Luna was stunned that Nico hadn't mentioned it, and saw him smile broadly. "It was for my film, *Amaru of the Andes,* about my initiation into the healing arts of the Q'ero tribe in the Andes. I told you about it."

Élodie laughed softly. "No you did not. I would have remembered this."

Nico huffed, "I told you. It won an award. You women just don't listen."

Élodie smiled politely and turned to Luna. "I do business with The Rails, here and in London. I am not at liberty to name my clients, but we have relationships with galleries around the world and have purchased the work of leading contemporary artists like Cui Ruzhuo, Gerhard Richter, and Richard Prince."

Impressed, Luna chimed, "How interesting! My husband and I go often to the galleries, and recently saw a Richard Prince exhibit. And did you by any chance see the amazing light sculptures by Frank Gehry?"

Élodie perked up. "Oh my God! Yes! I saw the exhibit last year with the fish lamps. They are spectacular!"

The women had finally found common ground. Looking over at Nico, Luna saw he wasn't pleased, but when Élodie turned to him and said, "I like this friend. She has impeccable style," he couldn't help himself, and winked at Luna, tossing her the small bone she needed.

Luna laughed and purposely caught a glimpse of Élodie's left hand. Seeing the ring, she chose to comment. "Oh! The ring is lovely. May I?" Luna took her hand, knowing it was presumptuous, but she wanted to see Élodie's reaction. "It's beautiful, Nico! Congratulations to both of you! Did you set a date?" Luna couldn't resist probing, even as she saw Nico squirm in his seat.

Élodie didn't brighten the way a newly engaged woman would, instead glancing furtively at Nico before answering, "It is all very new. We will date for a while…"

Luna turned her attention to Nico. "It's nice to see you, Nico. You look happy, and your hair got long."

Nico raked his hair back with his fingers and smiled flirtatiously at Luna, teasing, "Do you like it longer? Élodie likes it. Right, baby?" He reached around Élodie's shoulders and hugged her to him. Luna observed that she resisted slightly, and wondered if she was just shy with public displays of affection.

The banker was getting impatient with all the personal chatter. He got Nico's attention refocused on the document, which gave Luna an opportunity for more conversation with Élodie.

"Are you staying in L.A. for a while?" she asked again, since she never got an answer.

"I can stay only two days more. I have been here a week, and I have work in Monaco."

Luna pressed, "When will you return? Nico's birthday is next month. Will you come back then?"

Nico pounced on that quickly. "She'll be back for my birthday. Isn't that right, Élodie?"

Looking at him reassuringly, Élodie nodded. "Yes, baby, I will come for your birthday—of course."

Nico stood and shook the banker's hand, signaling the meeting was over. When Luna got up to leave, Nico asked her to wait, giving her an admiring once over. Luna smiled at him, sure her eyes reflected how much she had missed him. Nico came close to her and spoke softly. "She's beautiful, isn't she?"

Luna squeezed his arm, leaning in to his ear. "Yes, beautiful, and she has an impressive job, doesn't she?"

Nico shrugged, saying dismissively, "I don't know…but her clients are billionaires, and we've been talking about getting the sheikh to invest in my center."

She looked at him inquiringly. "What do you mean? What sheikh?"

Nico tilted his head, confounded. "My client I trained in the crown chakra meditation…the one who paid me half a million dollars. Élodie will pitch him first. He's on the board of a museum she works for. These are the richest people in the world! They spend millions on art, so they should invest in my center."

Luna gasped. "Nico, I didn't know anything about this. What are you talking about? We haven't spoken in months—how would I know anything?"

Nico shook his head. "I forgot, Luna. I think you know everything I do. Don't you?" he said sarcastically.

Luna was incredulous, and walking Nico away from Élodie, whispered, "Nico, I'm very happy for you. I mean, Élodie is beautiful and cultured. And you got paid all that money?!"

Nico looked at her smugly. "See, you left me, and I still did all this without you."

Luna sighed. She'd hoped that he wouldn't dredge up the past. "You deaded me, Nico. I wasn't available on one day, and you discarded me like a dirty tissue!" But as soon as she said it, she was sorry. "I'm sorry, Nico. Really, I am. Just forget it, please."

"No, Luna, you left me hanging when I needed you most! I lost important business because you needed to have lunch with your friend and dinner with your husband." When she looked into his eyes, they were cold. "I warned you the next time you did that to me would be the last time."

Luna sighed. There was no point in belaboring the point. After months of waiting, she was here with him now. "I missed you, Nico." She didn't need to say more. He would never see her perspective or admit that his punishment was excessive.

Looking thoughtfully at her, Nico's eyes softened. "I'll give you another chance, Luna. You keep fucking up, but I'll let you back in if you promise to listen and do what I tell you. I have a lot going on now, and I need you. The sheikh liked me. I helped him with something I'm not permitted to discuss. You know, that meditation can be very dangerous, and used for ill purposes." Nico took a breath. He was wound up tightly and had been talking fast. She could see how excited he was, full of promise, but it made her apprehensive. He became solemn and his face took on an intensity. Hearing a hint of desperation in his voice, as if it was her responsibility, he implored, "We need to get this investment." Nico held his eyes on hers as he spoke hypnotically. "For all of us," he added, including her in his dreams—making her a part of him again.

Luna nodded, unable to voice her thoughts. Though she believed in him, she felt it was a long shot.

"I'll call you later. I need you to get a proposal together for Élodie to bring with her when she leaves. She needs something to hand to him. I don't want her to improvise."

Luna reached for his hand, but he pulled away, "Not now, Luna," he admonished her, glancing over at Élodie, who was waiting for him by the door. "Let's make this happen, Luna. Don't fuck this up, OK?"

Luna felt a pit in her stomach. She'd missed him and now he needed her. "I want to, Nico, but I'm so scared of you abandoning me again. I know you want to drop the subject. I would dedicate myself to you forever; actually, I already have. But I need to know that no matter what, you won't leave me again."

"You're crazy, Luna. I never left you. You are the one who left me. Many times."

Tears welled up in her eyes and she looked away, not wanting him to see. "Of course I'll help you, Nico…you know that."

"Be there for me, Luna, and everything will turn out for us. I promise."

Leaving the bank, Nico and Élodie walked to a Moroccan Blue Bentley convertible, and Élodie got into the passenger seat. Luna wasn't surprised. It appeared Nico hadn't exaggerated at all. He did find the woman of his dreams.

Maya cut the engine of her black Jeep Wrangler. The rain had stopped, but before heading into the studio, she rested her chin on the steering wheel. Watching the steam rise off the shimmering asphalt, she thought about how devastated she'd been when Nico told her about Élodie. Indelibly etched in her memory, she visualized the moment Nico had fiercely pulled her to him and held her close in an almost desperate embrace. Nuzzling his face into her neck, he had called her his jaguar princess, whispering her name as if he were reciting a mantra. The recollection was so vivid, she unconsciously reached up and rubbed her neck where his bristly jaw had burrowed, causing a pleasurable tenderness. In a low and throaty voice, he had explained he wasn't ready for a relationship, but he didn't want to lose her from his life. He implored her to trust him—that he was making things happen and to be patient. Enfolded in his arms, she had been almost certain she felt his hot tears on her skin.

The familiar stomachache that accompanied feelings of betrayal came on strong. She'd been suppressing her wildly erratic feelings, afraid of pressuring him—afraid of losing him. Feeling nauseated, she took several slow, deep breaths, clutching her stomach, which was now doing somersaults.

Maya had anticipated the text from Nico informing her Élodie had left for Paris that morning and to come directly to the studio after work. At first, when Nico would tell her to stay away, she felt demeaned and inferior, but she concealed her feelings. Instead she would spitefully leave a little trace of herself at the apartment, even if it was only a used tampon in the bathroom trashcan. It wasn't much, but it was her meager expression of retaliation. But now Maya felt Élodie was just a younger and prettier version of Alexa, and had nicknamed her the ATM machine. Like Alexa, Élodie spent lavishly on gifts for Nico, picking up the tab for everything with what appeared to be an unlimited expense account.

Maya paused for only a moment before she continued walking into the studio. Nico was yelling at someone, and she quickly assessed he was on the phone, then heard him say Alexa's name. Maya had been wondering how long it would take for Alexa to blow up about Élodie. Seeing Maya, Nico put his index finger to his lips, warning her to be quiet. She could clearly hear Alexa's booming voice screaming at him through the phone to fuck off, threatening to no longer help him secure an investor for the center in Tulum. But Nico, unruffled, easily turned the tables on her. Venomously yelling how she damaged his business with her jealous and possessive behavior, he demanded she close the deal or she would be sorry.

Maya took a deep breath and walked into the kitchen to start dinner, while Nico paced back and forth like a caged lion. Still harping, he switched his tactic and began sweet-talking her, saying Élodie was an important client and bringing in a huge investment from the Middle East, and that if Alexa wanted to be a part of him, she needed to make things happen.

When he hung up, Maya mumbled, "Nico, is it wise to yell at her, since she's the one who got you the gig in Abu Dhabi?"

Nico erupted, "Shut the fuck up, Maya. You're an idiot. Mind your business, I know what I'm doing!"

Maya put her head down and quietly finished cooking him dinner. Later, they watched a movie on the big flat screen Alexa had bought him for Christmas.

After dinner, Nico went into the bedroom and called Élodie while Maya cleaned up the dishes. When she finished, she sat quietly at the kitchen counter, eavesdropping. She had no trouble overhearing Nico's side of the conversation. Weeks had gone by since Élodie had promised to pitch Nico's deal, but apparently she hadn't done it yet. Maya had read the new inflated business plan, which was now for a global chain of exclusive spa hotels and healing centers in Abu Dhabi, London, Paris, and the French Riviera.

"It's not that difficult. I gave you the proposal. Besides he knows me, and it shouldn't be a hard sell. I'm a world renowned shaman and yoga guru."

Élodie must have balked, because Nico responded sharply, "Listen to me. If I go to him myself, it will look like I'm begging. It will diminish the value of the investment. We're doing him a favor. Offering him a great opportunity to be part of this business. Don't you see the difference?" He paused.

She must have contradicted him. "No, Élodie. If you recommend this investment, it carries more weight. He looks to you for investment advice. You tell him you're letting him in on the ground floor… that it's a special deal."

Nico paused, then she saw him pacing back and forth again before he continued in a softer sexy tone, "Baby…of course. You know how much I love you. This is an opportunity that we can't let slip through our fingers. He has the money and he trusts you! Baby, I want us to be together, and I can't keep working the way I am. It's important I get this deal. If you love me and believe in me, then you need to do this."

He paced back and forth, tugging at his hair, obviously listening intently to what she was saying. Then he continued assuringly, "Of course…I'll come there and meet him after you've made the pitch and he says he's interested. Otherwise, it's no good, it's like I'm crawling…and the deal is worthless to him. He has to be jumping at this opportunity. Don't you understand that?"

More hair pulling. More pacing. "You promise? OK." His voice got low and husky, "I love you, too…but don't fuck this up. Yes…of course. I love you. Bye."

Storming out of the room, he barked, "She'd better do as I say, or I will destroy her." His tone, angry and desperate, made Maya cringe. Raking his hair with both hands, his eyes defeated, he stormed, "She's lying…I can tell. She has no intention of getting me that money!"

Maya poured him a cup of chamomile tea to soothe his abraded nerves and reassured him that if Deepak Chopra and Dr. Oz could be big celebrities, Nico Romero surely could, too.

27

With her head resting on Nico's shoulder, Élodie sounded convincing. "I promised Nico I will return in a few days. I am going to do what he asks of me and speak to my client about investment."

Listening intently, Luna sat across the booth from them at Stout Burger and nodded her approval. Élodie hadn't touched her burger, and Nico was eating the remaining french fries off her plate.

Nico rolled his eyes so that only Luna could see. He had been asking Élodie to do this for months, and she always made an excuse. Nico didn't believe Élodie had even tried to present the sheikh with the investment, claiming she only cared about her own business, not his.

Nico warned, "Élodie, if you don't ask him this time, don't bother to come back to me. I won't see you."

Élodie snuggled deeper into his chest and tipped her head up to kiss him on the jaw line. "I love you, and I am going to get this dream for you—for us to be together, always." Then, looking at her gold Rolex, she said she'd miss her plane unless she left for the airport right away. Nico got up so she could slide out of the booth, and Luna stood to embrace Élodie who, even without her Christian Louboutin high-heeled pumps, stood a couple of inches taller than Luna. Dressed eclectically in Saint Laurent black skinny pants, a white T-shirt with a graphic of the Eiffel Tower, and black fox vest, Élodie was strikingly chic in her effortless understated style.

Luna wasn't sure she believed Élodie would try to get the investment for Nico, either. Though she could tell Élodie was infatuated with him, she sensed her reluctance to insinuate her lover's business aspirations with her role as an investment advisor.

Luna hung back while Nico kissed Élodie good-bye. Her driver, a tall imposing sandy-haired man who looked like a Viking body-guard, helped with her bag and then opened the rear door of the black Escalade. Luna wondered why he glanced over at her more than once, first removing his black baseball cap, then putting it back on as if he were trying to tell her something. When the car edged into the traffic, Nico looked back over his shoulder to make sure Luna was still there.

Taking her arm, they walked toward his studio on Ventura while Nico vented. "Just watch, Luna. Mark my words. She's doing it again, toying with me. She won't ask for the money, and she won't be back in a few days, either. She promised she would stay…and move in with me. I need her with me, but she just comes and goes as she pleases."

Luna tried comforting words. "Nico, you aren't being fair. She has a business…and she's here as much as she can be. As for the invest-ment, maybe she just needs to find the right moment."

Luna knew her words were hollow, and was thankful when Nico abruptly changed the topic. "Luna, come to the house with me to-morrow morning. We can spend a long weekend. It's already June, and I need to work on the vegetable garden and fix things around the house. We can spend time together, and we'll cook on the fire pit."

His invitation was compelling. "Sure, I'd love to go," she said without much hesitation.

∘   ∘   ∘

When Nico had bought the five-acre cabin in April, Luna men-tioned she had a lot of stuff in storage from when they had a house in Lake Tahoe. After checking with Tyler, she told Nico he could take whatever he needed. There were extra sets of dishes, pots and pans, and odd pieces of furniture. Luna had kept most of the sentimen-tal things, but there wasn't room in the condo for everything. Nico rented a truck, and Élodie and Luna unloaded furniture and cartons of thrift shop treasures that Luna hadn't seen in years.

Élodie couldn't believe all the things Luna had given him, and with each item she unpacked, she'd ask, "You are not keeping this?"

Luna shook her head. "No. We don't have room for all this stuff, and Nico has nothing. This will give him a home with personal things."

Élodie had smiled wistfully. "You give him so much—so much love."

Many of the picture frames still held photos of Luna that Élodie had begun removing when Nico interceded, "No. I like them." Then pausing, he looked over at Luna. "Is it OK? Can I keep them?"

When she had nodded her consent, he began arranging them on a bookshelf.

Luna was packing a few things in her overnight bag when Tyler walked into the bedroom. Looking up, she said pointedly, "Nico asked me to invite you to come, too. He's really trying, and he wants you to like him…" Then she added nostalgically, "Ty, it reminds me of our old cabin. When I see all our things, I feel like I'm there again. It will be fun, and it's relaxing to get out in the country."

"I'll come another time," Tyler answered dishearteningly. Since Nico had gotten the house, Luna had unwittingly become his frequent companion when Élodie wasn't in town.

"He hates to be alone, Ty. When she's not there, he's anxious and doesn't even want Maya around."

"You can go if you want to, Luna. But set boundaries. I don't want all that nonsense to start again. You can be a friend, but not an object he uses. And remember, I'm your husband, not Nico. As long as he treats you with respect, I'm OK."

o   o   o

Luna refused to make the two hour trip on Nico's Ducati. He'd had the house for a few months, but still couldn't decide between a pickup, an SUV, or a sports car for driving there. He missed Sofia's Porsche, and now seemed to bask in the luxury of Élodie's Bentley.

They piled into her green Land Rover and stopped first to get gas. It bugged her that he never offered to pay, but she didn't say anything. As they approached Dick's Sporting Goods in Pasadena, Nico squealed like a little kid for her to pull in. He had the catalog that had come in the mail, and they were having a sale. Walking into Dick's, Luna asked what he needed, but Nico didn't answer, instead heading straight to the gun counter.

Luna had never held a gun, and was reluctant at first, voicing her objection, "Nico, why do you need a gun? You don't need a gun! They're dangerous."

Surprising Luna with his knowledge, he asked to see several rifles by name and bullet caliber. As he deftly sited one rifle, checking the chamber, he scoffed at her. "Luna, everyone needs a gun out in the country. There are Mojave rattlesnakes out there. They're deadly! Plus, the deer are eating my garden."

After three hours of discussion about rifles, Luna's head was spinning. She soon became fascinated enough to ask to see a break-action shotgun. "Can I look at that Annie Oakley gun? I think it would be fun to learn skeet shooting!" The salesman passed her the shotgun as she said, "I love those English movies where they go on picnics and shoot clay pigeons." Playfully, she mimed, "Pull!" and pretended to shoot the pigeon.

Even though he was slightly embarrassed by her antics, Nico couldn't help laughing. "Enough, Annie Oakley!"

Just as she was about to faint from hunger, Nico finally settled on a Tikka T3, made in Finland. Luna conceded that in stainless steel, it was very pretty. She was relieved he had finally come to a decision, until she realized he was embarking on another hour-long conversation about bullets—learning that a 130 grain by Hornady was both economical and effective against an innocent deer.

Starving, they stopped at McDonalds before getting on the Corona Freeway to Temecula. Luna mused that no one she knew would believe she had spent more than four hours gun shopping.

Settling into the cabin, Luna unpacked the groceries and started browning sausages and cutting onions and garlic. Nico was busy with his new rifle, and now, eager to try it out, turned off the stove and literally pulled her out the door. As he darted up the hill, she raced after him. He set a few large, plastic milk jugs into the crooks of trees, then counting paces, lay down on the ground about 200 yards away and summarily picked them off, one by one, impressing Luna with his marksmanship. Walking back to the house, she asked him when and where he learned to do that. He just smiled without answering.

Luna pulled placemats and napkins from the painted sideboard, and set the oak dining table with the familiar old set of blue and white china. If she squinted her eyes, she might have thought she was back in her lake house.

Just as Luna was testing the rigatoni, Nico walked in carrying an arm full of wood for the fireplace. Gently warning her not to over-cook the pasta, he popped one in his mouth, then quickly drained the whole pot into the colander before dumping the pasta into the deep cast iron dutch oven that held the sausages and wilted kale. After pouring wine into two crystal wine glasses, he carried the heavy pot over to the table and lit the taper candles in pewter candlesticks. In the dim light, the rest of the house fell into shadow, and Luna's vision contained only Nico, sitting across from her.

With Nico, Luna always felt transported to a different place and time, especially now, amid all her former possessions. After dinner, Nico lit a fire and they settled in two adjacent arm chairs. Luna had a novel she'd brought with her, and Nico pulled out a book on rustic cabins that Luna had stored along with books on gardening. They propped their four sock-covered feet on a painted milk stool in front of the fireplace, and their wine glasses sat on the tripod table between them.

The only light was the glow from the fireplace, and she glanced over at him, seeing his hair falling over his face as he turned the pages. Comfortable with the silence, Luna thought how peaceful Nico was in this house. She never saw him sit so quietly with a book. As if he read her thoughts, he said, "I like this, Luna. Just sitting and reading with you." He affectionately stroked her foot with his in an intimate gesture.

o o o

Luna was glad Nico woke up early, because she could never figure out the coffeemaker. If she attempted it, as she did once before, Nico scolded her. But he'd quickly apologized, repeating the instructions yet again. Nico emerged from his bedroom on the opposite side of the house from the guest room, wearing sweatpants and a torn T-shirt, making a beeline for the coffee machine. "You didn't make coffee, did you?"

Luna chuckled. "No way. Do you want eggs?"

She cracked six eggs into a mixing bowl and melted some butter in the pan. It was a glorious morning out there, away from the smog of L.A., and she carried two plates of eggs and toast outside into the sunshine along with her mug of coffee. While they ate breakfast, Nico made a verbal list of all the gardening tasks that needed to be done. When they finished their eggs, he and Luna, each with a refill of coffee, walked to the fenced-in vegetable garden to check on the progress of the plants. Nico began weeding, telling Luna to pull the weeds, not the plants.

They were mending fences when his cell phone rang. It was Élodie calling from Paris. "Why are you in Paris?" he snapped. Luna didn't hear her reply.

When Nico instructed Luna, "Hold this together while I attach them," she heard Élodie ask with whom he was speaking.

Nico baited her. "What difference does it make?"

Luna felt badly he was being cruel to her and called out, "It's Luna…"

She heard Élodie say hello before Nico abruptly got up and walked away to speak privately.

When he hung up, he wasn't angry at Luna, just frustrated with Élodie. "I miss her, Luna. I really love this woman…I've made love to her all over the house and on the grass, looking up at the stars."

Luna commented, "She's so beautiful, Nico, It's no wonder you love her."

"You don't understand. I love the way her skin smells. I love the taste of her pussy. We're made for each other. We built a bonfire way up there," he pointed beyond the hillside, "and we made love. She loves fire…she is so weird. But I need her to come through with her promises."

"Always with the promises, Nico. Why?"

"Because it is the proof I need that she loves me."

o　　o　　o

Nearing dusk, Nico carried out two bottles of Anchor Steam beer, untwisting the caps and handing her one. Luna tipped her head back and took a long pull. It felt rewarding after mending fences and gardening all day. She sat on the stone wall outside the kitchen door as Nico gazed beyond her at the hillside. Suddenly, he bolted inside, emerging moments later with his new rifle. Before Luna could remark, he pointed the gun past her and fired. Barking an order, he called out, "Come quickly," as he leaped up over the low stone wall and ran full speed, rifle in hand, up the hillside with Luna on his heels.

The young buck lay quietly breathing when Nico pointed the rifle at his head and fired at close range. Dazed, Luna didn't flinch. The deed done, Nico knelt down and looked at the animal. "What are we going to do, Luna? We can't just leave him here!"

Calmly, Luna collected her thoughts. "We will first give a blessing and thank the deer for giving us his life. Then we will butcher the animal and try to not waste any."

Luna placed her left hand on the warm chest of the deer. Leaning over, she said softly, "I see you, my animal brother, and we thank you. The water comes from the rain, the fire comes from the sun, and the meat comes from our animal brothers—who give their lives so that we may live. Let your spirit go to your ancestors and your body stay behind to feed the people."

Nico gazed into her eyes. "That was very beautiful, Luna. Now we must try to save as much meat as we can, and not waste this beautiful creature." He ran fast to the house, and came back with a box cutter and a few large kitchen knives.

Luna warned, "Be careful not to cut deep." She splayed the deer's hind legs, placing one under her knee, holding the other leg up.

Nico leaned in next to her, carefully cutting a straight line down from the bottom of the rib cage to the opening of the anus, careful to not penetrate any organs. While Luna held open the body cavity, Nico gingerly lifted the stomach out, scooping up the intestines without spilling their contents. Nico looked at Luna, letting out a sigh. "Have you ever done this before?"

"No, have you?" Luna answered, uncertain how they knew exactly what to do.

"Of course not." His voice trembled. "I'm a bit freaked out…are you?"

"No. For some reason, I feel completely natural doing this… It's like déjà vu, as if we've done this before. Do you know what I mean?"

"I think so," he answered, somewhat reassured.

Luna touched his arm so he would look at her. "We are doing something very sacred…"

Nico nodded and began cutting into the hip joint to remove the hind quarter. As he cut, a large amount of blood spilled into the ground. "Oh my God," he said, "All this blood!"

"It's OK, Nico. Just keep going. You hit the artery. The blood is going back to Mother Earth, see?"

They meticulously quartered the deer, using only kitchen knives and a box cutter. When they were done placing the large pieces in plastic bags, they were left with the carcass and the deer's head. Nico insisted they quickly bury it. Concerned, Luna reminded him, "Nico, we have a lot of butchering to do. I say we bury him in the morning."

Although he was unhappy waiting, he had to agree that saving the meat was most important, or the deer's death would be in vain.

Luna was grateful for the double sink. Piling all the meat to the left, she held the hind quarter steady as Nico cut steaks and cubed chunks. Luna rinsed them, dried them, and placed portions into freezer bags.

When Nico hit bone, one of the knives chipped, and he cursed. Luna assured him they were doing the best they could. Her arms and hands ached from the weight of the deer. Sweating, Nico removed his shirt. Using all her strength, Luna held the heavy deer's body up as if it were on a meat hook while Nico, bare chested, painstakingly worked the box cutter to remove the hide, carefully ensuring no hair became entangled in the flesh. Using only a dull kitchen knife, they carved every good piece of meat from the skeleton. Blood covering her hands, Luna pushed her hair back off her face. "Nico, we did it! We're done. I'm exhausted! How about you?"

Covered in blood and sweat, Nico stepped back to survey their job well done. Satisfied, he nodded. "I'll get the fire pit going. We may as well grill up some steaks!"

Luna took a long hot shower, thinking about what they had done while washing the blood from her hair. By the time she got back into the kitchen, wearing warm sweats, she could see Nico through the kitchen window stoking the fire. The bright orange flames danced in the darkness. She headed out to the fire pit carrying thick slabs of fresh deer meat on a metal pan, then went back to get a bottle of red wine and two glasses.

Seeing her approach, Nico called out, "That steak and a bottle of red wine is what we deserve after all that work."

Too tired to even bother making a salad, they sat next to the fire, dunking juicy pieces of flavorful grilled venison into a container of Nico's homemade chimichurri sauce. The June night was warm, and while finishing the bottle of fruity Malbec, they lay on the grass, gazing up at the stars, listening to the logs make soft popping sounds as the fire died down. Seeing fireflies, Luna gasped, "Make a wish, Nico!" They counted the glowing bodies floating above them, blinking on and off against the sky.

28

Luna was glad Tyler was in his office, out of earshot, when Nico called pleading for her to come out to the house. She had promised Tyler that she would set boundaries, but no matter how hard she tried, it seemed impossible.

Nico's voice was strained. "Luna…I have chest pains. I'm having a heart attack."

Luna didn't overreact. "What happened, Nico?"

Getting Luna's attention, he then began ranting about Élodie. "Luna, she's killing me. I don't trust her. She doesn't answer me when I call her."

"I'm sure she's busy…maybe she's on a plane…"

"Don't be an idiot! That's the point, I don't know where she is… what she's doing. I'm sure she's cheating on me! And she doesn't do what I tell her. She still hasn't spoken to the sheikh about the investment. Luna, I gave her my heart, and she lies to me."

"Give her some time. I'm sure she'll do her best."

"Just come here, Luna. I need you."

The last time Luna had been at the house, Nico had coerced her into writing a firm e-mail to Élodie, castigating her for not keeping her promises to Nico. She'd balked, not wanting to do it, but he pressured her relentlessly until she gave in. Though he'd insisted she type as he dictated a brutally harsh letter, Luna conveyed his message but softened the tone considerably. She quickly hit send before Nico could proofread it, and he became furious when he saw she hadn't included several of Élodie's supposedly egregious deeds in the message.

"Why didn't you write what I told you to write, Luna? You left out important things!" He paced back and forth, raging at her. Picking up a corrugated box that lay near the door, he charged at her like a bull and hit her over the head. Luckily the box was empty.

Luna yelped. Shaken, she countered, "I wrote it exactly as you said, Nico. The poor girl—she loves you. You are too hard on her. I told her to present the plan, as she promised to do. If she had no intention of doing so, she should tell you. I wrote it my way. I was firm, but told her nicely!"

"You're a moron, Luna. You lost this for me! She will never do it now, you were too soft on her! It must be done my way! I could just kill you right now….you've ruined everything!" He had come toward her again with fists in the air, but thankfully stopped before assaulting her. Crying, Luna had packed her bag, but Nico had taken her car keys away. In a panic, she had called Tyler and told him Nico wouldn't let her leave. Tyler had been baffled. Sternly, he'd insisted she get in the car and come home. He hadn't understood why Luna couldn't leave. He seemed oblivious to the power Nico had over her.

Now, safe in her own home, she remembered how terrified she'd been. Even though Nico had apologized, she was reluctant to go. She knew Tyler would be angry and resentful if she left again, and even her friends and family had begun questioning how he could let her spend the night there, alone with Nico. But Nico sounded desperate, and she wasn't sure just how distraught he was until he said Maya was there with him. "I don't understand, Nico. If Maya is with you, why do you need me?"

"Luna, I am very upset with Élodie. She hasn't answered my Viber calls, and I don't know where she is. I can't very well explain all this to Maya. Just come here. Please."

Feeling a sense of anguished urgency, Luna explained to Tyler that Maya was at the house and Nico wasn't feeling well and had asked for her. Tyler shook his head in dismay. Though Luna knew he disapproved, she agreed anyway. "OK, Nico. I'll be there in about two hours." What she didn't say aloud was she was looking forward to meeting Maya.

When she arrived, Maya was outside sweeping the walkway and

looked up, seemingly bewildered, as if Luna were an apparition walking toward her. Hesitantly, Luna kissed her lightly on the cheek. "Maya, it's so good to finally meet you."

Maya was a bit taken aback, but Luna felt Maya's warm lips on her cheek instead of an air kiss.

"I always thought you were an ex-girlfriend of Nico's," Maya said softly, watching the broom head move back and forth against the flagstone as she swept. "He keeps your note cards with the nice sentiments in them on display. He doesn't explain much to me. He just told me to get up and get dressed, that you were on your way."

Just then, Nico walked into the yard, and Maya nervously turned away from her and resumed sweeping. Luna double-cheek kissed him and they walked toward the hillside, near where the deer had fallen weeks earlier.

"Luna, Élodie's missing. Why is she doing this to me? She is supposed to be here with me. I bought this house for her, for *us* to live in, and have a *family*. How can she lie to me like this? Promising to get the investment for *our* future? I was fixing up the barn to be a guest house for her mother and sister to come stay."

Taking his hand, Luna began to console him, and from the corner of her eye she saw Maya retreat into the house. "What do you tell Maya?"

"I don't want to hurt her. She's a good person, and a good friend. But I've always told her I don't love her the way she wants me to. She knows I'm in love with Élodie."

"Well, what is she doing here, then?"

"I told her I want to stay friends. I don't want to lose her from my life."

"Are you sleeping with her?"

"Luna, I always told you how I feel about Maya. Don't worry about her, she's a big girl."

Luna shook her head. "You're right, Nico. I'm the one who encouraged you to have a friend with benefits! Besides, as much as I like Élodie, she's always coming and going, and it drives you crazy. Maybe Maya is the better choice. She might be the last soldier standing!"

Nico shrugged. "Maybe you're right."

They both smiled, and the dark cloud lifted momentarily.

Luna took her overnight bag into the guest room and dropped it in the arm chair near the dresser. Sitting down on the edge of the bed, she picked up a familiar red teddy bear that rested on the well-worn patchwork quilt and placed it on her lap, hugging it to her. These few former possessions of hers made her feel as though his home was hers, too.

Nico decided they needed supplies from the supermarket, so the three of them piled into Luna's Land Rover and headed to Vons. Maya pushed the cart, and while Nico meticulously gathered produce, she leaned in to Luna. "I'm worried about Nico. He's been doing a lot of coke again. Before Abu Dhabi, he forced me to do it with him for months. I had lost so much weight, I looked terrible, and people at work questioned me. When he came back, I told him no more drugs—but this stress over Élodie—of course I know all about her—he's been doing it a lot. I can tell he's high right now."

Luna was stunned. Nico had made flippant remarks weeks before that he was getting high and saying he was a sex addict. Not grasping the weight of what he was telling her, Luna had thought he was just being melodramatic. Then he quickly backpedaled and said, "I'm just pulling your leg. I wanted to see if you really care about me."

Obviously, he'd been more erratic and agitated. After all, he'd almost punched her in the head over that e-mail! But drugs? The incident with the hooker immediately came to mind. Abruptly asking, "Have you done coke with him lately?" Luna knew she sounded judgmental.

Maya nodded remorsefully. "Yes. I didn't want to, but you have to do what Nico says or he gets rid of you. I thought you knew that."

Those words stung, but Luna nodded her head. "Well, we have to get him to stop. Agreed?"

Maya agreed. "I told him I'm not doing it with him anymore."

The next day after breakfast, Luna drove them all back to town. It turned out that Nico and Maya had driven there on the bike, which made Luna wonder if Nico had really wanted to see her or just wanted a ride home.

o   o   o

The upstairs private dining room was warm and filled with the harmonious song of women's voices. Luna had been invited to attend a women's mentoring group, and was appreciating the camaraderie when she felt the vibration of the cell phone in her bag. Glancing at it, she saw an unfamiliar phone number. Normally, she would let it go, but something told her to answer. The voice on the other end was crying, and Luna moved down the stairs to better hear the caller.

"Luna, I'm sorry to call you…but I can't take it anymore. I know you care about him, and you were so nice to me. Can I meet you tomorrow? Please? There are things I need to tell you…I can't on the phone." The woman started crying more heavily now that the words were out.

"Where are you, Maya?

"The Belmont. I'm at the bar with my cousin."

"Isn't that on La Cienega, by Melrose?" Without waiting for the obvious confirmation, Luna went on, "I'm just finishing a meeting at STK. I'll be there in five minutes. Don't leave."

o   o   o

While Luna sat in stunned silence, Maya explained about Nico's obsession with porn and sex toys. She kept her head down as she described him forcing her to fuck him up the ass wearing a large strap-on dildo, and how he'd yelled at her when she cried, unable to do it the way he wanted. "He was never like this! We used to make love. He was sweet…romantic, even. I have a hard time talking about, you know…intimate things. But he was normal. No, he was great." Maya finally looked up at Luna, the mascara she didn't even need ran in black streaks from her eyes, resembling a tribal tattoo that suited her exotic countenance. "He bullied me! Threatening to send video of our Skype sessions to my job. Luna, I've heard him threaten Alexa, and Élodie too! But I never thought he would threaten me!"

Putting her head into her hands as she wept, her long obsidian black hair fell over her face. Maya picked up her iPhone. Quickly scrolling, she then held the phone up for Luna. There was a photo of Nico. A selfie. Only part of his lower face showed, but Luna knew his body well enough to confirm it was Nico. Her eyes widened as they darted between the phone and Maya. Nico straddled a chair, his legs covered by fishnet stockings.

"I don't understand," Luna said in stunned disbelief.

"Neither do I," Maya answered sadly. "But I am certain it has to do with cocaine." She continued, "When Élodie left, he called me to come over. As soon as I arrived, I was sorry. Again, he began pressuring me to do the drugs. He threatened to call a hooker if I wouldn't obey him. I pleaded with him. I said, 'I can't, I have work the next day, and you promised you would stop.' Luna, it's always an all-nighter…he can't come. It's exhausting—and painful."

Luna kept her head down, listening. She sensed Maya was deeply humiliated. "So what did you do?"

"I knew he wanted me to use toys to pleasure him and I just couldn't—it's disgusting to me. That one time I tried, I just cried until he let me leave. It was awful. I said no, and he stormed into the bedroom and slammed the door. He must have thought I left. But I went into the bathroom and closed the door. I sat on the floor and cried. It was quiet, but I knew he was using one of those anal toys on himself. Then I went and slept on the sofa until he came out. It must have been hours, he was soaked in sweat. He looked at me, but it was as if he didn't know me—like a crazy, wild man. I was so scared. He said nothing. He took a shower and went back into his room. That's when I left. I just needed to know he was alive."

Luna finally looked up. Maya looked drained, as if everything in her world had vanished. Luna had no words to console her. But she realized they were both trying to reckon if he had always been this way, or if his desires had driven him down this dark path.

o　o　o

"What are the three books that affected you the most?"

Luna had just given Nico a copy of Jack London's *Call of the Wild*. They had watched the 1993 version starring Ricky Schroder at his house, curled up on the sofa with a bottle of wine, and they both cried at the end. A classic tale of love and redemption, Luna had written inside on the fly leaf, "It was never about the gold—it was always about the journey." It struck her how similar she was to Buck—compelled to the mysteriously thrilling and luring wild, but equally bound to the comfort of immutable love.

They were sitting outside drinking beer and eating guacamole and chips, on the antique wicker chairs that had once lived on her sun porch. Things were peaceful. At least for now.

Luna was momentarily stumped, "Do you mean as a child?" Before Nico could answer, she chimed with enthusiasm, "*Island of the Blue Dolphins*! That book transported me in so many ways!"

"Why?" he asked softly, "What was it about?" She could hear genuine curiosity in his voice.

"Well, first it's the story of a twelve-year-old Native American girl, in the early eighteen-hundreds. She is accidentally stranded with her little brother on an island off the coast of California when the entire tribe leaves. It's about loss and survival. It's beautiful."

"Ah…so a lot like *Call of the Wild*."

Luna smiled at him. He was naturally intelligent and intuitive, making him excellent at his chosen profession. "You are a lot like her, aren't you, Luna bella?"

"Who?" She'd been thinking about that night, how their feet were touching on the sofa.

"The girl in the dolphin story. Never mind. What are some other books that made you who you are?"

In high school, I read *Siddhartha*. I had always questioned traditional religions…and that book, about finding spiritual meaning in our existence…well, that was huge for me…"

"Me too! I like spiritual stories. Like the poem you sent me. The one about the ocean. It reminds me of Malibu…"

She just wanted to kiss him right then and there, but that wasn't possible. She missed walking along the beach with him, their feet caressed by the surf, with the smell of the salt water clinging to their skin and hair. The memory of Nico holding her hand, the wind blowing her hair and him suddenly gazing at her, mystified. How the sunlight reflected in his eyes when he said she looked wild and beautiful there on the beach. It was where they talked, confessing to each other their fears—and their dreams—unsure which would come to pass.

That was before she knew the truth about him. About the drugs. And his brutality. Still, they were as eternal as the waves, enduring beyond her lifetime. A constant reminder of time's continuum.

The poem she'd given him was one she memorized in college, by the Indian poet Tagore.

> *Ceaseless life floats on the stream of ceaseless death.*
> *To reach what nameless, purposeless shore.*
> *Does this tiny raft cross the perilous sea?*
> *What unseen helmsman in my heart is issuing commands*
> *without end?*
> *I know that millions are moving on—*
> *Something remains, when all is ended.*

"I can't believe you memorized that!" His eyes beamed admiringly and he laughed. It was a natural, hearty laugh that came out when he wasn't trying, but was actually fully entertained. "Ah, Luna. I know you've read a great many books, but what books changed you?" Luna got the feeling he was searching for something.

"*Lord of the Rings,*" the title burst from her lips. "It's a timeless story that makes you think deeply about human nature…free will… and immortality."

"Yeah! I never read the books, but I love the movies."

Luna loved that Nico was drawn to the spiritual teachings of yoga with its Hindu origins and the knowledge of the Q'ero paqos that consequently had become integrated into his life. Long ago, she had written him about Taoism, saying Yoda was really a Zen Master, and quoting from *The Phantom Menace* about fear being the path to the dark side. It was shocking and disheartening to discover that Nico was manipulative and abusive, an emotional vampire who suffered from an uncontrollable craving and pervasive emptiness that could never be filled. His inner turmoil and persistent anxiety were palpable.

Her own unrest was the result of the ephemeral nature of youth and beauty, over which *she* had no control. Luna supposed that everyone, other than the most spiritually developed souls, was gripped by desire, hence the Buddhist principle that if you aren't free from attachment, you are suffering.

"Nico, you always seem to dig deeper and make me think about things. I love you for that, honey. Your turn. What books influenced you?"

"I asked you the question, Luna, for a reason…I want to try to understand you better. You're a great mystery to me."

Luna didn't press further. They sat silently. Neither one commented on the pink halo that hung over the hills, yet they both remained fixated on it. For some reason, with Nico she didn't feel the need to speak to fill a void.

o   o   o

The greeting in Facebook Messenger was seemingly innocuous:

> *How are you, my dear?*

She'd accepted her friend request, and was now pleasantly surprised to see a private message from Élodie. Luna typed back:

> *Fine, thank you. How are you?*

Seeing the location feature was turned off, she added:

> *Are you here in L.A.?*

> *London on business. Please, do not tell Nico I text you, OK?*

Luna felt an instant twinge of guilt—and fear—carrying on this clandestine correspondence. Especially after having written such a harsh e-mail on Nico's behalf.

> *Um, yes. He would be angry. Please delete our conversation when through.*

Élodie cautiously began to open up, referring cryptically to Nico's "problem."

> *Everything was so good in Abu Dhabi. He was sweet and loving; it was beautiful. When I came to L.A. the next time, he asked me to bring something from a pharmacy here. A hormone, for anti-aging. I know this is in demand and very expensive there. I brought with me 4,000 euros' worth. He didn't give me back my money. He tells me to wait for him to sell it.*

Luna was flabbergasted.

> *Wow…I had no idea he was doing that. It's illegal here.*

> *I know you are his best friend. Maybe you cannot speak with me. When I was there, he gave me a love potion. I know, because I felt it. We made love, like magic. I never felt like that before, with anyone. But days later, he was angry. I am confused. He wants me to live there. He insists I bring money for a big center. But I just met him. I need time. He became rough. I left and went to—how do you say this—cloister.*

Luna was more stunned by her candor than by her words:

> *A church? A monastery?*

> *Yes, I needed to think. I fell very fast in love with Nico. I never loved so much before. But then he showed a different face. I have been crying nonstop. Do you understand?*

> *I understand you very well. Nico gets very anxious.*

Élodie signed off. Luna sat stunned, still looking at the screen and the typed words in front of her. A wave of panic washed over her as she became terrified Nico would see it.

o   o   o

Luna waited with Nico at Amaru for Élodie's plane to land at LAX. They had met up in Cannes, but he had come back to L.A. without her since she had business in Paris and London. He'd been frantic all week, fearing she wouldn't show up. But now he was sitting on the sofa entertaining Luna with a joyful tune on his new guitar. To make up for being away so often on business, Élodie had bought two round-trip tickets to Maui, and Nico was looking forward to surfing there again. Playfully, Nico asked Luna if she wanted to smoke some pot, but she gave him a critical eye. "Nico, you told me you want to clean up your act, why do you tease like this?"

"Luna, pot relaxes me. I have this under control. Élodie is coming, and I'll use this trip to Maui like a spa and cleanse my body and soul."

"Well, you better cleanse your mind, too!" she teased.

Luna heard the click, click, click of a rolling suitcase and Élodie's musical voice ringing out, announcing her arrival.

"Baby, in here," Nico called out. "Why didn't you text me?"

"I did. Look at your phone!"

Nico stood up but didn't immediately embrace her, so Élodie approached him and put her arms around his neck, kissing him, then nuzzling. But Nico remained aloof. Luna speculated about the game he was playing with her.

"What, baby? I'm here now—are you happy?"

"Overjoyed," he mustered sarcastically.

Luna found his behavior deviant, or at the very least curious. "What's up, Nico? Give the girl a kiss!"

He obliged Luna and kissed Élodie.

Satisfied, Luna announced, "Well, I'm heading home and leaving you two love birds. Besides, I'm tired and might be coming down with a cold."

"Wait, Luna. I will make you a special tea. It will keep you from getting sick."

Élodie piped up, "Ah! Like the potion you made for me? Let's see…what does he put in the tea?"

Luna inhaled sharply, afraid Nico might realize she'd communicated with Élodie, but he didn't. He just went to the kitchen cabinet and began filling mugs with herbs while the kettle heated up. Within minutes, he was handing each of them a steaming brew.

Speaking to Luna, Élodie announced nonchalantly, "Nico made me a love potion, and now I cannot resist him."

Embarrassed by the turn of the conversation, Luna laughed lightly. "I will drink mine and head home to bed—and my husband." She emphasized the latter. "Nico, give me a hug. I'm not going to see you again before you go. And you'd better behave yourself," she scolded.

Taking Luna in a much too passionate embrace, he pressed his body against hers, obviously to annoy Élodie. Laughing, Luna gently pushed him an arms-length away, shaking her head. "You are trouble, Nico." Looking at Élodie she allayed, "He's only goofing around." Wishing them a great trip, she left as quickly as she could.

o   o   o

When Luna saw that it was Nico calling her from Maui, she picked up right away. "Luna, did you see my watch?" he asked brusquely.

"What watch?" she asked matter-of-factly.

Angrily, he assailed, "My Breitling. What do you think I mean?"

"Nico, I don't know what you are asking. I've seen you wear that watch. But I don't recall the last time. I don't think you were wearing it the night Élodie arrived. Did you bring it with you?"

"I thought I had, but it's not here."

"Then maybe you left it in the apartment, or maybe at the house."

"No, I'm sure it is not at the house. I remember. It was in the apartment. You were there. Did you take it?"

"Did I what?! No! Why would I take your watch?"

"You were the last person with me. The last person to see it."

Furious at the accusation, Luna snapped, "Élodie was with you. Did you ask her if she saw it?"

"Do you think Élodie would steal my watch?"

She was getting flustered. He was baiting her, and she was unintentionally becoming defensive. "I didn't accuse anyone of stealing, I'm sure you just misplaced it."

"Luna, I'm warning you. Tell me right now if you took the watch." His voice was tight and threatening.

"Nico, I did not take your watch. That's a ridiculous accusation. I'm hanging up." The conversation was bizarre, and even though she was safe in her home, she was frightened.

She was about to hang up when she heard Élodie's voice sobbing in the background. "Nico, what's going on there?" Luna demanded.

"It's none of your business. We're working." Then she heard the phone disconnect.

Luna was shaken. He was definitely terrorizing Élodie. A few minutes later, another call came in, this time from Élodie. She was screaming and begging for help. "He took my phone! He saw the messages!"

Luna was paralyzed. All her efforts to regain his trust were lost.

Nico snatched the phone from Élodie and railed at her, "You did it again, Luna. Inserting yourself in my life. Causing me trouble!"

"Nico, she messaged me! I didn't start it! She told me you made her bring human growth hormone into this country illegally! Are you crazy? She could be arrested, and you could, too!"

"Fuck you, Luna!" The phone went dead.

Days later, Nico texted:

I'm on the plane. She left me.

At least he was speaking to her. She texted back:

I'll be here.

Élodie's message came soon after:

> *I am in hospital in Paris. He kicked me in my head. I have a concussion. All my friends see the bruises on my face and say never return to him.*
>
> *I'm sorry Élodie. Truly I am.*

29

Setting aside her fear of the motorcycle, Luna embraced Nico, wrapping her arms tightly around his waist as if to prevent him from unraveling. When he pulled to a stop, she dismounted too quickly, and Nico caught the bike as it became unstable. Instantly, his eyes blazed and she noticed the momentary glare of admonition, but uncharacteristically, he didn't scold her. Killing the engine, he inhaled deeply and his body uncoiled upon hearing the sound of the waves. Luna took off her helmet, releasing her hair into the cool mist blowing off the ocean. Closing her eyes, she could taste the salt on her tongue. All her previous attempts to get through to him had been abruptly curtailed. Ranting, he had called her an idiot and crazy, or he'd just hung up on her. Alone with him now, she hoped he would confide in her.

Holding hands, they walked silently along the deserted beach until Nico began to speak. His words spilled out like a confession, the way they did when he was in church with her. "I did a lot of shit, Luna, and I've distorted myself…I don't even recognize who I am anymore. I'm more depressed than ever."

"Please, Nico. You are a medicine man. A shaman. Great healers are often wounded. This is who you are, but you don't have to destroy yourself."

"Luna, I let everyone down. I fucked up. But I'll get myself back together…and I *will* earn their respect back."

Luna kissed the back of his hand, knowing the intimacy of an embrace would make him uncomfortable. "I'm here for you, Nico—whatever you need."

When he turned to face her, there were tears in his eyes. "Luna, she's a liar and she played me…she broke my heart."

Luna understood he meant Élodie, and she could feel the weight of his sadness. There weren't any words to say that would make it better. This time, she held him close, her cold nose against the warm skin of his neck.

o   o   o

Nico had recently hooked up with a young model named Sloane, who he said was an aspiring actress. Boasting that he was going to make Sloane a big star, he invited Luna to join them to look at a space on Hollywood Boulevard that he said he wanted to convert into a sports bar.

"A sports bar? Really, Nico? What happened to the wellness center?" Luna asked incredulously.

He had enticed Sloane with promises that Alexa would get her an agent, but Luna knew it was a lie. Alexa wanted Nico for herself. There would be no way she would help some struggling actress he was fucking. When Luna met them at the office of the realtor she'd introduced to Nico, it was obvious they were high on something. Sloane was tall, with waist-length highlighted brown hair. She wasn't model thin, as Luna had expected her to be, but rather big-boned and athletic like a racehorse. She giggled incessantly, drawling Nico's name each time he stuck his hand down the back of her tight white jeans. Thoroughly embarrassed, Luna departed hastily, saying she was late for a meeting. A few hours later when Nico called, she erupted, castigating him. "I was mortified! I'm sure the realtor noticed you were both stoned…and that girl is trailer park trash! How could you, Nico?!"

Nico hung up, but called her back later, trying to sound convincing.

"You're wrong, Luna. She's a very sweet girl. You don't know anything! And you owe her an apology. She heard what you said; you were on the speaker. You're showing your age…we smoked some pot…big deal!"

"Nico, she is a bad influence on you. She does drugs with you, and I think that's why you're with her."

"You're an idiot, Luna! She's the most beautiful and pure woman I have ever met. The others are all sluts."

"I don't believe you." As much as she would have liked to believe him, her gut told her otherwise.

"She loves me. And is devoted to me. And she doesn't leave me."

"Whatever…Nico, please be the healer you're supposed to be… please…" she begged, practically in tears.

Devastated because Nico shut off his phone for days at a time and missed sessions at the studio, Maya began calling and texting Luna every day. Blaming Sloane for corrupting him and accelerating his rapid downward spiral, Maya maligned her, effusively casting her as a low-class drug addict. "Luna, I'm certain he's dealing. I never told you that Nico asked me to deliver drugs to clients for him, but I refused. I told him he was crazy! That's why he's hooked up with that girl. I wouldn't be his mule…but she obviously will. Then he had the audacity to ask me if I would do a three way with them!"

Luna welcomed her camaraderie. Maya's calls made her feel connected to Nico and fueled her with a purpose. Saving him was their shared goal, and they sent each other articles about drug addiction and personality disorders. They created the story of what they believed must have been Nico's traumatic childhood, and it didn't matter if it was true; it was close enough. Together, they surmised Sloane not only had become his drug mule, but was fulfilling his compulsion for cocaine-infused all-nighters. Maya knew Nico's password from paying the bills, and playing detective, she began tracking his cell phone calls, proudly boasting she'd found evidence—the cell phone number of his drug supplier.

When the gossip about Alexa traveled through her office, Luna called Maya right away. "I just heard Alexa was fired—and that she's in rehab! Nico had told me she was an addict, but I wasn't sure it was true until now."

"I believed him! I'd hear her on the phone with him…she was a fucking mess, that bitch!" Maya spat, unleashing her obvious hatred.

Luna chuckled. "Yeah, their relationship was toxic!" She thought about all the conversations she'd had with Nico about Alexa, begging him to sever his ties with her. But Nico wouldn't forgo the money and connections she afforded him. She loathed Alexa and blamed her for Nico's demise. Resigned, she sighed, "I suppose they destroyed each other…"

Now distraught and worried that Nico was going to get arrested, or worse, kill himself with drugs, Luna wrote veiled e-mails pleading with him to go into rehab and get rid of Sloane. Possibly in denial, but definitely paranoid because she was communicating with him over the internet, Nico accused Luna of being crazy and imagining things. Obsessed, Luna angered him further by badgering him and repeating the things he had told her, until he stopped replying altogether.

Luna couldn't reconcile Nico's drug addiction with the spiritual healer she'd met four years earlier, Confused and at a loss for what to do, she sought Tyler's counsel, divulging everything—Nico's cocaine use, Élodie smuggling in the human growth hormone, and Maya's detective work exposing Nico's drug dealing. Completely in shock, she beseeched, "Was he always like this? A drug dealer? An addict?!"

"I'm not surprised, Luna. Nico never did the real work needed to be a healer. He wasn't ready." Pulling books by Carl Jung from the shelves, Tyler explained the Greek myth of Chiron, the wounded healer, "The greatest healers are wounded themselves, but they use that suffering to heal the pain of others. Nico lacks empathy and uses people as objects for his own gain. He is broken. And you, as much as you have tried, cannot fix him." Tyler was right, but it felt dispassionate.

"He won't speak to me, but it still doesn't feel right to abandon him when he's in trouble. Maybe Maya can get him into a program…"

o   o   o

Luna texted Nico a photo of the red glass votives in the Saint Francis of Assisi Cathedral in Santa Fe. She wrote she was praying for him, and then playfully added a picture of the statue of Kateri Tekakwitha, a Mohawk woman from the seventeenth century who had been canonized as a saint. The effigy resembled Luna wearing a turquoise necklace and earrings, and she hoped Nico would find the irony funny. Lately, she'd irritated him so much that he ignored her, but this time he texted back: LOL.

A few weeks later, on a warm September day when the sky was a cloudless blue and the air crisp and clear, he called. "Meet me at the bank. I need you."

Hearing the urgency in his voice, she asked, "What's wrong? Is everything OK?"

Nico answered curtly, "Not on the phone…" Then he abruptly hung up.

Luna was relieved he had chosen a safe place to meet instead of the studio. When she pulled into the parking lot, she immediately spotted Nico outside the bank frantically pacing back and forth with his cell phone on his ear. Then she noticed Maya leaning against the side of the building with her head down in her phone. Chuckling to herself, Luna thought how good Maya was at disappearing—like she was wearing an invisibility cloak to shield her from the impending incursion. Nico looked red-faced and puffy; he obviously wasn't doing well. When he saw Luna, he waved her over. Visibly agitated, he declared, "Luna, I'm being audited. As if I don't have enough problems."

"I'm sorry, Nico. What can I do to help you?"

"Make me receipts," he instructed calmly, as if it was a reasonable request.

Luna looked back and forth between Nico and Maya, flabbergasted. "What do you mean make receipts? You mean fake invoices?"

"Yes, that's it. Some invoices that I paid to you for the business plan…and the book proposal. Make them total twenty grand. I need to show how I spent money. Otherwise, I have to pay more taxes."

"Nico, that's fraud. You go to prison for something like that," she blurted much too loudly.

"Don't be stupid, Luna." He grabbed her by the arm, pulling her toward him. "And keep your voice down!"

"Oh, I'm not stupid, Nico! And I will do a lot for you, but not commit tax fraud. That's a federal offense!" Luna got in her car, but Nico held the door, not allowing her to close it.

"That's what I'm saying, Luna. You're never really my friend. You always leave me. This time, don't ever try to contact me again."

Tyler's words ricocheted in her head, *Nico uses people as objects…* "I won't, Nico. That's an outrageous request. Those receipts would point straight back at me! You don't give a shit what could happen to me!"

Later, she received a text from Maya, as if she was apologizing for him:

> *Luna, he doesn't think. He just wants what he wants.*

> *I'm not going to do it, Maya. I can't. It's illegal. And besides, Tyler would kill me. It proves to me how selfish Nico is. He doesn't care if I go to jail. He would throw me under the bus! I'm done. I've had enough!*

o   o   o

Élodie called when she landed in L.A. "Luna, I don't know if he will see me. He's with that slut girl who does drugs with him."

It didn't surprise Luna that Élodie wouldn't give up on Nico. He'd been not only verbally abusive to her, but physically abusive as well, yet she was as inescapably tethered to him as Luna was. Élodie claimed she was worried about him, but Luna knew it was more than that. Élodie's messages became more desperate. Mostly she blamed Sloane, but she didn't trust Maya either, saying they both must be doing drugs with him as well as whatever else he demanded—and because she wouldn't participate in these things, he was punishing her. She was determined to get back the Nico she had met while sitting by the gulf waters, gazing at the full moon; the enchanting lover under whose spell she had fallen.

Nico hadn't spoken to Luna in over a month, since her refusal to help him with the audit. Still appalled, she told Élodie what Nico had enjoined, "I told him it was illegal…an outrageous request! And he told me to fuck off and leave him alone! He didn't care that I could be arrested for committing fraud. I'm horrified!" Still, concerned for him and bonding with Élodie, she asked, "Does he know you're here?"

"I went directly to Amaru, but he wouldn't let me in. He knows I will stay in the bungalow at the Beverly Hills Hotel. Do you want to come by the hotel and have a drink?"

"Sure, I'll be there in about an hour. He won't come, will he?"

"I don't think so. If he does, I don't care. Do you?"

"At this point, no. How can you come all this way and he doesn't even open the door?"

But Luna knew Nico would seek her out. Élodie was his prize. So when he walked into the hotel bar, both women followed him with their eyes. Nico would not meet Luna's gaze. She said a quick good-bye to Élodie and left.

Élodie texted Luna the next day that she was meeting with a client and then leaving for the Emirates. She wrote:

> *He stayed with me in the bungalow all night. I know he loves me by the way it felt when we made love. Sloane is a drug addict, low…in the gutter. He is with her because she does the drugs, and sells drugs for him. I will win him, and help him to get better.*

Spurred by Élodie's passion, Luna private messaged Sloane on Facebook, telling her to leave Nico alone and writing:

> *He is a healer, a medicine man—and you are destroying him.*

Enraged that Luna had contacted Sloane, Nico wrote her:

> *Stop interfering in my life! Do not contact any of my girlfriends again. You don't know Sloane, she is a good girl. She does as she is told, not like Élodie. You know that Élodie lied to me, and hurt me. Why*

Desperate for a solution, Luna looked online and found the nearest Narcotics Anonymous open meeting. Feeling nervous and out of place, she sat in the back and listened in stunned silence, hoping she was invisible to the group. Unexpectedly, she was moved to tears as each member shared heartbreaking experiences, yet each was also hopeful and surprisingly grateful. When the meeting was over, she humbly joined the circle for the Serenity Prayer. Afterward, she stayed and spoke with the leader. Clean more than twenty years, he was now an addiction specialist and explained that aberrant sexual behavior, such as addiction to porn and hookers, commonly coexist with cocaine addiction. Even married addicts regularly paid prostitutes to get them off because of the skill and duration involved. Luna shared her findings with Élodie, who promptly broke down, whimpering, "Mon Dieu, mon Dieu," afraid Nico would soon die of a heart attack from the combination of Viagra and cocaine.

Maya seemed tougher. Yet Luna wondered if it was a façade. Maybe Élodie was right, and Maya concealed her compliance. After all, she'd admitted she'd taken part in the past. But now, instead of falling apart, she told Luna she was pleading with Nico to dump Sloane and go to rehab—appealing to his reputation as a guru and telling him everyone would admire him for coming forward; that the admission would even elevate his stature.

Now caught in a whirlwind vortex between both women, Luna sought the cause of his addiction. What pain was he compelled to mask? Revisiting Sofia's speculation of bipolar, a mood disorder, Luna considered the diagnosis. The swing between his outrageous grandiosity and his morbid lows fit. His unstable relationships that split between extreme idealization and devaluation, and his frantic efforts to avoid abandonment were characteristics of borderline personality disorder. But at his darkest, his lack of empathy and remorse, the manipulative self-serving behavior that views others only as a means to an end, and the violent outbursts of rage that led to punishment and abuse were all signs of a classic sociopath with traits of narcissistic personality disorder. Regardless of the label, his pain and wrenching emptiness were palpable, as was her own obsessive need to soothe him.

o   o   o

Luna nudged gently. Nico held a grudge against her and accused her of having selfish interests. Though it was apparent he twisted this indictment for his own benefit, she was bent on proving him wrong. Just before Thanksgiving, she e-mailed him a well-known passage from Corinthians, assuring him that her love would never fail.

> *If I speak in the tongues of men or of angels, but do not have love, I am only a resounding gong or a clanging cymbal.*

Endeavoring to regain his affection, she explained that real love is unconditional and given without any stipulations—and the greatest gifts are valueless without love.

Surprisingly, he called to wish her and Tyler a happy Thanksgiving and said he and Sloane would be cooking at the house, then hung up quickly.

But the following week, a frightened Maya called Luna from Nico's house.

Her voice trembling, she whispered, "I'm with him at the house. When I got here, he was lying in a fetal position, crying. Now he's locked himself in the bathroom. There's all these empty packets…I don't know how much he's done. I'm scared, Luna. What should I do?"

Luna's anxiety soared, but she steadied herself and asked calmly, "Do you know what happened? Where's Sloane?"

"He confessed he'd done a lot of cocaine on Thanksgiving, and he mumbled something about being mean and not eating the beautiful dinner she'd prepared. He admitted that he went off on her and hit her because she wouldn't stop crying. And then he kept screaming at her when she called her mother."

"He's terrible with holidays…they always trigger stuff for him."

"He said that the next thing he knew, there were police at the door, along with Sloane's parents and brother. They drove from El Paso, packed all her things in a truck, and took her home! When they left, he called me and told me to come right away. He said he was going to kill himself. Luna I flew here—don't know how I didn't get a ticket!"

"Just keep talking to him through the door. He just needs to know you're there. He'll come out."

"He keeps ranting that he hates himself and wants to go into rehab. But then he started crying again because Sloane won't answer her phone."

"Well, he called you…that's a good sign. And, thank God, Sloane is gone. Maybe now we can get him the help he needs."

Luna felt bad for Maya, whose love remained enduring. It had turned out that she was, after all, the last soldier remaining on the blood-soaked battlefield.

Tyler never spoke about Nico. He'd had his fill of the drama, and Luna knew that it was coming to a head. When the doorman rang up to announce Élodie, Tyler gave Luna a stern look, though she was as perplexed as he was. Élodie's eyes were swollen with tears. But the fear in them was paramount. "Luna, I thought he was going to kill me. He's dément…lunatic. I'm afraid. It is only a bungalow, and he can break down the door!"

Luna rushed to console her, feeling responsible because she had relayed Nico's plea for her to come. "Élodie, it's fine, you're safe here. You can stay here and leave tomorrow. He's not himself."

"I know, it is the drugs. He takes them and is up all night. He wants to fuck all night, and no sleep. If I say I have to sleep, he yells. The security came to the door. I was so embarrassed because they know me, and it is my client's bungalow. It was awful!"

Luna gave her a cup of chamomile tea and waited until she calmed down before asking, "Why do you keep coming back, Élodie? He's a drug addict, and he abuses you!"

"I have other memories…of sweet Nico. This is another face I do not understand. I want to help him to stop these drugs and go back to the man I fell in love with. He only blows up because I say no. I will not do drugs and have crazy sex. So he becomes violent."

"He's dangerous, Élodie. I fear for you. I never knew about the drugs until recently. Maya told me, but she said he never hit her. Why is he like this with you?"

"If she does the drugs and sex all night the way he wants, then he's happy with her. I won't do this, and so he kicked me in the head, like a dog, giving me the concussion in Maui. That girl Sloane did everything he said. He told me. When I arrived he put out cocaine. I said no, I won't do this. He went crazy, screaming for me to give him what he wants. This crazy sex. I cannot do this with him." She looked away, embarrassed. "And he did so much drugs that I thought his heart would explode." She began crying and slumped over, her head in her hands. Luna put her arm around Élodie's shoulders, leaning their heads together. Élodie's hair was knotted up in a loose chignon, and the tendrils fell down the back of her swan-like neck. Luna looked over at Tyler, who she knew felt compassion for Élodie, but wished none of this had been brought upon them. He mumbled he would go make up the bed in the guest room.

Now that Nico's destructive behavior had been unveiled, Luna, cleaving to and cherishing Tyler more than ever, promised him she would take her life back.

Nico had been her drug, and she had chased the high long after he had withdrawn the euphoric potion of his flattery, making her feel young and beautiful, feeding her vanity—and compelling her to him. But now she had to let him go.

Nico made it up to the condo, somehow bypassing the multiple doormen.

"Where is she?" His eyes were vacant as he pushed passed Luna.

Tyler blocked his path, and Nico stopped, assuring Tyler, "I'm fine. I would like us all to sit down and talk. Can we do that?"

Tyler nodded, relieved there would be no trouble, but displeased by the intrusion. Nico sat next to Élodie on the sofa, taking her hand. He did all the talking, explaining that he'd been frustrated by her promises and lies. "I would never hurt her," he stated, focusing his gaze on Tyler. "I just want her to keep her promise."

Élodie interrupted, ignoring his cautionary glare. "Nico, I gave the proposal to my client, but he does not know you. He said for you to go there and meet him."

"Come, Élodie, let's go. We're fine. I would never hurt you. I'm sorry if I lost my temper. You just frustrate me sometimes." When he pulled her to him, she rested her head on his shoulder unable to look at Luna. When Nico stood to leave, Élodie got up and left with him.

Élodie had apparently remained in L.A., but Luna hadn't heard from either of them. She and Tyler were driving to Santa Monica when Nico called. "Luna, you have to come to the house right away!"

"Nico, I'm in the car with Tyler. What's wrong?"

"She's sitting on top of me, punching me!"

Luna heard Élodie in the background. She couldn't tell if she was screaming, crying, or both. "Nico, that's ridiculous! You're a big man and she's a skinny girl. I'm sure you can handle it." It was such a senseless request that Luna presumed he was high as a kite and Élodie was forcibly preventing him from taking more drugs.

"Ow, Élodie! Stop it! Luna! She's hurting me! You have to come here!"

"Nico, I can't—we're busy. And you're being absurd. I'm not driving two hours to stop a fight between the two of you!" Tyler looked at her askance.

"Fuck you, Luna! I need you. What kind of friend are you?"

She couldn't listen to him berate her; it was too embarrassing in front of Tyler. "I'm sorry, Nico…I can't…not this time…"

He started to yell, "Don't ever…"

Luna hung up.

As hard as it was, she realized they'd said their good-byes long ago.

o   o   o

During her ongoing Reiki and acupuncture sessions with Kristi, Luna often wept. She felt her heart had been torn out and stomped on. Life without Nico was akin to being deprived of a life-giving drug, but life with him had become untenable. Kristi assured her she would begin to feel the deep despair lifting. Yet each treatment session concluded with Luna in tears. It seemed to Luna that there was no cure for her obsession. If she was to be free, she would have to *want* to be free.

Élodie Skyped Luna from Paris. She was emotionally distraught, and Luna had to concentrate to hear her weak voice between sobs. "Luna, he did so much coke, many bags…he was like a wild animal. His eyes they were black—and empty—like he didn't even see. He tried to force me…and he wanted crazy sex! I don't want this. I want to make love, the way it used to be. This is not love to me. I told Nico I was leaving, and texted my driver to come right away. Nico went crazy. He punched me and kicked me in the ribs…in my head…I thought he was killing me! I was frightened. When he saw the Escalade, he went crazy. He begged me to stay and tell the driver to leave. I pretended it was OK, but Max, the driver you have seen before—he came inside. My client pays him to look after me…protect me. Right away, he could tell things were not right. Nico was cursing at me and threatening me, saying if I leave, to never come back, that he was done with me! I was frightened, running away from him, and he was screaming at me and pushed me. I slipped and fell down the stairs. I broke my back…how do you say…coccyx bone. Max punched Nico and knocked him down to keep him away from me. Then Max grabbed me, got me into the car, and drove away. Oh, Luna! What am I going to do?" Élodie began sobbing, unable to continue.

Luna spoke calmly while waiting for her to catch her breath. "Élodie, he is too violent. You are lucky to have gotten away…he could have killed you."

"Luna, I still love…I will always love…even though I am afraid now."

"You have to stay away until he gets help. He's too dangerous."

"How is he, Luna? I am worried that he will have heart attack. I listen to his heart, and it is not normal. I am afraid it will explode. Is he alone? Who is with him? He wrote to me that Sloane is coming back…is this true?"

"I haven't heard that. Maya is staying with him at the apartment instead of the house because she has to go to work every day. He closed the studio, and there are no classes. She says he looks terrible and needs to restore himself."

"I don't trust Maya…You see, he always keeps her around…for what?"

"I don't know, Élodie…really…I don't know what to think anymore…"

o　o　o

It had been a long day on the set, and Maya couldn't wait to take a shower. Nico had called her at least a dozen times asking when she would be home and reminding her to use her keys because he was locking the front door. Grateful it was Friday, she stopped at the market to stock up on groceries for the weekend. Too exhausted to drive to Temecula that evening, she'd succeeded in convincing him to leave early in the morning instead by promising to make him her mom's baked chicken with beans and rice recipe. Her arms filled with shopping bags, she walked into the studio and saw Nico sitting cross-legged in Easy Pose, nose gazing. Ethereal harp music by Laaraji was playing, and Nico didn't acknowledge her when she hastened past him, headed toward the apartment. After unloading the perishables, she preheated the oven and seasoned the chicken, filled a pot of water for the rice that she set on the stove, then headed into the bedroom to take off her sweaty clothes and get into the shower. She'd been choreographing fight scenes and teaching them all week. Every muscle was sore. She would have liked to stay in town over the weekend and get a massage, but Nico wanted to go to the house.

The hot water felt delightful and she spent a long time shampooing her long thick black hair. After rinsing out the shampoo, she combed in conditioner with Argan oil, letting it absorb while she lathered her body and shaved her legs. She thought she heard voices coming from the studio. It sounded like Nico was arguing with someone. Maybe his father, she thought. He always yelled when they spoke. While rinsing her hair, she heard two pops, consecutively. Her heart raced, and images of her childhood flashed before her eyes. She knew that sound, and her immediate response was to get low. She turned off the water and listened—but now everything was silent. She wanted to hide in the closet, but she wasn't a child any longer. She was a professional fighter, and her limbs were weapons. Still dripping wet, she ran naked toward the studio. Peering out around the corner, she saw and heard nothing. Turning the corner into the main area where the classes were held, she saw Nico. He was face down, lying in a pool of blood near the threshold of the open front door.

Maya screamed and ran to him, cursing that she'd left her phone in the bathroom. He wasn't breathing…and there was a lot of blood.

A familiar fragrance hung heavily in the air. Suddenly, it struck her. Élodie! She bolted into the parking lot. Quickly taking in 360 degrees around her, she saw a black SUV pulling out onto Ventura, then ran back inside, this time back to the apartment for her phone.

o　o　o

Kristi called Luna with an invitation. "I'm taking you to see Amma, which means mother. She's a Hindu guru called 'the hugging saint.' People go to get hugged by Amma. Her followers call it receiving darshan.

"Oh great! Another guru. Are you sure about this?" Luna laughed. It had been months since Nico had been shot, and Luna was still recovering from the emotional trauma. "What goes on at this event?" she asked dubiously.

Kristi's eyes lit up. "Luna, it's much more than an event! It's an *experience*, called darshan."

"What's darshan?" Luna asked curiously.

"It's a blessing that brings good fortune and well-being." Kristi then proudly added, "I'm one of the few people to have been married by Amma."

After researching Amma on Wikipedia, Luna discovered she was world famous, having embraced more than thirty-two million people in just thirty years. She also noted Amma was from Kerala, where Nico had once lived. Not one to believe in coincidences, Luna was now eager to see the hugging saint.

Arriving at the convention center, Luna was stunned by the thousands of people trying to get into the event. As they merged into the mob of attendees, she began to panic. Sensing her distress, Kristi took her hand and walked through the door. Showing an invitation with a red stamp on it must have meant something, because they were let in ahead of the throng on the sidewalk.

After waiting for hours, with many more people still ahead of her to see Amma, Kristi asked Luna to hold her place while she went to get something to eat. Luna agreed, but after waiting so long, she was about to abandon her spot when a young woman approached, and without explanation, took Luna's hand, saying, "Come with me."

Startled and uncertain why this girl had singled her out, Luna resisted, saying she was saving the space for her friend. But the girl kept hold of her hand and led her forward.

Silently, she escorted Luna into a cordoned-off space at the front of the assembly hall, where Amma, ageless and ample, sat cloaked in white on a large pillow, surrounded by attendants. Bewildered, Luna realized there were only a handful of people between her and Amma now. The young woman said, "Wait here, and you'll be told what to do," then left.

A young man instructed Luna to remove her shoes and leave her handbag with attendants. Uncomfortable leaving her bag, she hesitated, unsure what to do. Rows of Amma's attendants knelt facing the area before her. Aware of Luna's discomfort, a woman reassuringly murmured, "Don't worry. It'll be fine."

Dazed, Luna wondered if Kristi was looking for her. Then she considered that maybe Kristi had arranged this intervention after detecting her desire to flee. The young man reminded her again to remove her shoes, a sign of respect in many cultures. Obeying him, she apprehensively removed her Rag & Bone ankle boots, mumbling to herself, "Great, I'm going to leave my six hundred dollar boots and go home in someone else's flip-flops."

Another attendant instructed her to kneel and crawl forward. As she got closer to Amma, she felt a tingling sensation throughout her body and couldn't say if it was just her nerves. As soon as the next person fell into Amma's arms, the attendant moved her closer. Luna could hear Amma murmuring in what she assumed was Hindi, but later read was Malayalam. As she crawled on her knees closer to Amma, the auditorium full of thousands of devotees dissolved, leaving only the sound of Amma's unremitting enigmatic chanting. Shrouded by the warm, divine energy emanating from the holy woman, Luna's euphoric state reminded her of the San Pedro ceremony so long ago. Here, again, it was as though she observed herself from outside her body.

Bewildered, Luna wondered if she was supposed to say anything, or be thinking of something in particular. Listening to the sound of her own breathing blending with the soothing, monotonous tone of

Amma's indiscernible murmurs, she crept forward. The young man before her fell into Amma's arms, and Luna was suddenly overcome by the palpable emotion radiating from the scene. She took a deep breath as that man moved away and the attendant tapped her shoulder, signaling her to go. Crawling forward on her hands and knees, Luna fell into Amma's arms, resting her face like a child against Amma's voluminous bosom. Though she couldn't understand the words, she felt an overwhelming shroud of love envelope her, and sobbed uncontrollably—rocked like a baby in the Mother's arms.

o   o   o

Did she choose him, or did he choose her? Either way, Luna had been compelled, inexorably bound to Nico before she fully fathomed he was incapable of love—his soul paralyzed without empathy, and the fire in his heart extinguished. Filled with despair, Nico's pain was excruciating, and his emotions were felt with such intensity that an unintended slight became a betrayal. Instead of sadness there was grief, and a simple annoyance turned into rage—the dysphoria mollified only by possessing another to fill the echoing emptiness and burning hunger.

Nico's inability to love, born of whatever curse afflicted him, was the cruelest inhumanity. Yet his damage had been part of the attraction. Drawn to the wounded healer, Luna believed him the elixir vitae, the water of life, granting her eternal youth.

She'd given herself over to him.

"What do you want?" his eyes penetrated quizzically, like Mephistopheles to Faust.

"I'm not sure…"

"Passion. It's what everyone wants."

She lamented, "I'm getting old. Becoming invisible."

Nico awakened her soul inflaming her with a bewildering sense of longing and urgency. She could never go back and endure the mire of complacency she once felt.

Teetering in the space between light and dark…awake and asleep…death and immortality, Luna was buffeted by the continuous ebb and flow of the tide. Where the white rippling surf had once gently kissed her feet, the undertow now swept her away. Even aware of his nefariousness, the fear of losing Nico had daggered her heart, leaving her for dead.

Time. Age. Beauty.

All abstract constructs hovering surreptitiously, sliding in and out of our self-devised paradigms. Nico said convincingly, "Time is of our own creation. Past and present…days and years…exist only through perception, as do daylight and darkness. A star in tonight's sky may have extinguished long ago."

His words washing over her were cleansing, dissolving, seducing. The infinite green pools of his eyes glistened, beckoning her to follow him into the timeless vale. It was dangerous, but not in a way that frightened her. He made her feel like anything was possible. What she had perceived as limitations, were merely illusions. Reasoning that nothing adverse could possibly happen because he was a healer, she took his hand and stepped through the looking glass…the wardrobe…whatever conveyance she'd conceived, erasing the past and the future, entering into a place more brilliant where magic overcame the mundane.

Like Icarus, warned to fly neither too low nor too high, Luna flew too close to the sun. Resenting the earthly constraints that bound her, she clung futilely to the ephemeral while desire engulfed her. Having placed Nico's truth above the deepest truth within herself, she'd scorched her wings and fallen into despair.

Lost in the chimerical realm, she'd forsaken the divine, until Tyler's enduring love and abiding wisdom reverberated. *Evolve spiritually, develop wisdom, and manifest eternal beauty—these are the keys to bliss.*

What she'd once known with certainty, but had fallen into shadow, her suffering had revealed in perfect clarity. Without love there is no humanity. Amma, the aura surrounding her, the soft murmur of her chant, resounded with unconditional love. Everything had changed—but was unchanged. What she had desired was no longer necessary.

Can we ever be certain we know what we want? The higher self always speaks the truth, but is sometimes hidden, veiled by expectations. Though its clarity may be obscured as dust on a mirror—love is eternal.

READING GROUP GUIDE

The Sleeping Serpent

Intelligent, accomplished women may think themselves inviolable, and find it implausible they could fall victim to a narcissistic sociopath. If they unwittingly did, they are certain they would be able to leave, especially when emotionally or physically abused. Victims often blame themselves, but narcissists are adept at compelling their targets and manipulating them, making it difficult to sever the bond.

Our research covered the gamut from scholarly abstracts and psychology publications, to online support groups and blogs. We learned personality disorders are difficult to diagnose and treat. There are a wide spectrum of symptoms, degrees of severity, and many of these disorders can exist simultaneously. *The Sleeping Serpent* web site, www.compelledbooks.com contains links to additional reading. Please visit us there to follow us.

QUESTIONS FOR DISCUSSION

1. Luna has a loving husband and an enviable job, but she feels her life is conventional and circumscribed. She tells Nico she is getting old and becoming invisible.

How has society fostered a woman's need for physical admiration?

What drew Luna to Nico? Why did she continue to stay involved?

How is Luna's addiction to Nico similar to a drug addiction?

2. Discuss Luna and Tyler's relationship.

What is passion versus love?

How do trust, fear, and jealousy affect love?

Tyler says that only Luna can sever the bond with Nico, and she has to do it herself. Why?

Do you think Tyler should have been more insistent that Luna end her relationship with Nico?

3. *The Sleeping Serpent* explores the significance of love and our expectations.

What is unconditional love?

Why does Luna send Nico Corinthians 13?

Why is Nico incapable of love? What is empathy?

What does it mean to be free from desire?

What does Luna expect from Nico?

What does Luna learn about loving herself?

What role does Amma play in the story?

4. The notion that only weak and desperate women fall for narcissists is false. Narcissists' egos are inflated by successfully seducing attractive, accomplished, and compassionate women who are fixers. Narcissistic supply is the sustenance drawn by the narcissist. It can be admiration, money, or anything they value.

What was each woman supplying Nico?

How does Nico react when supply is withdrawn?

5. Tyler explains that blood-sucking vampirism is a metaphor for draining life-force.

How is Nico able to compel his victims and lead them down this dark path?

What is love bombing? Do you recognize Nico's tactics for seduction?

Do you believe he can actually compel his victim with hypnotism or his special tea?

Do you think that being compelled by a sociopath or narcissist could never happen to you?

How might you recognize a sociopath?

6. Kristi explains the psychic connection called cording that draws life-force.

Had you heard of cording? How is Nico able to achieve this cording?

Why didn't Kristi's cord cutting work for Luna?

What are the butterflies in Luna's solar plexus?

What was the impetus for Luna to begin her healing journey?

7. The archetype of the Wounded Healer is evident in Nico's work as a yoga master and energy healer. The idea, according to Carl Jung, is a healer is most effective when he himself is wounded—his own hurt gives him the empathy to heal.

How has Nico's emotional wound affected his ability to use his powers wisely?

Was Nico ever on the side of light?

At what point in the story were you first aware Nico has a severe personality disorder?

8. Sociopathy lies on a spectrum of behaviors, but all those with such disorders are empty shells who are unable to feel love—they have no empathy. They use manipulation and mirroring to control the perception and behavior of others toward them. Luna recognizes this without pinpointing the diagnosis, and believes she can fix Nico with unconditional love.

Why does Luna believe she can fix Nico? Does this make her a co-dependent?

How does Nico palliate his emotional pain and suffering?

When Tyler tells Luna, "It's like blaming a snake for having fangs," what do you think he means?

9. A malignant narcissist is the most extreme and dangerous narcissist, often existing simultaneously with antisocial personality disorder (sociopath). Presenting a lack of empathy and remorse, it is characterized by grandiosity, paranoia, aggression, and sadism.

Why do you think Nico's behavior became increasingly more aggressive?

Do you think that Nico always had a drug problem?

Why does Nico abuse drugs?

10. Tyler's love for Luna never wavers. As a spiritual teacher, he is not controlling.

How do you feel about Tyler's spiritual nature and expression of love?

Do you think Tyler helped Luna sever the bond with Nico?

How does Luna's understanding of herself and her desires change by the end of the novel?

What did Luna learn through her relationship with Nico?